Bombproofed

A Thomas Pennywhistle novel

Bombproofed

A Pennywhistle Novel

By
John Danielski

www.penmorepress.com

Bombproofed by John M. Danielski
Copyright © 2020 John M. Danielski

All rights reserved. No part of this book may be used or reproduced by any means without the written permission of the publisher except in the case of brief quotation embodied in critical articles and reviews.

ISBN-13: 978-1-950586-55-4 (Paperback)
ISBN :-978-1-950586-54-7(e-book)

BISAC Subject Headings:
FIC014000FICTION / Historical
FIC032000FICTION / War & Military

Editor: Chris Wozney

Cover Illustration by
The Book Cover Whisperer:
ProfessionalBookCoverDesign.com

Please send all correspondence to:

Penmore Press LLC
920 N Javelina Pl
Tucson AZ 85748

DEDICATION

To my mother and father. One taught me learning; one taught me love.

Prologue

29 August, 1814. 12 miles north of Benedict, Maryland, USA.

Pop! Pop! Pop! The hollow rattle of musketry was as unwelcome as it was familiar, the column's flank guards engaging enemy pickets. "Not again!" muttered an exasperated Captain Thomas Pennywhistle. *The Fleet is so close! Why did these damned fool Jonathans have to stage another Forlorn Hope?* He could have avoided all of this unpleasantness if he had not pleaded with Rear Admiral George Cockburn to let him finish the Chesapeake Campaign by leading his Royal Marines one last time.

Organized resistance had collapsed after the Battle of Bladensburg, five days before. The British called the engagement "The Bladensburg Races" for the speed with which much of the Yankee Army had departed the field. Washington City, six miles away, had been captured immediately after. The Americans had ignored Major General Ross's request for a parley; instead, their commanders, including President Madison, had fled in disorder. Then renegade attacks by independent militia companies had forced upon General Ross the unhappy choice between allowing his men to be shot at or to set fire to the city. The conflagrations had effectively distracted the snipers.

Zippt! Zippt! Two bullets passed a foot over Pennywhistle's head, fired from 200 yards away, judging swarms of horseflies. Clouds of gnats and mosquitoes added to the misery. Cockburn had tartly observed, "If I owned hell and I owned Maryland, I'd live in hell and rent out Maryland."

Recent heavy rains had narrowed roads to cart tracks and caused the men to christen their current movement "the mud march." The men had marched 15 miles today on Maryland roads so deep in ooze that many of the men had run ropes under their soles to prevent the shoes from being sucked off their feet. Mildew had attacked their uniforms, and rust could be forestalled only by repetitive oiling of muskets and bayonets. Scratches and wounds festered. Movements turned slow and tempers grew short, but discipline held, for these men were experienced campaigners.

Their appearance was the utilitarian one common to hard-bitten soldiers. Grime and stubble covered most faces—unshaven cheeks provided some protection from insect predation. Exposed skins were tanned the color of old mahogany and possessed the texture of weathered saddles. Every man bore a scent that was a mixture of woodsmoke, gun oil, sweat and tallow. Lacquered black round hats bore dents of various shapes; the swallow-tailed brick-red coats had faded to a chestnut hue and showed numerous patches. Blue collars and cuffs were scorched from powder burns, and the greasy residue of salt pork rations streaked their coats. The sweat-stained linen shirts beneath had absorbed the rotten-egg smell of burned gunpowder. None of the men wore any drawers; the shirts' long tails were all that separated marine buttocks from the seats of their trousers. Some of those tails carried the scents and stains of chronic dysentery. Their frayed duck trousers, the color of oatmeal, were patched at the knees and seats. The black canvas gaiters that protected the lower portions of their legs were threadbare, and the soles of their shoes were worn and holed from heavy marching. Two dishwater-grey, formerly white belts crisscrossed their chests, and a scuffed rectangular brass plate bearing a fouled anchor marked their intersection. One belt supported a bayonet scabbard, the other a black cartridge box which hung just above the right hip. The cartridge boxes had recently been replenished from the ammunition carts and contained sixty rounds weighing 15 pounds. With the canvas pack carrying the one-sixth share of camp equipage, bedroll, haversack containing four days' rations, three wooden canteens, and the 10-pound musket he held in his hands, each marine stepped with a 70-pound burden.

No enlisted marine was over 28 years of age, save for G"ramps" O'Laughlin, who had seen five and thirty summers. None topped five feet ten in height, but campaigning in baking heat induced a tendency to slump and aged a man quickly. Mud speckled their uniforms and hats, but their muskets and bayonets worked just fine, and that was what mattered now.

Pennywhistle directed his horse back to Sergeant Andrew Dale, who had halted the column of 97 men; heat had reduced their numbers from the original complement of 120. The company's two subalterns roved half a mile to the rear, using the flats of their swords to awaken exhausted stragglers. Pennywhistle considered the number of marines present for duty as a tribute to sheer tenacity; Wellington had once told him that at any given time 30% of his army was disabled from health problems.

Seeing the array of American militiamen, his chief NCO had already instructed the men to fix bayonets, turning their .75 caliber Sea Service Brown Besses into 70-inch pikes. Pennywhistle and Dale exchanged weary looks.

"It's their usual production, and we shall have to give it the usual review, Sar't. I noticed a path two hundred yards back."

"I did as well, Captain," replied Dale. "It will serve our purpose. Even if the track does not go exactly where we would like it, the forest is thinner there, and I think our fellows can handle the underbrush without difficulty."

Dale and Pennywhistle spoke in verbal shorthand because they had done the upcoming maneuver so often that they could have patented it. Yet it never failed to surprise untrained opponents.

"Get the men in formation, Sar't. First Platoon stall, Second Platoon hook. I will take First; you take Second.

"Aye aye, sir."Dale snapped a smart salute and bellowed a command so loudly it might have been heard in Washington City itself. "Column of files at the quarter distance!"

The marines shifted into a formation in which each man was separated from his mate by four paces. With a pace reckoned at 30 inches, when the column shifted back to skirmish order just before commencing its attack, the platoon would have a front of 150 yards, sufficient to overlap the enemy line. Such spacing would give each marine plenty of room to thrust and cut with his bayonet. Marines were trained to employ initiative and select particular targets.

"First Platoon: skirmish order!" bellowed Pennywhistle.

Men loaded their muskets, but this would be a contest of steel rather than fire. Performing the complicated evolutions of reloading single-shot muskets increased time in the lethal zone, whereas a bayonet could be used repeatedly to slash or stab. And scarcely one in two of the Yankees had bayonets, so that advantage lay firmly with the Marines. A smartly administered bayonet charge could prove so effective that Major General Charles "No Flint" Grey had actually ordered his men to remove their flints before the Paoli Assault in the American War of Independence.

First platoon would be the "stall"—the shiny object designated to command the enemy's attention and fix them in place. Their bayonet advance would be at the ordinary marching speed of 75 paces per minute. The inexorability of such a methodical advance had a pronounced psychological effect: few men wanted to try conclusions with an advancing line of bayonets. Not without reason; wounds inflicted by the blades ran deeper and were harder to repair than those caused by bullets, and were more likely to cause infection. The unhurried movement gave the Jonathan's plenty of time for the most bloodcurdling parts of their imaginations to work on them. Second Platoon would be the hook, circling round the enemy flank and closing to the rear at 120 paces per minute.

Because they held no particular animus toward the Americans, there was a certain detachment in their wary eyes. There was also a menacing looseness in the way his marines held themselves, the hallmark of professionals whose movements would be as nimble as they were swift. The whole Chesapeake Expedition had been about adroit maneuvering, more a raid than an invasion: quickly in, thanks to sea power, and even faster out, thanks to hard marching guided by runaway slaves. The Yankees 3-to-1 superiority in numbers had been offset by the skill and experience of British soldiers and commanders. All that remained was to shepherd these men back to the transports whence they had come.

Veterans scoffed at officers who speechified, because most battlefield sermons were sheer bombast, bolstering the inner confidence of the speaker more than inspiring the conduct of the listeners. Pennywhistle thought stoic silence and sound leadership generally inspired best, but he was willing to chance a few words if they spurred practical actions. "Marines," he called out, "I am starved for a good meal, and so are you. Our scouts have informed me that there may be a cache of Smithfield hams at a farm three miles ahead, stockpiled to feed the Yankees who have pestered us all day. We do not plunder civilians, but those hams constitute a fair prize of war. I want to see *you* eat them, not the jackanapes in front of us. Let's not waste time! I'm hungry!"

The men were too fatigued to cheer, but he could see tired half-smiles and weary grins. They were indeed hungry. The expedition's Army Commander, General Robert Ross, had dispensed with a baggage train in the interest of speed, and had forbidden foraging. Heat and moisture had rendered their salt pork inedible and spawned a bumper crop of weevils in their ship's biscuit.

"I think it is time to commence a musical bombardment," said Pennywhistle to two green-kilted pipers, on loan thanks to his winning a wager with the colonel of the Royal North British Fusiliers. The pipers started a sprightly version of "British Grenadiers." While his ears had never decided if pipes were friends or foes, or whether they skirled or squealed, they served as rally points because their piercing tones could be heard above the *spit spot* of musketry. Most importantly, the men liked them, and they unnerved opponents.

"Second Platoon: forward march!" bellowed Dale. "Double quick time!"

His column marched at a perpendicular angle to Pennywhistle's line. Pennywhistle drew his Osborn cutlass and brought it to the point. "First Platoon: forward march!" Two fifteen-year-old drummer boys *rat-tat-tatted* the command. The second platoon proceeded with neither drums nor pipes; Pennywhistle wanted all of the attention focused on the first. Now both platoons moved as handsomely as if they were on a parade ground. Pennywhistle's men stepped off smartly as the Yankees discharged a poorly timed volley. Inexperienced, they aimed too high, savaging nearby pine trees but sparing flesh. The whizzing of lead provoked a natural instinct in amateurs to seek cover, but veterans knew the faster they advanced the fewer rounds they would have to face.

Pennywhistle cantered two yards ahead of his men. Clever tactics meant little if they were not matched by an officer willing to take the greatest risk himself. Men should never be driven like cattle: they would perform miracles for "come on" officers, and do the bare minimum for those of the "go on" variety. He felt the familiar surges of anxiety and excitement but treated them like unruly children. He acknowledged their shouts but put their raw energy under the stern discipline of an uncompromising mental nanny. Ghillie Gunn's words spoken on his tenth birthday came back to him: "What you do with fear is far more important than fear itself."

He mopped cascades of perspiration from his brow with a silk handkerchief; the air was as heavy as a towel from a Turkish bath. His heart skipped a beat as he saw his fiancée's face in his mind. He had detailed three marines to conduct her to Benedict, and though his men had doubts about escorting a Yankee, they did so out of respect for their commander. A strong-limbed freedman of sixty years named Gabriel Prosser served as their guide. A veteran of the Colonial Marines, he was handy with a gun; and as a long time resident of the Maryland tidewater, he knew how to avoid the local militia rally points. He would protect Pennywhistle's love with his life. Yankee frustration increased after every failed skirmish against the British. Inflamed by strong drink, young sparks might seek to relieve their frustrations with the nearest woman available, and one viewed as a traitor would pose no moral dilemma.

His fiancée should be arriving in Benedict about now, and by tomorrow afternoon they would both be on a packet bound for Bermuda. He shoved the beautiful vision aside—

love distracted from the job ahead, and distraction could prove fatal.

Siss! Siss! Siss! Three rounds narrowly missed his temples. But these rounds had not come from anything resembling a volley. Yankees were reloading and firing at will. Their fire was spotty and decreasing in volume.

The pipers blasted out "Heart of Oak." The drummers counterpointed with a low, heavy beat of *babum, babum, babum bum bum* that steadied the marching cadence even as it sounded a funeral dirge to the Yankees.

"Boil the lobsters! Fry in hell, bloody-backs! Piss on your mothers!" The shouts increased in an inverse ratio to the volume of fire. They provoked an icy silence from his men. Yankee reloading became frantic and careless: many were spilling so much of their powder that any rounds fired from their weapons would have little striking power. Others were not using ramrods and were simply dropping the ball down the barrel; the flight of those rounds would be erratic.

Two Yankees abruptly broke from cover and took to their heels with the speed of deer spooked by a bobcat. Panic was contagious—Pennywhistle expected an epidemic of fleet-footedness to break out shortly. That was fine with him; he was looking to disperse the Jonathans, not compile a long butcher's bill.

Second Platoon had vanished into the forest at a quick trot. Just a minute more and they would be at the Yankees' rear. First Platoon continued its advance. Four more Jonathans popped up and ran. Pennywhistle could now see individual faces, and most looked like men who devoutly wished that they were back at the dull business of guiding a plow. Their earlier boisterousness had been replaced with stunned silence; the sight of steely British faces had changed death from something that applied only to others into something intensely personal. Dreams of glory had become living nightmares.

He had a certain respect for them. Unlike the other bands of militia he had faced today, the majority of these men were staying put. He almost felt sorry for them. Almost.

Phut! Phut! Two of his men recoiled as bullets punched their shoulders. No blood blossomed; they had been stung by rounds so lacking in velocity that they barely broke the skin.

Shouts of surprise and panic erupted from the rear of the Yankee line. Second Platoon had launched its attack, appearing out of the thick underbrush like forest goblins. He spied a fat man targeting him with what looked to be the sole Pennsylvania Rifle among his opponents. He was taking his own good time, trying to line up the perfect shot; at 30 yards' range it should be an easy one.

Pennywhistle whipped out a pistol version of that same rifle from his saddle holster, the gift of a dying half-brother. In a blur of motion, he brought the .44 caliber piece to the point, sighted, and snapped off a shot born of desperation rather than deliberation. Luck blessed the shot; the round caught the surprised man square in his oversized chest. He gave a yelp, then collapsed, dropping his rifle to clutch his chest.

A quick volley would ratchet up the confusion. Pennywhistle holstered his pistol and twirled his cutlass. "First Platoon! Halt. Make ready. Present." Marines opened their mouths to accommodate the forthcoming acoustic pressure, and tightened their musket slings under elbows to steady aiming. Since .685 lead balls traveling at 1,200 feet per second rose quickly and dropped equally fast, his men aimed for enemy knees to strike Yankee chests."Fire!" Forty-five Brown Besses discharged. Pennywhistle saw faint movements in the green behind the militiamen, and a flash of faded red. Time to snap the trap shut. "First Platoon: Charge bayonets. Advance! Quick Time!"

Private Crouchback of the First Platoon executed a perfect low lunge that caught a rising Yankee in the stomach. With the full force of Crouchback's calf muscles behind the 17-inch blade, it lanced through the man's backside as if it had passed through congealed porridge.

Private Blandon parried aside a tomahawk thrust aimed at his head; many Americans carried them instead of bayonets. He reversed his blade and slashed a wide, deep gash along the base of the American's neck.

Private Hobson thrust his musket horizontally above his head, the classic block against an opponent using his musket as a club. The enemy Springfield glanced off Hobson's Brown Bess with a resounding *kachunk!* Hobson swung the butt of his own weapon smartly and it crashed into his opponent's chin, crushing his jaw.

An American possessing a bayonet stabbed his Springfield viciously at Private McCarthy's belly. McCarthy leaned back and countered with a "parry and force down." Holding his musket horizontally at waist level, he brought the stock down hard on top of the barrel of the advancing weapon. As the Springfield descended, he slammed the butt of his musket into the man's solar plexus—a blow that stopped the man's breath. He then slashed at the American's left thigh, ripping a trench that severed the man's femoral artery. Blood erupted like lava and the American, struggling to breathe, brought his hand down upon his ruined leg, then touched it to his face in disbelief. His shoulders shuddered, his heart seized, and he farted. He gave a rasp that was part rattle and part wheeze, then collapsed.

One American madly shadow-boxed with an invisible opponent, using his bayonet in lieu of fists. Mirages sometimes plagued panicked men. A glassy-eyed Yankee slowly rose, turned, and shambled toward the rear. Liquid valor was common among undisciplined troops, and it evaporated swiftly in the heat of battle.

A swarthy corporal sighted his weapon on Private Richardson at point blank range. The round should have had Richardson's name on it, but the American's trigger finger hesitated for a second. Natural enough: killing someone for the first time was contrary to the instincts of most men. Richardson used that second to execute a "parry and force up." The American's piece discharged into the sky as Richardson drove the point of his bayonet into the man's sternum. The bayonet stuck fast; Richardson had to brace his foot on the fallen man's chest to extract it.

"Thrust, develop, gore, recover." Private Jones recited the words of the bayonet drill out loud as he disemboweled a baby-faced American who looked too young for a razor.

Suddenly, it was done. The Yankees broke and ran as if some survival instinct had taken over all the militiamen at the same moment. Instead of being heroes of the Republic, the Jonathans were plucked eagles.

Pennywhistle commanded the drummers to pound out "cease pursuit" and ordered the pipers to stop playing. The mens' bloodlust was in full cry, telling them that a battle was never done unless the enemy had been utterly wiped out as a fighting force; but he needed to conserve their energy. The men obeyed, but he saw disappointment in many faces.

A marine pointed his musket toward the back of a wounded militiaman who was slowly hobbling away, a worse wounded comrade gripping his shoulders. "No!" shouted Pennywhistle, and he emphatically shook his head at the startled marine. He respected what must be a remarkable friendship, since it was worth your life to stop for a wounded man. There was no point in adding one more death to a battle whose outcome was already decided.

Cirrus clouds of smoke drifted at shoulder level and the heavy, stale air reeked of brimstone as well as urine and feces: men wetting themselves and voiding their bowels were common side effects of battle. Some of his men would suffer delayed stress in the form of constipation, but that might prove a temporary antidote to the "bloody flux" that had plagued them since leaving the transports.

Pennywhistle shook his head. The landscape was straight out of Bosch's painting, The Last Judgment: bodies twisted like old rope, heads caved in like smashed pumpkins, torsos furrowed by bayonets. Half of the casualties were either old men or boys; the scrapings of America's manpower barrel. One body had been hit so hard by bayonets that it had scoured a groove on the pine tree against which it was jammed. The red-grey coils of its intestines dangled and swayed. Muscle spasms that occurred in the moments between wounding and death curled some bodies into fetal positions and caused their hands to ball into fists. Bodies appeared oddly smaller after death. Because eyeballs were moist, they were typically the first anchorages for the flies that swiftly converged.

One tableau of death consisted of an officer, a private, and a horse. The horse had likely been shot first and his rider had been struck as his mount collapsed. Lashing out in its final struggles, the beast's front hooves had smashed the spinal column of an unlucky private.

Tendrils of smoke rose from a body lying in smoldering grass ignited by musket wadding. Like sailors leaping from a burning ship, lice tried to escape the fate of comrades exploding like Indian corn popping. Lice caused typhus, the killer that had done more to defeat Napoleon's invasion of Russia than the czar's armies. Pennywhistle had kept the lice population among his marines to a minimum by thoroughly boiling all uniforms at the start of the campaign. It shrank the uniforms and made his men look like gangly adolescents undergoing a growth spurt. Their uniforms were all, he reflected, in dire need of another boil, including his own.

Several forms twitched spasmodically and a few faint voices moaned for water. One man missing a V-shaped portion of his skull shrieked at random intervals. An Aberdeen terrier barked frantically at his prone master, trying to rouse him from a sleep that would never end.

It bothered Pennywhistle that his tear ducts remained dry, but he had seen such things so many times before that he gave the carnage a back bench in his mental parliament. The awful detritus of battle had a cumulative effect: each battle chipped a little off the soul, and his was missing some very large chunks. Many newly commissioned officers fresh from England never had a chance to suffer psychic wounds because they died in their first fight, believing the deadly nonsense that war was simply a more demanding version of the sports they had played at school. He had seen men break down all of a sudden, or go slowly to pieces, their mental walls eroded by the frequency, duration, and intensity of combat experiences. Pennywhistle himself had experienced a bad case of the shakes after his last fight. At least now his hands and shoulders were steady.

Dale's men, he reflected, had performed particularly well. Once back at Benedict, he would speed Dale's promotion to sergeant major.

Something odd caught his eye. One middle-aged American had not fled. He brandished a sword that looked like an Osborn and was dressed in an ornate blue uniform that belonged in Grand Opera. Outsized gold epaulettes and an ostrich-plumed *chapeau de bras* proclaimed him a bandbox soldier, yet there were volcanoes in his eyes and Pennywhistle saw defiance in his posture. He was daring Pennywhistle to take him on, like the knights of old in a jousting match. Pennywhistle had no wish to kill a man with the heart of a warrior. He decided to take him prisoner, grant him his parole, and send him on his way.

He swung his horse toward the man and cantered forward. There was a large square of furrowed earth in front of the American that seemed out of place; it was as if someone had tried to farm the forest but had given up when the going got too rough. As Pennywhistle approached, the man's sneer changed to a triumphant smile.

Pennywhistle knew the expression and suddenly understood the significance of the dirt patch anomaly. It explained why the Yankees had been baiting him to attack. He had ridden into a trap.

The officer swiftly turned and bounded toward the deep woods.

Pennywhistle's mare tripped a thin wire connected to a mechanical contraption called a *fougasse*: a fragmentation mine, a cone-shaped apparatus filled with scrap metal, lead balls, and nails. The wire triggered a flintlock several feet away that ignited its fuse.

Boom! Pennywhistle did not so much hear the detonation as feel it: the *whump* of a pressure wave battering him like a giant hand crumpling paper. The blast gutted Pennywhistle's horse, tore off her hind legs, and tossed him ten feet in the air as if he were a badminton shuttlecock. As he cart-wheeled towards the earth, he had the sensation of being a twig in a tornado. And then he struck the ground.

The shocked company walked slowly toward something that none of them wanted to see.

"Step easy and careful, lads," said Dale. "There may be more of those damned things about." They heeded his words as they circled their officer's body, some shaking their heads in denial as others cursed. Many pleaded for divine intercession. A few dropped to their knees in despair.

Captain Thomas Pennywhistle was dead. For twelve years he had tricked his way out of death and had seemed destined for high rank and great honors. "Clever" was the contemporary distinction applied to him by his fellow officers. Cockburn had spoken of him as "a man of many wiles." The ancients would have called him "crafty" because he could substitute measured ingenuity for blunt force, preferring the cool-headed planning of an Odysseus to the hot-blooded impulsivity of an Achilles. His men considered him a military conjurer whose audacious tricks lay just beyond the scope of his audiences' imagination. Moreover, he had long enjoyed the lush favors of that most fickle of all females, Lady Luck; and his luck had become his men's. Now that luck had run out.

"Maybe he ain't dead; maybe it's just heat pros... pros... pros..."A beet-red O'Laughlin could not quite recall the term.

"Prostration, heat prostration,"said the cynical Crouchback. "That's what you mean, but you saw what happened. Those bruises on his face and that wreck of a horse over yonder weren't caused by heat."

Dale bent down close to the body, hoping to detect the faintest breath, and placed his fingers on the carotid artery. He willed a pulse, even though after 20 years of combat he knew the signs of death: mouth agape, eyes fixed in surprise, and cheeks blackened by pressure waves. He gave up and rose sadly to his feet.

The men saw his expression and any flickers of hope died.

"He went out doing his duty," said 17-year-old Private John Snodgrass, a sniffle in his voice."It's a shame t'was a cursed infernal device that brought him down." The cornstalk-tall private had only been in the marines a year, but the captain had taught him duty was a sacred word.

"I'd have followed him to hell blindfolded a'cause I know he would have brought me back without a single scorch mark," said Private Matthew Blandon, a thrice-wounded veteran whose life Pennywhistle had saved in the Adriatic.

"I will miss him," said Private Mark Hobson in a husky voice. He was a sentimental heart in a company of unsentimental men..

"What will we do now?" Twenty-year-old Private Sean McCarthy spoke the bewilderment of many marines who regarded Pennywhistle as a father figure even though he had been but thirty years of age.

"I shall pray for his soul," Private Luke Richardson said piously. He was a Baptist preacher's son, nicknamed "Parson" and the sole "blue lighter" in the company. "I shall ask God in his great mercy to forgive his trespasses and grant him eternal repose."

The men glowered at Richardson. n'Cap" don't need none of your prayin, Parson," growled Private Jeremiah Jones, a stubby, choleric Welshman with eyes the color of a sea storm. H"e were a good man, plain and simple, and don't need no forgivin'. Any God who can't apprehend that without a broken down marine pleading for Him to do so, ain't a father worth prayin' to. If his name be not writ large in St. Peter's book, then when my own time comes I just might turn my back on them Pearly Gates."

*****

A rush of colors that made rainbows appear drab enveloped Pennywhistle while he was still airborne. Time slowed, became elastic, then irrelevant. It was as if an invisible door opened. In an instant, he was experiencing his entire life, images projected boldly by a *camera obscura* mounted in his soul. The extraordinary thing was, he felt not only his own emotions but the emotions of others affected by his actions.

What he saw was not the life that he thought he had lived. It was as if someone had given him a pair of glasses that allowed him to view the world with the omniscience of a divine being. The events re-experienced had nothing to do with traditional ideas of success concerned with wealth, fame, and power. No images of his military triumphs appeared, and he saw not a single face of the foes that he had slain in battle. Neither did he see any of his own men who had died because of his mistakes.

Rather, the life review was about little things that he had mostly forgotten: small kindnesses that changed lives, thoughtless actions that damaged souls. Motives mattered fully as much as actions.

He felt the surprised joy of a blind beggar for whom he had bought a decent meal; the deep gratitude of a Spanish mother whose children he had defended against French renegades; the healing peace that he had given a dying marine who, in his painful delirium, had mistaken Pennywhistle for his father. He had held the man's hand patiently and responded to his babbling with soothing words a parent might speak. The marine's wheezed last words had been, "Bless you, Papa."

Actions raced by which brought him pain. He saw himself as a newly commissioned second lieutenant berating a hapless private who was not a bad man, just slow of understanding. After his tirade, the man had deserted and shot himself. He felt the lonely despair of the private's final moments and his horrible realization that suicide was not an answer.

He experienced the profound devotion of a naïve Scots heiress who had directed her considerable passion toward the capture of his heart. The searing agony caused by his equally profound indifference felt like a fire applied to tissue paper.

His mother had wronged him often, but near the end of her life had tried to make amends. He had responded by saying that he never wanted to see her again—and had proven as good as his word. She had passed badly into the next life because of her anguish.

He understood with terrible clarity that you reaped what you sowed: throwing stones in the form of hurtful thoughts, words, or deeds was like hurling a boomerang. They eventually returned to harm the sender.

Pennywhistle crashed into the ground with bone crushing force, yet felt no pain. He heard a low *zinging* that reminded him of a taut steel wire buffeted by winds and felt a pull, like a handkerchief being yanked from a pocket. He moved his left hand tentatively, shook his head, and hoisted himself to his feet. He felt fine—splendid actually. Then he looked down and saw that his body had not moved at all.

He felt he was seeing the world clearly for the first time: a prison inmate suddenly freed from confinement. His senses had never been sharper and their range was greatly extended.

Neither Christ, nor Mohammed, nor Buddha appeared to pass judgment. His only judge was the harshest of all: himself. He intuitively understood that the images were provided to instruct rather than punish, so that he might understand that Earth was a classroom, not a purgatory. The visions sought to help him answer a question that he felt rather than heard: "What was the point of your life?"

Marines stared at his corpse in shock and sadness. He wished he could tell them their grief was wholly misplaced. The pipers began playing "Amazing Grace."

He realized that he had passed through a veil that sages had called the threshold or "The Great Divide." He was uncertain as to whether this was the Afterlife or merely a staging area, but he was certain that this was no dream. The physical body was apparently no more than a suit worn by the spirit. He appeared to be entirely alone, but that might be only temporary; he would just have to wait and see. He literally had all the time in the world.

Bunyan looked to have been misinformed. No trumpets heralded his arrival and no angelic choir sang welcome. There was no Celestial City, nor was there any Slough of Despond.

Milton had it wrong, too. Neither Satan nor his chief lieutenants, Beelzebub, Belial, and Moloch, appeared present for duty. Neither had the archangels Michael, Gabriel, Raphael, and Uriel reported in.

There were no Pearly Gates and there was no Lake of Fire. Could it be that death was the greatest humbug of all? He had avoided church, because he disliked seeing spirituality degraded into an instrument which kept the masses in their place and reassured the ruling class that they deserved theirs. Was this beatific calm a condition granted all men, rather than a saved or select few?

He stood in a circle of soft white light: everything outside of that was a fuzzy grey. The silence was profound, but he felt no fear; rather, the opposite.

A long tunnel formed in front of him with a pinprick of brightest light at its end. He advanced into it because death had not killed his curiosity. He realized that the velvety blackness inside was a living presence, humming quietly with pleasing tones that almost constituted a voice.

The incandescence grew in intensity as the pinprick changed gradually into a large ball. At the end of the tunnel, the light shone brighter than a thousand suns. It would have blinded earthly eyes, but here it enlightened and comforted because it was love, peace, and justice condensed into one mighty orb. There was nothing like it on earth, which was likely why earth was a place of pain, turmoil, and corruption.

The light evolved into a rapidly spinning pinwheel of stars that resolved itself into a valley, beautiful beyond measure. Splendid meadows, plains, and hills containing perfect waterfalls, streams, and ponds were framed by grasses, plants, and trees. It was as if Constable and Van Ruisdael had blended their talents, creating the perfect landscape into which the Almighty breathed life.

He caught whiffs of jasmine, lavender, and sandalwood, ideal olfactory accompaniments to the wondrous panorama. Everything had an earth-like appearance, but the scents, colors, and textures were more vibrant and dynamic than anything he had ever encountered. The vision was accompanied by music that made Mozart seem an amateur, though the instruments it was played on could be found in no earthly orchestra.

He felt like the man in Plato's parable, who had spent his life in a cave facing away from the light of the entrance, believing reality was the images reflected from his camp fire on the far wall. Was this the Valley of the Shadow of Death?

He saw a group of figures advancing to meet him. They were family and friends who had preceded him to... should he call it The Promised Land? He saw dear little Molly at the edge of the group. She had been a seven-year-old camp follower whose death he had caused through carelessness. The crushing guilt he carried vanished when she flashed him a grin that was pure joy. Mercury, a huge mastiff who had given his life to save Dale, bounded happily at her heels, providing an answer to a question asked by all bereaved pet owners. Carlotta, the great love of his life, led the procession, and his father followed closely behind.

He broke into a run but halted when he came to a small bridge over a shimmering silver stream. He instinctively knew it was the River of Life; unlike the River Styx, its waters were clear, not dark. He could make out distinct drops: each had a slight color difference that he guessed represented individual souls, yet all merged together in a harmonious flow. His father and Carlotta stopped abruptly on the far side of the bridge as his foot touched the first plank of its near edge.

Carlotta's stately figure and expressive face seemed even more beautiful here. "*Caro mio,*" she said, her voice lilting with the sensual vowels of Venice, "I have missed you so, my Tomas!"

"Not a day goes by that I do not think of you," said Pennywhistle, with tears in his voice. "It was I who sent you here prematurely and deprived the world of a wonderful light. I blame my own stupidity for what happened. If I had not been distracted and been just a little quicker..."

"Stop!" said Carlotta in a commanding voice that yet overflowed with kindness. She placed her hands on her hips and thrust her chest forward, just as she had done in life when she had had something important to say. "Tomas, blame and regret have no place here. Your soul is hobbled by guilt in the manner of a peddler bent low from a cargo of lead bars strapped to his back. Your spirit has been unable to rise from its burden and wearily lurches through life, though it is capable of joyously running. You see the darkness in everyday things, not the light, and have treated life as something to endure rather than something to celebrate. Laughter is a stranger to you, while sadness has become a close friend. Like an innkeeper who gives featherbeds to his guests while he lies on a pallet of straw, you forgive others but will not extend that understanding to yourself.

I made the choice to surrender my life for yours of my own free will. I do not regret it, because I made my decision from love alone. There is no need for me to grant you forgiveness, *caro mio*, because you did nothing wrong. Love is the greatest force in the Universe, and you can only do right if you always strive to honor it."

She gestured at the waters flowing between them. "The fabric of existence is like a fisherman's net, with pearls tied at every knot. Everything that exists is a pearl in this net and is connected with every other pearl; harming yourself harms the universe.

"Guilt has poisoned your soul, Tomas, and has robbed the world of the man you were meant to be. Tomas, the only person you need beg forgiveness of is yourself." Carlotta favored him with a smile that radiated the joy of redemption.

He smiled back like a condemned prisoner granted a pardon. "If that is your wish, then I shall consider it my heart's command."

"Because of my love for you, *amore mio*, I bear a message requiring you to make a solemn choice. You have completed most of the goals that you were sent into the earthly plane to accomplish. You may cross over now and be welcomed, but, if you do, there is no going back.

"However, *Tomas*, some tasks remain only partially completed. There are those who would benefit from your presence in their lives. It is no exaggeration to say that you could play a role in altering many life paths for the good. You are being offered a chance to return and finish what you have begun.

"It will not be an easy road. Pain, suffering, and sadness lie ahead if you chose to return, yet you will also be granted a chance for your heart to flourish. You have worried that you are the last of an ancient line, but that outcome is by no means certain." She smiled roguishly.

"A woman has entered your life who will rouse your heart from its joyless slumbers if you will allow it. You have worried that loving her might be a betrayal of me, and thus you harbor grave doubts about joining with her in marriage.

I wish only for your happiness: it would distress me if you missed a chance for bliss because of a misplaced reverence for my memory. Love is welcoming and seeks expansion, not restriction. Just as a parent may love two children equally but in different ways, so your heart may find its perfect content with more than one woman."

Pennywhistle stared at his foot on the bridge. Stay or go? Pleasure or pain? He was sick of war; he had seen enough bloodletting and destruction to fill a dozen lifetimes. Everything here was poetry for the soul and a song for the heart. Here was the lasting peace he had fruitlessly sought for years. He was used to maintaining a reserve of nervous energy to use in an emergency, but here he could finally relax because here no one was an enemy. Here truth banished suspicion.

It would be the easiest thing imaginable to advance over the bridge, kiss Carlotta, hug relatives, shake hands with friends and forget the realm of sorrow that was the Planet Earth. Spending an eternity with Carlotta promised an ecstasy beyond imagining.

And yet, he was a creature of duty. He had always thrived on challenges and was happiest when he was of service. His men needed him: they had looked like bewildered children when he had departed. His fiancée had forsaken her country to be with him. He could become a bringer of light rather than a herald of darkness. He could never completely beat the swords of his nature into ploughshares, but he could fight just as hard for peace as he had for war.

The profound love that permeated this remarkable kingdom was a balm to every wound on his tattered soul. For years he had been suffering from increasingly severe tics and tremors caused by too many battles; now he felt a profound calmness healing him. Mankind's greatest terror no longer held sway over him. If he returned from Shakespeare's

Undiscovered Country, he would have a unique ability to reassure those dying on the battlefield that death was not an end but a portal to something wondrous.

His life was like a novel with a premature ending. He was being offered the chance to issue a revised edition.

"Carlotta, is any of this real? Am I dreaming all this?"

"My love, what you see before you is the fullness of reality. Elements here are in their purest form and never decay. It is the earth plane that is the kingdom of the chimera, for it is filled with barriers and blocks to ensure its inhabitants do not experience things for which their souls are unprepared. It is akin to a horse given blinders so that it only concerns itself with what lies directly ahead. Life on Earth is a pen and ink sketch drawn by child's hand. This realm is an oil painting by Rembrandt." Pennywhistle smiled at that; Carlotta knew he loved painting.

"Every life vibrates with a distinctive resonance: only the faintest echoes of those sounds can be perceived on earth. There you are in the position of a man trying to appreciate the richness of a symphony when all he can hear is a simple melody played on a lone,"—merriment sparkled in her voice—"penny whistle."

Pennywhistle laughed softly at the pun, and it struck him that laughter was the first cousin of joy: functioning as soap for a soul dirtied by worry and care.

"What you see here, *mio tesoro*, is experienced by each new arrival in such a way that their best understanding and impulses will be engaged."

"Will I remember any of this, Carlotta, if I return, or will it be as if it had never happened?"

"*Caro mio*, when souls incarnate on the earth they agree to have their memories of higher realms wiped clean: it is like forbidding a school child from using notes during a test. But you will carry back full memories of this for the purpose of helping other souls evolve at a faster pace. You will be changed by this glimpse of a larger reality in ways small and great that I am not permitted to explain. Pay attention and you will discover new abilities and perspectives when the time is right. It will take seven years before all of the changes are fully integrated into your second life.

"Search your memories for what Aadi taught you long ago, *caro mio*. You will find that all you need to know to use these gifts wisely is already in place." Aadi had been an ancient Hindu on his grandfather's Tweedside estate who had taught him meditation as a boy.

"Hearts and minds of similar disposition attract each other, my love. You chose to learn from Aadi of your own free will. That particular decision, along with thousands of small ones, set you upon a path that has brought you to this place."

He gazed on her loveliness, then spoke with sorrow mixed with hope. "The choice is both easy and hard. Easy, because I can see that the Universe is provisioning me with the insights for an earthly voyage of promise. Hard, because all I have ever wanted is right here, right now."

He slowly rotated his head, drinking in the delights of this supremely harmonious panorama as if he were savoring the last drops of a bottle of Glen Livet Whiskey. The sweeping majesty and subtle splendors of this place made the gardens of Versailles seem weed-choked wastelands.

He frog-marched his thoughts from freewheeling bliss to disciplined common sense. Being a marine did not end with death. "I have often marveled at marines bravely volunteering for dangerous missions; faced with the same choice, I can shirk my duty no more than they did. I choose to return."

Carlotta's smile reflected wisdom as well as love. "I was sure that you would make the difficult choice! Selflessness is why love transcends death. Never forget that my love will be with you, always!" She blew him a kiss.

A deep voice flooded the valley. If Niagara Falls could talk, it would have sounded thus. "It is done." Pennywhistle could not say it was the voice of God, but its majesty was as great as its compassion. He had always thought of God as a prime mover: a sublimely creative mathematician who had set in place mechanistic laws and then stepped away. This dominion seemed controlled by a deity that was considerably more personal. As if in answer to that thought, a voice whispered in his head. "Never forget to laugh."

Pennywhistle felt himself flying back down the tunnel as if he were a hawk caught in a hurricane. He crashed back into his body with a painful *thump* that was followed by a searing pain in his back and shoulders.

He blinked, then brushed his parched tongue against his arid lips. He carefully massaged the contusions on his cheeks. He felt like an old piece of clothing that had just been slapped against a washboard.

Blarney, the company bloodhound, cautiously sniffed at him and let out a surprised *woof*.

He opened his eyes to see Dale standing over him with dilated pupils and an open mouth, paler than a moonbeam. In his hand Dale held Pennywhistle's Swiss watch; likely he had been in the process of gathering up his officer's effects to forward to his relatives. Pennywhistle sat up and calmly asked, "How many did we lose, Sar't?"

"Uh, uh, uh..." Dale stammered. He had always been unflappable in even the tightest of spots, but this was beyond him. "None dead, three wounded."

"Good, good. You pipers: stop. I have never liked 'Amazing Grace.' How long was I out?" His tones were matter-of-fact, as if inquiring about the weather.

"According to your watch, five minutes," Dale replied automatically in the tones of a good NCO, but his voice had risen from its usual bass to that of a baritone. "But, but, sir: *out?* You had no breath and no pulse. We were all sure that we had lost you!"

Pennywhistle realized that the blackened condition of his face and charred uniform made him resemble a roasted red pepper, while his burned and swollen hands looked like nothing so much as black strawberries. His hearing was muted: Dale sounded as if he were speaking from the bottom of a rain barrel.

An officer was nothing if not backed by a good NCO. If Dale was rattled, the rest of the men must be considerably worse off. Most were as pale as their sergeant; their expressions ranged from terror and disbelief to shock and amazement. Fearful murmurings coursed through the ranks.

Pennywhistle was overwhelmed by the alarmed uncertainty that he felt from his marines. He had always tried to understand the men he commanded, but now he was experiencing their feelings as powerful electrical currents rippling through his body.

He'd have a panic on his hands unless he squelched the fearful talk immediately. He corkscrewed himself to his feet, ignoring the shooting pain in his lower back. He stamped a smile onto his face and pressed his considerable acting talents into service. "Don't look so startled, lads. I assure you, I am no ghost." He grabbed O'Laughlin's hand and clamped it firmly on his left arm. "See, Gramps, I am still flesh and blood!" He spoke cheerfully while his mind searched for a lie that made sense.

"You all know I was in medical school once. I saw extraordinary things there—queer happenings and strange circumstances beyond the imaginings of most men. They have given rise to legions of fantastic stories and yet..."—he paused gravely—"...and yet, some of them are true." Men looked at him with a combination of trust and awe, hoping that science might supply an explanation for the fantastic.

"There is a very rare condition called Cephalagic Shock," he improvised—cephalalgia was the medical term for a simple headache—"something that happens once in a hundred thousand cases and answers exactly to what you observed in the minutes past. It pushes a body that is on the point of extinction into a temporary preservative state that mimics death: no breath, no heart beat. It mostly happens to drowning and freezing victims, but can also occur if a shock is terrible enough. I think an explosion qualifies! It rarely lasts more than five minutes. Isn't that so, Sar't Dale?"

"Indeed it is, sir!" said Dale with feigned certainty, understanding his officer's intentions perfectly. The trumpets of The Great Beyond were irrelevant to the drum beat of The Service.

"You did not witness a miracle, men, but you did observe something so rare that I should probably write it up for a medical manual," said Pennywhistle. "By God! I believe I shall do that tonight, after I have seen you safely aboard the transports. Now, let's have no more of those shocked looks that make me think you just saw a witch fly by on her broom!"

He laughed loudly, wanting to drown the extraordinary nature of the event with humor: show the men that they should feel little alarm because he felt none at all.

His tones turned serious. "Marines, we need to reach saltwater at Benedict by nightfall, so hard marching lies ahead. We are almost home, but that is sometimes when the gravest threats appear because men relax their vigilance. Keep your eyes peeled for any Jonathans, be the guardian of the marine next to you, and keep yourselves hydrated with regular sips from your canteens."

He slowly panned his eyes over his men, carefully assessing postures, expressions, and equipment.

Because his words were spoken with the honesty of a plain dealing gentleman, their lack of drama underscored their impact. The hint of a sunrise in his normally phlegmatic eyes told his men that he was pleased with what he saw.

"Sar't Dale! Have the men fall out and fill their canteens from that creek over yonder; it is one of the few that we have passed that does not seem to be brackish. Make sure each marine has three full canteens, then form them up in a column at the half distance. We march in fifteen minutes."

"Aye, aye, sir," said Dale loudly as he snapped a smart salute. He knew it would be reassuring to the men to perform rote actions rather than fret about things not of this earth.

Pennywhistle's throat felt drier than a fossil, causing him to greedily gulp water from the clear stream. He then splashed several handfuls onto his face. At least now he could pass as a vagrant instead of Death's manservant.

An overwhelming feeling of being a penitent on a pilgrimage caused him to fill three canteens and walk a hundred yards into a bloody world of which he had been the chief architect. It did not matter that the recipients would be Americans: they had "met the lion" and so were brothers-in-arms.

His tear ducts gained a new lease on life but he dismissively wiped away the wetness as he focused on three militiamen who were rapidly fading from life. He knelt beside each one, brought him to a sitting position, and put a canteen to his lips. "Sip it slowly."

The sparks of surprised gratitude in their eyes reminded him of flickering candles flaring with unexpected brightness just before they went out. He now understood why Jesus had washed the feet of his disciples: little kindnesses and quiet acts of humanity were what made God smile.

The last of the three, a ragamuffin boy of perhaps sixteen years, expired in his arms after he had taken a single sip. He held him close for a few seconds, wondering what he might have become, then shut his eyes gently. He rose and covered the corpse with a coat, hoping to shield it from the buzzards that were already circling.

His men made no comments, though their approving eyes acknowledged his action. What he had just done might puzzle bloodthirsty, "no quarter" civilians who had never been near a battle, but made perfect sense to combat soldiers who had more in common with their fallen foes than the people who sent them out to fight.

The march resumed and the miles ground slowly past, and his men's confidence returned. The column settled into its usual routine. Bonaparte had said that what each of his Imperial Guardsmen saw of Russia was the pack of the man in front of him, and so it was with the Marines and Maryland.

The men's mood improved greatly when a flank guard located the barn containing the Smithfield hams. The arduous marching of the ten-day campaign had ensured that an overweight marine was as rare as a white peacock. The barn also contained a food locker full of fresh cornbread. Dale located several stone jugs of hard cider stashed behind it and permitted each man a cupful. The men gorged themselves on ham and cornbread, then reaped the literal fruits of victory by sacking a nearby peach orchard and raiding a strawberry patch. At the end of their feast, his men still had plenty of ham and peaches left to fill their haversacks. They seemed more than happy to toss away rancid salt pork and weevily biscuit.

Pennywhistle thought he had never tasted such fine meat and excellent fruit; even the cider sparkled with an unexpected effervescence. Enhanced sensitivity of taste was an apparent side effect of his recent experience. But spiritual enlightenment, however, came with a price: he directly experienced the power of his men's unadulterated emotions. Crowds, he realized, would be a problem unless he quickly devised some mental protocols to filter out the rawest of passions.

When they resumed marching, Pennywhistle forced himself to walk at a steady pace, even though daggers of pain stabbed at his back and arms. He was far more aware of colors, textures, and scents. The ash white of oak trees, the soft texture of cardinal flowers, and the comforting aroma of boxwood all seemed especially powerful. He wondered what other changes would result from his Other World journey, but realized that he could not chase the transformations as an academic chased explanations in an experiment. Things would unfold in their own good time.

So much of what he had held dear counted for little, and so many things that he had dismissed as trivial were of supreme importance. People mattered and titles did not, save for one: Good Samaritan. Man was a steward of most things rather than their owner.

A stray horse with an expensive saddle wandered into the path of the column. She was a docile white mare of medium height whose ancestry included an Arab progenitor. She was likely an orphan of war, possibly belonging to an American officer killed in an earlier skirmish. Dale won her trust with a handful of peaches that she eagerly accepted. He deemed it wrong that an officer should walk, and brought the beast over to Pennywhistle.

Pennywhistle thanked Dale, but his aching back felt gratitude beyond the power of any words to convey.

The mare responded well to Pennywhistle. He had never been a particularly good horseman. He had always distrusted horses, and suspected that in some way the beasts intuitively sensed that. Now his seat seemed surer than usual. The mare seemed to sense his intentions before the reins transmitted them. He wondered if his enhanced sensitivities extended toward a deeper understanding of animals.

O' Laughlin and Crouchback conversed quietly as they marched. Normally the men stepped in silence, but the Captain had bent the rules a bit in light of the heat and extraordinary circumstances.

"I believe him, Gramps. I don't hold with that 'back from the dead' nonsense." Crouchback was a hard-minded Cockney who scoffed at mystical explanations and called them the refuge of a weak mind. He took a large bite of a ripe peach. "What difference does it make, anyway? He has just shown us he is still lucky—that's what counts. You and me ain't going to die anytime soon! Why, he is bombproofed!"

"Bombproofed... bombproofed!" chuckled O' Laughlin. "I like it," he mumbled as he stuffed a strawberry into his mouth. The nickname that started as a single voice soon became the voice of the column. "Bombproofed, bombproofed," the men spoke it *sotto voce* as they marched in rhythm with their drummer boys. Pennywhistle had acquired the sobriquet that would follow him for the rest of his career. Bombproofed Pennywhistle.

Two miles before the column reached the safety of the fleet's guns, an emaciated old woman limped to the side of the road, leaning heavily on a stout cedar walking stick. She had a stern face, though her eyes hinted at a kind nature. She carried a pitch fork defiantly in the other hand, a black top hat fixed in one of its tines. The hat had a hole through it that could only have been made by a Brown Bess round.

She was dressed in the black of mourning and shouted with the indignation of those who have unfairly lost a loved one. "You lobster bastards!" she proclaimed. "You murdering sodomites! You killed my only grandson. He was all I had." She flourished the hat. "I curse you rotten sons-of-bitches to hell: may your souls be cast in front of Satan's throne!"

She dissolved into incoherent mutterings and sobs. The directness of her powerful emotions had nothing to do with allegiance to flags and struck a chord in the hearts of the marching marines. His men cast their eyes at their feet, since she looked the sort of grandmother that everyone wished to have. She was probably a good woman driven to her wit's end by war. Even pointless little skirmishes like the one just concluded killed men who mattered to someone.

Her pain crashed over Pennywhistle like a tidal wave. She represented an archetype that would always be a sad concomitant of war: the old burying the young when the reverse should be true. He could not take away her pain, but he could acknowledge it.

He halted his mare in front of the woman. She looked up at him with a mixture of hatred and confusion, surprised that a lordly officer would pay her attention. She quivered for a moment as if expecting violence, then relaxed when she saw understanding in his eyes.

"I am sorry for your distress, ma'am. I am sure your grandson was a fine man. It is said that a man never really dies as long as his memory lives in the heart of a loved one. I would be obliged if you would take this coin so that your grandson may have a proper headstone. I feel certain you can compose a suitable epitaph which will ensure that his life is not forgotten."

He reached into his pocket and pressed into her hand a golden guinea. She examined it carefully, as if uncertain of its authenticity. Her sobs ceased. She looked up at him in puzzlement.

"I don't understand."

"We British are not the monsters you believe us to be." He touched his hat in salute.

A hundred yards down the road, Richardson collapsed. Jones and McCarthy rushed to his side, and Pennywhistle trotted over. Jones examined Richardson's chest, then his legs. "He's wounded, sir: just above his right shin. Ain't going to kill him, but I bet it hurt like the very devil," said Jones. "I can't think how the Parson made it this far—maybe it was his faith. Don't you worry none, sir; me and McCarthy will hoist him up and get him home."

"No," said Pennywhistle shaking his head. He remembered Marlborough sometimes gave rides in his carriage to private soldiers too exhausted to march any longer. "I appreciate your regard for your mate, but we are all in this endeavor together. It's ridiculous that you should assist him to walk when he can ride. Hoist him over the back of my saddle and strap him down."

Arriving in Benedict, he shook the hands of everyone in his company one last time. There were sniffles, moist eyes, and choked voices aplenty, but the revelations of their faces were nothing compared to the emotions he felt from their hearts. He said he would never forget them, and he meant it.

When he boarded the packet *Aemelia,* his fiancée's first words were, "God Almighty, what happened to you?" She looked as shocked as a Bedouin finding a lion in his tent. She gently stroked his bruised cheeks as if her touch could heal. "You must be in a world of pain. And... your eyes! They remind me of witch balls."

"I have absorbed worse blows," he responded, as if discussing nothing worse than a scraped knee. "It's a long story, but right now I really don't want to talk." He kissed her, and she huffed with laughter. The kiss deepened, becoming passionate. "That's the kind of painkiller I need. Why don't we settle into our cabin?"

Lovemaking was the best anodyne for physical distress, and sleep was the fastest way to calm an excited mind struggling to understand insights not often granted to living men. As he drifted off in his fiancée's arms, the boundaries between reality and dreams blurred.

His relaxed consciousness opened a door, and a powerful surge of electricity shot through. All of the hairs on his body rose. He sensed the arrival of a presence, and somehow knew it was intended as a guide; it was unsentimental and did not judge. He understood that communication with it would be non-verbal, but he was too damn tired to figure out just how that might work.

He told himself not to worry. He would puzzle things out tomorrow. After all, he was bombproofed.

Chapter One

Royal Mailship Vesta, *English Channel, 29th September, 1814*

"Damn it!" growled Pennywhistle. He had been daydreaming in a haze of post coital bliss and the return of reality felt like chiggers on the genitals. Visions of sky, sea, ship, and sextant had granted the admiral of his imagination a pleasant voyage and he did not want it to end. Actively visualizing pleasant prospects had provided a welcome relief from the pain that had been his constant companion over the last month.

The long climb up the maintop in the crisp dawn air had invigorated his senses. He had enjoyed the sunny three-week passage from Bermuda and had been hoping for a glimpse of the Cornish coast when a black and yellow hulled specter popped out of a dissipating fog bank.

The intruder ship was five miles off the port beam with a rapidly freshening wind at her back. He watched her captain tack expertly. Wearing ship, putting your stern into the wind rather than your bow, was a slower but more reliable way to execute a turn if your crew lacked training and experience. This one clearly did not. The intruder confidently swung round to a new heading that was definitely an intercept course.

He'd thought that he had left war behind and what lay before him was a nasty reminder of his misapprehension. The view from the maintop masthead revealed an approaching emergency that would cause most civilians to shudder, wail, or pray for a miracle. He instead unfurled his Ramsden and examined his opponent slowly, searching for any sign of weakness.

His practiced eye appraised the interloper as carefully as a gambler would a thoroughbred before the Epsom Derby. She was a flush-decked schooner, of one 115-foot length and three hundred and fifty tons burden. He counted sixteen yellow gun-ports dotting her sleek lines, probably concealing 12-pounders.

He blinked as a wisp of salt spray stung his left eye, but the discomfort accelerated the reemergence of the old drives. His emerald eyes blazed, his pulse quickened, and his mind unfurled several courses of action. His breathing deepened and his sense of smell increased in acuity, detecting an oily scent that sparked a useful memory. Emergency reserves of blood reddened his face as his mouth purged moisture, and the sugary taste of quick energy flooded his tongue. The tiny hairs on his forearms snapped to attention from the jolt of electricity coursing through his veins.

He panned his glass slowly over the intruder. Her mainmast was set further aft and her foremast was proportionally taller than most ships of her size, marking her as a clipper. She carried a massive press of canvas in a fore and aft rig, to which was added a square topsail and topgallant. She had not yet hoisted an ensign, but her two steeply raked masts, low freeboard, and the sharp lines of her hull indicated one point of origin: The Fells Point Shipyard in Baltimore, Maryland. Her design sacrificed stability for speed: her narrow beam and soaring masts increased the danger of capsizing, but they also made a skilled captain a jockey riding a magnificent racehorse.

Clippers were designed for running blockades with expensive, low-bulk cargos, but this unusually large specimen was armed as a privateer and meant to take Pennywhistle's vessel as a prize.

Pennywhistle scowled and heartily wished that his mentor, Cockburn, had proceeded immediately against Baltimore after burning Washington. More than 100 privateers called that city home, and the inhabitants boasted that John Bull had not yet built a frigate fast enough to catch a clipper.

His ship, *Vesta,* was a Bermuda-built, two-masted schooner chartered by the Royal Mail Service. She was 68 feet long and reckoned speedy by British standards, yet she was no match for ships that were the fastest in the world. One clipper had made the 13,000-mile run from Canton, China, to Baltimore in a remarkable 96 days. *Vesta* might extend the chase, but the outcome was not in doubt.

Vesta's four 3-pounders fired a broadside so small it could be carried in a captain's coat pocket. Effective against brigands in small boats, it was ineffective when hurled at any ship built with American Oak scantlings; 18-pound shot had simply bounced off the USS *Constitution's* hull and earned her the nickname "Old Ironsides."

Even if *Vesta's* thin timbers survived a long-distance slugging match, she had no chance at close quarters. Her opponent probably carried twelve times her dozen-man complement—the extra men to be detailed as prize crews. Any reasonable captain would be well within the conventions of honor if he surrendered as soon as a privateer of superior force dispatched a few rounds over his bow.

Though he was a passenger and not *Vesta's* captain, Pennywhistle could not permit her surrender. Duty and love both demanded that not a single American boot gain *Vesta's* deck. He carried vital dispatches: it was imperative that Whitehall receive news of the capture of the American capital. The dispatches were in a weighted canvas bag that could be dumped over the side in an emergency, but he was determined not to let it come to that.

He also bore a silver reliquary chest containing the heart of an American half-brother born on the wrong side of the blanket. That brother had been a United States Marine Corps captain who had fought on the field of Bladensburg. His dying request had been that his heart be laid to rest in the family sepulcher in St. Cuthbert's Church.

Most importantly, he was joined to an American wife: a twenty-three-year-old, tart-tongued beauty from the backwoods of Maryland. Yankee tars would probably regard his bride as a traitorous tramp. The consequences to her might prove brutal.

Ambition was a consideration as well. Delivery of these critical dispatches practically guaranteed him a promotion to major. Even a knighthood was possible: news of a surprise victory would be welcomed by a Prince Regent weary of a misbegotten little war that had dragged on for far too long.

He assessed the American ship's approach and concluded that, based on wind, sail plan, and skill of handling, he had ninety minutes before the intruder closed to a critical distance. Her much larger ordnance considerably outranged *Vesta*'s popguns: the mail ship stood no chance in a contest of force, but in a battle of mind against mind he might just prevail.

A memory of the overwhelming peace of The Other Side flashed through his head and he winced at what he was about to do. He might aspire to be Francis of Assisi, but the situation demanded Richard Lion Heart.

He had reviewed the ship's cargo manifest at the start of the voyage as a matter of habit. Wellington at Salamanca had taught him that amateurs attended to tactics while professionals focused on logistics. *Vesta* chiefly hauled mail, but one unusual shipment bound for Edinburgh University from Pennsylvania had caught his eye. This shipment contained a curious array of chemical components and half a dozen foul-smelling barrels containing something called picula.

Even in war, men of science maintained international cooperation because they were dedicated to discovering universal truths that transcended political concerns. The intended recipient was chemist extraordinaire Angus Maxwell, a man Pennywhistle greatly respected. He had been Maxwell's star pupil at university, and he recognized that the chemicals were part of the professor's long quest to find a new source of lighting by modifying a Byzantine weapon.

Pennywhistle descended the ratlines, and by the time his booted foot reached the deck he had refined his ideas into a plan, the necessary first step of which was to win approval from Captain James Russell. Pennywhistle had dined with Russell on several occasions, and he had concluded the man was a Hotspur and a master marine. He had left the Royal Navy only because he had been unlucky in gaining prize money and hauling mail paid much better. He guessed Russell would resist capture strenuously—if only someone could show him how to wring advantage from meager resources.

Russell stood just aft of the bowsprit with his spyglass extended. He shifted his position every few seconds, never letting the American out of the focus of his lens. It was as if each new viewing angle might be the one to supply a way out of his hopeless position.

He jammed his glass shut when he heard Pennywhistle approach. He faced the marine with the exasperated look of a man in need of an audience in order to vent his frustrations. He spoke in short, hard bursts and his hands stabbed the air. "Curse the Gods! She's the *Dapper James*. Last I heard she was prowling St. George's Channel. The Admiralty has been hunting her for months. They have almost had her half a dozen times, but she is just too bloody fast."

He rattled off an impressive string of curses. "My *Vesta* could outrun any other ship, but I can't summon a miracle. I think you'd best tell your wife to prepare herself." He noted Pennywhistle's to-be-expected look of disapproval. He was startled when that look evolved to a sly smile.

"Captain Russell, you don't want to give up, any more than I do. Science might just be able to deliver that miracle. We don't have to outrun *Dapper James,* just outthink her captain. Might I explain?" he said conspiratorially.

"Please, Captain, favor me with any ideas you have. My life is this ship, and I will lick the Earl of Hell's riding boots if someone will show me how to save her!"

"Thank you, Captain. We need to lure *Dapper James* in close. We will seem to make her task easier rather than more difficult. Now here is what I have in mind..."

Three minutes later, Russell wore a startled expression as he rubbed his chin in wonderment.

"Our blue emergency signal rockets used as detonators? That's the damnedest plan I ever heard, but it will be deuced difficult to counter. Virgil McClarty commanding the *Dapper James* is much feared by those of us who carry the mail and military payrolls. I met him in Falmouth before the war—an arrogant man who boasts that he is half swordfish and half shark. A hard customer, too. His men call him Old Flintheart, and he relishes the nickname! A few months back, he sent a proclamation through the lines to be posted on the door of Lloyd's of London. He declared the whole of the British Isles to be under blockade by his ship alone. Drove the Admiralty into a tizzy. He is at least as tall as you, but consumption-thin; he should be easy to spot."

Pennywhistle formed his fingertips into a steeple of satisfaction. "Captain, I could not ask for a better opponent.

A man with outsized hubris is a man poised on the brink of a fatal lesson. We can fuel McClarty's overconfidence by giving him exactly what he expects. I just hope the wind holds."

Russell massaged his scalp as if his brain hurt from absorbing too much knowledge. "You are a clever man, Captain. Not sure I grasp it all, but I can see you have thought this through. I can manage the seamanship, if you can manage the chemistry. But is your wife really that good with a rifle? I have never met a member of the weaker sex who knew one end of a firelock from the other. I do not think women have either the instinct or resolve to fight in battle. Their field of honor is the family hearth."

Pennywhistle's expression soured.

"But forgive me, sir—the Yankees are passing strange folk and confound everyone's expectations!"

Pennywhistle spoke reproachfully. "Captain, you fail to consider that there is no more fearsome creature than a mother defending her children from bodily harm. Women routinely handle the pain of birth, which would likely break the strongest of men. Yes, Americans are odd, but despite nasal speech, blunt discourse, and egalitarian philosophy, they are still branches sprung from the same tree roots that gave us birth. We could learn much from each other, but stupid politicians chose guns over pens. I have fought the Jonathans, but it is sheer folly to have two English-speaking peoples at war."

Pennywhistle stopped abruptly, realizing that he had been lecturing, a habit his wife was working hard to cure.

"Captain, my wife grew up hunting all manner of animals. She knows weapons as well as you know the sea, and a rifle is as much a part of her as your spyglass is of you. I have seen her kill six men, five with a rifle and one with a tomahawk.

Russell's mouth puckered in surprise. "I shall take great care not to get on her bad side."

BOMBPROOFED

"A wise decision, her bad side is a very dark place to be! My batman Gabriel can assist as well. He is a stout-hearted fellow and has acquitted himself well in battle."

Russell started in astonishment. "I find it remarkable that a black man serves as a gentleman's gentleman, but a black man with a gun is even more extraordinary."

Pennywhistle flashed a sardonic half smile. "A black man with a musket is terror personified in the southern regions of America, and one with training is the worst nightmare of slave-owners. The Jonathans screamed long and loud when Britain formed the Colonial Marines from runaway slaves. But time grows short. Let me talk to my people, and then I shall require four of your smartest hands to assist me in the hold. Have them join me there at the earliest possible moment."

"Certainly, Captain Pennywhistle. I am just a Free Thinking, old shellback but... I hope to God this works!"

Russell departed aft and assembled his crew. There were confused looks when he said he wanted the handling of the ship to be slow and lubberly. It went against every ounce of the training that he had so diligently drilled into them, but he told them it was designed to send a signal—a misleading signal. Russell explained that the instant he bellowed "Belay!" he expected ship handling to return to its usual exacting precision. The crew nodded in relief and nudged each other, now that they grasped that the captain's odd instructions were part of some design to outfox the Yankees.

In short order, Russell put the helm over, almost missed stays, and clumsily brought the ship to a new heading. *Vesta* crested the waves and the intruder angled after her in pursuit, the response of a predator seeing the backside of feckless prey.

Pennywhistle headed down the aft companionway and alerted Dale and Gabriel. He gave them a quick resume of his plan and explained the role the chemicals would play.

"This stuff will actually burn on water, Cap'n?" Gabriel said in astonishment.

"Indeed it will," Pennywhistle replied solemnly. "The stuff is so dangerous that those who used it in war were often destroyed by it. We must be careful that such a fate does not befall us. Furthermore, we must use as little as will prove effective." Pennywhistle had a brief, unhappy moment, imagining the disappointment of Maxwell if his materials never arrived.

As Pennywhistle's bride emerged from their tiny cabin she spotted her husband. The former Samantha Josephine Matthews disdained her formal Christian names and always told people, "I'm just plain old Sammie Jo." It pleased her that he wore the robin's egg blue frock coat and buff pantaloons that she liked, rather than the scarlet jacket and grey trousers that he seemed to regard as a second skin. She wore the shamrock green dressing gown of silk, and burgundy slippers of satin that he had purchased for her in Bermuda before their improvised wedding. She had to stoop so that her five-foot, eleven-inch frame would not scrape the deck beams.

Her eyes caressed him from head to foot, and she grinned like a cat that had just gulped a bowl of cream. She stretched her arms downward and out; slowly and luxuriously. "Butter my butt and call me a biscuit! I feel really well fu—" She shook her head and stopped abruptly. "I know, I know, I need to clean up my language and be a lady, but it's plumb hard not to speak direct and frank when you feel good." When he didn't respond, she looked at him more closely.

Subtle worry lines were on his cheeks, the crow's feet flanking his vigilant eyes had deepened and his generous lips thinned, making him appear older than his thirty years. She realized something far more serious than her salty language distressed him. Her breezy tones changed to those of concern. "Jiminy Christmas, Tom! Were you climbing the rat lines again? I told you not to push yourself so hard."

He shook his head. "A spot of unpleasantness, my dear, nothing more," he said quietly, trying to sound nonchalant.

Her eyebrows arched in alarm because his "spot of unpleasantness" translated to "disaster" in the lexicon of civilians.

Pennywhistle dropped his pretense as he saw worry envelop her face. "Oh, blast!" he said, and ran a hand through his hair. "A fast privateer is closing on us and has to be stopped. I am going to need your rifle and the return of your Hawkeye self." The nickname he had given her for her shooting skills had also become one of endearment.

"Well hissy fit with a tail on it!" she snarled as she slapped her hands together in frustration. "It sure seems that a passel of my countrymen don't want us to be happy! I was looking forward to promenading around the deck in those silver-buckled pumps that made every lady in Bermuda pea green with envy, twirling a parasol, and letting the sun sparkle off that gold dress you like so well." She twisted her lips as if she had just bitten cactus dipped in castor oil, then growled, "I knew there was a reason I didn't throw out my working gear!"

Sammie Jo preferred the brutal honesty of the frontier to the Englishman's penchant for courtly understatement. He could see in her vexed eyes that she was on the verge of saying, "Don't give me that who-shot-John stuff," one of her favorite expressions, which translated to "speak plainly and get to the point." Now was clearly a time to do just that.

He explained his plan and her expression of anger changed to one of concentration as deep as his own. It pained him to put his ruthlessness on display, but emergencies demanded frankness rather than polite circumlocution. "The American crew will burn or drown, you understand? Mercy has no part to play."

She nodded calmly, listening carefully but saying nothing. Only the widening of her pupils betrayed any excitement.

Pennywhistle groaned in frustration. "I thought that we had left war behind, I truly did. I feel a complete hypocrite, since I have been making such a fuss about you learning peaceable ways and gentle manners." He pounded his fist into the flat of his hand in frustration. "Damn it, the last thing I want is to drag you back into your former life. I would do this thing myself, but I will be aiming the rockets." He shook his head. "Neither Dale nor I can match your shooting. Plunkett of the 95th knocked General Colbert off his horse from five hundred yards, but what I am asking will require an even greater level of skill." He hesitated for a fraction of a second. "You are going to kill the enemy captain."

"What distance and angle did you have in mind?" Her voice was businesslike and detached, betraying not a syllable of vacillation.

"Two hundred and fifty yards, 65-foot elevation, firing downward at a 45-degree angle. Both ships will be in forward motion, as well as pitching and rolling; there is considerable chop today. You should fire on the down roll." Pennywhistle realized that he sounded like one master craftsman consulting another, rather than a husband speaking to a wife. Still, couples were supposed to rely upon each other.

She massaged her chin slowly as she visualized the mechanics of the shot. Her face assumed a frigid, marble-like cast of utter implacability. She said quietly, "I can do it."

Fire followed the ice: her unfashionably tanned visage darkened with the heat of impending battle. The thin mask of civilization that she wore so uncertainly dissolved, revealing a truer self forged by a hard life of hunting—the ferocious beauty of a forest Zenobia. Her full lips compressed into a thin line of dark purpose. Tension tightened the skin on her high cheek bones and the light in the cornflower blue eyes shifted from comforting to cruel.

She spread her long, supple fingers wide apart, moved her muscular shoulders backward in slow half circles, and flexed her powerful legs, an athlete limbering up before a match. She winced faintly at the tug of a not-quite-healed sword cut on her left hip, a souvenir of her congress with war.

"Damn right I can do it, Sugar Plum!" Her favorite endearment came out as *shugah pluh-umm* in her heavy rustic dialect. "Any varmint trying to ruin our happiness deserves a bullet!" She spat the words, then breathed in and out deeply several times, as he had taught her, a lioness worried about her mate but trying to calm herself. She softly ran her fingers through the sandy red hair on his temples, then placed her hands firmly on her hips to emphasize her resolve.

Her voice turned husky and determined. "I ain't no innocent, Tom, so don't ever try to spare me. Hard as I aim to be a moral, upstanding lady, I ain't likely to pass muster with St. Peter at the Pearly Gates anytime soon. One more sin won't make no difference, so don't tucker yourself out trying to protect my hide or my conscience."

Pennywhistle grimaced. "This was going to be a pleasant ocean voyage to a better life. You were supposed to rest and let the sun and sea breezes heal you. I am so sor—"

She put a finger to his lips. "Hush, sugar! Lovin' me so deep and fine like you done a bit ago is the best medicine of all! Most folks run under a table when danger knocks, but you and I meet it right at the door and punch it straight in the face. We done plowed the furrow of respectability these last few days. It's time to give that mule a rest."

Her eyes blazed and her voice became as sharp and menacing as a guillotine's blade. "My rightful place is at your side, scrapping like an angry polecat and making damn sure that *we* decide our future, not those Baltimore bastards. Those sailors will curse the day that they ever saw this ship, though they will not do it for long."

Pennywhistle kissed her passionately, relishing her fire and candor and drawing strength from both.

While honesty was praised, it often starved but he valued her ability to look things in the eye and speak the unvarnished truth about them. Years spent in the forest caused her to reduce problems to their most basic components and fashion solutions that reflected a tough practicality too often absent from members of his class. He hoped that her New World naturalness would never be lost when she confronted the artifice of English aristocrats. But that presumed they would survive this present mess. It was, he realized, important to maintain an optimistic cast of mind. Those who believed they would prevail in a tight spot generally did, and those who believed they would fail usually brought about exactly that result.

He drew back, his eyes delighting in her womanly curves. "You once said that we were like a pair of tough old shoes, ready to weather any hard road; but I think we are more like sturdy bookends. We force the people around us to stand straight and tall and do what is right, rather than what is easy." He stroked her hair gently. "I need you in my life. After all, what good is one bookend?"

She caressed his cheeks slowly. "Bookends—I like that! Though I reckon we are more like pencil and paper, since we have a marriage to write. Besides, we just might get from strength what we sure as hell won't get from mercy." Her crooked smile indicated predation rather than mirth.

They re-entered their cabin and laid out the garb of war. Their bodies generated considerable heat in the confined space, but it was preparatory to battle, not lust. She dressed in brown bib and brace overalls, red plaid wool shirt, and men's jockey boots, then bound her hair up in a bun and covered it with a wide-brimmed black slouch hat. She checked her rifle carefully and made sure that her possibles bag was filled with the necessary accoutrements.

He was determined to be conspicuous and defiantly visible to the enemy. He had left his dress uniform behind in Bermuda before the Washington Campaign had begun, and now donned it with the care of a knight suiting up for battle. The military cloth gave him a psychological protection nearly as great as the physical one chain mail furnished to a knight. Military life was about rituals, and he treated dressing as a priestly one, though there was nothing holy about what he was about to do.

He swapped out his buff pantaloons for newly fashionable navy blue trousers and traded his cotton shirt for a silk one, because silk carried less risk of infection if pressed into a wound. He replaced his charcoal-colored wool socks for bone-white silk specimens, for the same reason. He removed his gold-buckled shoes and replaced them with Hessian boots that gave better purchase on blood-soaked decks. Next, he tied a black silk stock round his neck. Unlike leather, it caused no chafing from rapid head swivels during battle. Its softness was a stark contrast to the heavily starched uniform collar that would contain it.

He smiled briefly at the exactness of the fit his scarlet jacket. Gieves of Savile Row had tailored it from superfine broadcloth, and its high blue collar, short swallow tails, and closely cinched waist flattered his athletic figure. He brushed its gold epaulettes, buttoned up the double-breasted coat flap on the right side, and suspended his gorget from a blue ribbon round his neck; the crescent-shaped object signified an officer on duty. The arms of King George emblazoned on it gleamed with golden majesty. That same golden hue was reflected in the fouled anchor of the Royal Marines on his buttons and the tops and tassels on his black boots.

Then he wrapped his 88-inch crimson silk sash tightly round his waist, and tied the twin ball tassels on his left side. He hoped that he would never have to employ its secondary function as a stretcher.

He fastened on a white sword belt under his right epaulette. It crossed his chest at a forty-five-degree angle and ensured that the black scabbard suspended from it was held hard by his left hip. His Osborn would find no employment if his plan worked, but a sword was a hallmark of command like his sash, and symbols were important in battle.

He stretched his buff kidskin gloves until their tops touched the edges of his blue cuffs, then topped off the whole with the red and white plumed black coachman's hat that was a distinctive mark of his Service.

He turned to face Sammie Jo, who nodded crisply in approval. They smiled briefly at each other, then their faces set in stern determination. The final transformation was remarkable; less a change of clothing than personas. The newlyweds had departed and the warriors had returned. And yet, for those perceptive enough to detect it, it could be seen that love lingered in their eyes. He took her hand firmly. "Let's go!"

Chapter Two

Captain Virgil McClarty observed his quarry through his expensive Dolland spyglass. He recognized *Vesta* by her lines and sail plan, although he knew nothing about her captain save that he seemed unskillful. Odd that an incompetent man commanded a Royal Mail ship, but the British sometimes favored nepotism over ability and gave safe assignments to favorites who would be liabilities in more demanding arenas.

Vesta had set every ounce of canvas, yet he closed the distance with each passing minute—a thoroughbred chasing a pony. Currently he estimated the distance at nearly three miles; at a quarter of a mile, he would lob a few balls in her direction, her captain would see reason, and he would be a substantially richer man. Royal Mail ships had a reputation for reliability, and so private citizens often used them to carry substantial quantities of gold, silver, and jewelry. American clippers wreaked havoc with expectations, however. McClarty grinned, his eyes burning with avarice. The *Dapper James* had already taken twelve prizes in her eight-month career, netting him and his shareholders more than $1,000,000 in prize money. Thirteen was his lucky number. This ship would be his within the hour. Nothing could prevent that.

The dark, cramped hold of *Vesta* stank with a variety of smells. It was packed to bursting with stores, and not a place for the claustrophobic. The slowly swinging lanterns cast an eerie, malevolent glow on the assemblage of strained faces and tense bodies. A large rat raced off into the shadows as if frightened by the dark human emotions.

Four sailors babbled with a nervous energy that the battle-hardened Dale found annoying. If they had been under his command, he would have enjoined strict silence. Gabriel said nothing and was the picture of patient reserve.

Everyone moved to rise when Pennywhistle and Sammie Jo appeared, but the marine motioned all to stay seated. His own six-foot, two-inch frame was stooped and he saw no point in having men bang their heads merely to show respect.

"I brought the largest powder ladles I could find, just like you asked, sir," said Dale.

"I done just like you told me, Cap'n. I brought six brooms from the hold. They are made of this new American broomcorn stuff and stout ash," said Gabriel. "They will be good mixing sticks and should work fine as shafts for the rockets."

"Capital!" proclaimed Pennywhistle vigorously, hoping his enthusiasm would fire up the entire group. "I see in your faces that you wonder what I intend. We are going to be doing some cooking today, hence the utensils. We will not be preparing food, but a weapon. We are going to re-create an ancient substance, Greek Fire. It was the secret weapon of the Byzantines, and it destroyed entire fleets sent against Constantinople. I believe we have the requisite elements in the hold to create a good facsimile."

The sailors blinked in surprise, but Dale and Gabriel smiled, used to their captain thinking his way out of tight spots. One eager sailor voiced what was on everyone's mind. "Just what does it do, sir?"

"It is fire amplified tenfold, flame rendered almost supernatural: a fast-traveling holocaust that will burn on water and is virtually invulnerable to extinguishment. Furthermore, its jelly-like consistency will stick like iron filings on a magnet once it attaches itself to a hull."

The sailors looked uncertain, wanting to believe that ingenuity gave them a fighting chance of avoiding capture, but still not sure. One inquired, "What's in it, sir?"

Pennywhistle pointed to six barrels in the corner. "Those barrels contain an oily substance commonly found in Pennsylvania. It sometimes called picula, or burning water, but my old professor christened it "petroleum." He is a visionary who believes it contains a vast potential for the future. For our purposes, once lit, it burns hot and it will float on water. I propose to mix it with part of a shipment bound for Sir Humphrey Davy: antimony, resin, coal tar, and rock flakes coated with aluminum. The mixture will require something to ignite it; I believe the ship's signal rockets will serve the purpose."

"But how are we going to deliver it?" Gabriel asked.

Pennywhistle warmed to his subject like the academic that he'd almost become. "Two ways. We are going to mix the ingredients in the petroleum barrels and transform them into bombs. We will puncture the barrels just before we dump them over the taffrail. They will merge with the slip stream and flow toward the enemy. Once we ignite them, the enemy will sail into a sea of fire. As an added refinement, we are going to coat some cannon balls with the substance. Our three pounders ordinarily can't do much damage, but we can use the balls as fire-starters."

"Almost like hot shot, sir?" said Dale. Hot shot was fired from land-based installations after being heated in furnaces, and was deadly to wooden ships.

"Exactly so, Sar't Major! You are going to sight and lay each cannon, since I will be handling the rockets."

"Aye, aye, sir." Dale touched his hat in salute—difficult though it was in the close quarters.

Pennywhistle turned to Gabriel. "I want you to supervise dumping the barrels in echelon at thirty-second intervals so that we leave a solid trail in our wake, one the enemy absolutely cannot avoid."

Gabriel nodded. "I won't let you down, Cap'n!"

Pennywhistle addressed the sailors. "I believe men perform best when they understand the overall design of an action, so I will favor you with some additional details. I am banking on surprise, shock, and..."—he pointed to Sammie Jo—"and my wife." Sammie Jo bowed her head gravely in acknowledgement.

"When we ignite the barrels and fire the cannon, she will eliminate the enemy captain with her long rifle. There will be panic and confusion on the enemy deck; the indispensable man will be gone at the critical moment. Once the fires are established, there will be no stopping them. We then hoist every ounce of canvas and dash for Plymouth."

He looked each sailor hard in the eye. "I have complete respect for your captain's judgment and trust that you will disappoint neither him nor me. For this engagement, I need you to follow my instructions exactly. Are you with me?"

"Yes, sir!"

Pennywhistle's eyes sparkled with satisfaction, though his plan contained too many "ifs" for his liking. "Splendid!"

The sailors proved as good as their word and assisted Dale and Gabriel in assembling and laying out all of the necessary components. Each sailor took charge of a single

BOMBPROOFED

ingredient. They loaded the ladles with whatever amount of ingredient Pennywhistle requested. He filled each barrel with the requisite condiments, assigned one sailor to each barrel to thoroughly stir the mix, Dale and Gabriel taking care of the other two. The resulting muck smelled to high heaven and made the men's eyes water.

The ghostly light of the swinging lanterns made his helpers appear to be demonic imps reveling in the knowledge that they would confound the enemy with their devil's brew.

"Double, double, toil and trouble, sir?" said Dale with a wry half smile. Pennywhistle nodded, but worried that he was merely a sorcerer's apprentice, not the master magician that everyone assumed him to be. He believed that he had created a crude copy of what Theophanes the Confessor had alluded to in his ninth-century *Chronicles*, "a fierce and obstinate flame that instead of being extinguished by water is nourished and quickened by it." Yet he had no idea in what proportions the ingredients should be mixed. He hated guessing, but battle allowed no time for the systematic experimentation favored by academics.

As the wind strengthened, *Dapper James* closed rapidly on *Vesta*. McClarty ordered the ship to clear for action and ran up an oversize Stars and Stripes, even though the British ship undoubtedly knew their nationality.

Yankee gun crews raced to their stations as other sailors doused the galley fire, sanded the deck, and filled the blue buckets next to each cannon with water for swabbing. Two cartridges were brought up from the magazine for each gun, shot garlands were filled with cannon balls, and the flintlocks atop the cannons were unsheathed. Portfires were lit as backup methods of ignition and placed in tubs of sand. Tompions were removed from cannon muzzles, and the 12-pounders loaded with brisk efficiency. The gun ports were opened and the trucks of the cannon squealed as the guns were run out. Sailors designated for the boarding party brought the weapons chests to the deck and armed themselves with pikes, tomahawks, pistols, and cutlasses.

McClarty calculated that one or two shots should overawe *Vesta*'s inept captain. He had no wish to damage her with a full broadside since it would reduce her value as a prize. Through his Dolland he could see men hefting barrels onto *Vesta's* deck from the hold and rolling them toward the stern. He was puzzled, but the mystery was irrelevant because the ship-handling continued to be amateurish and un-seamanlike.

He noted two scarlet coats on deck—Regulars. He was briefly alarmed and carefully checked the deck for Marine sharpshooters. Seeing none, he decided that they were probably just passengers. He did not detect any activity near the cannons, a sure sign that *Vesta* would capitulate quickly. He rubbed his hands together in anticipation when *Vesta's* crew prepared to reduce sail. The sailors were slow; clumsy crewmen were to be expected of a clumsy captain. He fully expected to see the British colors hauled down in the next few minutes. The enemy captain probably just needed him to play his assigned part: it would look bad in the newspapers if he surrendered before even a token shot was fired. The British public would need to be convinced that the captain had bowed to the inevitable.

Pennywhistle and Russell both extended their glasses and carefully observed the *Dapper James*.

"I am glad that I heeded your suggestion, Captain Pennywhistle, and postponed the beat to quarters. If he is being slow to fire, deeming us no threat, we buy time. What do you reckon, about fifteen minutes, then get the crew to action stations?"

BOMBPROOFED

"Sounds about right, Captain Russell. Sar't Major Dale will make every shot count."

Sammie Jo paced impatiently behind the two; her long fingers pulling her rifle's chocolate brown sling tight against her shoulder in frustration. Her nervous energy finally got the better of her and she defiantly walked up to Russell and stared him square in the face. "Cap'n, I heard that you said a woman should be rocking a cradle instead of shouldering a shootin' iron."

Russell's face turned as red as his hair. "Forgive me, ma'am, but the women I was raised with knew as little about firearms as I do about electricity. Your husband has acquainted me with the particulars of your talent and—"

Sammie Jo cut him off. "I ain't faultin' you for worrying about buying a pig in a poke, but selling women short is as foolish as jabbing a wolverine and expecting it not to bite. I aim to give a powerful good demonstration of what I can do."

"The confidence in your voice reassures me, ma'am, and even an old sea dog can learn new tricks. Your rifle is certainly impressive, Mrs. Pennywhistle." Russell looked with genuine admiration at a weapon that was a triumph of the gunsmith's art. The tiger-striped maple stock was polished to a glass-like finish the color of campfire embers, the octagonal barrel glistened with gun oil, and the rectangular brass patchbox sparkled from careful attention. Yet what fascinated most was the downward curve of the butt stock: much like a Roman nose. He decided that was probably an American innovation. "What caliber is your piece?"

Sammie Jo smiled like a parent discussing her child. "Forty-four caliber! Always happy to talk about my pride and joy! The Widowmaker is 58 inches long with a 42-inch barrel and fires a .422 ball. A rifle should never be taller than a person's chin because otherwise the length blocks your vision when you load."

"A rifle with a name? Extraordinary! The only people I have heard of that give names to confections of wood are the owners of Stradivarius violins."

"Never ran into that particular fiddle maker, but all of the best shooters give their little darlin's names: Daniel Boone calls his rifle Tick Licker because it is so accurate he can shoot a tick off a buck without touching its hide. You lose hitting power as the distance increases, so the usual .36-caliber used for plinking little critters ain't a good choice against larger game or two-legged varmints. My baby only weighs eight pounds and is real well balanced because it has a swamped barrel." She saw puzzlement in Russell's eyes. "That means the barrel is wider at the breech and muzzle than it is in the center, allowing the stock to be thinner and lighter."

She placed the piece on her left palm, the metal and wood achieving a perfect horizontal equilibrium. "Maple don't warp near as much as other woods, no matter how bad the weather, giving you better accuracy. My piece was made by a real famous gun maker, Joseph Henry, in Nazareth, Pennsylvania. It's why folks call 'em Pennsylvania rifles. I added twin swivels to take a sling. That ain't usual, but long hours in the forest can wear you down and you need to have your best energy ready when that special shot jumps out at you."

"You certainly know your weapons," said Russell in surprise, realizing that Pennywhistle's boast about his wife had not been frivolous.

She pointed to 25 small Union Jacks carved into the butt. "Each represents a British officer that my Pa killed in the Revolution, which is why folks came to call this weapon The Widowmaker. The two Union Jacks to their right are mine. I thank God my group does not have a third flag. That was the one time in my life that I missed. Tom ducked at the last second."

Russell blinked in puzzlement. "I don't understand."

"That's all right, Captain. I think it was the good Lord moving in mysterious ways. Sometimes you find the biggest piece of gold buried deep in a pile of shi... uh... manure. Anyway, my piece also has a double-set trigger. That makes your control a heap better."

Sammie Jo turned to Pennywhistle. "I think the time's about right, Tom. I'd like to get in position and get used to the rocking of the mast. I want to make estimates of the arc of fire relative to the enemy ship's course, rate of closure, and angles of pitch and roll." She blinked and laughed, slightly puzzled. "Jiminy Christmas! I sounded just like you! Your fancy book learning's done wormed its way into my head!"

He kissed her strongly, caring not a whit about a public display of passion. "I am glad you are here," he said softly.

She looked him sternly in the eye. "You will owe me the best dinner in Plymouth!"

Pennywhistle nodded. "And a new dress to honor the occasion."

Sammie Jo sprinted to the foremast and began climbing the rat lines, her quick, lithe motions reminding him of mountain lions that he had seen in the Appalachians. Her destination was a tiny platform just above the point where the triangular flying jib joined the mast.

Directly below her, Gabriel yelled in exasperation, "Careful there! Don't roll those barrels so fast. Cap'n said handle them like they be glass. We don't want even a small tear and any of this devil's tea leaking onto the deck." The sailors nodded, realizing their enthusiasm had exceeded their good sense. Pennywhistle had impressed upon them the fact that the contents were deadly and any spark caused by accidental friction could set them off. They had already traded their shoes for slippers to eliminate a possible source of sparks.

Gabriel opened Pennywhistle's Swiss Blancpain, gratified that the captain trusted him with such a valuable timepiece. Pennywhistle was keen about the barrels being hefted overboard at thirty second intervals. He had made a guess about the enemy captain's course and he wanted the barrel positions to cover the maximum amount of sea.

Dale stood over the twin starboard 3-pounders and began surveying places on the *Dapper James* to direct *Vesta*'s fire. He decided just aft of the jib boom should do just fine. The loss of the jib boom and the attached jib and flying jib would make the ship hard to control. And if the captain were no longer alive to immediately give new orders, the ship would sail into the sea of fire ahead instead of veering away from it.

Sammie Jo reached her undulating roost 65 feet above the deck and surveyed the tiny figures bustling about below. She had no fear of heights, having frequently climbed tall trees as a girl. She fastened her legs round the topmast crosstrees, two horizontal spars used to anchor the shrouds.

She would have a clear shot at the enemy deck but the captain might well be moving about or hidden by the sails, so she would have to keep a sharp eye out. The stitches in her hip ached but she used the pain to increase her already deep concentration.

She brought her rifle to the rest position astride her thighs. The main charge had been loaded on deck but the pan remained empty. The lock plate glistened with a coating of gun oil, but the browned barrel would not reflect light to give away her position.

She swept out the pan with a camel's hair brush and pushed a wire pick through the touch hole: a meticulous loading ritual. Next she checked the tension on the main and

BOMBPROOFED

frizzen springs, and decided to tighten the frizzen spring with a screwdriver from her possibles bag. She ran her index finger along the edge of the flint to make sure it was properly beveled. She smiled—the edge was sharp and uniform. When it struck the frizzen that she had casehardened herself, a shower of sparks would result.

She had tested her powder before with a pistol-like device called an eprouvette, loading a charge of black powder into a small cup, then pulling the trigger. The force of the discharge moved a wheel with teeth against the tension of a strong spring. Markings on the wheel indicated the strength of the explosion.

It was a pleasure using British military grade powder; it packed 20% more punch than its French counterparts because of the quality of saltpeter from Bengal. It was also mixed wet to ensure greater element cohesion. Cheaper powder sold to civilians was often blended dry and lost potency when stored in barrels, partially separating into its component elements.

She removed her priming horn from her possibles bag and carefully filled the pan with eight grains of #3 fine-grain powder, making sure that the touchhole remained uncovered for the fastest possible ignition. The main charge was composed of 130 grains of #2 small-grain powder. It was a heavier load than she used for target shooting, but it would maximize the hitting power of the ball at distance. The large charge was necessary because even with the best powder only a little over half of it burned, the rest turning to a black sludge that had to be cleaned out every twenty shots or so.

Like most dedicated riflemen, she cast her own rounds. Each Pennsylvania rifle was unique, so the balls that gave it the best performance could not readily be purchased from the average gunsmith. Casting a 280-grain ball left a sprue; she always filed this off with the utmost care to ensure roundness. She had chosen the ball that to her practiced eye had the best shape. Like a surgeon examining his scalpel before an operation, she rolled it slowly in her hand one final time and then wrapped it in a patch of greased leather.

The Widowmaker was not just a confection of wood and metal, but an extension of her very self. This was her craft, her calling, her glory and her genius—her enhancement of excellence in the Universe. She was as skilled an artist in her field as Rembrandt had been in his.

She mated the crescent-shaped brass butt plate to her muscled shoulder—a trusted friend resuming her proper home. She considered the rifle a living being, a wrathful goddess with the power to upend a status quo that required women to be obedient and vulnerable. She swept The Widowmaker slowly over the enemy deck like a lighthouse beacon. *Dapper James* was still far away; she could only discern globs of color rather than individual features.

That would change soon enough. A keen-sighted hunter could make out the shape of a fast-diving kestrel at one hundred yards; she could discern the black dots on its yellow belly.

She adjusted herself to the rhythm of the swaying mast, which reminded her of the pendulum on a case clock. She sought a tall scarecrow of a man who would be gesturing energetically as he barked orders. Her target, she had been informed, habitually wore a maroon cocked hat decades out of date. Sailors were a superstitious lot and favored good luck charms. McClarty's was his hat, and it would be the death of him.

She breathed deeply for a full minute, slowing her racing heart to a steady beat of power rather than a fluttery one of anxiety. The joy of the stalk with the quarry finally dead to rights had always excited her, but now she fought for

BOMBPROOFED

something much greater: a husband she loved with a depth that continually surprised her.

He had cautioned her that in battle a cool head was worth more than a furious heart, but she could not help but view the enemy captain with anger. She did not care what kind of a man he was or if he had a wife and children—he sought to kill her future. His men would burn with him because they were complicit in his design to destroy her happiness.

It mattered not at all that they were American, because her loyalty was to a husband who treated her like royalty, believing her a gift to humanity rather than a freak of nature called to torment it. Her Baptist father had called her a spawn of Satan, and her countrymen had regarded her as a backwoods hoyden with no future better than as a rich man's plaything. She realized that she had not just a chip on her shoulder but a whole woodyard. *Good riddance to the whole goddamned lot!*

She shook her head slowly to dissipate her anger and focused on the mechanics of the shot. The best shot that she had ever made had been at two hundred and fifty yards, but she believed that with this advantage of altitude she could manage three hundred and twenty five today. Though her present platform was tiny, it was always better firing from a stand. She found her hips had adjusted and moved in intuitive synchronization with the mast.

The stakes were high and she felt the pressure, but it was also the supreme test of the marksmanship on which she prided herself. She believed in her gift and she believed in The Widowmaker.

But more than anything, this shot was for her husband's safety. She would kill for love.

Chapter Three

Pennywhistle attached the signal rocket heads to broom shafts, giving the rockets an appearance similar to that of the Congreves he had employed at Bladensburg, which made aiming much easier. He needed them traveling downward in a straight line.

He next trimmed the fuses with his dirk. The rockets normally ignited ten seconds into flight so they would reach a height from which they could be clearly seen. Given the distance today, he needed that time to be closer to three seconds.

"Sailor! Use those tongs carefully," shouted Dale as he jabbed a finger toward a startled seaman. "Yes, you, Blake—I mean you! Damn your eyes! Don't drop the bloody ball; handle it like an egg. We can't have a speck of this stuff on the deck." Like the other five balls already placed in the shot rack, this round shot was slippery from a coating of Greek Fire.

There was another reason Dale did not want them dropped. A drop would deform a ball ever so slightly, altering the trajectory. Every cannon ball was a little different from its mate, despite the apparent uniformity of weight. He had chosen six specimens for their nearly perfect roundness and then sanded them carefully to ensure a surface free of any trace of rust.

Bombproofed

The flannel cartridge bags filled with #1 large-grain powder were color-coded: black, red, and white for long, medium, and close range. Russell ran a tight ship, but since his business was delivering mail rather than fighting, Dale did not quite trust the accuracy of the loads. He ripped open a single white cartridge bag and examined the quality and amount of powder. Quality was fine, not a speck of moisture, but the load was slightly too small.

He procured a small powder ladle and a quantity of powder from the magazine, then methodically began the process of increasing the close-range charges. He would probably only have time for two shots, perhaps four, but he always liked to keep a reserve and increased the charge in six cartridges. It was slow, painstaking work, but Pennywhistle had taught him that anticipating the unthinkable meant that when the impossible happened, a solution would already be in place.

McClarty noted with pleasure that the wind had stiffened from a sprightly breeze to a steady zephyr. The *Dapper James* trimmed the sails to take advantage of the change and had closed the distance to a third of a mile. He felt a surge of pride that ingenious Baltimore shipbuilding and seamanship would once again humble the arrogant British lion.

Surprisingly, *Vesta* made no move to haul down her flag. McClarty was eager to open fire, but decided to wait until she was within hailing distance of his speaking trumpet. If she did not accept the inevitable after he commenced firing, he would steer directly for her quarterdeck and board. That contest would likely be over in minutes.

Pennywhistle tracked *Dapper James* through his Ramsden. It was time to start dumping the barrels.

Sammie Jo noted her husband talking to Gabriel and knew what it portended. She could see the enemy captain's face clearly now, and a jolt of vitriol made her eyes razors and her blood racing lava. His cruel, heavy-browed visage looked much like that of a lascivious backwoods preacher who had once tried to give her a very personal baptism.

She took four deep breaths through her nose, held them for three seconds, then exhaled slowly through her open mouth. She focused on a calming image that her husband had taught her: a soothing sun over a still pond. She reminded herself that just as she had administered lethal justice to the preacher, she could do so again, but only if she remained disciplined and focused.

Her equanimity returned, and she decided that the red, white, and blue cockade on his hat made a perfect aiming point. She full cocked her piece. She was ready, and so was The Widowmaker.

Dale's gun crews loaded the 3-pounders. They fitted gunlocks to the vent holes and full cocked them. Dale took the lanyard of cannon one. He would have only a few seconds to sight and fire when the ship pivoted.

McClarty watched the loading with astonishment. "Damn me, the fool means to fight us!" he exclaimed to his first officer, John Semmes. "Pea shooters against 12-pounders! Hell's teeth! Does he fancy himself David facing Goliath?"

"Orders, Captain?" inquired Semmes.

"Maintain our present course for three minutes. Fire two shots as soon as soon as we are within pistol shot if they have not already struck their flag. We shall give him a smart lesson in Yankee superiority."

"Now!" said Pennywhistle decisively. Gabriel stove in the side of the first barrel with a mighty swing of a boarding ax.

Bombproofed

He put his heart and soul into it. Two eager sailors dumped it over the taffrail a second later.

Pennywhistle could see the slicked surface glistening astern as the contents of the barrel spread over the sea. He waved to Sammie Jo and then to Dale. They waved back, signaling they were ready.

Russell walked quickly over to Pennywhistle. "My men have their orders and know what to do. I will take the helm myself. I certainly hope that you are right, Captain Pennywhistle."

Pennywhistle wanted to say, "So do I," but a show of confidence was important to bolster morale, and admitting doubt would help no one. "It will work, Captain." He spoke in a calm voice at odds with the bilious rumblings of his stomach.

McClarty was pleased that the chase was driving *Vesta* out to sea, away from her probable destination of Plymouth. A powerful gust filled the sails of the *Dapper James* to bursting and her sharp bow sliced powerfully through the water. She heeled to starboard as her speed increased to thirteen knots. *Lucky thirteen!* thought McClarty.

Her gun crews anxiously gripped their lanyards and the second mate told the boarding party to stand to arms.

The last barrel had just departed *Vesta*'s stern when Russell bellowed, "Belay! Hands to the braces, smartly now! Cross the 'T' on that Yankee bastard!" Russell pushed the wheel hard to starboard and the ship swung her bow round to a new heading.

Vesta's anemic ordnance now challenged the American at a ninety-degree angle, like a mouse turning on a cat. Pennywhistle fired two rockets at the closest barrel. The first zigzagged too far to starboard, but the second hit. And the world erupted in flame.

A shower of staves shot skyward, accompanied by jets of greasy, red-black fire. Large plumes of inky, vile-smelling smoke followed. Lances of scarlet darted toward the remaining barrels and their spreading contents. They ignited at the first kiss of flame, the dragon's cocktail making an unearthly sizzling sound. The sea erupted into a carpet of raging, unstoppable fire.

The heat and flames froze McClarty for the few seconds that remained of his life, the complete surprise stealing his powers of decision. One minute a fine following sea, the next a lake of fire not unlike the description he remembered from the Bible.

The speed of his vessel worked against him: the forward momentum of the *Dapper James* could not be stopped in time. Flames kissed the cutwater and an instant later red hot arms squeezed the hull. Long fingers of flame clawed their way upward to the main deck.

Sammie Jo focused her V sights on the cocked hat as soon as she saw the first gout of fire. She set the rear trigger, timed the down roll, then flicked the front trigger with the lightness of a baby's breath. She heard the comforting *clack, woosh, bang* as The Widowmaker barked its deadly message.

Dale's cannon flamed, thundered, and leaped backwards on its tackles. The first shot glanced off the netting below *Dapper James*'s dolphin striker and did no damage, but the second cannon landed a flaming ball square on a cartridge box behind the bow chaser and set off the contents with an ear-splitting bang. The fire darted across the deck like lightning seeking a lightning rod. Water racing through *Dapper James*'s scuppers acted as rivers of flame. Droplets of spray landed on the deck like incendiary measles. General panic followed because nothing was more feared at sea than fire, and this one had materialized without warning.

The captain had just opened his mouth to shout when Sammie Jo's shot penetrated the front of his cocked hat. The bullet smashed downward, compressing his brain. The pressure caused McClarty's eyeballs to pop out, then blood flowed from the empty orifices.

"Damn!" screamed Semmes. The death of his captain had happened so quickly that disbelief and disorientation left him unable to comprehend that he now had the conn. No orders issued from his mouth in the next critical seconds as flames sprinted up the ratlines.

Sailors screamed as the fire darted in every direction like the tentacles of an incendiary octopus. The flames had a strange, sticky consistency that clung tenaciously to clothing.

"Help me! Help me! Help me!" screamed dozens of victims.

Flames jumped onto the trousers of the boarding party. The seamen flailed madly at them, but the fiery lances shot up their legs. The flames not only set the 25 sailors ablaze, but the heat caused their pistols to discharge randomly, killing a number of their mates.

The fire's gusts were like the breaths of a living entity with evil intelligence and an uncanny intuition, seeking out the most destructive targets. The cartridge boxes behind the cannons detonated, blasting most of the gun crews into clots of gore. The heat cooked off the charges in the cannons and a broadside blasted out, two balls narrowly missing *Vesta*.

Greek fire generated a far more intense heat than a usual fire. The tar in the ship's miles of rope acted as a powerful accelerant. The shrouds and stays supporting the masts melted, causing them to sway like men who had had one too many beers. Men's faces disintegrated; eyeballs popped and skin puckered and boiled before sloughing off like tissue paper. Flesh liquefied moments later and flowed like streams of pale tears down bony faces. Hands curled into black claws as men fell to the deck and shriveled into fetal positions. The wind suddenly turned combative and funneled energy into a raging vortex that plucked the last gasps of oxygen from lungs even as it fried them. Those who could still breathe coughed and wheezed. The tornado hurled buckets, barrels, and belaying pins skyward. The ship's cat yowled frantically as he suffered the same fate. Deck planking warped and caulking evaporated. Treenails popped and seams ruptured. The flaming sea entered the hull, and the ship sank lower in the water.

Sammie Jo had the clearest view of the dreadful spectacle. She saw men slap crazily at themselves and jump about like fiery puppets performing some other-worldly spastic dance. Two blazing human comets trailing steam and cinders plummeted from the main top, their end marked by two crimson flares of sea spray.

She recalled ticks that she had seen children set afire. It was better to think of the burning sailors as insects. When she reminded herself that they were men, she felt the vomit rise in her throat.

She saw a few flaming creatures leap overboard, but the water did not extinguish the flames because the sea itself burned. Two men free of flame jumped into the sea, only to ignite when they hit the water. But even if the sea had not been aflame, most sailors could not swim. Her husband had been right: burn or drown.

The stench of burning flesh hit her, smelling uncomfortably like the bacon that she had had for breakfast. In that instant, insects became men. The contents of her stomach violently erupted.

BOMBPROOFED

Dapper James became a terrible spectacle, a Flying Dutchman of flame. Pushed by the wind, the Yankee ship continued her aimless forward momentum.

Sailors on *Vesta* knew that they should not look, but they could not help themselves and simply stared. Gabriel said a silent prayer for the dying men, remembering what the Good Book said about forgiveness and regretting his earlier wish to harm them.

Pennywhistle panned his Ramsden slowly over the privateer's deck. The unearthly heat had carbonized a score of sailors, shrinking them to the size of five-year-olds. Nearby, three members of the boarding party had partly melted and fused with the metal in their weapons, a repellent slag heap of black and silver flecked with bits of red and pink. He slammed his Ramsden shut in revulsion as his stomach shot geysers of bile. *My God, what have I done?* Two sailors standing at his side wept. "A Viking funeral ship," he muttered in awe. A part of him wondered if his soul was so blackened by death that he had no honest idea of where the mask of command ended and the man began.

He spoke urgently to Russell. "Time to show a clean pair of heels, Captain. It won't be long before the flames reach her magazine, and we don't any of that debris touching us." Russell nodded emphatically and gave the appropriate orders. The wind had shifted and now was almost directly behind the ship. *Vesta* picked up speed and dashed through the waves. The burning *Dapper James* fell rapidly astern.

Pennywhistle watched through his glass as *Dapper James* sank bow first. The ship shimmered like a mirage for a split second, then the magazine detonated with a blinding flash and an ear-crushing boom. A large, dome-shaped cloud of lurid scarlet settled over the roiled waters pock-marked with brown blotches of timbers and bodies. Splotches of fire would mark the privateer's grave for the next hour.

Dale was glad that as an NCO he had not had to make such an awful decision; he sympathized with the pain that manifested briefly on Pennywhistle's face. It frustrated him that he could think of no way to ease the suffering of his commander, to whom he owed his life many times over, as well as his recently added fourth stripe. He had sometimes heard his officer cry out during fitful bouts of sleep—the more conscientious the officer, the worse the nightmares. Remorse not only murdered sleep but caused a slow necrosis of the soul. Yet Dale knew that being a good leader was less about acting gallantly than having the moral courage to make a choice that was right rather than humane.

Sweat gushed down Russell's pallid face. His mouth opened in preparation for a long scream, but shock caused his vocal cords to freeze. *God, I need a tankard of rum!*

The only sounds were the *crack-crack* of swelling canvas and the *swoosh swoosh* of water racing past *Vesta*'s hull. Not a single cheer of victory rose: the men looked like supplicants at a requiem mass. The Yankee sailors were enemies no more but fellow travelers who had lost their struggle with the sea.

One sailor gently grasped Pennywhistle's arm. "Thank you for saving us, sir," he said quietly, his blue eyes wide and grateful. "Most of the men have wives and children back home, so you have saved them, too. You are a true hero, sir."

Pennywhistle stared at the sailor in grim puzzlement. A real hero would have found a less monstrous way to remove the privateer. He recovered himself after a few seconds and pasted on a smile of acknowledgement.

His right index finger commenced twitching and he felt the start of a violent shudder in his shoulders. Four deep breaths slowed the reaction, but it was the recollection of a supremely peaceful place that stilled it.

He had accepted the nickname "Bombproofed" because objections would have recalled attention to the event that had resulted in its bestowal. Word of his flirtation with eternity had spread during his brief time in Bermuda, and it had caused his fellow officers to regard him with curiosity, usually mixed with awe but sometimes tainted by fear. His eyes became objects of gossip; his irises were twin volcanic calderas centered by abysses of immeasurable depth. He had no wish to appear either a lunatic or a figure of fun, so when asked he always responded in the same fashion: with breezy denial and a scientific rationale.

"Those stories you speak of are the recollections of exhausted men whose minds played tricks on them. Once a story like that gets started, the fantastic is more entertaining than a conventional explanation. What happened was an obscure medical condition whose details would only bore you. If you were hoping for an account of a miracle, you are speaking to the wrong man."

But what had happened fit the definition of a miracle exactly: "a surprising and welcome event that is inexplicable by any known natural or scientific laws and suggests the presence of some divine agency." The profundity of the event was ineffable—words like "extraordinary," "incredible," and "amazing" were starvelings tasked to describe a royal feast.

The aftermath was transforming him in ways that he was only starting to understand. He had become less judgmental: his capacity for compassion had increased as his intuition had sharpened. He sensed lots of little things about people and why they acted as they did. Sometimes that flow of information and emotion became an overwhelming torrent that was painful. He was becoming a man who knew too much, sometimes wishing that Donne had been wrong about no man being an island.

His most notable revelation was that intuition and rationality were allies, not enemies. The logic that had always guided his actions was a beginning not an end, a doorway to wisdom, not its great hall. His ability to express honest emotion had improved markedly, though he still preferred thoughtful silence to voicing the impulsive impressions of the heart.

None of the tales told about his apparent death had found their way to the ears of Sammie Jo. She had remarked that he had changed somehow, though she could not say in exactly what ways. He wanted to tell her, but he had not yet found an ideal time, though there was probably no perfect moment to explain an event which might well change someone's view of the universe.

The Other World's chief lessons were that love was the glue that held the universe together and that a soul's primary duty was to give love to those closest to him. That extraordinary voyage had extinguished any doubts about marrying Sammie Jo. When he'd said, "I do" in His Majesty's Chapel of St. Peter in Bermuda, his voice had radiated confidence because he had for once listened to his heart.

Sammie Jo descended the ratlines torpidly, every movement measured yet uncertain. Like a drunk trying to navigate a straight line, she did not quite trust her feet to find the deck. She plodded toward Pennywhistle like a cripple with invisible chains, deathly pale and looking completely spent. Pennywhistle recognized the blank stare that he had often seen in men after a desperate battle. His expression one of tenderness, he took her hands in his and squeezed them gently.

"Holy Mother of God! That was plumb awful, Tom. I ain't never seen a fire like that and I damn sure hope I never see its like again. I didn't think I could be shocked anymore, but that smell was bad enough to make a maggot puke." She grasped her stomach. "I... I..." she stammered, her usually strong voice frail and reedy. "Fuck!" In her distress she

BOMBPROOFED

resorted to a favorite expletive that she was working hard to banish.

"I know," said Pennywhistle in soothing tones. "I had no idea that an ancient weapon could be the breath of St. George's dragon. I would not for a minute attempt to beguile your pain. You bleed for the fate of strangers because you understand that we are all passengers on the same benighted ship of life. But consider, my dear, that we are safe and free. We have saved not just ourselves, but every man aboard. We have a lifetime ahead to heal our wounds."

She caressed his cheeks softly. As she did, color returned to her own. "I want that lifetime, Tom."

"I would allow no man to deny it to us," said Pennywhistle firmly. "My decision was a terrible one, but I would do it again if I felt your life were in danger." His voice remained comforting but his eyes betrayed surprise. He had thought only about fighting for her and had completely forgotten his responsibility to protect the dispatches. Love had eclipsed duty.

She craned her head and perked up her ears. "I never thought rowdy sailors could be so quiet that you could hear a moth piss on cotton." She lapsed into thoughtful silence, struggling to banish the shouts of burning sailors from her memory. Her troubled expression gradually brightened as a supreme effort of will quieted her thoughts. When she spoke, her voice resumed some of its melodious quality, signaling the return of her self-confidence.

"I love you, Tom! Everything else just don't signify. When awful things happen, you take a hard look at what really matters and make sure to never let go of what you hold dear." She threw her arms around him in a great bear hug. "Just the sight of you makes me smile. That's something *you* don't do near enough."

Never forget to laugh. The Voice came back to him.

She drew back and gazed into kind eyes filled with understanding. Though her husband's soul was as dark as hers, their union generated light. "I have never felt more certain that we belong together than I do now," she said in an earnest voice at odds with her usual prickly self-reliance. "You think things to death while I don't think them through near enough, but together we balance things out. We both call out bullsh... uh... nonsense when we hear it, though you do it with a lot better words than I do."

She squeezed his taut biceps hard, her grip as much that of a warrior as a lover. "It's easier for us to confront life with a fist instead of an open hand. Yelling 'Charge!' comes a lot more natural than whispering 'I hurt.'"

Pennywhistle stared at her in amazement because she saw his soul as it truly was, mottled with warts, scars, and holes. Yet she loved him because of those flaws, not in spite of them. Tears started to his eyes, but he brusquely wiped them away, struggling to regain lost dignity.

"I once overheard a conversation of two of your friends, Sugar. I ain't never forgot it. One said that a prize bull should never be allowed to jump the fence, and the other replied that you don't mate a thoroughbred to an ass. I know that you don't hold with gambling for money, but I thank God that you were willing to gamble with your heart."

For a split second, Pennywhistle beheld a starved backwoods girl asking for a treat and his heart glowed. His soft voice became salve gently soothing a wound. "My military experience has taught me what my upbringing did not: greatness of fortune and greatness of character are not often shipmates. The second is always to be preferred to the first, but my friends miss this entirely. For them, marriage is a duty tied to property and pedigree; passion is a lucky accident. The love that we share is as much a stranger to them as a palm tree is to a Greenlander. *Omnia vincit amor,* I say."

He saw the puzzlement in her eyes.

"Love conquers all."

She removed her slouch hat and undid her bun. She shook her head, her hair falling sensuously to her shoulders. "I heard many a buck talkin' fast and fine about love, but seeing me as nothing 'cept a country jam pot to poke in the back of a barn. From our first meet, you gave me something more valuable than gold: dignity. You treated me like someone who mattered. You believe in me like no one else ever has. You see what I can be rather than what I am. You have given me the best gift of all: a future with hope." Her eyes misted and her voice took on the sweet tones of a silver bell. "You are showing me so much about books, manners, and gentle ways, but there is so much I want to teach you about love and the outdoors and..."

"Dance with me!" Pennywhistle blurted out, as he impulsively pulled her close. He saw the confusion in her face: spontaneity was not his forte, but he was learning that joy and over-planning were bad companions. Having just witnessed indescribable death, he felt compelled to do something which celebrated life. "Just follow my lead. The only music we need will come from our hearts."

He guided her in the steps of the waltz, and it took only a few moments for her to grasp its rhythm and follow his lead. Her feet proved as nimble as her motions were graceful, and she gradually aligned her movements with his as they slowly whirled round and round. The pain of the world faded and the sparkle in their eyes spoke of the dreams that each had for the other. Their sense of touch seemed amplified to an exquisite degree and their imaginations transformed a humble deck into a grand ballroom.

He began humming Diabelli's Landlier Waltz, pleased that his Other World journey had greatly improved his singing voice. He matched the ¾ time of the melody to their steps, as their bodies radiated a heat that grew in intensity with each turn. The Puritans had been right in saying that dancing was sexual touching set to music, but they'd missed the part that it stirred the heart just as much as the loins.

As two became one in motion, rhythm, and soul, joy blossomed on Sammie Jo's face and the merriment of dance chased away her pain. When they stopped a few minutes later, she breathlessly exclaimed, "I declare, Tom Pennywhistle, you have been holding out on me! You are full of hidden talents!"

"It is my belief that Prometheus actually stole dance from the Gods, not fire," he replied with mock solemnity.

"I always thought it was the gift of hair dressing!" Her eyes twinkled with whimsy; she had no idea who Prometheus was but could think of no more valuable prize than the wonderful coiffures that she had seen on the quality ladies of Baltimore.

"Awk! Awk! Awk!" The sudden screeching was accompanied by a flurry of wind, and something landed heavily on Sammie Jo's shoulder. Pennywhistle blinked in surprise and Sammie Jo burst out, "Shit!"

A parrot with a badly singed right wing had alighted on her shoulder, likely the only survivor of the *Dapper James*. It was eighteen inches long, with wings of iridescent green on the dorsal sides and sky blue on the ventral. It had a pinkish forehead, white eye rings, flame-red cheeks and throat, and a belly of lime green. It moved slowly and uncertainly from side to side, cocking its head as if appraising them.

Sammie Jo turned her head cautiously and regarded it with her peripheral vision. "Is that a... uh, uh, parrot, Tom? I ain't never seen one." He heard wonderment in her voice, a good sign. After a battle, people numbed by terrible emotions could more readily empathize with the plight of animals than men.

"Yes, it is, Sammie Jo. This is an unusually large Grand Cayman. Likely it was someone's pet. Sailors consider them fine souvenirs of tropical climes and see them as good luck talismans. They are perceptive creatures who form strong attachments. They are long-lived, and mate for life. I'd say this one is young, perhaps five years old."

Pennywhistle remembered that he had a cashew in his pocket, a relic of yesterday's dessert. He cautiously held it up to the bird's beak, hoping that he was not risking a finger. The parrot took it gingerly and began to chew. He consumed it quickly, then fluffed his feathers and wagged his yellow-green tail rapidly. He turned his head to the side and regarded Pennywhistle with one eye.

Sammie Jo smiled. "I think he likes you, Tom."

As if in answer, the bird spoke. "Thank 'ee kindly, sir."

Pennywhistle and Sammie Jo laughed, mirth rising like a spring breeze after an April storm.

"They are excellent mimics, but I believe they understand much of what they say," observed Pennywhistle. "One captain told me that his bird knew 1,000 words and greeted visitors by name. This chap's master must have been a polite fellow."

"Let's keep him, Tom," she said with girlish delight. "Since he likes you, I am already quite fond of him."

" Help you, I can !" The bird extended his left foot for Sammie Jo to touch.

It pleased Pennywhistle that the bird had buoyed her spirits. "No reason why not," he replied. "He is rather like us as a couple—hurt, yet bursting with life. He is going to need a name. What shall we call him?"

Sammie Jo reached up and gently touched the bird as he moved closer to her face, happy to be nurturing an animal instead of inflicting death. "I ain't sure. Maybe we can make this one of our first decisions as a couple."

Vesta surged ahead as the wind freshened, sun warmed the day, and the water sparkled brightly.

Pennywhistle and Sammie Jo spent the next hour discussing the thoroughly prosaic matter of the bird's name. The bird seemed content to stay on Sammie Jo's shoulder, tapping his foot from time to time to mark his territory. He feasted happily on nuts supplied by the newlyweds and a bond was established.

The masthead lookout's shouts ended their conversation. "Deck there! Land ho—Plymouth!"

Pennywhistle put his hands gently on Sammie Jo's shoulders: the bird transferred his perch to the Marine's right forearm. "Plymouth," he said gently, "England, your new home—no, *our* new home—is just ninety minutes away."

She looked at him thoughtfully, then kissed him hard. "Let's call our parrot Plymouth and remember the moment."

"Done!" said Pennywhistle enthusiastically.

She smiled mischievously. "You know, we could put those ninety minutes to a good use."

"I gather you are not suggesting an extended discussion of moral philosophy."

"Sugar Plum, all that tension you've built up ain't healthy and needs to be burned off." Her eyes sparkled with devilment and she inclined her head toward the companionway leading to their cabin.

"Far be it from me to argue with such wise counsel," he replied in amusement. "I have always believed that vigorous exercise is beneficial."

She took his hand in hers. "Come with me," she said in a honeyed voice that possessed the imperiousness of a sergeant major. "Folks back home called me a bad girl, and right now I want to do bad things with you!"

"Just how bad?"

"Let me show you!"

CHAPTER FOUR

Their coupling was short and violent. Sammie Jo was very bad and made Pennywhistle feel very good. Each drew back slowly and reluctantly, both with silly smiles, tranquil muscles, and shining spirits. Like a rogue wave at sea, the union had swept away everything but elemental emotions.

Carlotta's death had nearly broken him. To save the remaining fragments of his soul, he had resigned himself to a life without love, planning to fill the void with a string of meaningless affairs. But everything had changed when Sammie Jo had crashed into his life. She was as different from Carlotta as an apple was from a peach, yet the sheer power of their passions would have made them sisters in a different existence.

"I want to know something, Tom," said Sammie Jo, sprawled languorously on her side. She cupped her cheek in her left hand while she gently stroked her husband's hair with her right. "It's bothered me for a spell and I want to understand you. You've gone to a heap of trouble to do right with your American brother's heart, though he was a bastard and you hardly knew him. But you ain't spoke of your legitimate brother Peter more than thrice since I know'd you, yet you grew up with him and have inherited his property. He ain't been in the tomb but a few months, yet I get the idea that he had been dead to you long before the news reached you in the Chesapeake.

BOMBPROOFED

"I'm guessin' there was bad blood there and I'd like to know why. You ain't the kind of man who carries a grudge. You've always told me the man who lets anger fort up in his heart is like a man drinking a cup of arsenic and expecting someone else to die. Now, mind you, I ain't judgin', but since I am part of your family now and walkin' into a world I don't understand, I'd like to know the story."

Pennywhistle cast his eyes skyward, as if trying to translate a foreign word layered with multiple meanings into a simple English equivalent. "I don't know where to begin. I could give you a catalogue of our numerous spats over the years, but I doubt it would supply you with insight into the heart of our problems. Perhaps it's best to just say we looked at the world from different perspectives. We shared some of the same qualities of character, yet our odd upbringing conspired to turn those similarities into instruments of estrangement." He looked ruminatively at her face, as if seeking a golden thread through the maze of his memories.

"I have always been a seeker, while Peter was a grasper. I value knowledge for its own sake; Peter cared only for the knowledge that might help him snatch up any riches which crossed his path. To me, the Universe is a magnificent enigma that merits my highest intellectual attention. My personal motto has always been, 'the mysterious can be understood.' Peter laughed at science and metaphysics, saying I would do far better to invest my time studying actuarial tables, bank statements, and the finances of joint stock companies. He counseled me that instead of wasting my time exploring the wonders of Creation I should focus on the complexities of human motivations, particularly the ones most subject to manipulation." He sighed.

"I believe that while we have a great power of free will, we are also born onto this earth with a purpose and a destiny; to the extent that we discover and embrace that destiny we achieve fulfillment, if not necessarily happiness. Peter deemed God a myth to beguile the childish. He believed men were mere shadows and dust and born blank slates with no other destiny than that written by their own hands.

"I have always pursued that which delights my curiosity and poses questions that stimulate my intellect. I have turned those impulses to mastery of the profession of arms, even though they would have been better used in the realm of medicine, my initial choice for a calling in life. I like to think that I have never done anything purely for material or financial gain." Pennywhistle smiled sardonically. "You have no idea how that last statement upset my brother."

"Tom, I love you, but it's easy for folks who have never wanted for anything to say that money don't matter. I admire your book learnin' and heavy thinking, but a practical turn of mind can be a good thing. It ain't wrong to make money from a good idea, long as you are honest with folks. I think God gave Peter a gift and God don't give a talent to a man lessen' He intends for him to use it. I know you see life as a puzzle to be solved, but you live too much of your life in your head. Not everything is part of some hidden pattern. My aunt once said, 'Let your heart fill in what your mind don't know.' You don't have to allow your brain to turn warm feelings into orphans. Love ain't a distemper."

"You are right, my dear. Never having been in want of material things has sometimes made me forget that the leisure to study is a great luxury. I know that much of society spends every waking moment just trying to put bread on the table. You are helping me see that I am sometimes a prisoner to the thinking of my class, and that I often turn honest emotions into outlaws.

"But you will understand that it was emotions run riot that caused me to fight a foolish duel that changed my life forever. Absent that one shot, I would probably be enjoying a comfortable medical practice, healing people instead of killing them. For all of our differences, my brother came through and saved my neck with a marine commission. It placed me beyond the reach of the old duke, who was quite adamant about bringing me to a nasty end."

"Campbell challenged *you*, remember?" said Sammie Jo indignantly. "I know your code—it ain't in your makeup to duck an affront to your honor. That he was a duke's grandson didn't signify. All you saw was a high and mighty scoundrel beatin' on a defenseless girl."

Her lips curled and her brows knitted in anger.

"You gave him what he deserved, what the law could not. That weren't the act of a fool; that was the act of a Galahad. And you offered to postpone the duel when the coward showed up reelin' drunk. You gave him a chance to live and he threw it away."

Pennywhistle abruptly sat up and crossed his arms.

"A more civilized man would have fired his pistol into the ground. Honor would have been satisfied and no blood would have been shed. Truth is, at that point I was not reasonable. I was consumed with rage and succumbed to the temptation to play God, deciding that Campbell would never again harm another innocent. Even as I felt satisfaction seeing him fall, I knew that I had betrayed the ideals I claimed to stand for. I had taken the Oath of Hippocrates: *Do no harm*, and yet I allowed raw emotion to overwhelm the reason that should have stayed my hand. After that I imprisoned my passions, and it is only now, with you, that I am finally starting to establish a peace treaty between them and my rationality."

"Tom, you did right," said Sammie Jo fiercely. "Campbell were a bad 'un, plain and simple. He would have gone on to hurt others so you killed to prevent more killing. You gave him justice of a kind that ain't found in no law book. You gave him real Old Testament justice. You used might for right. Isn't that what King Arthur told the Knights of the Round Table to do? You could no more have walked away from that duel than you could have walked away from the fight at Bladensburg. Face it, Tom, when things go wrong, people look to you as a champion."

"A champion? Ha!" Pennywhistle snorted a derisive laugh. "I am Lancealittle not Lancelot; just a man who hates bullies. At any rate, let me return to my somewhat dour assessment of my brother's character. I must confess that talking about him and my past feels like fumigating an attic filled with bats and insects."

"Tom, I would call you a brave man slowly wise." She stroked his hand in reassurance. The comforting warmth encouraged her to drop her hand lower and stroke a more sensitive appendage. He gasped, wanting what she promised, but finally stayed her silken grip by some gentle taps on her fingers, letting her know that right now talk was a better way than touch for him to reveal himself.

"Where I could have lived contentedly in a world of books and theories, my brother carried on a highly practical romance with ledgers, stocks, and bonds. He was quick and sharp, certainly my mental equal, but he had a skill with mathematics that I lack, and he possessed an ability to memorize documents that was little short of phenomenal. He turned his penchant for calculus and probabilities into a series of successful investments in mills and mines.

"I felt that he squandered his gifts in relentlessly chasing after things which conferred wealth and prestige but did nothing to make the world a better place. It seemed a self-serving, wasteful employment of his considerable talents. I regret to say I frequently tweaked his nose by telling him so. He returned my censure by saying that I was the worst sort of feckless dreamer, one who thought only of himself but pretended it was elevated philosophy that claimed his attention. He said our family's future lay in the possession of wealth and power, and that the knowledge and self discovery I pursued were the self-indulgent distractions of a dilettante. He repeatedly schooled me, 'Ideals do not pay bills.'

"When I mentioned the pitfalls of avarice, he acerbically cited a merchant follower of Jeremy Bentham: 'I create wealth and that serves the needs of the many. The needs of the many outweigh the needs of the few.'

I must give him some credit. He never held with the belief that gentlemen should not soil their hands with trade and industry and was good at making money, obtaining influence, and catching the eye of the right people at the right moment. He applied his mathematical gifts to his dealings with people. He opined that once you understood the basic motives of a man, you could turn his cast of mind and emotions into mathematical variables. You could transform his future behavior into an equation whose outcome could be predicted with a high degree of certainty."

Pennywhistle shook his head, not in denial, but in a refusal to reduce mankind to mathematics.

"He liked to present himself as the gentleman amateur in all of his endeavors. We British are fond of that archetype, but in truth he was a calculating professional manipulator, both of finance and folk. He never acted without planning and foresight. None of it was my cup of tea, but he brewed his expertly, using affability and plain talk as metaphorical cream and sugar to sweeten the taste that he left in people's mouths. When *we* conversed, we seemed to summon the worst in each other, but with everyone else he seemed a gentleman looking out for others' welfare before his own."

"A friend to all mankind?" said Sammie Jo cynically. "I have always found those gents the most dangerous. More than a fair number are in the God business, which is why I ran away from my Pa's church. Those preachers would flash their pearly whites oh so prettily as they spoke honey-coated words beckoning you to trust them; meantime, one hand would be moving toward your privates while the other was stealing your purse."

"Peter was honest enough, Sammie Jo. He would have shared your disdain for men of the cloth who actually worship Mammon. He had a diplomat's instincts and excelled at convincing people that their best interests and his own enjoyed a unique and almost predestined intersection. He shone brightest when persuading people that he knew their minds better than they did themselves. He had a particular skill in obtaining lucrative government contracts for the manufacture of cloth for uniforms and was on a first name basis with many of the leading lights of government. He could have had a second career in Parliament, but he preferred the steady praise of the powerful to the capricious accolades of the public."

Pennywhistle stopped abruptly. "Damn it, I wish I'd had the character to simply make a blanket apology to him, to forget the past and banish blame. I should have embraced forgiveness and understanding, but I was too stiff-necked. Deep down he was enough like me that he would probably have accepted my apology as eagerly as I would have accepted his. Perhaps my concern over Tracy's heart is a way of atoning for conflicts left unresolved with Peter. My dear, you know the greatest epitaph for a tombstone, one that shall most assuredly not be emblazoned on mine?"

"What is it?" asked Sammie Jo quizzically, wondering how an event that she hoped lay long in the future had entered the conversation.

"'No regrets!'"

"Confound it, Tom, only a perfect person or a fool don't have no regrets. I think it makes more sense to admit mistakes direct and try never to make them again. Most people on their deathbeds don't regret the things they did so much as the things they never had the courage to do. A problem that ain't fixed because people could not decide on a perfect solution causes more hurt than one where the solution only worked a little bit."

Sammie Jo blinked at the change in Pennywhistle's face triggered by her last sentence. His expression darkened; troubled eyes, a tight mouth, and a far-away look indicated that he was haunted by ghosts whose nature she could only guess at. He did not speak for a full minute.

"I should have told you before, Hawkeye. I was wrong to withhold this. I am so used to keeping my own counsel that I have forgotten that I am now blessed with someone with whom I can share my burden. There is something very... wrong about my brother's death, something that just does not add up. I do not yet have any proof, only anomalies, intuition, and an acquaintance with my sibling's habits." He took a deep breath. "I am beginning to suspect that he did not die of natural causes."

Sammie Jo voiced a word that he seemed reluctant to speak. "Are you sayin' he was murdered?"

"I have more speculations than facts. I have no idea what the motive would be. He was a busy man, yet his life was as disciplined and well ordered as it was safe and dull. He did occasionally depart on trips without warning, baffling his wife, but I put that down to new strikes at his copper mines in Cornwall. A newly discovered vein meant considerable capital investment, and he always liked to see things for himself. As far as I know, he had acquired no dangerous enemies."

He debated whether to tell Sammie Jo one other piece of information that he had acquired on the Other Side. He had seen Peter holding aloft a bright red ledger and waving it in his direction. Unlike the smiles worn by everyone else, Peter's expression had looked troubled, as if he were trying to convey an urgent message but knowing that he was not succeeding.

Sammie Jo was puzzled by the dreamy expression that passed briefly across Pennywhistle's face. She looked him fiercely in the eye. "I ain't never seen you go off half cocked, so if you have your suspicions I will allow you have good reason for them. I'm a member of your family now, and I am damn well concerned if one of us left this life before his time."

Pennywhistle's voice became brisk and businesslike, as if reading from a legal brief. "His solicitor told me that he died at sea, the result of some kind of holiday boating accident—odd for a man who regarded leisure as a distraction from the pleasure of making money. The body was never recovered, and it is very hard to have a man declared legally dead. That can typically take a good year to accomplish, and yet Peter was declared legally deceased within a month of his disappearance. Almost as if..."

Sammie Jo finished his thought. "...someone wanted an embarrassing loose end tied up quickly. You once told me that he never carried large amounts of money on his person. Maybe he carried something more valuable in his head: secrets. You said he knew a lot of important people; it's my suspicion that the higher up you go in society, the more skeletons you add to your closet."

She scowled thoughtfully. "From what you say of his careful nature, he might well have kept a written record of special knowledge. Dirty laundry, I would call it."

The image of a red ledger flashed into Pennywhistle's mind. "I sensed the hand of the government behind the swift execution of his will. That it happened so quickly and assisted the fortunes of his wife and daughters suggests that it was an act of atonement. But atonement for what?"

Pennywhistle scratched his head as if trying to comb out insights from his brain. "Peter's contacts in government were of a commercial rather than a political nature. Copper is a valuable commodity in wartime, since it is the chief element in cannon barrels used by the army. He has held appointive office from time to time, but those were sinecures, ancient posts that were purely ceremonial yet carried a modest salary. I gather they were awarded as plums, but... his last post did not fit the pattern. How a connection with the Postal Service could be considered anything other than trifling is beyond me. He implied that he did something important, yet he was reticent about it, which struck me as odd. It was not that he sought my approval, but he was always keen to show me that his approach to life had been right—and mine wrong."

"Tom, your brother sounds like one of those men whose routine is so predictable that you can set your watch by his daily actions, so those unexpected departures of his trouble me. What if you brother's last post was a cover for something else? Like a rich woman concealing jewels inside a hollowed out Bible, figuring that thieves wouldn't be likely to snatch something commonplace."

"What are you suggesting, my dear?"

"Here is how I see it, Sugar. You have said in some ways your brother was a stranger to you. Maybe he weren't just a stranger to *you*, but to the whole world 'ceptin for a few bigwigs in Whitehall. You said that Peter's energy went into fortune-building and that he was of a mild, unadventurous outlook—a gent who liked to sit peaceful and content in his easy chair, looking close and loving at his piles of money." She began to tick off the points on her fingers.

"If I were picking a man to do dirty work that needed to be kept secret, I'd want a man that seemed mannerly and agreeable, but dull as dishwater and no braver than a gelded bull. If I wanted people looking left when something important was happening on the right, I would set out something showy for all to see. Same way a conjurer at a county fair gets you to focus on the crimson handkerchief he is flourishing about, not his other hand that is planting a coin behind your ear. If a matter of principle was concerned, I'd choose a man who appeared driven only by greed. A soldier or a diplomat doing the government's work would be obvious, but a man of business known chiefly for his mining and milling interests could use those interests to cover up something nasty that the government wanted done but could not appear to be involved in. This is just a country girl's perspective, but when I was out hunting, the game that was hardest to spot was them animals whose hides and coloring blended in with the trees and bushes where they made their homes. It might just be that your brother was picked to do extraordinary things because he appeared so damn ordinary."

Pennywhistle rubbed his chin compulsively, as if massaging a magic lamp of intuition that would summon the genie of insight. When he spoke, his voice bore the determination of a man who wanted answers and who had finally figured out the right questions to get them.

"I think someone important pressured Peter's solicitor to say that he was lost at sea. My brother hated the water. As far as I know, he never journeyed abroad, doing his traveling through books and newspapers. He got seasick at the sight of an incoming tide. A pleasant ocean voyage would have been his idea of hell, not heaven. No, the explanation was fabricated, not to fool my brother's friends, but to send a distinct message to a specific audience. The question is, what men were in that audience?"

Chapter Five

Five months earlier

"*Bwaaaah! Bwaaah!*" Peter Pennywhistle's mouth dropped open and his stomach blasted out a torrent of half digested meat, bread, and potatoes, the grey mass accented with the yellow of bile. The violent contractions pitched him forward and his stomach struck the port gunwale; the noxious effluvia cascaded into the English Channel.

He wiped his mouth with a silk handkerchief and tried to resume his pose of gentlemanly sangfroid, but his stomach muscles continued to heave and his rapid breathing refused to slow. After thirty seconds, an ominous gurgling rose from his belly. *Oh for God's sakes, not again!* His digestive diva deciding one last curtain call was necessary, he again lurched toward the side.

"The Channel be right neighborly today. I ain't seen her so calm in months. Such a peaceful blue, and the breeze strong and steady. Those pretty crests remind me of horse's manes and are telling me we will have good weather ahead for at least a day." Jeddidiah Tompkins boomed his words in a voice used to hailing boats over long distances.

It puzzled the ancient, hawk-nosed coxswain that others might not love the sea as he did. The strongly muscled right forearm that guided the tiller bore a tattoo of a large fouled anchor with the word "Victory" emblazoned below the flukes, proclaiming service on Nelson's flagship. He liked to think this enterprise was serving his country, too, because he suspected the government was behind his passenger's mission.

Pennywhistle's stomach rumbled another loud protest.

Tompkins ignored his passenger's distress in the hopes of raising his spirits. "Yes, sir, nothing like a pleasant voyage on a fine day to put a man in mind of what's important in life. The sea is like a woman—she has her moods, but when she is like this you think of her as a bride. Yes indeed, I would not trade the life of a sailor for that of a landsman if you offered me the Crown Jewels." The weathered crows-feet next to his lively blue eyes crinkled and his old-shoe-leather lips widened into a broad, if nearly toothless, smile.

Peter Pennywhistle wondered if the helmsman were mad. The 25-foot cutter bobbed about as violently as a thimble in a whirlpool. He would have gladly traded places with the lowliest digger in one of his mines and would have compensated him handsomely for the exchange. His six-foot, four-inch frame felt cramped by the thwarts, which his hands gripped so tightly that his knuckles had turned white. His rosy cheeks had turned gray, his pinched lips had assumed the pallor of a corpse, and his clammy skin was beaded with sweat. The worst hangover he'd ever had was but a ripple compared to the tidal wave of misery engulfing every nerve ending in his head and stomach.

"So says I to that gent beset with The Gout, if you want to regain your health, sir, you should take a long sea voyage. Nothing like salt air to bring strength to your constitution and joy to your spirit."

Blast! Would the damn helmsman never shut up? The sailor's droning voice set his already painful head to throbbing. Why did stupid people feel so eager to loudly share their lack of wit? He himself relied on tact and soothing language, and wondered why he could summon neither to silence the chattering tar. He decided it was less his present physical complaints than the fact that he was used to dealing with people who were intelligent, even if of flexible moral fiber.

He grudgingly acknowledged the true source of his discomfiture sprang from anxiety about his current mission. No matter how well you planned events, clandestine expeditions sometimes had an agenda of their own. Trying to anticipate what could go wrong aged a man quickly: he felt a hundred years old, with a head full of scampering spiders.

"Lovely day, ain't it, sir? It were a red sky last evening, so I'll wager this weather will be with us for a spell. I remember one day back in '98..."

Pennywhistle's stomach continued brewing cauldrons of acid, causing him to wonder if animals miscarried in the presence of the helmsman's voice. This was the first time he had had to leave Britain to ply his unusual trade, and his angry stomach was lecturing him, saying that he should have declined this particular undertaking. But Lord Castlereagh had pressed him hard to accept, saying "the safety of the realm" was imperiled.

"Now, I always say, women are like good shoes. It makes a lot more sense to choose for comfort rather than looks."

Lord help me over a fence! Now the sailor is an authority on women! Pennywhistle fingered the .62 pistol in the pocket of his russet coat, a last-ditch expedient if his primary defense of a clever tongue failed. He was a careful man, not a violent one, and had never discharged the pistol in anger. Still, there was a first time for everything.

Pennywhistle filtered out the incessant voice and focused on the details of his mission. He carried the temporary title of King's Messenger and the permanent one of Assistant Comptroller of the Post Office. The Postal Service was a key player in the British espionage establishment; like a number of important offices in the British government, its innocuous title obscured its vital function.

Since the 17th century, The Secret Office of the Postal Service had routinely opened, deciphered, and resealed foreign diplomatic missives. Its cryptographers were the most skilled in the country. That function had expanded during the Napoleonic Wars as the Office had begun to run agents abroad, easy enough when you routinely chartered ships reaching the four corners of the globe.

The duties of his position were stimulating and allowed him access to highly classified materials. Those duties were not burdensome, nor did they require long absences from his business interests. Yet the close study of cryptography had absorbed most of his leisure time for the past four years. A deep part of him loved puzzles; codes and ciphers constituted their most complex forms. Cryptography was chiefly mathematical and appealed to his facility with numbers. He had read everything published on the subject as well as many handwritten monographs that would never see a printer's ink.

Code breaking was personally profitable, since it provided information that was useful when buying stocks associated with the Army. He was often able to anticipate major overseas expeditions, such as the intervention in Portugal in 1808. Such martial developments always increased the demand for copper for cannons and cloth for uniforms. He considered himself a Free Thinker, but his brother had astutely observed that he had much of the Jesuit about him. Though a pen was his cross and a notebook his surplice, he tackled every enterprise with a breadth and depth of focus that found significance in the seemingly unrelated, well served by his eidetic memory, and he never let any matter pass until he had mastered its core. His ability to quickly assess the merits and applicability of key secret intercepts, in the manner of a pawnbroker valuing baubles and bric-a-brac, made him a frequent backchannel confidant of numerous officials, including Lord Liverpool, the Prime Minister.

His official titles were less informative than the unofficial one he had devised for himself: "Fixer-in-Chief." His education, pedigree, and business connections made him the perfect odd job man to fix thorny and delicate diplomatic matters that eluded official resolution. His war with Napoleon had been a conflict waged in the shadows with words, pens, and guile as the chief weapons. Then, as now, intellect, ingenuity, and special knowledge had counted far more than physical courage.

The potential blackmail of a member of the Royal Family certainly merited the employment of his unusual talents. The exchange today would be conducted in French, a language that, of necessity, he spoke nearly as well as his native tongue. His current mission was a payoff and he was the bag man: gold in exchange for a collection of damaging letters written by a damn-fool woman with an appetite for money and no palate for patriotism.

The Post Office had already recovered two letters; half of each was in plain text and half in code. The first part of each was an outline of the second and acted as a salacious appetizer. The main course promised details apparently so lurid that they could not be presented directly. Though postal clerks could only read the plain text portions, they were appalled at just how damaging the information was.

The Foreign Secretary to whom he reported had not alerted The Duke of York, who was featured in the letters. Frederick was George III's second son and Commander-in-Chief of the British Army. He was currently busy with that service's post-war reorganization, and Castlereagh had no wish to reopen an old wound. The very mention of the letter

Bombproofed

writer's name caused the duke to sputter and fume. This was something best handled discreetly, without either the duke's or the prime minister's involvement, giving credible deniability to both in case something went wrong. His mission was akin to clearing an obstructed harbor channel, while making sure that the surface waters remained calm.

Mary Anne Clarke had been the duke's mistress from 1802 to 1806. Before that, she had been an actress of skill, and her life revolved around drama and extravagance. Though the duke had given her (£1000 a year allowance, she had spent £2000 on furnishing her kitchen alone.

To satisfy her expensive tastes, she'd started a black market in the sale of commissions, using lists filched from under her lover's nose. She would jump candidates ahead of the queue for fees ranging from £100 for an ensigncy to (£600 for a majority. Emboldened by that success, she had expanded her purview to include the sale of civil and ecclesiastical offices, extending her reach so far as to include the appointments of the vicars and rectors of individual parishes.

She had caused a public scandal so great that the duke had to resign as Commander-in-Chief, even though his attorney had secured a parliamentary acquittal. His brother, the prince regent, reinstated him two years later, everyone believing that she had already caused all the damage possible.

No one had imagined that her insatiable demands for money would lead her to reach out to Bonaparte, promising him access to all manner of royal family skeletons. Bonaparte paid generously for her help since there was no more highly placed spy than one who had occupied the pillow next to an important target. Napoleon's abdication had prevented him acting on the information, but the explosive material remained in the hands of his Bourbon successor.

Peter had been able to read the second part of the two letters because Mrs. Clarke's cipher had been fashioned from an obscure volume, a copy of which had once resided in his father's library. He had used variants of the book's codes often enough that all ten of its decryption tables were fixed in his memory. Though basic in nature, Clarke's code was sufficiently random to make it unbreakable to someone who lacked the proper decryption chart.

He had used the code himself to confide his thoughts on this mission and others to a red ledger that functioned something like a diary. Clandestine work was stressful and he treated his ledger as the friend and confidant who could not exist in real life: someone to whom he could speak freely about matters that must never be spoken of freely. That ledger needed to be passed on to his brother in case something happened to him, and he had left instructions behind to ensure this. He had stowed his pride and written a long letter to Tom, hoping to heal old wounds and protect him from possible consequences if any mission went wrong. The letter rested now in his pocket, but as soon as this job was over, he would make the final changes and post it.

When he had first read the two letters in the Postal Service's possession, Clarke's gushy style had annoyed him: she alternated between being a gossip and a scold. Her rambling discourse told him that she was a vexed voluptuary, not a master blackmailer. Yet putting the second part in code displayed craftiness. He guessed that she would only furnish the code key after she had been paid a second sum of money. She had never been prosecuted because a court case would have brought out secrets embarrassing to numerous members of Parliament. Nevertheless, she had evidently retained her correspondence with the duke as an additional insurance policy. The new government of Louis vIII had acquired the letters after the fall of Napoleon but had simply sat on them, chiefly due to incompetence. The corpulent Bourbon king finally offered to return them as a gesture of good faith, France wishing to bury the past and inaugurate a new era of peaceful cooperation. Britain's good will would be critical at the Congress of Vienna. The gesture was officially gratis but there was an unspoken understanding that the French messenger would expect heavy compensation: he had been given the job by a cash-strapped king who lived beyond his means.

"We should beach in about ten minutes, sir," said his assistant, the Honorable Algernon Grosvenor.

Finally, a piece of useful information instead of the old sailor's endless musings! His heart began to race, but this time it was not from seasickness. The usually phlegmatic Castlereagh had been unusually agitated when he had given him this job, and that had set warning bells to ringing. He wondered if the letters were not just embarrassing to the royal family but could also be instrumental, in the wrong hands, in bringing down the government itself.

The French government considered the matter sufficiently important to send the Marquis de Louvois as their representative. Louvois suffered from a reputation as a silly sot, only distinguished for his wit and pursuit of odd sexual pleasures, but his family was old and well connected. Before the revolution, they had been the worst of lay-about lords, privileged bloodsuckers who quaffed the tears of the poor from goblets of gold. But the man mattered far less than the symbol of a restored *ancien régime*.

Louvois spent like there was no tomorrow, just like Louis; to Peter Pennywhistle's way of thinking this was a warning that Louvois should not be trusted, for a man who cannot live within his means is easily tempted. But Louvois was skilled as a fawning courtier, and he had been given the job as a way to cancel most of his debts.

Pennywhistle did not suffer fools gladly and, apart from any other concerns, he wondered if Louvois would be sober enough to get things right. He had to make absolutely sure that not a single letter was missing. He found himself strangely missing Bonaparte; the Emperor would have sent an experienced messenger chosen purely on merit.

The more his mind became engaged upon the permutations of the mission the more the seasickness retreated. His intellect rebelled at idleness, and it sometimes chased puzzles at the expense of domestic bliss, something his dear wife repeatedly reminded him was a bad thing. He had never considered that that faculty would prove the perfect antidote for a severe case of *mal de mer*.

He took out his spyglass and panned it slowly over the Normandy beach. It was remote from the nearest village, as he had specified. He spotted the French delegation moving towards the 150-foot bluff that led to the tidal flats, though at this remove he could only make out blobs of color rather than distinct individuals.

At least they were on time, a good sign. Punctuality typically meant less to the French than to the British. If he had been in Louvois's position he would have arrived hours ahead of the meeting time. Though secrecy had theoretically been maintained on both sides, there was always the danger of an interloper. A careful man would make sure that the immediate area was clear of any unwanted presence.

Louvois halted the horses of his caravan at the spot where the Vierville-sur-Mer road met the beach. His servants began offloading camp chairs, foldable tables, and a substantial quantity of expensive food and drink. His considerable belly was not wholly concealed by good tailoring and showed just how much he loved gastronomic and alcoholic excess. He reveled in the extravagant life, but regarded the tradesmen

BOMBPROOFED

who made it possible as annoying little people, impudently demanding money at regular intervals. Bonaparte's rule had undermined the deference usually shown aristocrats.

His ruddy cheeks and red nose were inflamed by a bottle of champagne imbibed en route. Sober, he was aloof and nasty-tongued; under the influence of the only monks he liked, Dom Perignon's effervescent messengers, he turned outgoing and witty. He wanted the exchange to be a celebration of Anglo-French amity rather than some sordid cloak and dagger affair. A little pomp and ceremony would let the British know that the grace of the *ancien régime* was restored indeed.

His footman Andre approached. "Monsieur le Marquis, most of the ice has survived the journey and I have begun chilling the champagne. However, I fear in the short time available it may not be at the right temperature to do honor to our guests."

Louvois frowned for a second, then smiled. "It is probably of no moment, Andre. The English have crude palates and probably will not notice the difference. So brave, yet *trés gauches* about the better things in life! Still, my tongue will recognize an incorrect temperature, so please make sure that you comb the packing straw for every last filament of ice."

"Oui, oui, Monsieur le Marquis," replied his footman. "I shall set out the pastries directly. Fifteen different ones, just as you requested, all freshly baked before dawn."

"And Monsieur le Marquis," chimed in the apprentice footman Etienne, "I made sure to bring only the best glasses, for you have told me that fine wine in cheap glasses is like putting a diamond in a ring of tin."

"Very good, both of you. The *roastbifs* know nothing of good pastries and nothing of the proper presentation of food and drink. They are content with awful mince pies and sour ale. We must show them what they are missing!"

He hoped his English counterpart was not one of those puritanical types who refused to see that business went most smoothly when mixed with pleasure. This meeting should unfold with the graceful languor of aristocrats rather the uncultured, clipped pace of the bourgeoisie. Some English tourists whom he had met in Paris recently had sought out the city's historic sites with a scholarly zeal that reminded him of inquisitors seeking heretics, completely oblivious to the relaxed delights of food, fashion, and fornication.

His fondness for long nights of exquisite repasts, witty repartee, sensual conquest and erotic adventure could never be indulged in a prim city like London. The magnificent architecture of Parisian palaces was the proper setting for splendid women. The ready availability of wines, pastries, and cheeses made Paris the ideal place for gastronomic joy to evolve into hedonistic abandonment, possible only in a truly cosmopolitan city. His favorite bedroom practice, "the Varnished Turk," would likely baffle the stunted sexuality of the English.

He was curious about his English counterpart. He bore no title other than "mister," but enjoyed the confidence of the British foreign secretary and so must be a man of influence. A leisurely meeting that had elements of a picnic might get the Englishman talking and furnish insights into the frame of mind of his government. Those insights could be profitably passed on to Louis.

His aide, the Comte de Vergennes, strode over to him, waving his unfurled spyglass. The tall and stately-looking twenty-year-old had a discordantly high voice. "Monsieur le Marquis, I have spotted the English boat. They should be landing in five minutes or so. I am honored that you have chosen me for this expedition, and even more grateful that you are granting me the privilege of making the introductions."

Bombproofed

Louvois smiled like a patient uncle. "I may not know you well, young sir, but I know your family well. Their connection with mine goes back centuries. I find good family is the best guarantee of discreet and gallant behavior. Though my expectations for you were high initially, you have already exceeded them. You will go far in the king's service."

"*Merci beaucoup, Monsieur le Marquis.*" Vergennes bowed graciously. "I wish that we had an artist present to render a watercolor of this meeting."

An artist *was* present, three hundred yards away. He had carefully concealed himself in a fold of ground near the top of the bluff. But he did not work with the tools of the atelier: his brushes were guns, swords, and knives. He had not come to commemorate life, but to inaugurate death. He was a man on a quest that had nothing to do with money but everything to do with family and winning back the Palatinate of Reichenau. Napoleon had stolen his patrimony and then, in 1806, had incorporated it into a much larger entity known as the Confederation of the Rhine.

Klaus von Steinwehr, the once and future Graf von Steinwehr, was a professional soldier who had served in the armies of Prussia and Austria, and was now in the service of Russia. His chiseled, broad face had once been deemed a subject worthy of Michelangelo but now reflected the sculpting of his varied service: trenches from bullets and swords on his cheeks, proud flesh from a fire on his chin, and a long nose that had been reset more times than a boxer's. The whole commanded instant respect and more than a little fear; you never turned your back on such a man.

He hated Napoleon and had switched allegiances as countries fell to the Corsican's power. His current employer welcomed experienced foreign officers; he had quickly obtained the rank of colonel in the Russian service, attracting the attention of Czar Alexander himself for his assassin's skills and a willingness to employ them with no questions asked.

He had found out about the Clarke Letters while serving with the Russian occupation army in Paris. He had struck up a conversation in a 6th *Arrondisment* tavern with a drunken man who was an important clerk in King Louis's government. The man boasted that he was in possession of an important secret and was dying to tell someone. He did indeed die when von Steinwehr snapped his neck, but not before he had milked him for every drop of information.

The clerk had told him that part of each letter was encoded with a cipher that French cryptographers had been unable to break. However, what they *could* read contained details that the British would definitely not want known. If those secrets were half as valuable as the clerk seemed to think, they would be highly useful to Czar Alexander.

Alexander wanted to redraw the map of Europe at the Congress of Vienna, and anything that gave him leverage over the British would be welcomed. And Alexander was the one man in Europe who could put Reichenau back on the map.

Von Steinwehr preferred jobs where he worked alone; few men had his skills and even fewer had characters worthy of his trust. But today he had to employ three assistants since the mission could not be managed as a solo effort without leaving loose ends. The three hirelings were all ex-Prussian Army officers—experienced, but down on their luck because they were warriors without a war after Napoleon's downfall. They thought of themselves as soldiers, not killers for hire, but their ethics had evaporated when he'd promised payment in gold. It never occurred to them they might not be able to collect. Unfortunately for them, the first rule of assassination was: when the job is done, kill all the assassins.

Bombproofed

He felt a tingle of excitement and it worried him. He needed to be calm, and the tingling presaged a mood swing. The mood shifts sometimes rendered him unstable. He had learned to mask them from employers through disciplined self control, though the cost was very hard on his family. His wife acted as a sounding board to make sure his powerful emotions never trumped calculation.

His mood swings followed monthly cycles, as inevitable as the phases of the moon. In the first week, he would behave as a calm, rational individual noted for his brilliance. This gradually transitioned to a second week were he was boundlessly optimistic and hatched schemes that were not quite tethered to reality. During that week, he would sleep little and talk compulsively. In the third week, he would sleep much and be so plagued by despair that he found it hard to even leave home. In the fourth, he became world-weary and reflective. Today was the start of the second week of the current cycle

He checked the positions of his three assistants through his spyglass. They could sweep the beach with gunfire, and their concealment made them nearly invulnerable to return fire, though it was unlikely that diplomats would offer any armed resistance.

He watched the French servants setting up two tables with food and drink, and realized that he was hungry and thirsty. No matter, he could have his fill of both after his work was done. His assistants could share in the bounty: he had a very special bottle of Calvados prepared for their celebrations.

"Now remember, today you and I ARE the British government," said Pennywhistle to his assistant. "It is our conduct that Louvois will judge, not that of our masters in Whitehall. Follow my lead. You don't have to say much; just look pleasant, bow deeply, and nod in delighted amazement if the Marquis delivers a *bon mot*. Laugh quietly if he jests, cup your chin and cock your head in deep thought if he offers political wisdom, and compliment any offered food and drink. Your title will speak for you when I make the introductions. Your job is to act well bred and important without overshadowing me. Your presence conveys the message that this outing is important enough for the king to be sending men of rank and consequence."

Pennywhistle's seventeen-year-old assistant nodded vigorously. The Honourable Algernon Grosvenor, third son of Earl Grosvenor, possessed a cast-iron stomach, and though the boat had pitched like a whore faking an orgasm, he wore the annoyingly bright smile of one chasing the God of Adventure. His contemporaries had nicknamed him "Blinky," because his eyelids flickered. While he was physically ungainly, with a homely face that put women in mind of a poached egg, he was a talented linguist who was proving a quick study in the arts of clandestine diplomacy.

Pennywhistle had taken him along as a favor to his father, who had asked him "to provide some seasoning and a spot of adventure." Pennywhistle hoped it would provide none of the latter. He wanted things to unfold with no more drama than a housewife purchasing victuals for an evening meal.

"I checked the locks on the strong boxes, Mr. Pennywhistle," said Grosvenor. "The gold is secure. Pardon me, sir, but it seems strange that we are giving such a substantial payment to a government that craves our friendship."

"The transfer of gold will never be recorded in any government ledger, and the treasury in Paris will not see a shilling. It is a private consideration for the marquis."

Grosvenor looked outraged.

Bombproofed

"The situation is this, Algernon. Many of those staffing the new Bourbon government once lived in penury as the cost of backing a royal house that might never see a throne again. Louis now rewards that loyalty by turning a blind eye to outrageous financial behavior; jobbery, bribery, and embezzlement run rampant in the new government. Many officials charge extra fees for performing tasks they are already well paid to do."

"This has not gone unnoticed by the French people. Their longing for Bonaparte's return increases with each passing day. Louis knows he is unpopular, and that is why he hopes doing a favor for the British will ensure their continued support. Bonaparte's government might have been a tyranny, but it was an efficient tyranny that rewarded merit. The Bourbons have forgotten nothing—and learned nothing." Pennywhistle had to school himself to keep the scorn he felt out of his voice.

"So we are abetting bad behavior, then, Mr. Pennywhistle? The New Order is to be the same as the old?" said Grosvenor with the disappointment of an idealist confronted with idealism's ancient enemy, necessity.

"Sadly, lightly principled men and diplomacy go together like drums and orchestras; the background beat of corruption is always present, no matter how lovely the melody. But the New Order will *not* be the same as the Old. The upcoming Congress of Vienna will redraw the map of Europe, and many of the changes forced by Bonaparte will remain. More rights will be granted to the lesser orders, though it will not be a brave new world. Many of the more hidebound aristocrats will find themselves out of jobs, and the antebellum *status quo* that the Bourbons want reinstated will never return. At least the new boundaries will be drawn by pens, not by swords, so I believe we have made some progress."

Von Steinwehr could not hear Pennywhistle's words, but he would have disagreed strongly with them if he had. Violence was still the ultimate arbitrator: there was no thorny problem that the application of a well placed bullet could not solve. He was confident Alexander could reconstitute one remnant of the Old Order, Reichenau, and that was all that mattered.

The vision of a restored Reichenau shot a jolt of electricity through his veins. Damn! Just what he did not need! He could feel the mood swing swelling. There always came a tipping point where the surging optimism felt good and right. Yet such feelings of confidence were those of a drunk enjoying a boozy high, and what seemed fine in the moment usually did not appear so during the next morning's hangover.

He panned his glass along the beach. There were five in the French party and three in the British. Including his own weapons, his band of killers commanded twelve shots. Even allowing for misfires, he had more than enough bullets to do the job.

In the unlikely event that anyone survived, he would administer the final *coup de grâce* with his Kleigenthal blade. Death by sword made things more personal; you were close enough to watch the light drain from a man's eyes and hear his death rattle. It was emotionally messy—he preferred death distant and removed from what remained of his humanity.

Yet as the mood swing heated his blood, the prospect of slaying a man with a blade began to seem pleasant. It would be a chance to exert a personal dominance over pampered aristocrats who had never struggled as he had to maintain membership in a very exclusive club. He had once been a minor sovereign, a Graf of the Holy Roman Empire. His

Bombproofed

territorial enclave had been about one and two thirds the size of Prince Johann's Lichtenstein, valuable because it controlled a key chokepoint on the Rhine, thus guaranteeing a substantial income from tolls. Damn that Napoleon! If he could not reach his real enemy with his blade, he would settle for these mincing minions.

Louvois watched the British boat stop abruptly, caught on a sand bank. The three men inside conferred. A tall man in a russet coat pointed to two iron strong boxes. The other two nodded, lifted one with stout rope handles at both ends, and stepped into the surf. They walked five yards or so and deposited it on the sand. The russet-coated man motioned for them to return and attend to the remaining box. Once it was landed, sets of wheels were affixed to the undersides of both boxes for easy movement.

The helmsman guided the lightened boat over the bar onto the beach—when they returned, his passengers would not have to wet their boots a second time.

Louvois's grey eyes sparkled with avarice. Bank notes were fine, but there was nothing like the luster of gleaming gold. Unlike paper, the heavy metal would only increase in value. It distressed him not at all that the upstart Emperor had replaced gold louis with coins bearing his image, naturally calling them napoleons. Gold was gold, no matter the likeness stamped upon it. He thought nothing of the debts he should repay, only of the glorious pleasures he would experience in incurring new ones.

Von Steinwehr spent the next few minutes reviewing his preparations one last time. Like a chess master, he saw the full game in his head before the first move was made. He believed that he had accounted for most permutations, and that surprise was on his side. He struggled with rising excitement, calming himself with visions of his wife and two young daughters. He had promised them gifts and would shop in Bayeux after today's affair concluded: French lace for his beloved Ingrid, and china dolls for his daughters. He also owed himself a good dinner. *Le Lion d'Or*, a block from the cathedral square, served a delightful *tripes à la mode de Caen*..

The French and English parties approached each other 50 feet below von Steinwehr's perch. Louvain advanced in slow, waddling steps, unsuccessfully trying to project an air of easy grace. He was attired in the most *au courant* fashion: ruby red top hat, peppermint-striped trousers, and a double-breasted royal blue frock coat with a collar so high and stiff that he could barely turn his head.

Pierre, his batman, followed a dutiful four paces behind, holding the reins of a grey pack horse. He extracted a small portmanteau from the left saddlebag. Andre bore a silver cooler containing a bottle of Bollinger Champagne. Etienne brought up the rear, holding a silver tray with Saint Louis les Biches crystal glasses.

Pennywhistle kept his face dignified but breathed easier. The smiling Frenchman looked a jolly fellow, not a devious one. His physique was the dumpy one of an aging rake. The champagne he'd brought was an elegant touch. A French noble would not waste champagne on a foreigner unless he had amicable intentions.

Could it be that he had worried for nothing? No, in his business worry was never unwarranted. Things were often not what they seemed, and the unexpected could ambush you with as little warning as a footpad in a dark alley. The talkative helmsman had gotten one thing right: "A rising tide is a lovely gift, but never forget that your boat still needs a firm hand on the tiller."

He glanced over his shoulder to make sure that Grosvenor had kept up with him. His assistant towed the

BOMBPROOFED

wheeled strongboxes as seriously as if they contained the riches of Araby. Each sixty-five-pound box contained 453 napoleons; each individual coin weighed 6 grams and consisted of 90% gold. They were untraceable to Great Britain and constituted part of the Postal Service's discretionary funds buried in the annual budgets of ordinary departments.

Pennywhistle and Louvois made sweeping bows to each other. Vergennes bowed toward Grosvenor, the second in command saluting his opposite number. Grosvenor returned the gesture, recognizing a fellow aristocrat. Formality satisfied, the two principals shook hands. Vergennes was about to introduce his master, but Pennywhistle spoke first.

"Monsieur le Marquis, I am Peter Pennywhistle. It is an honor to meet you. My assistant, the Honorable Algernon Grosvenor shares that honor." Louvois started slightly on hearing the name Grosvenor. That family owned much of the West End into which London was rapidly expanding. "The Prince Regent is grateful that your king has sent such a distinguished noble to treat with us." Pennywhistle spoke the trite phrases with a convincing sincerity. "The reputation of your family is well known throughout Europe." True enough, but the original reputation had been built by men long since turned to dust.

"Monsieur Pweny'istle,"—Louvois found the Englishman's name taxing to his Gallic tongue—"I am Francois-Michel le Tellier, 8th Marquis de Louvois, at your service. The honor and pleasure are mine. Your reputation for discretion, intelligence, and probity precedes you. My assistant, the Comte de Vergennes, had an ancestor who faced one of yours at Fontenoy and has told me of your family's love affair with valor." Vergennes nodded in assent. "Had you been fortunate enough to have been born a Frenchman, I feel certain you would now be my king's right hand." Louvois sounded as though his delight in his new acquaintance were real rather than feigned.

Pennywhistle understood that Louvois meant the words as a compliment, not a back-handed insult. "Monsieur le Marquis, perhaps the new era of peace will give our civilizations a chance to learn from each other. You have much to teach us about proper dining, and we might show you useful details about finance. Today is a diplomatic milestone. Two governments, formerly bitter enemies, solving a delicate problem together—the House of Bourbon and the House of Hanover reaping the rewards of peace."

"Très bien, monsieur, très bien! Such fine words demand an immediate toast." Without waiting for Pennywhistle's response, Louvain summoned Andre. The servant handed Pennywhistle a flute-shaped glass, a sure sign that the Bourbons were back. The wide mouthed coupe glass, popular under Bonaparte, had been derisively associated with the shape of Marie Antoinette's breast; it also had the disadvantage of dispersing bubbles, thereby reducing effervescence. Louvois merrily popped the champagne's cork. He half-filled Pennywhistle's crystal, allowing space for the bubbles to foam up, then poured a glass for himself. They clinked their glasses. "May prosperity always smile upon the prince regent," chortled Louvois.

"To King Louis, a long life and a happy reign," responded Pennywhistle. He took a slow sip. The champagne was excellent, superbly chilled. The ice necessary to cool it must have cost a fortune in the recent hot weather. The Frenchman was willing to spare no expense to get things right; that largesse probably did not extend to paying tradesmen, however, given his family's reputation.

Louvois threw his arm around Pennywhistle in a typically impulsive Gallic gesture of friendship. Pennywhistle recoiled slightly, unused to such naked emotion.

BOMBPROOFED

"Come, come, my new friend," said Louvois, directing Pennywhistle toward the two tables that Andre had covered with a dazzling array of delicacies. "I have always believed that excellent libations should be complimented by the best pastries. You will find the *canelés* and *clafoutis* particularly memorable, though it would be unwise to neglect the *gateau Basque* and the *far Breton*. My own favorite is the *tarte tatin*. I simply adore caramel."

Von Steinwehr shook his head at the blather—the shifting winds had wafted their dialogue in his direction. It strained his patience to watch the two diplomats eat their way along the tables for the next twenty minutes, taking samples of everything as they quaffed champagne. Their assistants showed less restraint, merrily taking farmhand-size portions. He himself had not eaten breakfast. An empty stomach limited the effects of peritonitis, if shot.

He suppressed his appetite and focused on the strongboxes, estimating the value of their contents by their size. A handsome sum, though trifling compared to the wealth the packet of letters represented. This would be a very productive day!

Pennywhistle handed Louvois two coins. The marquis examined them perfunctorily. "This is completely unnecessary. Your honor is the perfect guarantee of what the strongboxes contain. An English gentleman lying about such a matter is inconceivable. But Monsieur Pweny' istle, it seems a shame to waste this lovely day in matters of politics. Please, my servant has an additional bottle of Bollinger, and I propose that we explore its delights."

Pennywhistle had had three glasses already and felt more relaxed than he wanted to be. The marquis was no particular friend to his country, and occasions such as this were merely warfare disguised. He wanted to make the exchange now, but refusing another glass seemed boorish. Louvois might be a useful person to know for future missions, so it made sense to conciliate him.

"Very well, Monsieur le Marquis, but only one glass. Any more and I shall certainly burst out into a chorus of *Au Clair de la Lune*. Like the candle in the song, the Bourbons have rekindled a fine old flame."

"Ha, ha, ha!" bellowed Louvain as he poured two more glasses. " We shall make a Frenchman of you yet!"

Von Steinwehr watched the Englishman and the Frenchman laugh loudly at some joke. The next twenty minutes were spent merrily emptying the second bottle of champagne. Then—at last!—the men's faces turned serious. Documents were exchanged and signed on an elegant portable writing desk. Grosvenor brought the wheeled strongboxes forward and handed their rope pulls to Vergennes. Louvois's batman opened the portmanteau, removed a large silver box inlaid with numerous pearls, and gingerly handed it to the Englishman.

Von Steinwehr made hand signals to the three Prussians: he would take the English diplomat, Major von Bulow would take the French one. The other Prussians would kill the underlings.

Pennywhistle's long fingers closed around the box. He thought of checking to make sure of the contents but decided against it, believing that he had read his opposite number correctly. The marquis might be a voluptuary, but the House of Le Tellier was famous for its fidelity to honor and the Frenchman would behave as he was raised.

"Please accept this small token as well, a symbol of the amity between our nations rendered into a bond between our families," said Louvois with enthusiasm.

Bombproofed

The "small token" was a gold ring, its square shield emblazoned with the leopard rampant, which was the crest of the Le Tellier family. Pennywhistle slipped it on his finger. "I shall wear it with pleasure in memory of this historic event, the royal repast, the delightful company. I am desolate that I have no gift to give you, but when I return to England, I shall have a twin made with the Pennywhistle crest and will dispatch it to you."

"I would wear such a ring with equal pleasure. It has brought me joy to make your acquaintance, monsieur. A pity amiable chats such as this did not happen between our diplomats years ago."

Von Steinwehr centered his v sights on the Englishman's chest and gently squeezed the trigger.

"I look forward to a peace between our nations that—" a bullet tore into Pennywhistle's chest and lodged near his heart. He staggered but did not fall, reeling like a drunk, trying to stay upright. His pallid face wore a look of stunned disbelief as he touched the purple stain on his chest, wondering why it was spreading so fast. *God, it was a trap after all. Who would do this? He had to get the boy out of here. The chattering sailor, too; they were no part of this.* "Run, Algernon," he gasped, "run! Back to the boat fast as you can!"

The shot of von Steinwehr's chief flunkey exploded Louvois's head like a porcelain pomander.

Pennywhistle saw that Grosvenor had drawn his pistol and was looking about. *Damn, the boy was playing hero and trying to save him.* "Algernon! No!" His shout wheezed out as little more than a whisper.

As Grosvenor dashed in front of him, he was hit by a bullet that would have taken Pennywhistle in the sternum. The impact whisked the boy off his feet and he landed hard on his back. His eyes blinked in horror and surprise as his breath came in spasms. "Why?" he gasped. Then his pupils turned fixed and staring. *God, he wished he could tell the earl his son had died a hero. Who were these blackguards?"*

Vergennes and the two French servants blinked in incomprehension. Von Steinwehr's men killed them with efficient shots to their chests.

Tompkins reacted quickly, because he had seen death in battle. He raced along the beach, darted in front of the cutter's bow and gave the boat a violent shove that freed it from the sand. He leapt inside and was just starting to hoist the mast when von Steinwehr's bullet took him in the back. He fell face down into the surf.

Von Steinwehr's eyes swept the beach. Everyone was dead save the tall Englishman, who was crawling toward the boat.

It was time for his sword. Then he would examine the Englishman's body carefully. A diplomat might have letters on his person which could interest Alexander.

His three assistants were greedy. They raced down to the beach and began searching the bodies for coin and treasure. They would be happy in the few minutes before they died.

Von Steinwehr walked quickly downhill toward the crawling Englishman, who had nearly made it to the boat. The man displayed a dogged refusal to yield up his life. The English were a peculiar people, far tougher and more resolute than their personas suggested.

Von Steinwehr picked up the pearled box, and deposited it in a large haversack that he wore round his neck. He then drew his sword and advanced toward the Englishman, who had hoisted himself to his feet. He staggered into the surf and threw himself over the gunwale of the drifting boat.

Von Steinwehr waded into the sea up to his thighs, his sword arm cocked. The Englishman braced himself against the stern-sheets, one hand on his chest, the other trying to

BOMBPROOFED

work the tiller. Their eyes locked, each man assessing the other's mettle.

Von Steinwehr admired his opponent's defiant resolve. His faced showed no fear, only anger. Von Steinwehr rammed his sword through the Englishman's left pectoral, savoring the sensation of steel lancing flesh. He could feel the singular resistance of the heart's muscle as his blade pierced it.

Pennywhistle coughed violently and slumped sideways. He saw his brother's face in his mind's eye. *Why had he not mended fences with Tom? Pride goeth before a fall... and he was certainly falling.*

He summoned up his last remaining ounce of strength. He forced himself slowly to his knees. He crawled painfully over the thwarts toward the bow.

One final action to perform.

He drew his pistol from his coat pocket and aimed at von Steinwehr's heart, but his hand wobbled and his eyes saw three enemies. The startled look in his foe's eyes gratified him.

Bang! The gun discharged as his hand shook violently. Instead of hitting the chest, the bullet merely nicked his opponent's shoulder.

"Your marksmanship is unequal to your spirit. You are like an opera singer with laryngitis trying to perform one last aria before the curtain falls."

Pennywhistle's gun slipped from his fingers. He fixed von Steinwehr's eyes with a gaze of amusement and contempt. His voice was hardly more than a whisper, yet the derision in it was clear. "Joke's on you, fool. All that trouble for a safe without a combination. Your destiny will be the nail and the rope." Bubbles of pink froth foamed from his mouth. "Pennywhistles never yield, you scarred freak. *'Frangar non flectar'*..." The light faded from his eyes like blinds being closed.

Von Steinwehr recognized both the curse and the quotation. The nail and the rope was a Roman curse: a nail used to fix a rope to a tree so a man could be hanged. The other was Cicero: *I break but will not bend.* Though von Steinwehr bristled at being called a fool, he respected the Englishman's courage.

"Safe without a combination"—the Englishman had known the letters were encrypted! How had he understood that without seeing them? Were there other letters back in London? Did he have the key on his person in order to immediately verify their authenticity, or was it back in London?

He searched the body but found no code keys or cipher charts. He refused to take the gold ring, disgusted by the decadence of Louvois. Besides, it might be recognized or traced.

He did discover two unsent letters and read them quickly; hoping that they might provide clues to a decryption protocol. One was to a wife named Jane, the other to a brother, Thomas.

The Englishman seemed to have had some presentiment of tragedy. An apologetic letter to his brother spoke of a red ledger. "It contains secrets that will give you advantage. Should I disappear, a dead man's switch will operate and you will receive it through unexpected channels. I am confident that you will solve its riddles."

A red ledger containing secrets? Tantalizing! thought von Steinwehr. From the references in the letter, he deduced that the younger brother was a Royal Marine Captain serving in America. It was quite possible that news of his brother's disappearance would cause the British government to grant him compassionate leave to settle his sibling's affairs.

BOMBPROOFED

Red ledger, red ledger. The words gripped his mind. That volume might be forwarded to an officer overseas once his brother had been declared dead—he might have them on his person when he arrived in England. A dossier would have to be assembled on Thomas Pennywhistle.

He wondered what sort of life the dead man had lived and if he had children. He stopped his speculations after a few seconds because they humanized his opponents.

He had already begun to think of code books and ciphers. As he walked along the beach, he made a mental list of people whom he might consult. He only needed them to deduce a pattern and furnish a key; he would do any deciphering personally. Information thus obtained would be kept in tight compartments.

Von Bulow bounded up to him and arrested his speculations. "We have found much, Colonel—a real treasure trove. Plenty of coins, and a bundle of letters on the marquis."

"Excellent, major. Let us go back up the beach and partake of a very special bottle of brandy that I have brought for an equally special occasion." Von Steinwehr's lips stretched in mirthless cheer. He clapped his hand on the major's shoulder and the two walked the beach like old comrades in arms. They walked toward the horses that Captain Shaffenhausen had brought forward.

He and von Bulow bound the strongboxes to von Steinwehr's chestnut mount with stout rope and deposited the inlaid pearl box in the right saddle bag. The remaining two men deposited their miscellaneous booty into the saddle bags of their own mounts.

Von Steinwehr reached into his left saddlebag and produced a bottle of Martell Calvados—apple brandy. He brandished it cheerfully. "Very fine stuff, and you have earned it! I follow the old custom that a commander sees to his needs only after he has provided for his men, so I invite you to eat and drink. A feast remains on these tables, and here"—he flourished the brandy—"is liquor such as a man counts himself lucky to taste once in his life!"

He removed the cork and passed the bottle to von Bulow, who took several greedy gulps. "Marvelous," pronounced von Bulow. He passed it to Shaffenhausen, who took an equally long pull on it.

"Hey, don't drink it all!' laughed Captain Dukenfeld, who had already taken a pastry from the table. He grabbed the bottle and upended it. There was little left when he offered the brandy to von Steinwehr. But von Bulow lurched forward and snatched the bottle, wanting more. Von Steinwehr shrugged, and walked over towards the table as if eyeing the remains of the picnic. Shaffenhausen followed.

The change started thirty seconds later. One by one, three faces paled to grey under their weathered tans. Forty-five seconds later, as they were stuffing their faces, the men began to gasp for breath. Then they clutched their throats in agony. A minute later they pitched onto the sand, jerking violently, until they lay unmoving.

Von Steinwehr kicked each body hard to make sure no trace of life remained. It would take an hour or so to clean things up.

His great strength came in handy. He took care of his assistants first, then the corpses on the beach. He carried each body over his shoulder and dumped it into the boat. The wind had picked up and the sea had become more active, almost as if she were angry at his conduct. But the rising wind was a good thing and would take the corpse-laden boat into the Channel.

The problem was that the Channel was heavily patrolled by British Revenue cutters. He punched a small hole in the

BOMBPROOFED

bottom of the boat. It would ride lower and lower in the water, then quietly slip beneath the waves. He hoisted the mast inexpertly, ran up the sail, and pointed the boat out to sea. The wind caught the sail and the boat rocked away from shore.

He watched for forty minutes as the little death ship disappeared over the horizon. Then he transferred his assistants' goods to his own saddle bags and slapped their horses and those left by the Frenchmen smartly on their rumps, speeding them off to parts unknown. The horse he rode was a gigantic Belgian, the Continental equivalent of the British Clydesdale. It was an inelegant animal, but necessary for a man of his six-foot-six-inch height.

He headed toward the city of Bayeux. He was ravenously hungry. And yet, he felt drained and old, as he often did after a major operation. To cheer himself, he fastened a red carnation to his lapel. He had once killed a man whose hobby had been horticulture and had appropriated his victim's trademark blossom as his own floral escutcheon.

He could not get the tall Englishman's face and dying words out of his head. His intuition said the name Pennywhistle would be significant to him, and he realized that his sixth sense was speaking about Thomas Pennywhistle, not Peter. He brushed aside speculations and concentrated on happier, more practical matters—lace and dolls. As he rode, he thought of the day when he and his family would return to Reichenau. His scarred face broke into a smile.

Chapter Six

Pennywhistle and Sammie Jo walked slowly up the cobblestones of Durnford Street. Her head had been turning in every direction since landing in Plymouth and she remarked upon things that were ordinary for her husband, but novel for her. This land was to be her new home. The brooding grey gatehouse of Stonehouse Barracks loomed a block ahead. Pennywhistle maintained lodgings there and needed to briefly report to the commanding officer of the district.

The noontime sun shone brightly, but a robust breeze off the Channel made the air brisk and bracing. Plymouth Harbor throbbed with activity and he delighted in explaining the various rigs and the differences in function and performance. She listened closely, excited to understand his world, and asked legions of questions. She proved a far quicker study than most midshipmen and soon grasped the differences between sloops, schooners, and snows.

"I don't understand why you would live in a barracks," she said in puzzlement. "You are a gentleman."

"My room at the Bachelor Officer Quarters serves perfectly well, my dear, and I like being in proximity to the men I command. I take my profession seriously and want to convey the message that officers and men must work closely together. Besides, I saw no point in expending money on quarters when I had no wife or family. My own needs are modest, and I am chiefly concerned with impressing people with my conduct, not my lodgings. Of course, with you in my life, these digs will never do. You have changed my life in many ways, and I want to give you a marriage that brings out the best in both of us. Whether that includes me continuing to serve in what will shortly become the peacetime marines is problematic."

"I love you, Tom, and I trust you. I know whatever decision you make will be for our mutual happiness. I am used to living a rough existence, so even rooms in the barracks would probably impress me. I don't want you to feel you have to change for me. I am perfectly happy with the man I fell in love with."

"It delights me to hear that, Hawkeye, but much as I have enjoyed the roving life of a sea-going soldier, it is time to put down some roots. I want someplace safe to raise a family."

Sammie Jo smiled. "I know you are worried that you are the last of your line. I promise you," she said devilishly, "I am going to bed you at every opportunity so that don't happen. Two boys and two girls—how does that sound?"

"Splendid, my dear!" He kissed her boldly.

A handsome officer kissing a beautiful woman elicited smiles from most passersby. People of quality in arranged marriages seldom displayed public affection. Had their attire indicated they were from the lower orders, their behavior would have been judged vulgar. A few old biddies did sniff in disapproval, but accepted that such deportment was the price of living in a port town where military reunions and farewells were common.

Pennywhistle drew back and once again marveled at Sammie Jo's appearance. Most of the women of his class had a physical dullness disguised by artifice and manners. But man could not put in what Nature left out. In Sammie Jo's case, God had not only left nothing out but had pulled extra duty in completing her design.

She wore a yellow muslin gown stiffened with a whalebone corset. An embroidered line of cream colored roses danced just below a gathered Empire style bust, and bands of avocado green French lace adorned the waist, cuffs, and bottom of the dress. The shoulders were puffed and the sleeves ran to just above her thumbs; white kid gloves covered her hands. Save for the high, modest neck, its general outline resembled those worn by the ancient Romans. It did have an extraordinarily wide bottom to accommodate her long stride. He wondered if she was using the extra width to conceal some sort of knife, since she frequently told him she felt naked without a weapon.

Thanks to the fashionable rejection of pockets on dresses, she carried her needful feminine items in a canary yellow and cerulean blue silk bag called a reticule. It hung suspended from a short gold loop wrapped over her forearm and was shaped like a large U. The design had been copied from the sabretache worn by hussars. Women's fashions inspired by military garments were all the rage. An azure bonnet covered her hair and she twirled a green silk parasol over her left shoulder.

Undergarments were disdained by some women as the stuff of prostitutes, but were a necessity with sheer garments. Knitted wool drawers covered her thighs and cotton stockings reached just above the knee. Chalk-colored silk garters held the stockings in place.

Even on an ordinary lady, her fashionable outfit would have garnered a few approving nods; on her Junoesque figure it caused passing gentlemen to stop and stare. It amused Pennywhistle that others envied him for a woman they would never have spoken to if they had met her in her native environment.

Bombproofed

She walked in a black pair of women's riding boots which were both comfortable and stylish. With their two-inch wedge heels she was only an inch shorter than he, and she worried that they might make her look freakish. He assured her men would find her many things, but freakish was not among them.

The only thing out of joint was the large red and green parrot perched on her right shoulder. Sammie Jo fed Plymouth nuts from time to time and stroked his feathers gently as she did so. He spoke to startled passersby at unpredictable intervals, saying either "Ahoy, mate" or "Good day, Captain."

Pennywhistle had sent Gabriel ahead with the luggage and instructions to secure the best room at the King's Arms Inn. The Inn had wonderful food, a splendid view of the harbor, and was close to their point of departure. They would begin the 225-mile trip to London in the early evening after snatching a few hours' rest. Gabriel also had a list to fill at the greengrocers for a hamper of food and wine. Dale was already on his way to Bolton's Livery Stable to charter the fastest post-chaise available, one that could manage close to 12 miles an hour. The journey would be nonstop, save to change horses and drivers. Pennywhistle wished to be at the Admiralty less than twenty-four hours after departure, and had told Dale to tempt the carriage's owner with a guinea bonus for each hour less than that.

At the entrance to the barracks, Sammie Jo asked Pennywhistle, "You said you could get a digest of your message to London before we have even left town. How is that possible?"

Pennywhistle pointed to a tall rectangular tower atop a hill half a mile away. "That's a semaphore station. You see those six large octagonal shutters?"

She nodded.

"They can be adjusted either vertically or horizontally to a variety of positions to send simple messages. There are twenty stations in the line, at ten-mile intervals. Once I give the commanding officer a summation of the dispatches—the bare bones, really—a message will be encoded and relayed to the roof of the Admiralty. It's an efficient system, although only useful when the weather is clear. We are fortunate in that respect today. Once the message is sent, I expect to have a response within ninety minutes. I want to use that time to do a little shopping with you. You are going to need some dresses for London."

Sammie Jo clapped her hands with joy. "I would love that!"

"I hate to say this, but they will have to be off the peg. There is not time for tailored creations."

Sammie Jo kissed him quickly. "Off the peg is fine. It is a dream come true for me that I will be able to dress like the First Lady! All the ladies in Baltimore envied Dolley's fashions!

Pennywhistle shook his head. "We are going to find you a proper couturier in London. You will need a dress for Court, and those have very particular requirements." He tapped his lips twice as if bidding his mouth to speak words he did not want to say. "The Prince Regent is a dissolute beast, and I worry that he will make ungentlemanly overtures to you."

Sammie Jo replied with amusement, "Don't you worry none, Tom. I've handled drunken swells before. You just have to understand their particular chain of command. Their brain is run by a midshipman, their long boat is commanded by an admiral."

Pennywhistle barked a quick laugh. "All too true! But I would never allow you to go unprepared. We will be staying with the Dowager Countess of Leith when we arrive in London, and I will have her instruct you. She is sharp-tongued and savage with the witless, but a resourceful ally to her friends. She has a remarkable fund of droll stories, some of which are quite naughty. While we stay with her, we must decide where we shall make our permanent home. I appreciate that you are a stranger in a strange land, and the process of adjustment will have plenty of ups and downs. I want your home to be a place of comfort and safety. The final choice as to where we live will always be yours."

"A fine building don't make a home, Sugar Plum. Bricks and mortar ain't near as important as the hearts and minds of the people who live there. As long as you are by my side, even a shack would be a grand home. But I know shopping with a woman is hard on a man. There ain't no reason why I can't do a round of shopping alone while you handle your military stuff."

"That is most considerate, Sammie Jo, but here a lady does not shop unaccompanied."

She made a face. "Hell! That don't make no sense. I want to fit in here, Tom, but maybe there are some customs that ought to be changed. Maybe its time to start a new tradition!"

An expression of revelation slowly panned across Pennywhistle's face. "God's grace, you are right, Sammie Jo! I married you for your independence of spirit, and it seems ridiculous to ask you not to exercise it." He reached into his pocket and produced a black leather purse.

"You can hire a shop assistant to transport your purchases back to the King's Arms. Meet me back at the semaphore gate in three hours; just listen for the chimes on the city hall clock."

As he handed her the purse, a dirty brown flash streaked out from behind some barrels and snatched it from his hand. "Damn!" He blinked in surprise and exasperation. It was a street lark, a young boy little more than four feet tall and running like a fox.

Sammie Jo's face became a thundercloud. "Shit," she hissed as she yanked up the side of her dress, revealing a flash of lovely leg—and a bullwhip, suspended from a small leg belt beneath the dress.

There was a blur of motion and the whip cracked through the air like a brown bolt of lightning. It wrapped itself around the boy's left leg, dropping him to the cobblestones. The purse sailed from his grip and he lay barely moving.

Sammie Jo angrily marched over, followed a second later by Pennywhistle. She scooped up the purse, then jerked the boy upwards to eye level. She shook him twice, and her blue eyes glowed with flame. "Somebody ought to tan your hide!"

The boy seemed dazed by the fall, and his face was dirty and haggard. He was painfully thin and his clothing was little more than rags.

Pennywhistle saw the confusion in Sammie Jo's face. This was the poverty of cities, not the farm and woodlands she was accustomed to. "According to our law, trying to steal something of more than forty shillings' value merits death. I have seen a ten-year-old boy hanged for the theft of a pen knife and a fourteen year old girl executed for stealing a handkerchief. *The Bloody Code* is unforgiving: 225 violations carry the ultimate penalty. It is our duty to turn him over to the authorities."

Sammie Jo was surprised that his voice lacked its customary conviction. The eyes he fixed on her were not the hard ones that he usually displayed when he talked of duty.

"I know he did wrong, but is that what you want for him? We have a choice to make here. Why don't you put the boy down?"

He was asking for her opinion! He had never done so before about an official matter, being always in thrall to "the other woman" in his life: the mistress called duty. Her expression softened as she realized that she held a waif, not a desperado. She gently set him on his feet on the cobblestones, and he collapsed limply. "He's no more than a pup, Tom. And he looks like the runt of the litter."

"My guess is that he is an orphan. Probably belongs to a street gang run by some local thief. Port cities provide particularly rich pickings. He may have marked and followed us as soon as we left the ship. Look at the black and blue welts just above his collar, Sammie Jo—hallmarks of a recent beating. He has been disciplined as well as starved.

"His face reminds me of a powder monkey I knew, although that lad was considerably better fed." Pennywhistle stopped talking abruptly. His expression turned wistful as his mind's eye saw a phantom from his past. "His name was William, William Borders. He was cut in half by a blast of canister at Trafalgar. He was a good boy."

A beefy constable came puffing up the street, a truncheon in his right hand. "Here now, sir, are you and the lady all right?" He knuckled his black round hat in deference to his betters. "Constable Bartholomew Perkins at your service, sir."

Sammie Jo nodded, and Pennywhistle said calmly, "A minor inconvenience, constable. But my wife is new to this country, and this an unsettling introduction to our land."

The constable looked at Sammie Jo with surprise and admiration. "Ma'am, I am much in your debt for helping me apprehend this little rat. I have been after him for months, but he always seemed to be one step ahead. He is one of Joe Hopkins' band of hellions that has plagued Plymouth for two years. I will take care of this straightaway, ma'am. I am sorry that he has darkened your visit to our fair city."

He reached down and grabbed the boy by the scruff of the neck. "Come along, you little guttersnipe," he snarled. "You have an appointment with Hanging Judge Pence. Hope you are ready for a round of dancing with a rope as your partner!" The boy looked into his eyes, his expression begging mercy. The constable's eyes remained hard.

"No!" Sammie Jo exclaimed. The constable was shocked that a gentlewoman had any regard for someone who had tried to rob her. Being foreign probably meant that she had strange perspectives.

She glanced quickly at Pennywhistle, who nodded his head. He had seen her turn strong men into candle wax on several occasions. Her beauty was every bit as much a weapon as her rifle and bull whip, and she wielded it with a sophistication that would have done credit to Lucretia Borgia.

She bade the parrot depart and he quickly deposited himself on her husband's shoulder. She removed her bonnet and shook her honey blonde hair free. She smiled sweetly at the constable, and her cornflower blue eyes danced with life, suggesting a way that more life could be created. She sashayed toward Perkins like a cat in heat. She placed her hand firmly on his shoulder and he shuddered slightly. She stared into his eyes and he began to sweat. "I'd take it as a great favor, Constable, if you would stand down and let my husband handle things."

Pennywhistle trusted her cleverness with men and would follow her lead.

"Right now this boy is about as useful as a ship's wheel on a mule, but my husband is always on the lookout for recruits for his service. The marines are short of drummers and this boy's hands move with a quickness that make me think he and drumsticks could become real fine friends. It seems a waste to execute him when his energies could be used to serve the good of king and country. Wouldn't you agree, Constable?"

BOMBPROOFED

The constable cocked his head in puzzlement: lust and duty in conflict. His limited imagination had never considered any alternative to the boy's timely death. "I suppose that is so, ma'am, but I have a job to do and..."

"My wife is, of course, correct, constable," said Pennywhistle imperiously." If you will release this boy to me I will explore the possibility that he might prove suitable for a military use. Royal Marine discipline would change him from a guttersnipe to a king's servant."

Pennywhistle reached into his pocket and pulled out a crown. "Constable Perkins, why trouble yourself with matters that my Service is better equipped to resolve? Take this with my compliments and enjoy yourself at the Tabard. Consider it a marine finder's fee."A very considerable fee—a hearty meal featuring the best cut of sirloin and plenty of alcohol could be purchased for a mere eight pence.

The constable's eyes brightened and he unconsciously patted his stomach. "That's right kind of you, sir. But do be careful, sir. He is a slippery piece of larceny. Don't let him fool you with his sad stories."

Sammie Jo put her hand on the boy's shoulder. Her grip was firm, though the boy did not struggle; his face was suffused with surprise. "He won't be going anywhere unless he wants me to jerk a knot in his tail," she said politely.

"I will be on my way, then," said the constable, "and I wish you and your lady a pleasant day, sir." He turned on his heel and waddled down the street.

Pennywhistle turned to Sammie Jo. She kept her hand clamped tightly on the boy's shoulder, though he moved closer to her rather than away, instinctively drawn to her warmth. "You did the right thing, Hawkeye, but now he is our problem. I warn you, gang life is probably the only existence he knows, so you must not expect too much from him."

"Give him a chance, Tom. Don't make no sense to expect much from a boy who is so skinny that I can't even see his shadow. We need to get him fed. "

He pondered for a second. "The Saracen's Head is a block away. It's not the best place in town, but respectable enough. I need to report in and get the message on its way. I will take you there, order a large meal, then leave him in your charge. I have no doubt that you can handle him, but it will mean less time to shop."

"That ain't no problem. The clothes from Bermuda will do until we get to London. I feel sorry for the young 'un, because I know what it's like to be so hungry your belly thinks your throat's been cut. You gave me a second chance at life when you could have had me killed. I aim to do the same for this boy."

Second chance at life. His eyes lit with recognition as a subconscious voice spoke: "What was given unto you, you will be asked to render unto others."

Pennywhistle turned toward the boy, who was trying to fight off a case of the shakes. He did not like seeing anyone filled with fear, yet he realized there was a profound difference between the chronic fear that broke a man and rendered him a craven thing, and the fear that was "the beginning of wisdom." He spoke in his sternest command voice. "I want your name, lad! Immediately! Snap to it!" His unforgiving expression matched his voice: an officer reprimanding a marine who had been late to assembly.

"John..."—the boy shuddered slightly—"John Tregallon. Johnny Jump Up everyone calls me." His voice was high and faint. "I .... I thought I was headed to the gallows." His fear lifted for a few seconds, replaced by a look of curiosity. "Why'd you do it?"

Pennywhistle did not relax his disapproving look. "I do this only for my wife. She is from America, where they view transgressions such as yours with more leniency than I would. Her sensibilities lead her to conclude there is hope for you. I am far from certain, but her kindness persuades me that I should give you the benefit of the doubt, at least temporarily. Whether that persists beyond the next hour depends entirely on your conduct."

"Please, sir," said Johnny desperately, "let me prove myself. I will do anything that you and the lady ask. Word will get around that the constable almost had me, and Mr. Hopkins will beat me within an inch of my life."

Sammie Jo spoke to the boy with authority mixed with kindness. "Johnny, nobody is going to beat you. When was the last time you ate?"

"Yesterday morning, ma'am. Just some bread and cheese."

"Well knock me down and steal my teeth!" exclaimed Sammie Jo. "This boy needs some real food—some steak or chops. And potatoes and peas to go with it."

Johnny practically salivated in anticipation. "Steak or chops, ma'am? Never had those. I just get the leavings of the older boys."

Plymouth flew back to Sammie Jo's shoulder and bobbed about. "Steak and chops! Steak and chops!"

Pennywhistle surveyed Johnny from head to toe and his nose wrinkled. "He needs be made presentable before you take him to an inn, Sammie Jo."

He looked around and spotted a ship's chandlery whose window displayed sailor's clothing. "I think a pair of brogans, socks, duck trousers, a checked shirt, and a pea jacket will do. Some sort of hat would be in order as well, something with a low crown and wide brim. Since ship's boys excite no attention in a port town, this garb will give him concealment from those who might recognize him from his past misdeeds. Then we can meet up at The Saracen's Head."

She put her arm around Pennywhistle and spoke in a whisper. "I don't know anything about servants, but can't we find some use for him?"

Pennywhistle looked dubious. "He would need a lot of training." He rubbed his chin absent-mindedly, lost in thought. "Yet inherent character matters far more than an unpromising background. Very well, Sammie Jo, we can take him on as a servant, but he may bolt at the first opportunity. I do not want you to be disappointed."

She kissed him quickly. "You took a big risk with me, and I trust you ain't disappointed?"

Pennywhistle laughed. "I will let you know. In forty years!"

Chapter Seven

One hundred and seventy miles up the coast, Royal Navy Captain Neville Palliser walked Marcus, his huge black Newfoundland, along Southsea Beach. Both man and dog reveled in the bright sun and warm salt air, a snappy breeze giving the Solent a fine set of whitecaps. The usually placid animal began barking and pulled violently at his leash. Newfoundlands had been bred for sea rescue, and Marcus never acted this way unless he scented a sailor in peril. Palliser untied his leash and the dog dashed toward the breaking surf.

Palliser gasped when he caught up with his dog. A headless torso had washed ashore. The ragged flesh was clad in the remnants of what had been an expensive russet frock coat of superfine broadcloth. The brined flesh on one finger bore a gold signet ring with the figure of a leopard rampant.

Palliser had seen enough sea duty to realize that the body must have spent months in the Channel, and bite marks where the thighs had been indicated that it had attracted the attention of a large shark. It was normally too cold for them, but a Greenland Shark had turned up on a Devon beach two weeks before. Perhaps this was its handiwork.

He bent down to examine the body, wondering if he could discover some sort of identification so that the family might be duly notified. He found a wallet of Cordovan leather in the inside coat pocket. It was waterlogged but contained £200 worth of Bank of England notes, as well as a smudged receipt for three hundred pounds of copper ore from a mine at St. Day in Cornwall. The receipt was dated five months before. His fingers dug under the remains of a silk shirt and grasped a small gold locket with the portrait of a pretty woman inside. It bore the inscription. "To my dearest Peter." This might have been a man of consequence; his Royal Navy superiors should be informed.

He thought that by consulting the mine, he might be able to discover Peter's last name. He hated to be the bearer of bad news, but most families of men lost at sea would rather know the truth than spend years pining for a reunion that would never happen.

Something caught his eye, and it was not a bite mark. He looked closer and put his finger into the hole. It had been made by a bullet. Now suspicious, he examined the rest of the corpse in a new light. He found a deep puncture wound that could only have been made by a sword. He whistled in surprise. The man had died a violent death.

Three hours later, the corpse lay on a long wooden table and was undergoing a careful examination by the Port Admiral, Sir James Samaurez, and his chief surgeon, Adam Craik. Craik agreed with Palliser on the cause of death and added, "We are looking at a murder."

Samaurez's eyebrows arched in shock when he examined the ring. He recognized the crest. On his last day in Paris five months before, he had met a dissolute nobleman sporting a similar ring. He could not recall the man's name, but he had dominated the soiree at the British Embassy. Samaurez had heard rumors that a French lord had gone missing.

What the blazes was the man's name? He cudgeled his memory and it came to him. Louvois! Yes that was it.

The corpse could not be him. He had been small and portly; this man had been rangy and tall. Besides, the cut of

BOMBPROOFED

the clothing was English, not French. Yet the ring suggested that the English corpse might be connected to something involving the inner circle of the Bourbons. The murder of a British gentleman involved with a high-level official of the fledgling Bourbon government was a serious matter and merited a careful search for the man's identity. Samaurez thanked Palliser and Craik, then dismissed them. He needed to be alone with his thoughts.

Twenty minutes later, the semaphore tower in Portsmouth flashed a message to the Admiralty in London. Thirty minutes after that, a courier from the Admiralty arrived at the Foreign Office. Samaurez had no way of knowing it, but his message would cause candles there to burn long into the night.

Sammie Jo and Plymouth watched Johnny as he ate in silence. He regarded them with eye flicks every few seconds, like a vigilant animal wanting to make sure that his kill would not be snatched away. He gobbled three pork chops, four potatoes, and a bowl full of peas, and washed them down with two large pitchers of lemonade before he spoke a word.

His hunger reminded her of the awful winter of 1800. That long, hard season had killed many of the animals that her family had relied upon, and they had been reduced to a diet of gruel made from boiled chestnuts and buckwheat.

"My husband thinks you are an orphan. Is that true?"

The boy's cheeks were stuffed like a squirrel's, but he swallowed quickly and replied. "I had a good family until a year ago. We lived in a cottage by the sea. I had a brother and sister, too. My pa was a blacksmith in Penzance, and my ma worked as a parlor maid for Squire Whelen. But there was a bad outbreak of yellow jack in Penzance. They say it came from a ship that docked from Antigua. It carried off a couple hundred people. My whole family died." His voice choked. "My ma bled from everywhere before she passed: not just her mouth and nose, but her eyes and ears, even her toes."

Sammie Jo nodded in understanding. An uncle of hers had died in the great Philadelphia Yellow Fever outbreak of 1793. It had been so bad that George Washington and the government had fled the city for several months.

"I was powerful sick, too, but I guess I am too bad for the Lord to take me." Tears formed in his eyes, but he brushed them angrily away. "Mr. Whelen did me a good turn. I could read, write and cipher a bit—my folks were Methodists and wanted me to be able to read the Good Book. He apprenticed me to Mr. Paul Dark, a printer, but he turned out to be a real servant of Satan, like I read about in the Bible. He starved me and beat me regular and..."

He stopped and gulped as if girding himself to explain something horrible. "One night he got real drunk, and it turned out that he was the kind of man that liked boys. I know a lady like you has probably never heard of such things, but he was bent on committing uncleanness and came after me. I kicked him hard, ran like the devil, and never looked back." His face brightened for an instant. "I did learn quite a bit about the printing trade in the eight months that I was there, though. I liked the work." His expression turned bleak.

"Because I broke an indenture, Mr. Dark set the constables after me, and they almost caught me a few times. Since my description was broadcast far and wide, it was not like I could be a printer's devil for anyone else. I stole from farms to eat. When I got to Plymouth, I met up with one of Mr. Hopkins' gang. He told me Hopkins liked to help out runaways. He treated me real well at first. The other boys became a new family. I got to be a good thief, but I knew from my upbringing and the Bible that what I was doing was wrong. But I could not see how to get out of it."

He looked at Sammie Jo as if some part of his lost innocence still lived behind his prematurely lined face. "I am lucky I fell in with you and your husband, ma'am. The Lord can be generous, even to those who done wrong."

Sammie Jo spoke with kindness. "That's an awful story, Johnny. But if you stay with us, you can become a man you can be proud of. You won't be sent to the marines, either. I just said that to fool the constable." She winked.

"Where did you get the parrot, ma'am? He is something to look at, and he talks like a man."

As if to acknowledge the boy, the parrot squawked, "Thank 'ee kindly, sir."

Sammie Jo's face turned grim for an instant, but she recovered quickly. "His name is Plymouth. He came off a ship that... uh... sank. I treat him as a wedding present from Providence. My husband and I have been married less than a month, and this is my first day in England. I come from a far piece away, but I'm thinkin' you already guessed that from the way I talk."

Johnny looked at her with eyes that were both knowing and innocent. He had indeed noticed. A boy who lives on the streets hears many accents. When Sammie Jo said "talk" it came out as nearly three syllables, and "far" sounded like "fur". "True, ma'am. I thought you might be from Scotland. But I noticed something different about you before I ever heard you speak. It is the way you walk. It is not like the gentle ladies who live in town, who take short, careful steps. You move with long strides. It's like you are stalking something. I once saw pictures of tigers in a book, and you move like I think they would." He cleared his throat in embarrassment.

Sammie Jo's face reflected satisfaction. The boy had good instincts and sized up people well. "I am glad that you think me a lady. My husband is a gentleman from a long line of them, but I am a country girl from the backwoods of Maryland. I know I don't talk like a lady, but I am trying hard to clean up my language and learn the customs of the country. It's god d—... uh, mighty hard. I am blessed that my husband is a wonderful and patient teacher."

Johnny looked at her with a mixture of puppy love and gratitude. "I think you are beautiful." He sighed, then realized he had spoken without thinking. "Beg pardon, ma'am. I don't mean to be impudent."

Sammie Jo flashed an earthy smile. "I ain't never offended when someone calls me beautiful. Now if you were a swell out for a good time I might take it different, but you are a boy speaking from a good heart. This country sure gets plum fussed about people using the wrong words."

Sammie Jo spoke to him with the serious tones of a forest woman skilled at observing the primal instincts and temperaments of animals. "I had a feeling about you, Johnny. Your story backs it up. Course you could be makin' it all up, but you don't strike me as a fibber, and I don't fool easy. Your eyes and the way you speak tell me that you and truth are friends. So I will ask you direct: do you want to come with me and my husband?"

Her expression was ruthless, warning *"second chances are not given to most."* She spoke from experience: bushwhacking usually got you hanged without a trial.

"If you don't, say so, and I will let you go. I don't think you want to go back to Old Man Hopkins, but there are some who get so used to trouble that they can't live without it. Like an old mule so used to being hit by his owner that he won't perform for a new one who don't believe in the rod.

BOMBPROOFED

"If you stay with us I will ask for your word of honor that you will never lie to us, and that you will follow my husband's instructions. My husband sets great store by a man's word. But he don't ask more of anyone else than he demands of hisself.

"I promise you will never be beaten or go hungry, nor do work that is anything but honest. What say you?" Her eyes were kind, yet there was no flicker of compromise in them.

"Cross my heart and hope to die," said Johnny as he crossed himself, and his eyes misted. "I give you my word, ma'am."

Sammie Jo extended her hand, which surprised Johnny. "Welcome to the family!"

"Family?" He missed his own badly. He shook her hand vigorously but the touch of a hand, so like his mother's, opened the floodgates. He cried quietly for a minute, flushing the emotional toxins from his heart. He stopped as it dawned on him that while the Hopkins gang might be a false family, it had brought about the chance to acquire a real one. The day that had almost led to the hangman's noose might actually be the day of his salvation.

"Thank you, Mrs. Pennywhistle! I never expected God would grant me a second chance. Its just like that song that they sang at Methodist Chapel: 'I once was lost and now I'm found.' I learn quick and I work hard. I could see by the way your husband holds himself and his manner that he is a fine, upstanding officer. I bet he is a real hero. He is a hero, isn't he?"

His eyes blazed with an eagerness to believe that mythic heroes might have real life counterparts.

Sammie Jo's lips curved into an ironic half-smile. "He is a hero, though he don't see it that way." She sighed. "I told him to speak honest and plain about his deeds and pay no mind to that manly modesty shi—... er... uh... nonsense. I think he uses modesty like a cloak, veiling his strength until his opponent is fully committed to an attack. Here is what I wish he would say."

Her eyes twinkled as her voice dropped two octaves and turned into a creditable imitation of her husband's, the languid vowels of the South becoming the crisp consonants of Northumberland. "It was a deuced close run thing, sir, and I am proud that my actions tipped the balance in favor of our side. By God, sir, I do not believe it would have succeeded if I had not been there!"

She resumed her normal dialect, but with a smile in her voice. "Johnny, I reckon it ain't a crime to do some self-promoting with the bigwigs."

"I could tell the first time I spotted him on the docks that he was something special," chirped Johnny. "Mr. Hopkins told us to target distinguished-looking gentlemen and I thought he fit that bill."

Sammie Jo's index finger sliced the air in emphatic agreement. "Well slap my head and call me silly: you nailed it, Johnny! He *is* distinguished! Though sometimes I wish he weren't oh so proper. But he don't like to talk about his past, so don't expect him to tell you much about battles. He sees no glory in them, only the deaths of good men." Her face became suddenly somber.

"He once visited the Haslar Hospital where a number of his men were recovering. They had been injured in a fight where they had been under the command of another. 'I am so sad to see you all here,' he said. One of his men spoke up. 'There would be a damned sight fewer of us here if you had been in command, sir.' He fled in tears.

"He don't never scream or yell. He hates boasters, blusterers, barrack room orators and sea lawyers. His eyes do his best talking: they are equally good at putting fire into the hearts of his friends and curdling the blood of his enemies."

Plymouth twirled twice on Sammie Jo's shoulder. "King's enemies beware!" Sammie Jo rewarded him with a walnut heart.

Sammie Jo stroked Plymouth's wing and continued. "He considers loyalty a guiding light and regards betrayal as the darkest of crimes. His sergeant major once described to me the harrowing consequences to one man who betrayed his trust, calling it 'the Gunwale Gator Grounding.' He will tell you the tale if you ask; but if he does, be prepared to be visited by nightmares."

Johnny shivered and his pupils widened in fear. "No, ma'am, I would never think of crossing such a man. Besides, I owe both of you a debt. Joe Hopkins is a bad man, but I did learn one lesson from him. You never welch on a debt!"

Sammie Jo sighed in self reproach. She had just told the equivalent of a ghost story around a campfire and had scared Johnny. She gently touched his forearm and his expression relaxed. But her husband had been right, frightened people could be molded to the whim of the frightener—dull clay transformed into fine sculpture. And yet, he would have hated the "sinners in the hands of an angry God" sermon that had scared her as a child. Unlike a Baptist preacher, he was only willing to use fear to get a person's attention. He did not seek to make a man a mindless zealot but wanted to train him to use his free will to choose worthy paths. He would start by granting Johnny dignity as he had done with her. He would visualize Johnny as he could be, not as he was.

Tom neither patronized nor condescended to her, as most men did. Though women were often referred to in legal documents as "wife of," "daughter of," or "sister of," he considered her an equal partner, not a piece of property. He never used the common husbandly endearment of "dear child" which implied dependence, but instead referred to her as "my dearest friend." He was always "Tom" or "Sugar Plum" to her; it never crossed her mind to address him as "Mr. Pennywhistle" in the formal manny her ma had spoken of her pa.

They were learning from each other and both were benefitting. She was becoming more respectful of tradition while he was becoming less hidebound by it. She was learning to restrain her impulsivity, while he was starting to liberate his spontaneity. She was learning to truly listen while he was beginning to stop lecturing.

Most of his friends had called their marriage a match made in hell. She smiled because she knew it had been made in the Other Place.

CHAPTER EIGHT

In the tap room of Sewell's Ordinary, just across the street from the expensive King's Arms Inn, Gabriel talked with Dale. Each held a tankard of beer. English beer was darker, with a sharper taste than its American counterpart. Gabriel liked it but was used to lager beer chilled from storage in his plantation's deep cold spring.

An ordinary only offered food and drink, not lodgings. This particular venue was a gathering place of yeomen and tradesmen rather than gentry. While most came to socialize, others came for information: numerous newspapers, broadsheets, and pamphlets were available free to guests. None of the customers communing with friends, beef pot pies, and Whitbred's Ale seemed to take any notice of a black man conversing with a white man as an apparent equal.

Gabriel had put his many years of working in stables to good use. While Dale had negotiated a price for hiring a post-chaise, Gabriel had inspected the many horses and identified the ones likely to be the fastest. Knowledge of horses was a skill always in demand, transcending national boundaries.

"You retiring, Sergeant Major? I don't believe it!" said Gabriel with astonishment. "The captain without you at his side would be like bread without butter. I can't imagine the Marines without you in their ranks."

"I have thought about this for some time," said Dale in a weary voice. "The idea of being a civilian frightens me, but though my mind says I am still a young man, my body has other ideas. The heavily lined face I see in the mirror each morning is that of a 45-year-old stranger. I have logged a quarter century in the King's Service and been wounded three times, the last time in the leg. The surgeon wanted to amputate, but I threatened to use his saw on him. Thank God I don't limp!" He rubbed the crown of his head and his lips wrinkled in distaste. "I am going bald as well!

"And yet, I consider my life well spent. I have traveled the world, known my fair share of women, and served under the immortal Nelson."

He massaged the back of his neck as if trying to iron out a crick in it. "Most of my friends are dead, crippled, or have succumbed to drink. Those who have left the Service believed their experience of command fitted them well for a variety of jobs, but many civilians were reluctant to hire them because they thought a military mind could not grasp the idea of a business run purely for profit." He shook his head. "The job market is flooded with veterans returning from the wars, and they must compete with experienced laborers out of work because military contracts are being cancelled." He scowled. "It is disgraceful that the nation quickly forgets the sacrifices of its warriors! The American war will end soon and my Service will contract no further: it is inevitable that the Admiralty will put an old warhorse like me out to pasture. A man has to adapt to changing times, Gabriel. As the Captain says, 'the man who can't change becomes irrelevant.'"

"Ain't that the truth!" replied Gabriel.

"I am fortunate,' continued Dalef. "I have chased an idea that has sustained me through many battles. I come from a long line of yeoman farmers whose land was stolen through an Enclosure Act. I wanted to be a man of property as my father had been, but I had no interest in tilling the soil. Owning an inn became my dream. I had in mind a place like this one, serving a similar clientele but being especially welcoming to returning veterans.

"Dreams do keep you going," offered Gabriel. "Mine was to be out of bondage. I never knew how that would happen but I had faith the good Lord would find a way. I never imagined that way would come in a scarlet coat. Now I know you ain't much for Jesus, but I think maybe he was whispering in your ear all along on just how you could make your dream come true."

Dale looked skeptical. "I would agree the Lord helps those who help themselves."

"Oh, He does, Sergeant Major, but often He ain't direct about it. It's like being lost in a forest and then discovering that someone has left little bits of twine along the way. If you look close, you find that those little bits are all connected and form a trail leading you out of the woods to a place your heart has always wanted to go."

Dale looked thoughtful. "I have saved all my prize money and will receive a small pension. The captain's brother invested my funds in government bonds and his copper mines and tripled it. The sum is not enough to buy anything grand like the King's Arms, but enough to buy something respectable, if I am careful. The captain made inquiries on my behalf before he left for America. The mail waiting for him at Stonehouse included a letter recommending The Black Robin, an inn near Canterbury, as a likely prospect. It is a fine old place patronized by farmers much like the ones I grew up with. It is named after a highwayman who had a reputation as a local Robin Hood. The owner is a retired naval officer whose gout grows worse by the day; he would like to sell to a military man. I cannot wait to see it!" Dale's weathered face lit up, but then his expression sobered.

"The captain has encouraged me to find a better half to help me run such a place, saying that he finds marriage an agreeable estate. He says I will be a good catch for any woman." Dale picked up a newspaper that he had been reading. "Gabriel, you once said that you believed when you are on the right path the Lord will open doors for you. Do you really believe that?

"I do, Sergeant Major! Just as I believe if you are on the wrong path, the Lord will start slamming doors shut. You just have to pay attention and have faith."

Dale smiled and tapped the newspaper. "Then I believe the Lord has just opened a very special door! I was reading this just before you came in from the stables, *The Laborer's Clarion*. It has articles demanding fair pay for farm workers, pensions for veterans with less than 14 years service, and price controls on wheat and rye. The headline caught my attention: 'Enclosure Acts Must Stop.' I wondered who would be so bold as to publish material that the government might term insurrectionist." He pointed to a line of print. "D. MacJarrow at Watling Road, Cornhill, London." Dale rubbed his chin. "That is a very uncommon Scots name, and all who bear it are related." He took a deep breath as if preparing to reveal a great truth. "I once knew a person by that name very, very well."

"It's always good to meet up with old friends when you've been away for a while," responded Gabriel cheerfully.

"She was an old flame, not an old friend."

"A woman running a newspaper? I ain't never heard of that!"

"The D. stands for Deborah. When I knew her, she ran a small press in Portsmouth. It's not uncommon for widows to continue their husband's business or trade. Nothing political back then; she mainly kept track of merchant ships coming and going and cargos being landed. She actually managed the business better than her late husband. Considering what she is writing about now, she is in dangerous waters. When

BOMBPROOFED

the government shuts down such papers, mobs often react violently. I can see why she does not want to call attention to her gender."

"From the look on your face, you look mighty worried about her. I get the feeling that she was once very important to you."

Dale sighed in pain. "She was. We were never formally engaged but had an understanding."

"That's real sad. Do you mind me inquiring what happened?"

"No. It's good to tell someone. I last saw her in April 1805, just before *Bellerophon* departed Portsmouth. We were going to marry when I returned from Gibraltar. The trouble is, I did not return to Portsmouth until December. In the meantime, the names of those killed at Trafalgar were made public. By some mistake, I was listed among them. She had been gone a month when I returned. Everyone said she was consumed by grief and sold her press to the first buyer she could find. Despite my best efforts I could discover no information about where she had gone. I spent five years trying to find her."

He stared at his lap in sorrow. "This paper is... a shock. I thought I had put all of this behind me, but seeing her name..."

"I'd say your heart is a long way from done with her, Sergeant Major. I know what it's like to lose someone. My wife was sold someplace in Louisiana. I don't know if she is dead or alive, but if I had any way to find her and get her back, there would be no power on earth to stop me!"

Dale stared at Gabriel. "But what if she has remarried? What if she has forgotten me? What if..."

"Hold on, Sergeant Major. Don't drown yourself in ifs and think the worst. I think Jesus guided your hand to pick up that paper. If her writing has offended the proud and privileged, she could be in danger and needs a warrior. And what better one than you?"

A thundercloud crossed Dale's brow and he looked like he might explode. "God's blood, Gabriel, you are right! She is not *a* woman, she is *the* woman. If there is even a small chance we could get back what we lost, I have to take it!"

Gabriel slapped the table. "That is fine news indeed! I'd be glad to help you in your search. Have you decided yet when you will submit your retirement paperwork?"

"I will not do so until I have seen the Captain and his wife settled properly. He will help me through the severance process to make sure that I receive all back pay, mostly prize money from vessels taken in the Chesapeake that has been awarded but not yet paid out. What about you? Are you ready for what lies ahead? London will be a big change for you."

"What's London like?" asked Gabriel, both excited and frightened by the prospect of seeing a famous city.

"Nothing like it on earth, Gabriel," said Dale. "Over a million people live there. It's dirty, foggy, and dangerous, but also amazing, exciting, and always changing. Not a place I'd care to live, but fine to visit, so long as you're careful of what hands reach in your pockets."

Dale and Gabriel had no idea their entire conversation was being monitored. The listener was John Smith, a short, greasy-haired man of 20 with a face as forgettable as his name. He had heard them charter a coach at Bolton's, where he worked as a full time stable hand and part time spy.

The comings and goings at Bolton's were of interest to his employers, whom he knew only as the Fox and the Whippet. They were celebrated highwaymen, though they always concealed their faces when he met with them. He had already alerted them about the charter and had been instructed to follow these two men to obtain additional information. He was expecting an extra golden guinea lay in his future.

The Fox and the Whippet were outlaws who specialized in ferocious play acting. They had patterned their conduct and attire on bandits they had seen in a Covent Garden opera. Their crimson capes and ostrich-plumed blue hats gave them a theatrical appearance that some of their victims had actually called dashing.

So far, their performances had been convincing. They were better at inspiring terror by brandishing their swords and declaiming, "Your money or your life!" than committing actual violence. Once the Fox had resorted to punching a man who objected to surrendering a gold locket that was the legacy of his recently deceased wife.

But tonight they would cross an irrevocable line, and both men wondered if they had sold their souls for 100 guineas. They had never worked for anybody, but their chief fence had persuaded them to meet an important gentleman from the Continent with "unique needs." That gentleman offered financial rewards too great to refuse.

"I loathe the idea of killing anyone!" growled a raspy voice, the result of the frequent smoking of tobacco. The heavy-set speaker was Robert Jeffers, who until eight months before had been a lieutenant of the 30th Regiment of Foot. He relished his sobriquet of The Fox. "But if we must kill this officer, we should act now. His men have left him, and so has his wife. Elfred's Alley is dark and close to the semaphore tower he just entered. We should take him on the way out. I bump and distract, you give him a quick thrust from the back with your stiletto."

"Don't be a damn fool, Jeffers. Killing a uniformed marine officer in daylight in a garrison town would be as foolish as striking a match in a powder magazine," observed a prune-faced man with a nose that resembled a harpoon and a chin as jutting as a ship's prow. Robert Pasco had also been an officer of the 30th and enjoyed his own nickname, The Whippet. Both men had been cashiered after it was discovered that they had been black marketing stores of powder.

"Loyalty to the Corps isn't just a saying to the Marines, it's their gospel. Remember, it took us a whole month to find a corruptible manservant to search Pennywhistle's room at the Stonehouse Barracks. His demise would not be handled by the usual constabulary that we fool so easily. The Marine Garrison would be turned out, and there would be a manhunt the like of which you've never seen. We'd be dancing at the ends of a rope before the week was out. Besides, he may not have what we want on his person. It could be in his baggage, or stashed elsewhere. No, it has to be done on the Dartmoor Road, when he will have everything of value with him."

"I don't like the idea of being lackeys for a German," said Jeffers. "I may be a highwayman, Pasco, but I am no traitor. The idea that we are doing the bidding of some Continental clown makes me uneasy."

"Vogel is Prussian, not German. And anyways, how can you object to Germans when our kings have been Hanoverian since George I? How can we be traitors if England has no enemies on the Continent? With Bonaparte gone, the Great Powers are now one big happy family. We may well be serving the diplomatic efforts of George III's friends, albeit in an oblique way."

"That maybe true, but I wonder if we have extended ourselves too far by taking this job. We make a good living robbing coaches, and we get away with it for two reasons: we do not act so often that we become a threat to good order, and we have never actually shed blood, apart from that one man's nose." Jeffers rubbed his knuckles at the memory.

BOMBPROOFED

"One hundred guineas sounds appealing, but I wonder if it would be bad for business. Gentlemen and ladies understand that we will offer them no violence if they surrender their belongings without protest. Should that change, our future efforts may encounter armed resistance."

Pasco grimaced. "I agree—perception is important. But there is a way to preserve our reputation. We rob the coach, then kill *everyone*. No witnesses. In for a penny, in for a pound."

Jeffers' face turned white. "More than one murder? My God! We will be no better than Tartars!"

"I don't like it, either. But if we leave no witnesses, the authorities will assume it was the work of some gang. They will pursue a band of brigands that does not even exist instead of coming after us."

"Has our usual source at Bolton's come through?" inquired Jeffers.

"Yes, he has. Pennywhistle's carriage will depart around seven this evening. Besides Pennywhistle, there will be four people aboard: his wife, his sergeant major, his blackamoor servant and a street urchin his wife seems to have adopted. We will also have to dispose of the two coachmen. They should pass the ambush spot at Princetown just after nine."

"How many will assist us?"

"Four. Charlie, Steve, Joe, and Bart have agreed to come and will meet us at the sign of the Crossed Keys at four. Don't look so downcast. We get paid twice: once with gold and once with booty. We have numbers, familiar ground, and surprise on our side. What could go wrong?"

"That's just the problem: it sounds too perfect. It's so much safer to keep things clean and neat by only robbing fat, fearful civilians."

"All things change, Jeffers. Sometimes excellent opportunities demand we move into territory that we find uncomfortable. I would also remind you of the eyes of the man who hired us—as cold as they were cruel. If we fail now that we have taken his money, I doubt that he would turn the other cheek. He strikes me as the Old Testament sort. No, we cannot back out now." Pasco shivered at the thought of Prussian vengeance. "I have already sent a messenger to inform him that Pennywhistle has arrived and is being followed. Vogel told me he would forward any communications to his master, and they would arrive in five days or so, depending upon winds in the Channel. Well and good. But, Jeffers, I am still unclear about what we have been set to find."

"Vogel told me to look for a red personal ledger, and any volume relating to codes or ciphers."

"That's pretty vague," said Pasco in exasperation.

"Perhaps it has something to do with accounts, or bookkeeping peculation that's been disguised by a cypher. We did come across some papers from the captain's room that could be codes. Perhaps this Pennywhistle has been managing investments and pocketing more than his commission. He certainly has more money than your average officer, handing out crowns and even sovereigns as tips to tradesmen and servants."

"So he probably deserves what he's going to get. I know it's a risk, but we only have to do this once!"

Half a mile away, Pennywhistle paced restlessly, like a tiger that had swallowed a barrel of coffee. The subaltern in command of the semaphore detachment had transmitted the message, now he awaited the reply.

Royal Marine Second Lieutenant Quinton Connors dashed down from the rooftop stairs, energetically flourishing a piece of paper. "It's here, Captain. I just got done decoding it and wrote it down for you. It's the best news!" He breathlessly handed Pennywhistle the paper, the grin on his youthful face at odds with Pennywhistle's neutral expression.

The message was simple and direct. "Report to First Lord at earliest possible moment. PM pleased with your news. Star for epaulettes, star with ribbon await." The first part meant he would be promoted, since a major wore a single star on each epaulette. The second meant he would receive a showy bauble of jewelry; a five-inch, eight-pointed silver star with a gold and red circle in the center emblazoned with the motto *tria juncta in uno*. That translated as "three joined as one" referencing both the crowns of England, Scotland, and Ireland as well as the Holy Trinity. The medallion would be worn with a long silken ribbon draped from shoulder to hip: the insigniae of the Most Honorable Order of the Bath. His calling cards would now read *Thomas Pennywhistle, KB*.

His conduct was being commended, yet the message distressed him because he was about to become a public figure of the kind he hated, a pawn in the power games of the high and mighty. Rather than celebrity, he sought the private life that his father had recommended, "filled with old wood to burn, old wine to drink, old friends to converse with, and old books to read."

His earlier meeting with Colonel Carstairs, the commandant of the Stonehouse Garrison, had given him a preview of the dubious rewards of fame that lay ahead.

Upon hearing a précis of the dispatches, Carstairs had clapped his hands together in satisfaction. "Finally some good news from the American cesspool! I lost my brother there. Damned fine revenge for the burning of York!" He had then broken into a quickstep of joy that resembled an Irish jig after one too many Jameson's. Casting all restraint aside, Carstairs had laughed loudly, poured celebratory glasses of cognac, and slapped him on the back several times, proclaiming him "a splendid fellow and an example to us all." They had never met before, but the news of a surprise victory had caused the colonel to act as if they had been bosom friends from childhood.

Though there was historical precedent for the awarding of a knighthood, Pennywhistle realized that it was a calculated political move, having as much to do with propaganda as propriety. The government required a handsome face in a scarlet coat to be the public face of success, and that man needed a suitable title. It was to be, he suddenly feared, a small-scale version of what Nelson had undergone, but while Nelson had reveled in the attention, Pennywhistle feared suffocating under the bouquets thrown by well-wishers. He knew that he had a certain reputation within the Corps. He valued that fame because it had been bestowed by peers who understood that the real renown belonged to the men under his command who had willingly shed their blood on his behalf. Hannibal had not crossed the Alps alone. Pennywhistle valued his privacy, and the accolades of an unpredictable public held somewhat less attraction than digging camp latrines.

In practical terms he would need new uniforms, new monogrammed writing paper, and new calling cards. He would probably have to buy some kind of coach and have an altered coat-of arms with the knight's helm emblazoned upon its doors. He dreaded submitting to a lengthy interview with the dull mandarins at the College of Arms, talking about what odd symbols should be added to his armorial bearings.

On the positive side, his salary would increase to £291 per year and he would be entitled to a military funeral with 200 men allowed to fire three volleys in his honor. As a captain, he would have only merited a company.

Sir Thomas. Yes, his vanity liked the sound of it. But then the acerbic voice of his Scots mother began hectoring him, saying that the new title would allow innkeepers to charge him higher rates and lead the servants of friends to expect extravagant tips when he called upon their masters. Her disagreeable tones also informed him he would be expected to entertain lavishly.

Outrageous spending was a cancer among the nobility. There was an enormous temptation to not only display wealth, but to flaunt it. Abetted by addictions to drinking and gambling, spendthrift gentlemen burned through their fortunes within a few years of receiving their inheritance. The Prince of Wales had set the pattern: despite a lavish income, he was rumored to be more than half a million pounds in debt. Then and there, Pennywhistle resolved he would not follow suit. He would force himself to live within his means, even if that meant disappointing would-be sycophants, jumped-up neighbors, and stockbrokers claiming a unique investment opportunity.

On the other hand, he reflected, Sammie Jo would be pleased. To his bride, a title represented a dream come true. Those silk-clad Baltimore scolds who had dismissed her as a backwoods hoyden would be shocked to the roots of their dyed hair to learn that she would soon be addressed as Lady Pennywhistle. Yet she would always be Sammie Jo to him.

He doubted that she would ever lose her New World honesty, frankness, and sympathy for those who sought to rise above their origins. She might one day conduct herself with ladylike deportment but she would never forget her roots on a hardscrabble farm she had described as "a place where people were ridden like horses, fleeced like sheep, worked like cattle, and dressed like swine."

She was adaptable, yet it would be on her own terms. She would incorporate American ideas of egalitarianism, hard work, and plain speech into her new life. The hardest part would be convincing her to let servants do things for her, because she was the model of self sufficiency.

"Sir, Sir? Are you all right?" A puzzled Connors interrupted his ruminations. He blinked; realizing that he had been so lost in thought that he had forgotten where he was. He tried to think of a response appropriate to the man of action that people believed him to be, rather than the unfashionable introvert he actually was. "Forgive me, Lieutenant. I was trying to think of who to invite to a celebratory party when I reach London." He forced a cheeriness he did not feel into his voice. "News of a knighthood is overwhelming! Not something that happens every day, is it? Ha, ha, ha!"

"Oh, I understand, sir, really I do," chirped Connors. "Let me congratulate you again, sir!" Connors extended his hand, which Pennywhistle clasped. Connors' grip was firm and his handshake vigorous, reflecting his earnest personality. "The duty here is dull, sir, though I allow it is important. It is not often I get to meet a hero who has gallantly met the challenge of battle that I so long to experience." Stars of admiration sparkled in his eyes.

Oh God! thought Pennywhistle. He did not want fawning admiration. Ordinarily, he would have regarded it as his duty to disillusion Connor about battle with hard, ill-favoured truths. But the lad had a part to play in the charades ahead, and now was as good a time as any to begin practicing responses to a situation that would likely arise often.

"You are too kind, Lieutenant, and I thank you for your felicitations." Yes, that was it—graciously accept what was offered. "Though it would be wrong of me not to give full credit to the gallant men who served with such fortitude, and to Dame Fortune for the singular favoritism she has bestowed on me." Good—be humble and acknowledge luck. "Now, Lieutenant, I must take my leave of you and prepare for my journey to London." He and Connors exchanged crisp salutes.

Pennywhistle exited the station and began walking briskly toward The Saracen's Head. It was a bright afternoon, he had just received happy news, and a loving wife awaited him a few blocks away.

A prickling of unease traveled up his spine.

It felt as if he were being followed. He had sensed eyes upon him ever since they had left *Vesta*. Even as he had walked with Sammie Jo, speaking of pleasant things, a part of his mind had warned him that something was off. He cast quick, wary glances in every direction. He had the feeling that a watcher had disappeared into an alley a second before he'd turned his gaze in that direction. And then he was at the entrance to the inn. The feeling faded.

Chapter Nine

"Yes, the shrimp is delightful, Countess, but I prefer mine with plenty of paprika. I like seafood that gives a sharp kick to the taste buds. But I understand the empress does not care for spicy foods." Von Steinwehr smiled pleasantly at his dinner companion. But despite the lavish spread of food and wines, he was not enjoying dinner and had begun to tire of Vienna. He was a man of temperate habits and did not like the bloated, sluggish feeling that followed overeating. He also felt light-headed from one glass too many of a one-hundred-year-old Tokay, a bottle of which cost more than a Viennese civil servant's annual salary. The whole occasion was an expression of the luxuriousness that his Spartan core disdained.

He tried to eat small portions, but, even so, eight courses caused even the thinnest person's waistline to distend and press against the confines of tailored garments. The courses were served by regiments of servants sporting powdered wigs and the Hapsburg livery, *très ancien régime*. The table tops gleamed with imported china, expensive crystal, and elegant silverware. Each carefully polished mahogany table featured a huge, elaborate bronze centerpiece specially made for the occasion.

His practiced eye counted 40 tables seating at least 500 guests. The largest of Schönbrunn Palace's 1,441 rooms had been specially decorated for the occasion, and all 139 of its

BOMBPROOFED

kitchens had been employed to serve up the feast. Hundreds of candles burned in scores of elaborate chandeliers. The light reflected brilliantly off the gold and silver buttons of the men and the diamonds, rubies, and emeralds of the women.

The ostentation was calculated, showcasing Hapsburg prosperity and stability so as to impress guests and never be forgotten. Europe had gone through many political and economic upheavals since 1792, and it was deemed time, by those who had survived, to show the world that those upheavals were at an end.

The first course had been soup and *hors d'oeuvres* served from blue china tureens and silver platters. He was no great fan of turtle soup, with its islands of floating green fat, but he had to admit the one prepared tonight had been delectable. Oysters with Chablis, boiled beef with *Spatsburgunder*, and roast beef with expensive clarets followed the soup. Ham, goose, venison, partridge, and pheasant rounded out the array of meats. Several varieties of fresh trout were presented for those who favored fish. The shrimp had appeared then. The *pop popping* of champagne corks reminded him of musketry.

Then dessert was served. Cakes, pies, pastries, fritters, puddings, jams, and jellies vied with each other for the attention of the guests. Ice cream and four varieties of coffee were served as well. For the few restrained diners, there were apples, oranges, and pears, ten types of cheeses, and cashews, walnuts, and almonds.

His present distress could not be helped. No one of sense would decline a gracious invitation that was personally issued by the Czar. Alexander and a select gathering of other royalty chatted with raucous merriment a few yards away.

Von Steinwehr eyed them. He himself was 39 years old, the ideal age to rule: the optimism and muscles of youth tempered by the experience and wisdom of incipient middle age. As he looked at the chattering geriatrics surrounding him, he realized how much better fitted he was than they to be Plato's enlightened ruler. It irked him that over twenty centuries had passed since Plato had written the *Politeia*, yet mankind still had not settled upon any reliable way for the men most fit to rule benignly..

For all his hatred of the Corsican tyrant, Von Steinwehr had to admit that in some ways Napoleon had come close with his enlightened reforms, but he had become so enamoured of empire building that he'd made the fatal mistake of invading Russia: extending his reach far beyond his capacity to grasp and hold.

Their host, the Hapsburg Emperor Francis, was a lantern-jawed, prematurely aged man with a scholarly bent. He collected maps, grew exotic plants in hothouses, and often walked the streets alone. Subjects waved to him during his perambulations, and he waved pleasantly back.

Von Steinwehr found Vienna attractive if contradictory. Its heart was joyous and sensual, a paradise for the aesthete as well as the epicurean. Medicine and natural philosophy flourished here without the restraint and oversight of church or state that stunted scientific advancement in many other countries. Other Viennese devoted their attention to their famous pastries; and their own dance, the waltz, was taking Europe by storm. The city's soul was musical, thanks to the legacy of Mozart, Haydn, and most recently Beethoven, whose rough manners and untamed talent fascinated everyone. Now, however, the intrigues centering on the recently assembled Congress of Vienna meant that wild speculations and fevered suspicions were replacing the usual atmosphere of *joie de vivre*.

The assembled emperors, czars, kings, nobles, electors, knights, and ministers, and their entourages, had swollen the city's population of 250,000 by at least 100,000. There were also legions of hangers-on: minor gentry, soldiers of fortune, and men of letters, as well as confidence men, pickpockets, and forgers. The Congress had attracted every power broker in Europe, and more than a few who were not, but desperately wanted to become so. It was a game of thrones whose glitter and glamour riveted the rest of Europe, as if they were watching a grand opera unfold.

The Congress was an unprecedented assemblage of political and moral authority. There were devotees of Machiavelli as well as acolytes of the Rights of Man. It was the first time a pan-European conference had been assembled to systematically compose a peace and devise instruments for its continuance, Enlightenment ideals finally moving from talk to action. The Congress would decide the fate of Europe for decades to come, and no one with a cause, constituency, or calling wanted to be excluded from the process. Much of the negotiation was being conducted in secret meetings, and there were cabals, intrigues, and conspiracies galore.

New businesses opened to cater to the extensive needs and wants of the foreign arrivals. Tailors, dress makers, jewelers, and florists became wealthy overnight. Likewise, numerous new messenger services facilitated fast communications between Vienna and European capitals. Switching horses and riders at regular intervals, couriers could get a message to London in four days, and one to Moscow in eight.

Czar Alexander himself had commissioned an entirely new wardrobe, since his once trim figure had acquired a paunch from all the summer banquets and parties. Tonight he wore a splendidly gilded white and green hussar uniform, bedecked with medals and emblems of various orders of chivalry that he had not earned but wore as a sovereign. The tailor had delivered his current outfit only two hours before the dinner.

Whole divisions of prostitutes took up residence in the city, from inexperienced country girls to sophisticated courtesans. There was a harlot for every budget, preference, and perversion. Though most were female, young men also made themselves available. Duchesses, countesses, and ladies of fashion were present as well and charged no fee, for they loved the attentions of the great and powerful. Von Steinwehr had never seen so many head turners in one place, yet he remained unbeguiled, since no finer woman than his wife existed.

The previous day, von Steinwehr had explored the city. It was his custom to familiarize himself with any new locale, since every location was a potential battlefield. The city was small in size, but superimposed upon the medieval town plan and within the decaying walls of the *Ringstrasse* was a Baroque city of winding streets and stunning palaces, a few of them royal but most belonging to the nobility. They showcased elaborate filigree and gilt ornamentation, huge bay windows, tall towers, elegant domes, and neoclassical columns. Most featured gigantic ballrooms designed to satisfy the Viennese passion for all forms of dance. Many also contained their own riding schools and fencing academies. At least ten had private opera houses.

The requisite cathedral, St. Stephen's, was of Gothic design, and a 446-foot spire commanded attention. Yet most of the city inhabitants paid the church little mind, for this was a city of secular concerns and earthly pleasures.

Vienna was also the greenest city in Europe, thanks to an extensive tree planting program and the careful retention of existing forest areas. There were bucolic promenades, places to relax or engage in discreet negotiation, whether of a romantic or diplomatic nature.

Bombproofed

"Do you enjoy Maestro Beethoven's music, Herr Colonel? I was present at the premiere of Wellington's victory and do so hope the Orchestra favors us with a performance of it tonight. I find the raw power of his melodies so much more satisfying than Haydn's measured cadences. I like... raw power." The Countess von Mellinthin was a tall, blonde woman with a prepossessing bosom, full lips, and features that suggested a formidable character. She was well into her forties, but extensive and artful makeup concealed her age from all but the most observant eyes. Her husband was nowhere to be seen, and she was trying hard to hold von Steinwehr's attention. The bold directness of her gaze indicated that she might be measuring him for her bed. His height and scarred face frightened many, but to some women the hint of savagery acted like catnip to a cat. Clearly she liked what she saw.

Since this was a state dinner, he was attired in his most formal uniform. He wore a tightly fitted midnight blue tunic with a high crimson collar and matching cuffs, closely cinched at the waist, with long tails, and lined in ruby-red silk. His gold epaulettes made his already broad shoulders seem herculean. His bone-white breeches fitted his long legs so tightly one could see the articulations of the underlying muscles when he tensed his leg, and his knee high boots were blacked to perfection. A gleaming gold gorget bearing the royal arms of Russia hung suspended from a black ribbon round his throat, and a yellow sash of the finest silk encircled his waist. Even seated, he literally was head and shoulders above the crowd, a figure not easily forgotten.

The countess's sky blue eyes sparkled like the diamond necklace she sported above her impressive décolletage, set off to advantage by her red gown, but he had no interest in her charms. Absolute fidelity to his wife was not just his nature, it was his choice. Ingrid was far more than a pretty face adorning a lovely form; she possessed a quick, insightful mind whose counsel had never led him wrong.

"I do like Beethoven's music, Countess," he replied, "but I prefer the subtlety of the *Moonlight Sonata*. A concert hall should be a place of relaxation, and the Wellington piece reminds me too much of battles in which I have fought." He was trying hard to be a good guest, but his purpose this evening was not making artful conversation with a countess.

He glanced over at Alexander. The Russian's handsome face was flushed with alcohol and the prospect of yet another romantic rendezvous. Von Steinwehr had never met a man as randy as the czar, and the Congress gave him plenty of opportunity to indulge his impulses. Alexander's arranged marriage had been unhappy from the start. At least he allowed the czarina Elizabeth the privilege of discreetly pursuing her own "outside interests."

Von Steinwehr had warned the czar to be more discreet, for each affair risked placing leverage in the hands of opportunists. Alexander did not seem to care. Indeed, it amused him to have his sexual prowess and ability to conquer even the most determined feminine virtue be widely known. His stalwart defense of Russia and frustration of Napoleon had brought him a considerable reputation, which acted as a powerful aphrodisiac when his natural charm did not suffice. He was particularly delighted that he had stolen a mistress away from Austria's chief minister, Prince Metternich.

Alexander thought of himself as the ideal enlightened monarch and military strategist, but in reality he was neither. His successful defense of his homeland was not about his superior leadership but the stubborn character of the Russian people, his troops' dogged willingness to die in droves, and the supreme command of "General Winter." He had indeed been educated in Enlightenment ideals, but he was head of a brutal, backward state that was heavily theocratic, with widespread serfdom.

He could be kind and generous in personal matters, yet turn vindictive and petty if his active imagination fancied a slight. He carried a certain exotic glamour about him as the son of the infamously murdered Czar Paul, and was undeniably bright, but possessed of a weak character. He was easy to flatter and influence, yet he changed his mind without warning: you never quite knew what might trigger an abrupt change of plan or mood. Von Steinwehr found extended time with Alexander exhausting. You constantly had to be on your guard. His delight in sexual conquest extended itself to prurience. He maintained a well organized Secret Service that kept tabs on all the principal players of the Congress and furnished him with daily reports; however, his primary concern was not their economic or political jockeying, but their nocturnal activities, which he read about religiously each morning.

The countess was merrily rippling on about trifles and laughing brightly at irregular intervals. Her eyes told von Steinwehr he was about to be favored with an invitation that he did not want.

"Would you please call me Daphne? Any man who sports a red carnation on a uniform is a gentleman I should like to know better."

"I will do so with pleasure," he replied, being careful not to suggest a reciprocal arrangement with his Christian name.

He caught the czar's eye.

The czar frowned slightly, but nodded. He hated to abandon business for pleasure, yet he respected von Steinwehr's experience and instincts well enough to consent to a short meeting in the usual place. The czar's guest apartments occupied two entire floors of the west wing of the palace. They would rendezvous in a quarter hour in the large library on the top floor.

Most guests still conversed animatedly in a wine-soaked, pleasant fog, but a few had begun to leave and head toward the ballroom. The dance would probably be attended by 10,000 people, a display of numbers and magnificence on a scale that made the balls of Versailles seem mere gentry dances. He could already hear the sounds of the orchestra warming up, and word was that Beethoven had written something special for the evening.

"Forgive me, Countess... uh ...Daphne. I must depart. Though it pains me to leave your delightful company, my czar is leaving and I must attend upon him. Perhaps we might continue this very pleasant conversation tomorrow."

"Tomorrow?" she said with disappointment. She clearly wanted him to say, "later this evening."

He refocused his thoughts as he left the banquet hall and walked purposefully toward the grand gilt and marble winding staircase. The light-headedness departed. He was all business now, and every ounce of his energies, intellect, and intuition focused on the prize—getting back Reichenau. The czar sought influence in the German states, so von Steinwehr's best course was to strongly imply that a reconstituted Reichenau would extend his influence.

He stopped abruptly at the top of the stairs. In his eagerness to meet with Alexander he was walking too fast. He needed to allow time for Alexander to arrive first, pour himself a drink, and settle down a bit. The audience would of necessity be short, no more than ten minutes, since Alexander's vision of tonight's *inamorata* was probably already dancing in his head.

Von Steinwehr felt his heart pound and his chest constrict, yet he must not seem too eager. His own case was of great concern only to himself and his family. He was far

BOMBPROOFED

from the only person seeking restoration of lost lands. The less concerned he seemed about getting his way, the more likely Alexander would respond favorably.

Tonight was not the denouement of the play, merely a forwarding action.

He was a devotee of Shakespeare, as were many Germans, and the Bard had taught him that a great play always had a strong opening scene, followed by a dramatic and unexpected revelation. He had one ready, and it was a bombshell.

The Congress, he reflected, was less like the chess matches the Russians loved than a card game of guile and bluff, where cards had no fixed value; instead, each card's value depended on whatever you could fox your opponent into believing it was worth. He walked slowly down the hall, lost in thought and barely conscious of the magnificent rococo mirrors lining the walls.

"Oof!" A drunken couple stumbled heavily into him, having emerged from one of the many alcoves in the hall. Old reflexes directed his right hand to the stiletto inside his coat. Only at the last moment did he stop himself from drawing it.

The couple staggered, blinked, and giggled; both slurred an apology. The man wore the apple-red breeches and lime green tunic of an officer of the Fourth Hussars. His butter-yellow sash was askew and his sapphire-blue shako tilted at a crazy angle. His partner wore a peach-colored satin dress that revealed considerable décolletage below a gaudy ruby necklace.

He wondered what they were doing on the same floor as the czar's apartments. Were they merely an officer and his lady enjoying clandestine revels? Or were they a pair of the Emperor's spies trained to blend in with the evening's celebrants? His trained eyes made a quick assessment of potential hiding places—no weapons, at least.

The guardsman laughed drunkenly, saying they were here to see the famous Cellini statue of Perseus at the end of the hall. The woman giggled again and added, "Oh, I do so want to see it!"

Their silliness and passion seemed sincere, so he relaxed slightly. He pointed toward the statue and wished them a pleasant good evening. He heard more titters and the rustle of clothing as he turned his back and walked quickly away.

He knocked on the door of the library a minute later and commanded his pulse to slow. He really had to stop jumping at shadows. Still, he had seen men die because of a single momentary lapse of vigilance.

The czar answered the door himself. As von Steinwehr stepped into the magnificent room, Alexander motioned for Boris, his general factotum and chief bodyguard, to depart. Boris was an albino built like a steel safe, and his outsized head squatted like a toad on his wide shoulders. His coarse features and Asiatic eyes marked him as a Bulgar. He was tough and stupid, but loyal in the manner of a good dog.

It pleased von Steinwehr that the czar trusted him sufficiently to feel no need of Boris, especially in light of what had been done to his father. The czar indicated for him to sit: another mark of esteem.

"You have the letters?" inquired Alexander. His face was bloated and puffy, making him look older than his thirty-six years.

Von Steinwehr nodded. "Yes, your Imperial Majesty. There are twenty-three in all. I have read them. There is more material than I originally expected." That was both true and false. He could only read the plain text portions. The words of the dying Pennywhistle haunted him.

What he could read made it clear that something extremely damaging lay concealed in the encrypted portions. The précis that formed the first part of each letter hinted that men associated with the Duke of York had unusual and dark sexual proclivities—prime stuff for blackmail and manipulation. But, without the code, the details were tantalizingly out of reach.

The czar licked his lips and flashed a lupine smile. He loved gossip; gossip that brought him political gain was particularly to be relished. "So the material in them is as provocative and useful as we hoped?"

"More so, Your Imperial Majesty, far beyond our expectations. Most of the letters were written by Mrs. Clarke to the duke demanding money, but several were written by the duke himself in angry—and, I must say, intemperate—response. There is a revelation so shocking that it has the potential to utterly destroy the commander-in-chief of the British army, and perhaps bring down the entire House of Hanover. I must admit, I have always found it odd that a Hanoverian Dynasty has ruled England for the past hundred years." He waited for the weight of his words to sink in. Alexander's expression became almost feral.

The czar huffed. "There is far too much talk of republican government at this Congress. Much as I seek leverage against the British government because of our disagreements about the future of Poland, I shudder at the thought of wrecking a legitimate monarchy. It is imperative that we reverse these tides of democracy that have swept the shores of America and France. We must use the information sparingly, at just the right intervals, to make the British dance to our balalaika. I must ask you now, what is this incendiary piece of information about the Duke of York?"

Von Steinwehr related the explosive secret in his calmest, most matter-of-fact tone of voice.

Clearly the czar was stunned. His voice jumped an octave. "How can a man lie with men as well as women? And the officers under his command? Incredible! Incredible! Utterly unnatural! Base and perverse!" For all of Alexander's sexual conquests, his bedroom tastes were conservative.

Alexander took a deep breath and his eyes bored into von Steinwehr's. "Do the letters supply unarguable proof? Is there a possibility that the letters are forgeries? It is such a monstrous thing that it almost seems the stuff of a deranged prankster or fabulist."

Von Steinwehr spoke gravely. "I realize that, Your Imperial Majesty, but I would remind you, the letters were written by a woman who *knew* that what she wrote had the power to bring royalty to its knees and bend kings to her will. That is the power of incontrovertible facts. Mere slander can be dismissed—and punished.

"For a handsome consideration I had one person who knows the handwriting of both principals carefully examine portions of the letters, though only sections containing innocuous information. He assures me that they are genuine. He says the words sound exactly similar to the way the duke speaks. Still, I believe in second opinions. I have the least explosive letter on my person. Tomorrow afternoon I shall meet with a former officer of the king's German Legion who once worked closely with the duke and get his estimation of the authenticity of handwriting and word usage. But, again, I shall share only those portions which contain no secrets. By tomorrow at this time I expect to have irrefutable proof that the letters are genuine. And I would ask you to remember the Baroness de Krudener's admonition that God's hand is upon you. God does not forget His chosen ones. The appearance of these letters is no coincidence, but His design and His will that they should fall into your outstretched hand. It is my good fortune that I have been selected to play a humble, yet honorable role as well."

Alexander nodded solemnly. He liked the idea of being God's instrument. "I must be absolutely sure before I use

BOMBPROOFED

them. There must be no possibility of error on our part or forgery on anyone else's. I trust they are in a safe place?"

"A very safe place, Your Imperial Majesty. I realized extraordinary documents deserved extraordinary protection. All correspondences to and from the principal representatives of the varied powers attending this Congress are opened, read, and re-sealed by the minions of Francis. That is why I have warned you to use the postal service for only the most mundane of exchanges and to use special couriers for sensitive materials. It is why I send you no written notices of what I discover and instead request personal audiences. Thus the information stays between the two of us."

Alexander looked concerned. "Do you think there could be some kind of counter move?"

"I think it unlikely, Czar Alexander. Talleyrand manipulated Louis into returning the letters. He knew the symbolic value of France's oldest enemy standing as its staunchest ally during these troublous times. Since the parties involved were either lost at sea or tragically overtaken by French bandits, no suspicion can attach itself to your august person."

Alexander flushed an angry red. "God damn that rascal Talleyrand. His tongue speaks three languages but one lie, and he always seems to have a trick up his sleeve. He seems friendly and direct, yet I never know what he is thinking." The czar pounded his fist repeatedly in frustration.

Von Steinwehr interrupted his tantrum. "I do feel compelled to say that if there is to be any trouble, it will come from the British. I would not be doing my duty if I did not inform you of the possibility. And yet, any interest they evince is one more surety that the letters are indeed genuine."

The czar's voice took on a hard edge. "Then I leave it to you to treat any inquiries from the British with,"—he inhaled deeply—"the firmest and most profound resistance. Do I make myself clear?"

"Quite clear, Your Imperial Majesty. I shall make sure that the British discover nothing. It is not just about my honor and reputation—" He could see the czar's attention slipping away, no doubt resuming its focus on the evening's *inamorata*. He would have to compress his rehearsed speech. "I have done my part, Your Imperial Majesty. Now about the matter of Reichenau..."

"Proceed," said the czar, looking slightly bored.

Von Steinwehr's face lit up. He was anything but bored.

Chapter Ten

A lemon-yellow post chaise with gigantic rear wheels bounced along the rutted road. Six horses pulled the coach at breakneck speed toward the final rays of a setting sun. To maintain the pace, the horses had to be changed every twenty miles. Luxurious red Moroccan leather lined the cabin, and newly installed springs cushioned the ride, but it was still sufficiently rough that Pennywhistle and Sammie Jo had no inclination to open the hamper and make an attempt at the wine therein. It would be hard to get any sleep in the hours ahead.

Dale and Gabriel sat across from them, and Plymouth the parrot perched on the window edge, seeming content to sway with the motions of the carriage and watch the scenery. He occasionally squawked a single word, "Pretty."

The luggage, sea chests, and portmanteaux were stowed on a large platform behind the cabin, secured with stout ropes and iron clasps. The two coachmen did not sit upon a buckboard, but rode the trace horses. Johnny, who had grown up with horses, also rode, and grinned with boyish glee. He was excited to see London and start a new life. This thrill ride was a wonderful way to begin.

Pennywhistle was tired, and inclined to make the long journey in stoical silence. He respected Dale and felt Gabriel to be a good man, but he had been raised to think that a gentleman never spoke freely to his wife in front of others.

Sammie Jo's emotions were under no such genteel constraints. She treated the traditional expectations of a woman—silence, obedience, and modesty—as suggestions, not commands. She burst out from time to time with breathless observations on both the scenery and English customs in general. In her excitement, she lapsed into her old ways of talking. "I ain't never ridden in such a fine coach. Hell, Tom, I ain't never ridden in anything better than a broken-down old buggy. I did think the roads would be a heap better here in the old country, though. Tell me what lies ahead in London."

He answered as calmly as he could through the jouncing. "I must deliver a personal message from Admiral Cockburn to his wife. After that, I will be tied up for a few days with official flummery. The Government will want to arrange interviews for me with newspapers favorably disposed toward Liverpool's administration, and I shall just have to endure them. As far as I am concerned, the only good to come out of the Washington Campaign was my meeting you. I—"

He suddenly found himself unable to breathe, for Sammie Jo was kissing him hard on the lips. Against his will, he felt her fire, and had difficulty letting her go. He flushed in embarrassment as Dale and Gabriel fought to suppress grins at his discomfiture.

He struggled to compose himself and regain his train of thought. "In the past I have avoided politics, but since my participation will make you a lady, it is a small price to pay."

Sammie Jo giggled with delight, like a little girl given a pony. "A lady! Me, a lady! Never in all my born days did I think a sow's ear could become a silk purse." But a second later, a serious expression on her face spoke of doubt rather than joy. "Tom, I don't ever want to embarrass you with my funny accent and damnable bluntness. I want to help you and complement you. I'm goin' to need some education in your ways right quick."

He looked at her and saw not a beautiful woman, but a confused little girl pleading for help, terrified of venturing into a world of refined human tigers whose mannered claws she little understood. She was queenly in courage and character, a feminine version of the natural man idealized by Rousseau. If she lacked manners and refined speech, that was of no moment. The windows to her soul were set with panes of the finest crystal and revealed a beautiful room bright with promise. The curtains might be too garish, but curtains were easily replaced.

Pennywhistle squeezed her hand. "I assure you, Lady Leith will be a good and patient instructor. If you can function in the jungle of war, you can adapt to the perils of civilized society. You may make a few missteps. That is to be expected, since one cannot grow without them: eggs must be broken to make their contents useful. I will always be proud to have you as my wife. Wherever we go, it will give me the greatest pleasure imaginable to have you at my side."

Sammie Jo's eyes glistened. "That makes me happier than a possum eating a sweet potato, Tom." She brusquely wiped away the wetness. "Damn, I don't want to start a waterfall." She took a deep breath. "Since we have a long journey ahead, ain't no reason why my education can't start right now. If you spit in one hand and wish in the other, it don't take a seer to know which one fills up first."

Pennywhistle smiled. "Certainly! Is there a particular topic that preoccupies your mind, one that you would like to have clarified?"

Sammie Jo rubbed her chin in thought. "Let's start with why people in Plymouth were afeared of speaking to me when I was visiting stores. Folks moved aside like I was carrying typhoid. Some of the shopkeepers froze, as if I was a Barbary pirate about to abduct their children."

Pennywhistle chuckled and held up his palms in amusement. "You misunderstood, my dear. It was about deference and uncertainty. The townsmen and shopkeepers behaved properly according to their lights, as you did according to yours; the two were simply out of synchronization. They have been taught that they should only speak if a lady deigns to address them. One with no apparent need of a man so startled them that they did what startled people do: they froze. In America, people think nothing of engaging strangers in conversation. Your direct manner probably confused the store clerks, because you were willing to ask advice and not simply order them about. You treated them as equals because it never occurred to you not to." He smiled at her.

"I am also sure that you surprised many people at The Saracen's Head with your kindness toward Johnny. It's not that people here don't have hearts, but a gentlewoman generally does not bestow attention on what looked to be a ship's boy. While I appreciate your willingness to decipher our ways, I hope that the knowledge in no way occludes your better instincts."

For the next two hours Pennywhistle patiently outlined the class system and the protocols and manners required by its various stations. He went through the degrees of nobility and explained that since a Knight of the Bath was not ranked as a peer, he could stand for the House of Commons. At first she was disappointed to learn that, although she would be a lady, she would only be considered gentry, until she realized how very constrained by social expectations the lives of peers could be.

His talk was punctuated by her questions. Sometimes she asked for clarification of a detail; other questions were more rhetorical in nature: "Who the hell thunk that up?" or "Hellfire and damnation, why would anyone believe that?" Sometimes her commentary was a single drawn out exclamation which began with an "F". Dale and Gabriel found it all vastly amusing, since her tart comments often mirrored their own feelings.

Pennywhistle had just begun to explain a butler's function when she raised a hand in an emphatic "stop" motion. She cocked her head, her nostrils flared and her eyes narrowed. An instant later, her face turned hard and cold. The world had changed to one she understood perfectly. Her eyes bored into his. "Gunfire!"

Chapter Eleven

Pennywhistle heard the sound a second later, unmistakable and close. Dale and Gabriel recognized the angry bee noise as well. Plymouth flapped his wings but did not leave his perch. "Bad! Bad!" he squawked.

Dale leaned forward and said quietly, "Highwaymen, sir?"

"Undoubtedly," replied Pennywhistle.

Sammie Jo gripped the door handle and craned her head out the window. The moon was visible and reflected brightly off a stream paralleling the carriage road.

"I see them. Six men on horseback, maybe a hundred yards behind. They have pistols, no carbines. Don't look to be in no particular order—not like a troop of cavalry, more like a swarm of skeeters." She jerked her head back in the coach. "Damn, Tom, I thought the death penalty would discourage this kind of mischief." Her expression turned vulpine. "Them bandits picked the wrong coach."

Pennywhistle nodded tersely. Had his sense of being watched earlier in the day presaged this attack? He cursed his foolishness for ignoring his instincts. He had stowed their weaponry with the luggage for the comfort of his bride, to give her more leg room in the crowded cabin. At least he still had the dirk in his right boot.

He plumbed the depths of his mind for every scrap of knowledge about highwaymen. He assessed his group's strengths and the probable weaknesses of their opponents. A sudden certainty that had no earthly source overwhelmed him: these bandits intended fatal violence.

He experienced a moment of panic when his mind went blank. Nothing showed on his face, but he felt the terror of knowing his love and friends might die because of his ineptitude. An eternity yet only a second later, the amoral part of his mind seized control and banished any notions of conscience or morality. All that mattered was survival. His face flushed a passionate crimson.

A small smile creased the corners of Dale's eyes. He knew exactly what that flush meant.

But then a vision of the Other Side popped into Pennywhistle's head and temporarily dethroned his ruthless self. He noted that circumstances seemed to be forcing him away from fully embracing that world's promise of peace. Perhaps this was some kind of cosmic test: to see if peaceful means could be employed where he had formerly used violent ones. If so, it was a test that he was about to fail. If he had his way, the brigands would face their own self-judgment on the Other Side. He frowned inwardly, wondering if his knowledge of what came after made him more willing to kill rather than less.

Like a bursting firework, a full-blown plan sprang into existence in his mind's eye. And now he could hear shouting outside the coach. He did not have time to explain the plan, but he trusted the others would do his bidding without hesitation.

Another shot rang out, and two horsemen neared the coach windows.

Plymouth squawked, "Deep six 'em! Deep six!"

"Sammie Jo, I assume you still have your whip?" She nodded briskly. "Good! Can you get the parrot to move on command?"

Sammie Jo immediately grasped the bird's value as a distraction. "Damn right. I just got to touch one spot on his burned wing and he will squawk like a banshee and sail into the air. That happened by accident yesterday."

"Gabriel, you bought a whittling knife at the market, did you not?"

"I sure did, Cap'n, and I got it on me." He reached into his pocket and pulled it out. It was cheap, but the blade was long and sharp.

"Can you whittle flesh instead of wood?"

"Since I be defending you and your lady, I can shave a man so sharp he won't even know he has a shadow."

"Excellent." Pennywhistle faced Dale. "Sar't Major, I know you are unarmed but I trust your pugilistic skills are in working order?"

Dale started in mock indignation. "I am not an old man yet, Captain. I still have a mean jab and wicked right cross."

"Age plus experience: a deadly combination!"

Two more shots rang out. The coachman shouted "Whoooaaa!" and the carriage ground to a halt. Pennywhistle hoped Johnny was unhurt.

"They may expect us to surrender and hand over our valuables without protest. That is exactly what we will appear to do. But I sense dark intentions and will take no chances. No quarter will be given. Agreed?"

The others nodded.

"I will focus their attention on me so that they will pay less mind to you. I am counting on the probability that they are accustomed to tame civilians and know nothing of how fast death can be administered by professionals. My timepiece is the key. The signal to act will be when I hand it to their leader; or rather, almost do so. Sammie Jo, at that moment, get the parrot to squawk and fly. Each of you needs to select a target while I talk so that you can strike immediately while they are disoriented. Weave at least once when you rush them. With luck you will be upon them before they can discharge their pieces."

There were the sounds of men approaching the coach door.

"We will prevail," whispered Pennywhistle. His hard eyes matched the certitude in his voice.

A man in an ostrich-plumed blue hat thrust a gun barrel through the window, literally right under Sammie Jo's nose. His other hand held a lantern. His eyes darted over the passengers as he bellowed, "Get out, move away from the carriage, and put your hands in the air. No tricks: do exactly what we say. Give us what we want and this will merely be an unscheduled stop on your journey to London. Disobey us in the slightest and this will be the last stop you ever make."

The voice puzzled Pennywhistle. The accent was refined and genteel. *Possibly an ex militia officer or cashiered regular?* Though its harsh tones were meant to terrify, he sensed a lack of conviction. Wait, had he not heard of some gentlemen bandits on this route? They had been styled the Fox and the Whippet by townsmen who thought of them as modern day MacHeaths.

Pennywhistle spoke as one gentleman to another, his tones reasonable, if meek. "A moment, sir! For the sake of my wife, I want no trouble and will obey your instructions. I appeal to your chivalry and ask if I may dismount first to assist her passage. We are newlyweds, you see," he smiled wanly, "and your appearance has shaken her delicate sensibilities to the very core."

Sammie Jo caught the cue and began to sniff and snuffle as if barely holding back a torrent of tears. The bandits dismounted, which puzzled Pennywhistle. Staying on horseback would be a logical way to achieve dominance over those on foot. He decided it was greed—they were probably planning to thoroughly search each passenger to make sure nothing of value remained hidden.

A tall man in a scarlet cape walked over to the one with the short plumed hat. Like Plumed Hat, Scarlet Cape wore a silk lavender scarf about the lower part of his face. He began urgently whispering in his companion's ear.

"I can't kill a woman, Pasco," Jeffers hissed. "I just can't do it. Especially not for some damned foreigner. As long as we get what we came for and hand over the books, we've earned our pay."

Pasco sighed, then nodded. "He does seem reasonable, I admit. And I've no stomach for killing a lady, either; it goes against our principles. If he gives us his word, I will accept it."

Pennywhistle could not make out the words, but knew vacillation when he saw it. These men had poorly developed killer instincts. Even so, he would take no chances; his wife's safety outweighed all other concerns.

The two bandits concluded their colloquy and turned to face Pennywhistle. "Will you give us your word, as a gentleman and King's Officer, that you will cooperate fully?" offered Plumed Hat. "If you furnish that, I give you my word of honor that my associate and I will spare you."

Bandits and honor seemed peculiar partners. Pennywhistle nevertheless chose his words carefully. "I give you my most solemn oath that I will follow your instructions." His promise did not preclude additional actions on his part.

"I am pleased that you are amenable to reason," replied Plumed Hat. "You have two articles that we covet. We will consider the rest of your valuables afterward."

Bombproofed

Pennywhistle blanched inwardly. Could they know about the dispatches? He kept his face impassive and replied with oleaginous politeness. "Pray tell, sir, what would those items be?"

Scarlet Cape spoke. "A red ledger and a very rare book. We don't know the title, but it is a small volume about codes and such like."

The red ledger! Sammie Jo's speculations about the true nature of his brother's work leapt to mind. Codes would be a given in that unusual line of work. He did not have the ledger, but he did have a book that was unique. It was President James Madison's account book for 1810 and listed the American's government's expenses in detail. Cockburn had taken it as a souvenir and had entrusted it to Pennywhistle to convey to the admiral's wife. Some of the entries were nearly as arcane as codes and would probably fool two brigands. He could try to bluff this out.

"Good sirs, I do not have, nor have I ever had, in my possession a red ledger. Perhaps you have been misinformed on that point, gentlemen. It is quite true, however, that I have a rare book which may be the object of your quest. It is stowed in my luggage. Allow me to retrieve it for you."

Plumed Hat looked as though disappointment warred with anticipation, but eagerness won out. "Please do so at once, sir."

Pennywhistle exited the coach and walked slowly toward the rear luggage platform. He bowed his head and forced a troubled expression onto his face, moving with the deliberation of a man bearing a great burden. He projected uncertainty and submission. He wanted the brigands to expect fearful cooperation.

As he walked, he assessed the gang's weaponry. Plumed Hat and Scarlet Cape held Light Dragoon pistols. Their effective range was ten feet in broad daylight. There were no long arms in evidence, though both carried the expensive small swords of gentlemen. He detected a hint of rust just below the guard on both blades. Neither had been drawn recently; the lack of maintenance suggested the weapons were for display rather than action. Four assisting bandits stood 20 feet to the rear of their leaders and appeared restive —probably eager to plunder the chests strapped on the rear of the coach. They had their pistols drawn, but held them dangling at their sides. They looked thin, and their threadbare clothing did not match the well-tailored attire of their leaders.

The two coachmen stood with hands up in front of the horses, their frightened eyes exchanging quick glances of uncertainty. They would supply no help. Pennywhistle searched in vain for Johnny. Had the boy been shot, or fallen off in the chase? A surge of worry shot through him, but he sequestered it. He could not afford to be distracted.

He opened his portmanteau and quickly located the small volume. He pulled it clear and walked toward the brigands. Plumed Hat snatched it out of his hand like a bear grabbing a salmon. He held his lantern next to it and began thumbing through it, though the expression on his face told Pennywhistle he had no idea what he was looking at.

"Is that it?" inquired Scarlet Cape eagerly.

Plumed Hat replied, doubt coursing through his voice, "I don't know. I just don't know. I can't understand it, but it looks important. It sure could be code stuff."

"Gentlemen," Pennywhistle said with feigned sorrow, "it is what you seek. I assure you, it is unique. I part with it only for the sake of my wife; otherwise I would have defended it to my last drop of blood. Admittedly it is complex, but a man with the right training will find it easy to understand."

The two bandits looked at each other. One shrugged, the other sighed in baffled resignation. Finally, Plumed Hat

BOMBPROOFED

spoke. "I thank you, sir, for your cooperation. Neither my associate nor I had any wish to make our brief association painful."

"I thank you for your restraint and your unwillingness to divorce yourself from the manners of civilized men," Pennywhistle replied as his pulse began to accelerate. "Allow me to escort my wife and servants away from the carriage. Then I shall give you and your partner a full and exact accounting of all valuables on the coach. Our business may then be concluded."

Scarlet Cape replied magnanimously, "Your request is granted, sir—honor among gentlemen. We respect the service against the Corsican Ogre that your uniform reflects."

Pennywhistle laughed inwardly at the irony of patriotic bandits.

He went round, opened the carriage door, and helped Sammie Jo down. Sammie Jo continued to sniffle tearfully, but he caught the hint of a grim smile on her face for a split second. Plymouth on her shoulder seemed calm and remained silent. He heard something rustling behind the tall ferns by the moonlit stream bed, directly behind the four flunkies. He wondered if it was a fox.

Gabriel and Dale followed Sammie Jo and slowly moved away from each other and the coach. Pennywhistle worried that the flunkies would herd them together, but to his relief two of them moved towards the coachmen instead, brandishing their weapons to remind the drivers to keep their hands up. The remaining two made the fatal mistake of focusing on Dale and dismissing Sammie Jo and Gabriel as of no consequence or threat.

In a dejected manner, Pennywhistle walked back to the two brigands and faced them. "My wife is much calmed, gentlemen, and I am grateful. Much as it pains me to part with a friend, allow me to keep the rest of my bargain." He produced his Blancpain watch, a product of Switzerland's most skilled craftsmen and worth more than a cavalry officer's mount.

He swung it slowly back and forth on its chain, like a mesmerist in action. The eyes of the two brigands were drawn to it. Scarlet Cape extended his empty hand; his finger tips stroked the gold surface with an almost orgasmic joy.

"God damn it!" yelled Plumed Hat. His hand flew to his head as a large rock bounced off his temple. Next there was a slithering sound, and he hopped violently. "Something bit me!"

Scarlet Cape dropped the watch, startled by his partner's bellow. The unexpected diversion could not have come at a more opportune moment.

Plymouth screeched and shot skyward. He flew in fast, low circles, shrieking "Borders away!" His antics captured the attention of the four accomplices for a critical few seconds.

Pennywhistle ignored an Other Worldly voice that whispered "Spare them." He slammed his Hessian boot down hard on Scarlet Cape's foot, crushing his toes. As the man's head reared back in pain, Pennywhistle rocketed his right palm heel into the brigand's Adam's apple. Scarlet Cape fell to the ground, gurgling horribly. Pennywhistle stomped down on his neck. A wheezing sound issued from the writhing brigand; his smashed trachea guaranteed death by asphyxiation.

Pennywhistle heard the crack of a whip and knew Sammie Jo had struck.

Plumed Hat leapt to face him. He started to bring his pistol to the point, but Pennywhistle's left arm lashed out and arrested the man's arm in mid arc. He chopped with his right hand at Plumed Hat's wrist, causing him to drop the pistol with a howl of pain, then grabbed his forearm and elbow to dislocate his shoulder. He raked Plumed Hat's nose with his left elbow, kicked him in the right knee, then backfisted him square in the Adam's apple. As his wheezing opponent fell forward, Pennywhistle's right hand grabbed the base of his neck while his left seized the man's chin. He twisted the head violently to the right and was rewarded with a snapping sound. The lifeless body dropped to the ground like a sack of tanner's offal.

Thanks to Sammie Jo and her bullwhip, Gabriel and Dale had an opening. Gabriel barreled into one of the bandits menacing the coachmen, causing him to drop his pistol and fall sprawling to the ground, while Dale engaged the bandit's companion, becoming the bare knuckle boxer he had been years ago. A nursery rhyme echoed in his head, giving rhythm to his actions. *One, two, buckle my shoe.* He sidestepped the man's pistol, then stomped hard on his left foot. *Three, four, shut the door.* He curtailed the man's yelp with a left hook to the chin, followed immediately by a right cross. *Five, six, pick up sticks.* He shot two quick jabs into the man's solar plexus. A desperate wheeze issued from the man's lips. *Seven, eight, lay them straight.* A left uppercut smashed into his opponent's chin, lifting him off his feet. A right cross hit the man the second his feet touched the ground. *Nine, ten, begin again.* Two straight line punches to the sternum completed the pummeling, stopping the brigand's heart.

Gabriel whipped his knife out and raced toward the remaining brigand. As the man was about to fire, Gabriel slashed at his wrist, causing him to drop his weapon, then he scored a deep trench along the man's neck. The severed carotid artery squirted blood, drenching Gabriel and blinding him.

The downed bandit Gabriel had thought was out of action suddenly rose and tackled him from behind. Both fell in a flailing tangle. They rolled over and over as each man struggled for dominance. The bandit came out on top and positioned himself astride Gabriel's chest. He screamed in wordless fury and raised both fists to slam them down into Gabriel's face.

Sammie Jo's whip lashed out and wrapped around the bandit's neck. He frantically tried to tug it free, but Sammie Jo stalked toward him, pulling the whip tighter as she advanced. Her teeth were bared and her eyes blazed. How dare this man threaten her man and her happiness! Rage unleashed bloodlust. She pulled and pulled with every ounce of her furious strength until the man's eyes bulged and swelled to the size of eggs. His tongue protruded; his head lolled to one side as his skin turned purple.

Dale's firm hand came down on her shoulder. "Enough," he said with uncharacteristic gentleness. "Enough. He is gone. Stand down, stand down, ma'am. Stand down."

She let go of the whip and the bandit sagged to the ground like a windless flag. She broke Dale's grip with a flash of her arm, spun round, and stared madly into his eyes, her own wild with hate. She resembled a malevolent Diana, ready to wreak havoc on mortals who had the temerity to interfere with the business of Olympians.

Dale stared steadfastly back, his eyes kind and firm. He would not be cowed. He understood; he had seen the like before. Battle did this to some people. It would pass in a bit.

He put a hand gently on her shoulder. "Breathe deeply, ma'am, like the captain showed you. Nice and slow, long and deep. Come on, you can do it." Dale's usual command voice could be surprisingly gentle.

She came back to herself slowly as she heeded Dale's words.

Pennywhistle dashed up, his face gaunt with fear and concern. "God's garters, Sammie Jo, are you all right?" He put his fingers to her temples and gently stroked her hair. "What happened? Tell me. Tell me. I want to help."

He searched his bride's eyes for recognition, but all they showed was a mixture of fear and confusion. He recognized the look. From years of battle, he understood that in her mind she walked a dreadful wasteland in a lonely dimension: a darkling realm where grief and pain reigned, where reality and fantasy were locked in perpetual combat.

He scanned her face and limbs for any physical damage but could detect none. Her tanned skin was deathly pale in the moonlight, beads of sweat stood out on her forehead, and he felt the beginning of a shudder in her shoulders. His heart choked. Many stricken thus lived physically but died inside. She needed a loving guide to call her back from that desolate place.

He took her hand. "Come back to me, Sammie Jo. Come back to me!" He repeated the words, steadily and rhythmically, almost as a mantra.

She coughed like a drowning victim expelling water. She inhaled deeply, and her eyes brightened. She tried to speak, but gagged on the words. At last she sputtered, "Oh God, Oh God, Tom, I love you so. I could not stand to lose you." She threw her arms around him with a grip like a shipwrecked sailor seizing a floating spar. She was quiet for a minute and her breathing slowed. Then she started to shake. The sobs came slowly at first, then intensified.

Her sobbing and shaking was lamentation of the psyche, a cry from the deepest depths of her soul. It would be a mistake to arrest the grief and shock; much wiser to let it bleed out. Letting pain hide caused it to fester and poison the soul. Catharsis might begin in pain but it ended in healing.

Pennywhistle had had a similar moment years ago after a particularly vicious little skirmish. It had proved a turning point in his moral evolution. Now, as Sammie Jo clung to him and wept, he held her. He did not attempt to trivialize her grief and pain with platitudes—understanding silence and touch spoke far better. He had been schooled by a cold Scots mother to shrink from comforting touch and kind embrace, but Carlotta had taught him better.

He stroked her hair gently and allowed her tears to drench his sleeves. He felt his love for her and hoped she could feel that.

The two coachmen looked at each other in surprise. "That fight was a sight to behold!" said the thin one.

"I have never seen its like!" said the fat one. "But I wish we had not taken this job. This is another fine mess that you've gotten me into."

"And yet we did not have to do a thing!" observed the thin one. "Too bad there wasn't a bookie around. I could have made a fortune betting on our passengers."

"They pay us to drive, not to fight!" replied the fat one.

"I got to say, it scared me so I wet meself."

"I lost twenty pounds in sweat." The fat one pulled out a small flask from his hip pocket. "This calls for a drink." He opened the flask and took a deep pull. "This French brandy really hits the spot. Care for a nip?"

"Don't mind if I do!" said the thin one.

What arrested Sammy Jo's crying was the boy. Johnny came out of the reeds—frightened, yet unbowed. He threw his arms around her waist in a hug as strong as she had given Pennywhistle: a child seeking the nurture of a mother. She let go of her husband and focused entirely on Johnny. "Are you all right?" she asked gently, kindness sparkling in her eyes.

He brought himself to parade attention, trying to imitate Pennywhistle's military carriage. "I am fine. I ran and hid when the carriage stopped. They didn't pay me no mind. I have a good throwing arm and strong teeth and thought I could put both to good use."

Plymouth dropped out of the sky and landed on Sammie Jo's shoulder. His eyes dilated and contracted rapidly several times, he held his feathers close, and his neck and body stretched upwards. "To Davy Jones' Locker they went!" he cried. Sammie Jo stroked his wings in an effort to calm him.

Pennywhistle let out a quiet "Ah," his questions about scarlet's cape's distress finally answered. "You acted bravely, Johnny. It is times like this that show a man's true character —whether he remembers others or merely looks after his own hide. It is an instinct, nothing that can be rehearsed or faked. It is an instant with implications for a lifetime. You have done well, and I am proud to have you with me."

Johnny grinned, puffed his chest, and stood on his tiptoes. It was just like the lady said: you had to earn the captain's trust. He had started the day a boy, and if he was not quite a man now, he had made exactly the right start to reach that destination. He wished his mother were here to see.

Pennywhistle surveyed the bodies. Their shabby clothing had once been naval slops. He guessed they had served the Fox and Whippet simply because they could not find other employment.

Pennywhistle's companions gathered around him. All were tired and ragged around their emotional edges, but proud and unyielding. Sammie Jo clamped her arm firmly to Pennywhistle's waist and would not let go. Though her eyes were bloodshot from crying, she managed a pale smile.

His customary reserve and self possession departed as his heart demanded voice. "I was thinking of Shakespeare just now, *Henry V*. 'He today that sheds his blood with me shall be my brother. Be he ne'er so vile, this day shall gentle his condition.'

"We are more than just fellow travelers and a band of brothers. We are a family, perhaps a peculiarly assorted, unexpected one, but one that nevertheless deserves recognition and celebration." He smiled because he had finally grasped a truth that had been in front of him all along. "And that family includes Plymouth!"

"Life is about family. A man's real home is not a physical structure but an idea that exists only in the heart: a remarkable place where he finds contentment and solace in the embrace of those who see him exactly as he is, yet give love rather than judgment. Their esteem is the real treasure in life, compared to which the Crown Jewels are trinkets and shadows.

"We come from different estates but that matters much less than the honor, courage, and depth of heart which have brought us together. We have all known death and suffering, but we have drawn strength from it. We have been through fire, but fire burns away barriers and falsehoods and pretensions and reveals the man beneath. Bonds forged in fire are the strongest of all.

"We have two families in life—one of heredity and one of choice. I believe Fate guides people who fight for the right towards each other and affords them the chance to become relatives of the spirit. I am proud, very proud, to call you my family." Tears clouded his eyes and silenced his voice.

"Family," Gabriel murmured to himself. It had a lovely sound.

Chapter Twelve

Von Steinwehr would have agreed with Pennywhistle's sentiments on family. In the long letter from his wife and children, which he had just reread for the fourth time, they pleaded for an opportunity to visit, and he was tempted to allow it. He had been out shopping for his wife and had found exactly the items that she had specified in her last letter from Berne. As a bonus, he had purchased a spider-shaped emerald brooch which would compliment her auburn hair exceptionally well.

It was a crisp, bright autumn Saturday in Vienna, perfect for a leisurely perambulation with family. He would have welcomed his wife's practical counsels, and her bedroom magic would mend most of the fault lines in his equanimity. Yet his affection for them would compromise his concentration; he needed his mind active, not his heart.

He lounged in a rattan chair in an outdoor café. The aroma rising from a steaming mug in front of him delighted his nostrils: a blend of coffee, chocolate, and citrus fruits. His right hand held a crescent-shaped puff pastry bursting with strawberry jam. It was a relief not to wear his heavy uniform, and simply go about in the black top hat, smoke-grey cloak and iron-grey trousers of a gentleman of leisure. But though he wore civilian clothes, he was never truly off duty. He pretended to be reading a newspaper and soaking up sidewalk sights and sounds of a Saturday afternoon, but his alert eyes swept the street for a man who had been following him all day.

His mood had been pleasantly neutral, a welcome relief from the driving optimism that had consumed him the previous week. But depression would follow in the inevitable sequence. His unwanted minder was triggering the onset of depression and it annoyed him.

His senses perked up when he spotted a flash of the same excessively dandified clothing he had seen twice before. He had not yet a gotten a clear look at the man's face, but was sure a little patience would remedy that.

Gilbert Fouché was new to espionage. He had been assigned a task suitable for an apprentice: observe and report. Follow von Steinwehr—keep careful track of where he went and to whom he spoke. His man was easy to spot, thanks to his height and the red carnation he habitually sported.

Gilbert had been given a training course in surveillance methods. Since he would not know the names of those contacts, he had been instructed how to describe faces and appearances exactly so that better men could puzzle out who they were. The word *discreet* had been stressed in his instructions: be ordinary and forgettable. Dress in the drab garb of tradesmen, take advantage of the mirroring effect of shop windows, stay in the shadows, use the concealment of crowds and any cover furnished by buildings.

He had obeyed his instructions in all but one thing: the artist in him would not countenance wearing clothing that lacked flair. The canary yellow tailcoat, peacock blue trousers, and maroon top hat flattered his figure and garnered admiring glances from women. His attire fit with his concept of espionage as a daring enterprise carried out by gentlemen of *savoir faire*.

Bombproofed

He owed his position to his uncle, Joseph Fouché, who had run Napoleon's secret police and now wielded influence along the same lines with Talleyrand. He resembled his uncle physically: tall and spare, with an angular face, hawk nose, and thin lips. Temperamentally, however, they were as different as night and day. His uncle was feared as much for his brutality as his cleverness, while Gilbert was a devotee of the arts, especially music. He lavished as much care upon his Stradivarius violin as upon his wardrobe. But like so many musical innovators before him, bourgeois critics had savaged his recitals.

He had lived extravagantly, as befitted a great artist, enjoying numerous parties, many mistresses, and spendthrift friends who lived as if there were no tomorrow. But *tomorrow* eventually came; he had found himself hungover, penniless, and with few prospects. His dreaded uncle was a crude man, but he valued family and regarded even such a errant sheep as Gilbert as one of the flock. His uncle had taken him in, but goodness of heart was not in his uncle's nature. He minced no words.

"Gilbert, let us not speak of family love. It does not require a seer to discern that you have come to me out of financial necessity. I do not hold self interest against you. On the contrary.

"I see in your troubled eyes that my reputation for ruthlessness precedes me. Though your effeminate face, narrow wrists, and delicate fingers might suggest otherwise, your daring to approach me suggests you have a dark side that might be willing to make hard, pragmatic choices.

"You are easily corrupted and your character is malleable. You are of an impulsive nature and have the temperament of a voluptuary. I have doubts about your physical courage. And yet... and yet..." His eyebrows furrowed as eyes narrowed.

"You have intelligence and a fine memory. You have a certain charm. Though it has no effect on me, I can see that it would allow you to ingratiate yourself with others. Something can be made of those varied gifts. You can be useful to me and to France in ways that would astonish your artist friends."

Fouché blanched at the memory of that damning assessment, yet he could not call it false. His current allowance might not be impressive, but it was steady and could be counted on, unlike the airy accolades that artists garnered from a fickle public and the derisive remarks of ignorant, captious critics. Just as he was a master violinist, one day he might just be a master spy. By the end of this day's surveillance, even his uncle might be proud of him.

He cautiously edged around a corner and studied the face of his target. It was a remarkably ugly face, yet its expression was pleasant enough. His target was focused on his newspaper and eating a pastry.

From the corner of one eye von Steinwehr glimpsed a bobbing maroon top hat. Now he knew where his minder was. The knowledge calmed him and he thought back to his recent audience with Alexander.

The czar had promised that Reichenau would be on the Conference agenda in the next few weeks. Reichenau was part of a territory that would probably be granted to the King of Wurtemberg, who had been a mere duke before Napoleon conferred honor upon him. Part of the price for keeping his kingship could well be the subtraction of a mere hundred square miles from his realm. It was a small thing to the Conference, but von Steinwehr's whole *raison d'être*.

The leaders of the Great Powers might be inclined to grant Alexander's request if left to their own devices, but they all had underlings with very distinct ideas of how the

BOMBPROOFED

map of Europe should be drawn. These underlings would later be called bureaucrats, and like sergeants in an army they often exercised more control than their overlords. Many of those underlings objected to the restoration of city-states, which they deemed anachronistic. Von Steinwehr was acquiring a list of their names and was thinking of ways to persuade them to his point of view. All were French and all anti-Russian, likely playing a large role in Talleyrand's foot-dragging responses to Alexander's initiatives. Some of his overtures involved entreaties to reason; others appealed to greed and baser motives. Words like blackmail and treason were distasteful to him, yet they had to be factored into courses of action. Violence was a last resort, but it could not be excluded.

He wanted to keep families out of his calculations, but a man's family was not only his greatest asset but his greatest vulnerability. He had already gone far down the slope of moral compromise in his quest and it troubled him. He wondered how far he was truly willing to go and he honestly did not know. The only way to find out was to pursue his goal wherever it took him and act as the situation dictated. Sometimes it was best for the darker parts of a man to remain veiled in mystery, yet only if a man understood the complete truth about himself could he act with the full power of his convictions.

Sunlight glint briefly off heavily polished brass buttons beneath that absurd maroon *chapeau*. The man had grown bolder and more careless. Von Steinwehr guessed his tracker was conducting a solo effort that did not enjoy high-level sanction. A high-level operation would have used a team of trackers, working in relays. He was most curious about his minder's master. It was likely the emperor, but it might be one of Talleyrand's people. It was even faintly possible he worked for the British. Von Steinwehr wondered what dossiers were being kept on him. He had always been careful to cover his tracks and was satisfied that his more delicate and violent operations remained unknown to all but a few of the czar's closest associates.

One advantage of the paranoia and obsession with secrecy at the Russian court was that most of its dirtiest secrets remained hidden. Those with loose lips met with retribution that was swift, final, and conducted in private. People sometimes just disappeared, because the czar had legions of informers in places both high and low.

Von Steinwehr trusted Alexander, but only to a certain point. He kept a private ledger of rumors and secrets that he had heard, as well as a careful record of missions that he had undertaken on Alexander's behalf. He had also made copies of a number of important documents and had ensured that all enjoyed the protection of a safe deposit box in Coutts Bank in London.

The British might be an odd people, but their banks were the most stable in Europe. Their bankers were discreet and would dependably execute any instructions he left behind. Should anything untoward happen to him, those documents would quickly find their way to the Foreign Office. He had also established a private account for his wife and children, to be activated in the event of his demise.

He had obtained information through diplomatic and private channels indicating that the younger Pennywhistle had indeed been granted compassionate leave. He assumed Plymouth would be Pennywhistle's first port of call, but if it was not, no matter. He had hedged his bet by hiring dock watchers in Portsmouth and London as well, who would carefully monitor passenger lists on arriving ships.

He had to admit the younger Pennywhistle was a long shot, but he had had dreams about the man of late. Those dreams told him that Thomas Pennywhistle and the code key were closely connected. It was nothing like the cold intelligence that generally guided his actions, but sometimes the universe rallied to a just cause in mysterious ways. Of course, it was possible that this was all just the optimistic component of his mania speaking.

Alexander probably suspected that von Steinwehr had made provisions for his continued good health, for the czar treated him with more than ordinary caution. That notwithstanding, von Steinwehr knew his best guarantee of continued prosperity was simply staying useful to the czar. But if things went as hoped, he would only have to play the lackey for a few months more. Then he would be free, in command of the people that he was born to rule and living the life that he was meant have. He would be independent and never again bow to anyone.

He could resume a life more in tune with the ethics he had been taught at university in Heidelberg. He would rule justly and benevolently and make sincere efforts to atone for past misdeeds or previous rulers. He had once been an idealist and devoutly hoped he could get that back. A thoughtful part of his mind feared the steps he had taken were irrevocable and that lost idealism was like lost virginity.

He had nightmares—always the same dream. It used to happen once a month, but now it was a weekly event. He dreaded sleep when he was deeply fatigued. Fatigue born of stress rather than exertion seemed to trigger those dark excursions.

In the dreamscape he was walking through a large pool of hot tar. He could move forward, but barely. His wife and children beckoned to him on the shore only yards away. He could see a castle with his family's banner waving from a turret in the far distance. The tar scorched his legs and tried to suck him under. He always woke up when the tar reached his chin and he began to scream.

Yet he realized that the dreams would stop when he had reached his goal. The dreams might frighten but they also motivated. He needed to get the job done as quickly as possible.

He glanced across the street. The telescope was still there. It was time to take care of his minder. He noticed an unusually tall waiter. His clothing would be a poor fit but an acceptable one. He was sure the man would cooperate. By simply sitting and reading a newspaper for an hour, he would earn more than he did in a month as a waiter.

Fouché watched his target rise, fold his newspaper, don his hat, and stroll back into the restaurant. His body tensed as he readied himself to move to von Steinwehr's next destination. He waited several minutes for his mark to reappear at one of the café's two exits but nothing happened. He grew impatient.

Finally after what seemed a lifetime but was really only five minutes by the pocket watch that he checked repeatedly, Von Steinwehr walked back out of the café, His hat was lower and concealed his face, but the outfit was unmistakeable. Von Steinwehr resumed his seat, commenced eating a new pastry, and went back to reading his newspaper.

Fouché watched his target intently for several minutes. A tall flash vanishing into an alley caught his eye. One of the waiters was dashing away, perhaps on an emergency errand for a temperamental chef. Fouché went back to observing von Steinwehr eating and reading, and wondered when he would move.

Von Steinwehr moved down the narrow alley with light steps, circling around the streets to re-approach the café. He sighted his quarry by the maroon top hat.

Fouché felt a massive pain at the base of his head. Stars followed, then dots, then oblivion.

Chapter Thirteen

The mists in front of Fouché cleared slowly. His head felt like a golf ball just whacked off a tee. When his vision returned to normal, he saw a face that was not just ugly, but menacing. It was beset with small tremors and tiny twitches as if the tortured soul behind it was struggling to calm itself.

He realized with a start that he was naked and bound to a chair.

Von Steinwehr picked up a heavy truncheon and walked to within six inches of his captive, towering over the seated man. His great height established a physical dominance that was aided by Fouché's nude vulnerability. His unforgiving eyes scoured his victim's terror-filled ones, assessing and predicting. His vision then moved lower, fixing his contemptuous gaze on Fouché's fear-shriveled penis.

He slapped the truncheon several times against the palm of his hand and it made a nasty crack each time. Fouché's eyes bulged and his face begged for mercy.

"You know who I am," said von Steinwehr, his voice pleasantly conversational. His lips parted briefly in a smile so faint it made the Mona Lisa's seem broad. "I have a few questions to ask. Answer them honestly and completely and our chat need not be unpleasant. I have no wish to harm you, but I do require your full cooperation. Lie or resist and your mistresses may find your bed an unhappy place."

The lack of overt menace in his interrogator's voice made it seem all the more threatening, as if violence was an everyday occurrence to its owner and of no particular moment. Fouché gasped for air like a beached fish. "I will do as you ask if you give me your assurance as a man of honor that your promises are not idle ones," he said in a voice tremulous with abject surrender.

Bargaining? thought von Steinwehr. *Very promising: his survival instinct is strong. He wants to yield. I just need to make things easy.*

As usual, the mere threat to an opponent's manhood was enough to compel cooperation. Men would sacrifice fame, fortune, and family long before they would submit to a de facto neutering. And persuasion was better than torture, since it generally brought honest answers. Pain might get a man to talk, but he would likely say exactly what his interrogator wanted to hear, whether it was true or not.

He had thoroughly searched his minder's clothing, emptying pockets and seeking hidden compartments in its linings. His search yielded much direct information and he deduced a great deal more. No professional would have carried so many informative bits of minutiae.

His captive probably owed his job to nepotism and so would have use beyond the information that he carried. He thought of ransom. Joseph Fouché was a wealthy man who had profited from the keeping of powerful people's secrets. He dismissed the idea immediately because he needed information rather than gold and because Fouché was sufficiently reptilian that he might throw his nephew to the wolves. His captive would have greater value as a double agent. He could be used to feed false information to his masters as well as provide von Steinwehr with insights into his opponent's intentions.

BOMBPROOFED

He needed answers to four questions. Who was young Fouché's ultimate paymaster? He guessed he was being sublet by his uncle to Talleyrand; that could be very useful both to him and to Alexander. How long had he been following von Steinwehr? Who were this young man's contacts? Could he provide information on the French bureaucrats who opposed Reichenau's restoration?

Urine leaked from Fouché's penis and dribbled to the stone floor. Sweat glistened on his chest and shoulders and his breathing came in short rasps. Shame and humiliation suffused his face.

"I am sure we can work something out," said Fouché in a pleading voice.

Von Steinwehr understood the five stages of interrogation from long experience. The order of occurrence might vary, but it was a rare man who did not evince all five in time. First was usually fear—as the imagination ran riot and speculated on how bad things could get. Next, denial—perhaps things were not as terrible as they seemed. Defiance followed—*I am going to be strong and brave and not tell them a thing*. Bargaining occurred as the interrogation wore on—*I will tell them this but not that*. Once a man bargained, you knew he would ultimately yield up everything. Finally, acceptance—*If I want to survive I must give them everything they ask for*. You wanted to break a man's resistance, yet not destroy his soul; bring him to the acceptance phase as swiftly as possible.

"I am not your enemy, sir!" said Fouché with barely concealed panic. "Could you please put that thing away!"

Some men were born confessors, eager to justify their failure to stay silent. Fouché fell into this category, for he had raced to stage four almost immediately. All von Steinwehr had to do was give him a small push to get him to stage five.

"Gilbert, consider my word given." He favored his captive with a smile of affable brutality. "I will put away the truncheon because I am not a barbarian, and I presume you prefer pleasure to pain. None of your employers need know of our little chat. In fact, I will help you earn their approval. You may actually get an increase in your stipend. I also know of your skill with the violin; an associate attended one of your recitals in Paris. At the end of our association, I may be able to secure you a position with the Austrian emperor's orchestra. How does First Chair Violin sound?"

Fouché's eyes widened in astonishment. "You could do that?"

"I could. I might even be able to secure you the position of Court Composer, a position that Mozart coveted but never achieved. I will give your masters enough useful material so that they assign you as my minder on a regular basis. It will contain just enough truth to convince them that you have a great future in covert activities. I will also ask you to obtain information on men who may seem unremarkable but are of interest to me."

Fouché looked puzzled. He had been thinking only about survival. But now there was a reward in prospect, both an immediate one that promised financial remuneration and a distant one that was truly consonant with his musical gifts. To obtain either would involve betraying his uncle's trust, and yet, his uncle would probably do as he was contemplating if placed in the same situation.

Von Steinwehr saw the conflict on Fouché's face. He understood the battle. He thought of his bouts of mood as twin sets of powerful magnets placed side by side: each rebelled at the presence of the other. Détente was not an option; it was a constant see-saw struggle, with each side achieving only temporary victory.

BOMBPROOFED

He felt his mood darkening, an expected concomitant of his actions, but wanted to act before its power unleased his more unpleasant impulses. The ancient Teutonic legend of the wolf-man came to mind: human rationality cast aside at the onset of the full moon and replaced with mindless savage appetite. His present action was a moral full moon and might have consequences just as dire.

He reminded himself that the purpose of this session was information, and that to acquire it he needed to remain detached. Sadists made bad interrogators because their real goal was their own gratification.

"In return for present and future patronage, I will do my utmost to advance your fortunes!" The resolve in Fouché's voice betrayed a hint of hesitancy, as if what he was hearing was too good to be true.

Von Steinwehr felt like a man who had hooked his fish but had not quite gotten him into the boat. It was time to reinforce Fouché's decision with some celebratory Russian vodka and measure the quality of his cooperation. But this vodka was heavily laced with opium to make things even easier for a tongue that was already eager.

"Gilbert, as a show of my good faith, I am going to free one hand. Do not take it as a mark of indulgence, and make no attempt to free yourself of your bonds. I am going to give you a drink, but do not consume it swiftly. Sip it slowly as I ask you questions."

He untied Fouché's hand, noticing that it was shaking badly. He turned his back and walked over to a small table where he poured vodka into a large mug. He took his time to see if the man would follow instructions.

When he faced round, Fouché had quieted his hand but done nothing untoward. Good: shocked apathy had taken over.

He handed the mug to the Frenchman, who took his first sip tentatively, as if it might contain poison. His eyebrows arched in surprise when he found that the taste was agreeable. He gulped desperately.

"Now Gilbert," said von Steinwehr in a schoolmaster's voice, "let us start with a few simple questions." It was best to get a man talking about little things, things that seemed harmless to reveal. Once he had divulged little secrets it was much easier to move on to big ones. "What time did you begin following me?"

"I took up my post outside your residence just before dawn. I had been informed you were an early riser."

"Where you operating alone?"

"Yes, just me."

"Did you at any time leave messages in any prearranged dead-drops?"

"No, I was only to deliver one report at the end of the day."

"Precisely what were you directed to report on?"

"I was directed to pay closest attention to those with whom you spoke. I speak German and have the ability to lip read—very useful when one plays in an orchestra—so I was enjoined to get close enough to observe you through a spyglass."

"And you kept track of my movements in this?" Von Steinwehr held aloft a small notebook.

"That is correct."

Von Steinwehr thumbed through the notebook slowly and carefully. "I must compliment you on the thoroughness of your observations. When did you first begin your surveillance of me? How many other notebooks like this one exist?"

BOMBPROOFED

"I began following you two weeks ago. I used one notebook per day. I cannot give them to you because I turned them into my handler on a daily basis."

"Understandable, and yet I would guess that a man who keeps such careful notes might at least retain a précis of each notebook. You strike me as a man who would want to have insurance against... shall we call it a rainy day?"

"Yes, I made a one-page summary of each day's events."

"Excellent. They will be most useful in preparing a new narrative that will point your masters toward threats that will move their attention away from me and my cause. Now tell me about your handler."

"I do not know his real name. He goes by the code name of *La Défense* and is a man of learning and character. I was assigned to him by my uncle, who said that he is a distant cousin of Talleyrand. I assume all of my reports ultimately find their way to that gentleman's desk. My uncle does not like Talleyrand but knows that more than anyone he kept France a player once Napoleon fell. Whatever I have done, monsieur, it has been for the good of France."

The answers from Fouché made sense and his justification that he acted for a higher good was as expected. Talleyrand had served the Bourbons, *La Révolution*, Napoleon, and now the Bourbons again. Most men would have literally lost their heads early in that process. Talleyrand survived because he was as adaptable as his morality was flexible.

Fouché might be a way into Talleyrand's inner circle. Talleyrand's niece acted as his hostess at official functions. She was personable and his trusted confidant. Though her relationship with her uncle was rumored be something less than platonic, she was unmarried and, as far as von Steinweher knew, unattached. Like her uncle, she was a skilled card player who regularly wagered large sums of money. She might give von Steinwehr exactly the leverage he needed.

Kompromat, the Russian word for damning, secret evidence sprang to mind. That is what he wanted: the sort of evidence that could set aside a man or woman's principles and loyalty. A plan began to form in his head.

"Change of tack, Gilbert. From your manner and looks, I sense you have a great affinity for the ladies. Or am I mistaken? Is it for the lads?"

Fouché looked indignant. "It most certainly is not for the lads, monsieur! I have been a bringer of pleasure to a great many ladies!" A smug expression flitted across his face.

"As I thought!" proclaimed von Steinwehr in tones meant to flatter Fouché's ego; he suspected it was fragile. "How would you like to pay court to a very charming young lady? Use your gifts to become close to her?"

Fouché's face showed confusion. This interrogation was going in an entirely unexpected direction. He took a long pull of his vodka and felt his confidence surge. "I should enjoy that a great deal, monsieur."

"And do you enjoy playing cards, Gilbert?"

"I do, though sometimes I have played with more daring than skill."

That tracked with what von Steinwehr suspected: the man was impulsive and reckless, the living embodiment of a foolish young rake in a second rate opera. Those qualities would be drawbacks at the gaming table, but advantages in seduction.

If he backed Fouché he might have to dip deeply into his discretionary funds. No, it could be presented in such a way that he could bubble that money out of Alexander. Like most Russians, the czar loved novels with multiple characters, complicated plots, and secret intrigues. He would just have to spin the right story, not necessarily the truthful one.

Bombproofed

Fouché continued to take long pulls from the flask of vodka, disobeying von Steinwehr's instructions but furthering proof his impulsivity. Fouché was at the stage where his conscious mind had quieted and his unconscious was clamoring to be heard. His ego had swollen as his reasoning had diminished.

"Gilbert, the opportunity I offer will be the making of you, and so far you have cooperated admirably. Once I release you, you must do my bidding without hesitation and give me the unstinting use of every portion of your mind and soul. Can you manage that?

"Yes, yes, yes!" The slurring of his words could not diminish the enthusiasm of the born toady in his voice.

"It pleases me that you have accepted my proposition, but I want to remind you that there is iron behind my pleasant words. If you disobey or tell your handler even a word of what has transpired here today, there are physical methods to school you in the consequences of straying from your commitment. Talk is cheap, so I think a demonstration is in order." He pointed to a foot-and-a-half-tall metallic cylinder on a small table. One long copper wire protruded from its top and one from its bottom. "This is a recent addition to my collection of mechanical curios. Do you know what it is, Gilbert?"

Fouché put down the mug and tried to focus his bleary eyes on the sinister-looking contraption. "I'd rather not."

"It is called a Voltaic Pile. The good Dr. Franklin would have termed it a battery. The power of lightning is stored within its discs of copper and zinc. If I apply the two wires to the legs of a dead frog, I can get those legs to jerk. When applied to a man..." Von Steinwehr pulled the wires to their full length then touched them to Fouché's genitals for an instant. There was a small spark and an acrid smell filled the air.

"Yeeooww!" Fouché jerked violently and his scream rent the air. His eyes betrayed shock as well as confusion. He tried to focus them on von Steinwehr, though he saw two men when he knew there was only one.

"A sample of my resolve, Gilbert. Should you disappoint, the next time your punishment will be more extended. Just as you were appointed a minder to me, so I have associates who will be minders to you. They will have you on a visual tether and can pull you in at any time should I so instruct them. Do we understand each other?"

Fouché nodded as vigorously as his drink-addled head would permit.

"Excellent. I do so prefer to give rewards rather than punishment." *Oh damn,* thought von Steinwehr, *I am going to lose him.*

Fouché's head lolled to the side and he passed out.

He had been a fool. The electric shock had been one thing too many. He had let his resentment of the man's libertine ways get in the way of clear thinking. Birth had given Fouché much and he had thrown it away, whereas von Steinwehr's portion had been stolen by Bonaparte. But his error need have no lasting consequences. Fouché would wake up with a headache and a tender groin, but he would listen and obey.

Von Steinwehr felt contempt for the man in the chair; then he took an inward look and realized that he was projecting some of his own self loathing onto the Frenchman. He wanted to believe himself a good man, a moral man, a family man, one chosen both by blood and instinct to rule as Plato's benevolent despot.

And yet he had lied, tortured, and murdered in his quest to retake what was rightfully his. He served a bad man who was more concerned with gratifying his ego than doing what was right. He had lost count of how many times he had betrayed the Ten Commandments that formed the core of his Protestant upbringing.

He slumped into his chair, fatigued more morally than physically. His head drooped onto his chest. Sleep approached, but it would not be restorative. He dreaded its arrival because it would arrive with the depressive aspect of his nature riding a dark chariot of torment.

After fifteen minutes of consciousness warring with sleep, sleep finally triumphed. The dreams that came were not pleasant, yet they were truthful. They told him what he had to do and suggested possible outcomes of his actions: his subconscious was weighing options devoid of ethical filters. The last dream was so horrible that he woke up with a start.

He checked his watch. He had only been out two hours. He did not like what he had learned in the last dream, but he would use that knowledge. If his soul suffered, so be it..

Chapter Fourteen

Pennywhistle's post-chaise rumbled slowly north along Borough High Street in Southwark, headed toward the square gothic tower of the cathedral, a quarter mile distant. London Bridge lay one hundred yards beyond the church. The City of London, the square mile that was the financial heart of Great Britain, began at the bridge's north terminus, marked by the Chapel of St Magnus.

The coachmen had all they could do to avoid hitting pedestrians who weaved in and out of the carriage traffic. A small religious procession passed by on the way to the cathedral. It was apparently the feast day of St George the Martyr, unrelated to the one who slew the dragon. Pleasant sounds of Bach and Mozart issued from Bedale Street, home to a number of violin makers who were testing products that occasionally rose to the level of an Amati, if not quite a Guenari. Other noises were discordant: the blare of coachman's horns, the shrilling of a constable's whistle, the songs of street vendors and shouts of newsboys, and the neighing, braying, and barking of animals.

The sun shone wanly in a pewter sky, obscured by a yellow haze caused by the tons of coal burned daily in the city. A thin coating of soot covered most doorsteps and had to be swept away by servants every few hours. The ever-present soot besmirched all-light colored clothing exposed to it; as a result, black was becoming an increasingly popular

BOMBPROOFED

color choice for fabrics. Much of Southwark was given over to industry. There were iron foundries, glass works, dye makers, distilleries, and tanneries, generating a bewildering array of scents, many of them unpleasant.

Sammie Jo gazed at the assorted spires, domes, and towers of London across the water. Pennywhistle looked at his pocket watch and noted it was just after 4. Despite the encounter with the bandits, he was not far behind schedule. He stuck his head out the window and shouted to the lead coachman, "Driver, pull over into that alley." The driver nodded and did as asked.

Pennywhistle turned to Sammie Jo. "I have to deliver those letters I spoke of to Mrs. Cockburn before we go on to Lady Leith's town home. The streets are constricted from here on. I can make it faster on foot. I hope you don't mind waiting?"

"Hard to imagine anyone loving that bastard Cockburn," said Sammie Jo tartly, purposely pronouncing his name as it was spelled rather than "Coe-burn" as it was properly spoken. She had once been one bullet and a hundred yards away from killing the admiral.

Cockburn might be the most hated man in America, but he was chivalry personified when it came to women. His usual stern expression softened when he spoke of his wife, which was often. Pennywhistle was glad to be his messenger, pleased to serve the cause of Cupid rather than that of Bellona. As a newlywed, it touched him that a man married five years could still regard his wife in the same way he had when she was a bride. He hoped he would feel thus about Sammie Jo until the end of his days.

Sammie Jo flashed him an unexpectedly sentimental look. "I guess there is a Jill for every Jack, and I will allow that even buzzards like Cockburn need love." She kissed him quickly. "We will just be fine here. It gives us time to watch the passing sights."

He stepped out of the carriage and walked briskly up the street. People seeing his scarlet uniform and his determined face moved out of his way. As he walked, a sense of being watched tickled like an itch between his shoulder blades. He glanced over his shoulder and saw a boy his peripheral vision had detected earlier. The boy was tailing him, and his eyes never left Pennywhistle's back.

A King Charles spaniel raced in front of Pennywhistle, rose on its hind legs, and began dancing backwards as if expecting some sort of treat. He could not help but smile, even though he realized immediately the animal was not there by accident. It was trained to put on an endearing show. Pennywhistle knew what this was. The animal was the stall, the boy the hook: the pickpocket version of the same military tactics he often employed. It was a shame the boy's ingenuity could not be put to a more gainful use.

He felt a small, deft hand insinuate itself into his coat pocket, intent on lifting his watch. Pennywhistle spun round, seized the boy's wrist, and drew the dirk he kept in his right boot. He pressed the flat of the blade against the boy's throat and held it there. The thief turned white with fear. The dog ran to his side and growled at Pennywhistle. The dog appeared better fed than the boy. It was probably the only creature in the boy's life that he could trust and who returned direct love.

London overflowed with pickpockets, unsurprising in a city where most of the wealth was concentrated in the control of 10,000 people. The most successful pickpockets were young and relied upon speed, agility, and delicacy of touch. They often worked in trios: one to bump, one to grab, one to run with the prize; only a few used an animal as a partner. This boy could not be more than eight years old.

Bombproofed

Pennywhistle wasn't sure if it was Sammie Jo's or Johnny's influence that caused him to do what he did next. He relaxed his grip on the boy's wrist and put away the dirk. He looked into the thief's eyes and said calmly, "You need to find a new profession. You have no future in this one. Continue in it and you will hang." He reached into his pocket and put a silver half-crown in the boy's hand. The pickpocket blinked in surprise. Then he spun the lad round, gave him a light push between the shoulder blades and said, "Be off with you." The boy scampered off into the crowd, the dog hard on his heels, and disappeared from view.

He had walked half a block when he felt a tugging at his coat tails. He turned and was surprised to see the boy and his dog again.

"Sir, I want to repay your kindness. There are lots of pickpockets about. Most of us know each other and have areas we work. Jewel and I want to give you an escort. As long as we stay at your side, none of them will molest you. Honor among thieves, sir."

Pennywhistle smiled. "I accept your offer of convoy." The Other Side had things right: that which you give to others will be given unto you. He had offered kindness and guidance, and was being offered both in return. "Since you know the streets, let me use you as a guide. Do you know the Cockburn residence?"

"I do, sir. Every day the lady there puts a basket on her doorstep: table scraps for boys like me." He gripped Pennywhistle's hand. "Follow me, sir."

The boy proved as good as his word. He guided Pennywhistle through a rabbit warren of twisting streets. More than once, Pennywhistle saw boys start to converge on him, only to fall away when they saw his guide. Presently, they stood in front of an imposing, half-timbered structure that looked to have been constructed at the time when The

Globe Theatre flourished mere blocks away. "That's it, sir. Glad to help, sir. And I thank you for the coin, sir. Jewel an' me can take the night off and maybe get a bed."

He saw the gratitude in the boy's eyes and wished that he could do more. He could not save the world; there were too many boys like this one and Johnny, but at least he had saved one lad for one night.

"Got to go, mister. Oh, one more thing. When you return to wherever you came from, don't go down Trent Alley. That's the worst den of pickpockets in the city." The boy spun on his heels and raced away.

Pennywhistle thumped the lion-headed knocker three times, and a butler answered the door. Pennywhistle handed his card to the butler and said, "I have just returned from America and bear important messages from the Admiral."

"Yes, of course, sir. Please come in." Pennywhistle was shown to the drawing room and waited until Mary Cockburn came briskly into the room. She had a pretty, heart-shaped face, which wore an expression of surprised pleasure. "Thank you for coming, Captain. I so welcome having news of my husband. It has been two years since I have seen him, and I am grateful for every scrap of information. Will you give me the pleasure of staying for tea and favor me with a full account of my husband's activities?" She smiled with eagerness.

He bowed. "Thomas Pennywhistle, your servant, madam. I am honored by the invitation, but alas, ma'am, I cannot tarry long as I have dispatches from your husband for the admiralty." He opened his satchel and handed to her a bulky, sealed pouch of canvas. "I believe that the many letters within will provide a wealth of information, madam. He also wanted you to have this." This time he handed over Madison's account book for the year 1810. "A small souvenir of your husband's brief visit to Washington City."

Bombproofed

She accepted both gratefully. He could see by her delighted face that she would begin devouring the letters as soon as he left. She looked into his eyes with frankness and understanding. "My husband would commend you for your devotion to duty and would admonish me sternly if I detained you. But do tell me: is George well? How did he look when you last saw him?"

"He is the picture of health and vigor, madam, and in the best of spirits. He is fit, active, and an inspiration to his men. You have every reason to be proud of him." He told Mrs. Cockburn two choice stories about her husband, which set her alternately laughing and clasping her hands in admiration of his exploits. "He did ask me to convey a simple personal message to you. It was, and I quote the admiral directly, 'I love you very much and I look forward to the day of our reunion with all my heart.'"

She blushed and tears came to her eyes. "Oh my! That declaration will make my entire week glorious! I see that you are married, Captain, so I am sure you understand."

"I think it would be the most difficult thing imaginable to be parted from my bride for any great length of time. You have my complete respect for your fortitude."

Pop! Pop! Pop! It couldn't be! But the report of bullets was like no other sound. Pennywhistle's body tensed as his blood began pumping hard. The sounds had come from behind the house.

"Oh, folly and flummadiddles!" said Mrs. Cockburn with more asperity than fear. "It's from the mews. A gang of horse thieves has been plaguing the area for the past month. My groomsman told me he thought he was being watched. They are after Daisy Belle, my mount—my husband's parting gift before he left for America."

Pennywhistle drew his sword. "Let me handle this, ma'am." Before she could reply, he raced through the doors, dashed down the stairs, and sped towards the rear of the house. As he flew down the steps into the courtyard, he saw that the groomsman was down, with a bullet wound in the shoulder. Two men were struggling to get a horse out of her paddock. She neighed loudly in distress.

"Let her go!" shouted Pennywhistle.

The two men turned toward Pennywhistle in shock and fear. They had counted on surprise, and their estimation of the males in the household clearly did not include an angry redcoat with a sword.

Pennywhistle judged the taller one of the two the leader because of his dominant body posture. He charged at him with his cutlass held straight and level. The shorter one jumped back.

Tall Thief instinctively put up his arms to block, as if flesh could stop steel, but Pennywhistle's blade dipped lower and plunged through the man's belly as if it were puncturing a cheese preparatory to slicing it. The thief let out a squeal that changed to a low moan. He toppled backwards.

Before Tall Thief hit the cobblestones, Pennywhistle felt a heavy blow on the back of his neck. It caused him to release the still-impaled sword as he crashed to the pavement. He was dazed but rolled away from his attacker.

He shot to his feet but his opponent shoved him face firsrt against the courtyard wall. His peripheral vision showed that the man had the build, stance, and crooked nose of a professional prize fighter. Pennywhistle countered with a backward jab of his elbow that connected with the man's solar plexus. He then kicked low, his boot heel thudding into the man's tibia. Small Thief wheezed and stumbled.

Pennywhistle faced round and snapped a back-fist into Small Thief's chin: a classic move of *savate*, the French art of street fighting. Ordinarily such a blow induced unconsciousness, but his opponent was used to absorbing punches in the ring and bounced back fast. He aimed a right hook at Pennywhistle's head. Pennywhistle ducked and kicked him hard in the shin.

As the man fell forward, Pennywhistle grabbed the back of his neck and rammed a knee into his stomach. The man's flailing hands connected with Pennywhistle's waist and shoved him backwards. Both men went into a boxer's stance.

They circled quickly, each assessing the other and looking for an opening. Pennywhistle stood on his toes and took fast, irregular steps, constantly shifting his weight from one leg to the other. He zigzagged forward and backward, then side to side. He was good at dancing and saw boxing as a destructive variant.

Boxing, like battle, was about movement; never stay in one position long enough to give your opponent a stationary target. Maintain a constant barrage of blows and allow your enemy not a second's respite. Just as there were four elements to the box step in dancing, there were four basic punches in boxing: the straight-line jab, the upper cut, the hook, and the cross.

He kept his elbows tucked in and pointing down, using more shoulder than arm when he fired a blow. He crouched and swiveled his hips to increase the torque behind his punches. He constantly bobbed his head from side to side as he mixed punches in random combinations interspersed with feints at different heights and directions from the punches that followed.

Pennywhistle connected more often than his opponent, but the smaller man was faster and evaded many of the marine's punches. Small Thief finally landed a solid left hook that missed Pennywhistle's face but connected painfully with his shoulder. He followed with a jab at Pennywhistle's chin that the marine sidestepped. A blow to the stomach made

Pennywhistle wince but he riposted with a right cross that lanced into his opponents teeth.

His opponent wobbled, then bent low. He pulled up his right trouser leg, revealing a knife in a leg holster. Pennywhistle fired a kick to the knee before the thief could draw his knife, spinning the man. He then shoved him face first against the courtyard wall.

He kneed Small Thief twice beneath the buttocks, grazing the testicles, but a lucky shot from his opponent's windmilling arm threw Pennywhistle back against a small storage shed. Small Thief jumped at the marine, but Pennywhistle twisted sideways. He grabbed Small Thief's arm at the wrist and elbow and slammed his back against the shed.

The man kicked at Pennywhistle, but he caught the leg, jerked it straight, and brought his elbow down hard on the knee. Small Thief shrieked but pulled a pocket pistol from his coat: a gambler's weapon, good only at close range. Pennywhistle pivoted and caught the thief's wrist before he could bring it to the point.

The two twisted in three complete circles as they fought for control, finally crashing into the courtyard wall. Pennywhistle banged his opponent's wrist hard against the wall. The pistol discharged and fell to the ground.

He yanked his opponent's right arm rigid then smashed the elbow joint with his fist. His encore was a side kick to the man's calf muscles. The man yelped and Pennywhistle grasped him in a headlock.

In one last convulsive burst of strength, Small Thief lifted him a foot off the ground and shoved him feet first into the shed. Rather than fight his opponent's strength, Pennywhistle redirected the kinetic energy and walked up the shed wall. At the top, he threw his weight back over the man's shoulders. As he descended, he let go of his opponent's neck and grasped his lapel. He dropped to one knee upon landing and yanked hard. The man did a fast cartwheel and crashed into the pavement. This time he did not move, though he was very much alive.

Pennywhistle's battlefield instincts told him that the only safe opponent was a dead one, but a memory of The Other Side restrained him. It was wrong to cheat the hangman: let the constables and courts finish the business.

Pennywhistle breathed heavily for a minute, calming himself. *So much for an errand of love!* He walked over to the unconscious groomsman, bent down, and probed the wound with his fingers. The bullet had passed clean through the man's shoulder and had not hit any bones. It would be painful but was far from life threatening. He pressed a silk handkerchief into the wound to absorb the slowly suppurating blood.

Daisy Belle had retreated back to her paddock. The Other Side had improved Pennywhistle's rapport with animals. He approached, patted her head gently, spoke a few soothing words. Then he assisted the reviving groom into the house, where servants took him in hand.

Pennywhistle told Mrs. Cockburn two more stories about her husband as she used soap, water, and a soft cloth to make him presentable. He accepted a tall glass of lemonade, which greatly refreshed him. He was running behind schedule, but if it hadn't been for Mrs. Cockburn's husband, he would not be carrying the dispatches in the first place.

"How can I thank you, Captain, for saving my horse from those thieves?" Mrs. Cockburn asked.

"No thanks necessary, ma'am. I am glad to repay a small portion of the debt that I owe your husband."

Mary Cockburn's smile was wistful. Then she clasped her hands and said, "Captain, allow me to give a small token to your bride, from one wife to another." She left the parlor, walking in her quick way, and soon returned. She proffered a small silver stickpin bearing a gold "C."

He smiled in delight as he took it from her hand. "She will be very pleased, madam."

He decided against telling Sammie Jo about the fight: her nerves were still frayed from the encounter with the highwaymen. But he was keeping a secret from her, and that was starting to become a bad habit. The effects of his Other World journey had occasioned probing questions from her, and so far he had answered them with half truths that obfuscated rather than clarified. She didn't miss much, and each day her skepticism about his answers grew. If he did not soon answer her honestly and fully, it would drive a wedge between them. He determined to do so, but it would not be today.

Chapter Fifteen

Pennywhistle strode along, reflecting how fortunate he was that his love was only a few blocks away, not thousands of miles.

Nothing pleased a hungry traveler more than fresh, hot food. He stopped at a street vendor's cart and bought a basket containing five Cornish pasties, which constituted an entire meal in a pastry shell, popular with miners. One side contained meat, potatoes, and vegetables, while the other contained a spiced fruit.

"I come bearing gifts," he announced cheerily as he approached the post-chaise. When he got inside, he passed the basket to Sammy Jo to distribute the contents, then shouted to the coachmen. The carriage resumed its slow progress.

Johnny wolfed down three huge bites in the time it took Gabriel and Dale to eat one. "This is the best..." he mumbled happily. Sammie Jo took a bite and chewed slowly. A surprised half-smile curved her lips. "Say, this ain't bad." She took another bite. "Actually, its pretty good."

"Why so surprised, my dear?"

"Truth be told, Tom, I heard an Italian gent at The Saracen's Head complaining to his English friend that while Italians treat cooking as an art, the English treat it as an afterthought. I got the impression from him that the main reason the English are glad Bonaparte is gone is that now they are free to cross the channel for a decent meal. But this is fine. Now, I was never any great hand at cooking, but I do have some recipes I would like to make for you sometime."

"You realize, my dear, that we will have a cook to look after our needs. You will never have to lift a pot or a pan."

"That'll be hard to get used to after a life of making my own meals. I will just have to give her some lessons in the cookin' of black-eyed beans, crab cakes, and glazed ham. Grits, too."

"I am sure your skills will bring pleasure to our table, but I must tell you, I tasted grits in Washington, and..." he hesitated, "...they were like a mushy porridge that had undergone a taste extraction ritual."

Sammie Jo shook her head like a master passing judgment on the work of an inattentive apprentice. "Whoever made yours probably didn't put in enough salt and pepper. And the secret is in the topping: put on some cheese, sugar, or syrup, and the taste is transformed."

"I will trust you to complete my culinary education," Pennywhistle said wryly, "but you are too hard on English food. Our food may be plain compared to that of the French, but it is solid and portions are generous."

"That maybe so, Sugar, but I kept an eye on the crowds while I was waiting and a heap of folks here don't look well fed."

He sighed and his expression darkened. "Sadly, what I said only applies to nobles, the gentry, and the middling orders. The average American is better fed than his English counterpart. The majority of the lower orders in London subsist on a diet of potatoes, since they are cheaper than bread. Should the potato harvest ever fail, the consequences would be dire. For those who still prefer bread, the price of a single loaf has gone from two to five pence, and two loaves are the minimum necessary to sustain a family of four on a daily basis." His tone of voice had become very serious.

"Agricultural prices are down since Bonaparte's fall because there is no longer the demand for military food and fodder. Many farm laborers have been let go, and those who are still employed have seen their wages drop from around 15 shillings a week to something closer to sixpence. When we are settled in, I will have to take a long, hard look at my brother's estates and see if I can play some small part in putting as many rural folk as I can back to work, and pay them wages that mean no family need go hungry. I know little of farming, but I believe science can be profitably applied to its practice."

"Farming is hard work, Tom, and I know from experience the awful results of a bad harvest."

"I heard of a riot in Brandon," Pennywhistle mused, "where an angry crowd armed with pitchforks shouted, 'Blood or bread!' and demanded fair prices for bread and meat. Things will only get worse now that we have thousands of soldiers returning from the Continent who will further depress the labor market. Rioting is common, Sammie Jo, and the results are sometimes brutal."

"Sounds like this country could do with a heap o' fixin', Tom. And all these notions of sucking up rub me the wrong way. In America, every man thinks he is just as good as the next."

"I agree that Britain needs reforms, and voices are beginning to speak out on key issues: penal codes, child labor, and working conditions in the mills and mines, to name but a few. We have those in Parliament who wish to do away with Rotten Boroughs and expand the number of people who may vote.

"Rotten Boroughs?"

"Old constituencies that sometimes have only five or ten inhabitants but are still entitled to representation in Parliament," Pennywhistle explained.

Sammie Jo looked thoughtful. "You know, Tom, maybe you could be one of those voices. You should consider politics. I remember what you said about your father's seat, and it sounds like you know what needs doing and have the gumption to see it gets done. You have the right background, you talk real fine, and folks trust you. And you've fought for your country, which I'm bettin' most of those MPs did not."

"Politics?" Pennywhistle put his hand to his heart as if about to be overwhelmed by an attack of the vapors. "Now, that is a frightening thought. At least on the battlefield you are facing uniformed men that you know are trying to kill you, and you understand that the men wearing the redcoats are on your side. Politics is not nearly so clear cut."

"But as you keep telling me, Sugar, times change and people must adapt."

"Just so, my dear, just so. You are entering a whole new life; perhaps I must do the same." He had a flashback to the Other Side that reminded him it was better to build than to destroy; distasteful as Parliament sounded, it might give him a chance to do the former. Seeking office for ambition struck him as ungentlemanly, but being called to it by duty was another matter entirely.

The carriage clattered onto London Bridge, which was choked with horse, foot, and wagon traffic. "In the old days," Pennywhistle informed the newcomers, "the gatehouse at this end bristled with the heads of traitors on pikes."

"For folks who love to tell others how civilized you are, you sure can be violent," said Sammie Jo with an amused air of Yankee superiority. She stuck her own head out the window to get a good look at the River Thames. She could see at least fifty ships: white sails and dark hulls, small ships and large, to-ing and fro-ing. She pulled her head back in. "I thought Baltimore was a big port, but I ain't never seen so many ships."

"The area in front of the bridge is called the Pool. Until sixty years ago, the large ships could not sail beyond this point. They finally widened the banks to build dockyards for the increasing traffic of the East India Company. The dockyards have grown in size and number during the wars with Bonaparte. Just look at the different flags out there: more than 14,000 ships call each year. There are vessels from nearly every seafaring nation. The only major nation whose ships do not call is the United States, and I devoutly hope that will change."

"I hope so too, Tom. We should be trading with each other, not shooting at each other."

The carriage finally clattered off the bridge after taking fifteen minutes to go a mere 400 yards. Late afternoon was a busy time; the streets were a cacophony of sound as people bustled about on errands great and small.

"Apples! Apples fresh and juicy, just picked. Pears and peaches too!" Costermongers hawked fruit and vegetables. Pie men and orange girls held up their products to passing customers. Girls hardly more than ten stood on street corners selling shoe and stay laces; even younger ones sold long kitchen matches.

You want this! You need this! Cheap jacks peddled trinkets like watch chains, whittling knives and metal toothpicks, hailing passersby and proclaiming the quality of their wares. Packmen slowly walked the streets, their packs stuffed with cotton and linen goods. Porters delivered coal, and dustmen collected coal dust to be turned into bricks. Rag and bone men went about collecting odds and ends that might be sold for a few pennies: rags to the paper mills and bones for mortar. A small crowd had gathered round an improvised theatre where a Punch and Judy show was provoking gales of hilarity. For a nation that appeared to be so high and mighty, low comedy seemed the choice of many.

The Thames was at ebb tide, so legions of mudlarks were out and about. These were children who roamed the tidal flats searching for bits of bone, copper, nails, and anything else that the river had left behind.

"Phew!" said Sammie Jo, holding her nose. "That river smells bad enough to gag a maggot! And it an't any of the right colors for water."

"Absorbing 200,000 tons of sewage every day will do that," replied Pennywhistle. "The aroma once got so foul that it caused Parliament to adjourn temporarily. London is the first European city since Caesar's Rome to reach one million inhabitants, and it is beset with the same baleful five Fs that plagued that ancient metropolis."

"Five Fs?" said a puzzled Sammie Jo.

"Fever, flooding, fire, filth, and famine. The hunger you have seen; various diseases run rampant, including typhoid; flooding from the Thames is frequent; and though we have not had a city-wide fire since 1666, frequent small ones occur because of the ramshackle construction of many wooden buildings. And I remember my father talking about a Parliamentary report his subcommittee received just prior to the construction of the Vauxhall Bridge. Compiled by the esteemed naval innovator Samuel Bentham, it stated that London city was generating 350,000 tons of urine and 100,000 of feces, as well as 150 new corpses each day; a veritable torrent of filth."

There were plenty of horses about, flipping up their tails and dropping excrement onto the streets. The stench reminded her of why perfumes and eau de cologne were so popular. Urchins armed with brooms dashed to and fro, clearing paths for ladies and gentlemen who did not want their expensive clothing soiled.

A wagon resembling an American Conestoga passed close to their carriage. It was filled with cages crowded with noisy, oversize roosters, all asserting their dominance with *er-er-er-errs*. It was followed closely by a similar vehicle bearing a single caged black bear. Dog fighting, cock fighting, and bear baiting were still popular pastimes.

"Hellfire and damnation!" Sammie Jo exclaimed with indignation. "The bear in that cage looks like he is a hundred years old. Now if you folks really want a contest, you should put a young grizzly in a pit with your dogs. Doubt they would last more than a few minutes."

A barker yelled confidently as he waved a stout hickory stick at a fierce-looking youth whose face was almost entirely covered in bushy black hair. "Hurry, hurry, hurry, ladies and gentlemen: Step right up and see Lupo, the wolf boy. Raised by wolves in Siberia, he can kill with his teeth and eats meat raw. He barks, he bites, and has lots of tricks to delight."

Rail-thin Johnny was fascinated by the quantities of food peddled by street vendors.

Gabriel blinked when he saw several well dressed black men strolling about with walking sticks. Their attire was not quite that of gentlemen, but it was of far higher quality than that of tradesmen.

Dale cast covetous eyes on inns they passed. Several had memorable names and equally unusual signs for those who could not read: The Silent Woman featured a headless serving girl with the caption "Soft words turn away wrath." The Drunken Duck featured an inebriated fowl frolicking in a pond. The Bucket of Blood depicted a startled man hefting a bucket up from a well—a reference to a mutilated corpse found on the premises three centuries earlier. But a London inn was probably far more expensive than he could ever afford Besides, his preference was for one near the coast where he could breathe salt air. He wondered if Deborah would approve of his becoming a publican.

"Strike me blind, will you look at that!" Sammie Jo yelled in wonderment. She pointed to a man dressed in a jester's outfit of bright reds and greens. "He is juggling knives! Don't that beat all!" she said in amazement. "And over there! That little monkey is dancing a jig to that man's accordion."

She smiled at the unexpected sights, and it pleased Pennywhistle greatly. She had been subdued since the fight, refusing to let go of him and dozing with her head on his shoulder. He was overjoyed that her customary high spirits and buoyant curiosity were returning.

The parrot eyed the dancing monkey and squawked, "Hornpipe! Hornpipe!"

"Street performers are found everywhere, Sammie Jo. Don't be surprised if you see an occasional fire-eater or sword-swallower. People enjoy having their days brightened by the unusual, and the performers earn respectable livings."

The carriage halted. Two wagons had collided, blocking the street. The owners shouted and swore at each other, but their assistants worked to clear the congestion.

"This is huge, Tom," said Sammie Jo, swiveling her head slowly and drinking in the mad, delightful chaos. "I seen Washington and Baltimore, but they seem like toy villages by comparison. This city don't seem to have no end!"

"It is expanding every year, Sammie Jo. You will see more wealth and extravagance here than exists in America. Sadly, you will also see extremes of poverty and degradation that you would never find back home. It is all very contradictory, deserving both admiration and condemnation."

A look of concern crossed her face. "Tom, what if Lady Leith don't like me? What if she thinks I am a stupid Yankee fortune hunter, a witch who cast a spell on you because you were too busy fighting a war to see me as the backwoods bi—uh... girl... that I am."

He kissed her in reassurance. "I'd bet all my prize money that you two will get on famously. She comes from a fine family, she has the proper accent and manners, but for all that she has always been a firebrand. She values honesty and depth of heart and enjoys skewering the great and mighty with her wit. Don't be surprised if she hugs you. Her penchant for touch has shocked quite a number of society people, but at her current age it is regarded as an amusing eccentricity. With sufficient wealth, lineage, and years, you can get away with flouting almost any societal convention." He laughed at a sudden memory.

"When she was young she made a reputation for a lifetime. She was a great beauty in her day. The Prince Regent, much thinner then, and less addled by drink, waylaid her at ball and sought to steal a kiss. He was rewarded with a slap across the mouth."

Sammie Jo blinked. "She hit royalty? Don't that get you beheaded?"

He realized that she was not joking but actually thought it possible.

He smiled gently. "We haven't done that for hundreds of years, and we don't draw and quarter any more, either. It did two things. It got her socially cut for years to come, but also earned her the undying respect of many well bred ladies who had been similarly put upon by Prinnie. She acquired a fearsome reputation as a headstrong lady not intimidated by rank or the admonitions of conventional respectability. The strangest part of it all was that, as the years passed, Prinnie came to recall the incident fondly, since no one else had ever had the courage to so boldly resist his advances. He came to admire her spitfire nature and finally invited her back to court. He publicly begged her forgiveness. She granted it, although by that time she had come to rather enjoy the role of a societal rebel."

"That's some story, but I'd have kneed him so hard that he would have been singing soprano!"

Pennywhistle's eyes twinkled. "I have no doubt. I suspect that if Lady Leith had grown up on the frontier instead of a castle in Scotland, she might have become your boon companion. Just as you always tell people that you are plain old Sammie Jo, she has always insisted that her friends call her Margaret, not Lady Leigh. She is much taken with the Utilitarianism of Mr. Bentham and will often ask of a custom or mode of behavior: does it serve any gainful purpose? Again, much like the attitude that you have evinced when I have shown you new things."

He sighed with regret. "She would have made a fine mother, but, regrettably, proved to be barren. She never cared much for my brother, but took a shine to me early on and considers me more a son than godson. And in many ways she was more a mother to me than my mother was. She is part of the family that has chosen me, and that I have embraced by choice. I have not seen her as often as I would have liked since I joined the Service, but she has told me to consider her home in London as my own when I am in the city. I have much of my dunnage stowed there, as well as a spare uniform. "

The carriage clattered through some narrow streets little wider than cart tracks and onto the wider thoroughfare of Fleet Street. They skirted the edge of the Inns of Court, home to the British legal establishment. He explained he would be going there soon to meet his late brother's solicitors.

She seemed fascinated to learn that the Middle and Inner Temples of the Inns of Court had originally been part of a giant courtyard used by the Knights Templar. Like many Americans, she thought knights were heroes who fought injustice, slew dragons and ogres—or at least nasty human versions of them—and rescued fair damsels from high towers. He smiled and explained that the real Knights Templar had been very rough and tumble fellows—good warriors, but less chivalric than the knights portrayed in the tales of King Arthur.

St. Paul's commanded her particular awe; she had never imagined a church could be so large. He gave her a quick summary of the Great Fire, Christopher Wren, and Nelson's entombment within. He found that seeing the City through the eyes of another brought him unexpected pleasure. He also enjoyed her impertinent observations. He answered her questions as thoroughly as possible, seeing how her native curiosity finally overwhelmed the lingering traces of melancholy from the encounter with the brigands. She was clearly focused on her future, and that was exactly as it should be.

Sammie Jo commented on the variety of small specialty shops. One shop, for example, was devoted entirely to plumes in nearly every hue of the rainbow: ostrich, peacock, and egret feathers for all manner of attire and occasions. The sheer volume of items to be purchased made her wonder if sufficient buyers existed, but the streets teaming with traffic gave her an answer.

"What the hell is that, Tom?" she exclaimed when she saw a man riding a saddle atop two wheels held together by an iron frame. It had no handles or pedals and the driver was engaged in a careful balancing act, propelling it by occasionally touching his feet to the ground.

"It's a velocipede and it is the latest fashion among eccentric young bucks. I find them outlandish and dangerous, but I suppose that is part of their attraction. I am told they can sometimes reach speeds of ten miles per hour. The trouble is they have no brakes."

He pointed out another odd conveyance. It was a sedan chair set atop what looked to be a wheelbarrow. The wheelbarrow's handles were bound to the shoulders of a man who huffed and puffed as he moved it forward. "The barridans are a favored method of transport for old women of the middling orders."

They passed the Temple Bar marking the edge of the City proper and continued down the Strand, as Fleet Street was styled beyond the city limits. They passed by Somerset House, which fit her conception of what a palace should look like. The carriage turned onto Charing Cross and proceeded up the hill towards Haymarket. Haymarket was the City's biggest open-air shopping area for agricultural products. The sights and sounds there were very familiar to Sammie Jo.

On the fringes of Haymarket she remarked, "Say, Tom, there sure look to be a lot of fancy painted up women strolling around. Are they...?"

"They are doing exactly what you think they are, Sammie Jo—trolling for customers. The city attracts all sorts of girls who for one reason or another fall upon hard times or into bad company. A learned Quaker once told me that he believed that more than 30,000 girls are involved in the flesh trade. There are those who judge them harshly, but I do not. Many are victims of my own class: gentlemen steal their virtue with false promises, then cast them off when they have lost their freshness. They become fallen women who cannot return to their families. The trade ages them quickly. You see that one over there?"

He pointed to a woman in a bright red dress with an outrageous amount of rouge on her cheeks. Sammie Jo nodded. "She looks thirty, but my guess is that she is a year or two shy of twenty. The evangelicals preach against them and launch campaigns from time to time to drive them from the streets, but they would do more to eliminate the problem by simply providing food and shelter. An empty belly and sleeping in alleys can destroy anyone's morals."

The carriage took a left at the top of the hill and headed into Piccadilly. He explained that the fashionable crowd loved to promenade in this area; as a result, it was a fine place to view the most prestigious, most *au courant* women's attire. She pointed excitedly at several fine ladies and said, "Love to get me some of them dresses."

"And I am determined you shall have them, my dear. However, I know little about women's fashion, so Lady Leith will have to assist you in that department. It pleases me greatly to know your beauty will be showcased properly. A splendid jewel deserves the finest setting."

"Lordy, Tom, your fancy talk makes me feel like I just won the beauty lottery! I'll be careful with your money, though; I won't never go hog wild. I lived so long on a pittance that I probably will never get used to the idea I don't have to worry about every red cent. One thing, though—what is a mantua maker? I heard some lady talking about one in Plymouth. Is it something I will need?"

"Dress maker," he responded. "Its from the French word for coat. Lady Leith knows the best ones in London. I have distinct opinions about what I like in women's attire but have no idea of what merits the appellation much sought after by women: stylish. Lady Leith can probably assist you to develop your own style."

It took him ten minutes to explain English money to her and she made a face, saying the decimal system of the United States was easier and more efficient. He agreed with her, but said England was stuck with pounds and shillings. He also told her he preferred the metric system as more logical than English weights and measures, but doubted England would ever adopt something devised by the French.

She was very impressed with the white-pillared neoclassical and Palladian townhomes when the carriage swung onto Portland Street. He told her the site had been a pasture five years before, but London was expanding quickly in the West End. When society mavens declared Marylebone fashionable, it had precipitated a rush of construction in the area. Small hills and fields lay directly behind the new homes and gave the impression of sophisticated urbanity in a country setting.

She did not really grasp his explanations of the Adam Brothers' contributions to architecture, and finally just said she found the homes beautiful, whoever designed them. She asked, "How come they are all so narrow in front? They are something like the row houses in Baltimore, although those are mostly red brick, and not nearly so fine. I thought the folks here could afford something with spacious lawns and the like."

He explained it was because of skyrocketing land values. It was cheaper to build vertically rather than horizontally, so the homes were built like layer cakes. "They follow a consistent pattern: kitchen in the basement, with a dumbwaiter for delivering meals to upper levels; morning room, dining room, and receiving hall on the ground floor; the formal drawing room on the first floor. A library, study, and women's boudoir occupy the next floor; and the upper floors are taken up with bedrooms, children's nursery, and servants' quarters. Water closets, what Yankees call toilets, have replaced chamberpots in many of them. Mews for the horses and a carriage house are generally in the rear. This reflects what Vitruvius wrote of in *De Architectura* : '*firmitatis, utilitatus, and venustatis.*'"

Sammie Jo shook her head in exasperation. "At least you didn't start with your favorite phrase *'Seneca scripsit.'* Land sakes, Tom! Most of us think Latin is a dead language spoken

BOMBPROOFED

by some long gone gents dressed in bed linen. I sometimes think you'd have been happier wearing a toga instead of trousers. Now, what was the old buffer trying to say in plain simple English?

"I think of Latin not as a dead language but as an immortal one. Stability, utility, and beauty are what Vitruvius required in a structure."

Sammie Jo stroked her chin in reflection. "Stability, utility, and beauty are also the characteristics of a good rifle."

Pennywhistle smiled in complete agreement, then continued. "Lady Leith's home has a sizeable area of open land behind it, which she owns. She had it surveyed and sectioned into parcels a few years back. I was thinking one of those parcels might be a suitable site for our own residence."

Sammie Jo looked over the land and proclaimed, "It's good farmland, but I don't suppose we'd be raising crops. One thing don't make no sense—why don't you just call the ground floor on these here buildings the first floor?"

"I really don't know, to be honest. *Tradition*, I suppose." They grinned at each other.

The carriage turned a corner and he excitedly pointed out the window. "See the one at the far end of the block, the one with the giant weathervane over the entrance portico? That's it—number 7: Lady Leith's."

She looked out the window. "I see it, Tom. It looks like a mighty fine place." She pulled her head back in the window and looked him in the eye. "I'm powerful scared right now, Tom. What if I don't measure up?" She had again become a frightened little girl.

He raised her hand to his lips and kissed it slowly, gently. The best way to help a woman feel like a lady was to treat her like one. His eyes found hers, and held their gaze. "I believe in you, Sammie Jo, and if I do, Lady Leith will, too." He saw her chest rise and fall with a deep breath, and felt her tension lessen.

"Whoa!" the blue-jacketed lead coachman yelled to the horses as he drew back on the reins. The carriage ground to a halt directly in front of the Corinthian-pillared portico which marked the entrance to Lady Leith's home. Both coachmen dismounted. One held the horses and the other walked round and opened the door for Pennywhistle. Pennywhistle alighted and spoke quietly to the coachman.

"As soon as I have alerted the household, the passengers can disembark and you may pull round to the mews in back so the luggage can be properly unloaded. The servants will take things from there. Once that is done, you may be on your way." He reached into a stout leather purse and extracted two guineas, which he placed in the man's eager hands. "I believe that your sterling conduct merits a tip. One coin for you, one for your friend." They had given good service, though they were only the final set of drivers.

"Thank you, thank you, sir," said the coachman in surprise. "That is most handsome of you, sir. No one ever gave me more than half a crown. You are indeed a generous man of the world!"

Pennywhistle nodded, turned, and stuck his head back in the coach. "Wait here a minute. Lady Leith will need a moment to recover from the shock of seeing me appear out of the blue. I saw her last just before leaving for America, and she has heard nothing since. I hope you all will back me up when I say I was occupied."

He took his leave of them and walked briskly up the steps. He banged the ornate ram's head door knocker three times and waited.

CHAPTER FIFTEEN

A minute later, the heavy door swung open. Grimsby, the butler, blinked and did a double take that belonged in a music hall. A second later he jerked to his best attention—a little off since he had a wooden leg—and snapped a smart salute. He had once been a marine sergeant and never forgot his roots. Pennywhistle returned the salute crisply, then broke into a broad smile.

"Captain Pennywhistle, a great pleasure to see you!" said Grimsby with an enthusiasm seldom found among servants. "We all thought you were in America."

"I just landed yesterday, Sar't. I bear urgent dispatches and will need to report to the Admiralty. However, I have friends with me who need accommodation. Is Lady Leith about?"

"She is indeed, sir, and will be overjoyed. She has worried a great deal about you and scours all of the newspapers looking for any account of you deeds. In fact, she is in the morning room now with a pile of them. Let me escort you to the drawing room while I get her." Grimsby did a smart about turn and limped slowly down the hall.

Pennywhistle followed Grimsby through the elegant neoclassical entrance hall and up the stairs. He took a seat on a comfortable, well-padded Sheraton settee. The settee sat upon a checkerboard marble floor in a room that was a study in subdued whites and golds—understated ionic columns, a plaster frieze ceiling of laurel leaves, and two discreet alcoves containing marble statues of Roman gods that he guessed were Mercury and Apollo.

Lady Leith burst open the doors and eyed him up and down several times, as if to make sure he was not a mirage. She was dressed in a high-waisted ultramarine blue dress that flattered her trim figure, and she wore her iron-grey hair unfashionably short—she had long ago ceased any attempts to dye it back to its original blonde. She had worldly brown eyes, the perfect aristocratic nose, a Cupid's bow mouth, and an imperious chin. She looked at least a decade younger than her sixty-two years and was the picture of cool, elegant refinement.

She began to slowly walk toward him. Halfway across the large room, she stretched out her hands and her face broke into a smile, which transformed her into a woman of warmth. She began to walk faster and faster and finally abandoned any pretense of reserve and broke into a run.

He had risen to his feet and she threw her arms around him and hugged him tightly. She drew back a second later, scowled, and slapped him smartly in the face. "That's for not writing, you rascal! I want you to remember this so it won't happen again. I have been so worried about you, and feared the worst. The reports the newspapers carry from America have not been good. I peruse the papers carefully for any report of an officer being wounded or killed. I was sad to see your old friend, the one with the outrageous name, Pine Coffin, among the casualties at the Battle of Chippewa. I even scour that rag *The Anti Gallician* for news!"

She looked deeply into his eyes, as he stroked his reddened cheek. "You look pale and worn, Tom. How many hours without sleep? Were you in some sort of altercation? You look thinner than last time—are you not eating well?"

Bombproofed

Pennywhistle knew she loved to fuss and tut-tut over him, and it was as well to simply let her have her head. It was exasperating, since he was tired from the long journey, but it gladdened a part of his heart to know someone cared so deeply for him. His cold, distant mother had never done so.

She absentmindedly ran her fingers through his hair and took a deep breath. "Forgive me, Tom, I want you to feel at home. It's just that I have so many questions to ask and do not know where to begin!" Her patrician face beamed with joy.

"You have quite a whip hand there, Margaret, and I have no wish to meet it again! But I will not have to write, for I shall be in town for some time. For now, I cannot stay long because I must report to the Admiralty, as I have dispatches."

"You bring news of a victory in America, I'll be bound." She was always adept at piecing the fabric of a story together quickly from even the most fragmentary bits of information.

"We beat them handsomely and captured their capital." He frowned. "Sadly, we burned most of it to the ground."

Her eyebrows shot up. "Why the deuce would we do that? It seems distinctly uncivilized, not at all consonant with British magnanimity and leadership of the modern nations of Europe. Not to mention impractical."

"It's a long story, and I don't have time to relate it just now. I really ought to report to the Admiralty before I launch into explanations."

"Don't be ridiculous. You have come a long way and need your rest. Most of the people at the Admiralty end their day at six. Do you really want to provoke the ire of cranky old admirals by tearing them away from an evening at cards? Be honest—is there anything in your dispatches that cannot wait until tomorrow morning?"

Pennywhistle looked pensive, then relaxed. "Actually, no. I already communicated the basics via semaphore from Plymouth. I suppose the realm won't collapse if I don't deliver the papers tonight. But personal feelings are certainly causing me to develop bad habits.

"Good! You are always so all-fired eager to have everything done yesterday. Besides, is it not better to deliver such important news when your faculties are unmarred by fatigue?"

Pennywhistle nodded in reluctant agreement.

"You can fill me in on your adventures over supper."

"You are doubly right, Margaret, for it would be well if I presented myself in a fresh uniform. I trust my clothing still hangs in the large wardrobe where I left it?"

"It does indeed, Tom, and I shall instruct Grimsby to give your uniform a thorough brushing. I can have the shower cistern filled with hot water in just a few minutes if you want to bathe. The maids are already heating a large cauldron because the new dresses my couturier's assistant was delivering got soaked when she was splashed by a passing hansom on my very doorstep. I have plenty of the lemon-scented soap you like from Floris."

The shower cistern was a new-fangled contraption which featured a large cistern of water suspended from the ceiling. A pull-chain would release a steady stream of it upon the person standing beneath. He always found it invigorating, and he would emerge with his both his body and outlook refreshed. He would be meeting the First Lord and wanted to appear his best. The theory that staying unwashed protected the body from noxious airs had always seemed insanity to him.

"That would be a blessed relief after all the grime of a long journey. But Margaret, I am not alone and I must see that my companions are taken care of first. And I must ask you to prepare for a great surprise."

"Surprise? I like surprises!"

"This is something you have long urged me to." He paused for few seconds, as if debating how to precisely state something delicate. "I think you will like her."

She noticed the gold band on his ring finger for the first time. "You didn't? I can't believe it! You took the plunge? After all this time and so many narrow escapes!" She smiled mischievously. "I am eager to meet this mystery woman."

"I must warn you, she is a Yankee and very... ah... blunt."

"Blunt indeed! How very refreshing! I have always said that our tired blue blood needs the infusion of fresher lines. Don't just stand there like a gawky new recruit from the country who can't grasp his first order. Fetch her in! Come on! Come on! Get moving! Right now! I am consumed with curiosity to meet the extraordinary woman who finally breeched your stout defenses!"

Pennywhistle responded as if he had heard an order from the Commandant of the Corps. He dashed out the door and down the steps. He gave the coachmen final instructions as everyone dismounted, then he addressed Dale. "You lead the way, Sar't Major. Sammie Jo and I will come in last." He chuckled. "We want to make a grand entrance."

Dale saluted crisply. "Of course, sir," he responded with good humor. He had been with his captain often when he visited Lady Leith, and liked her. The lady had been gracious enough to hire a crippled veteran as her chief domestic based only on his recommendation of the man's sterling character. Grimsby had had to learn everything on the job, but that bothered her not at all. Many aristocrats talked about helping veterans, but it was mostly rhetoric without results. Lady Leith had taken solid action, and in so doing she had earned the admiration of every marine at Stonehouse Barracks.

"Come on, you two, let's get moving,"Dale said gruffly to Johnny and Gabriel. Dale guessed Lady Leith would shower the boy with sympathy and would find Gabriel exotic and interesting. Johnny and Gabriel did as asked and followed Dale briskly up the steps.

A moment later Pennywhistle heard Lady Leith's voice boom out cheerfully, "Sergeant Dale, as I live and breathe, how are you? It has been far too long! Is that a fourth stripe on your sleeve? And who are these two fine fellows?"

Pennywhistle took Sammie Jo by the arm. The parrot flew twice around them, then alighted on his usual perch on her right shoulder. "We're on! All three of us. Chin up, you will be fine!"

Sammie Jo took a deep gulp of air and forced a smile onto her face. "At least she sounds friendly!" She locked her arm tightly around his. "I'm ready! Let's get this over with!"

They walked slowly, almost majestically, up the steps into the entrance hall. Sammie Jo wanted to be the picture of serene dignity, but feared she was failing badly. She fixed her eyes straight ahead, although she wanted to gawk at the splendor of the entrance hall.

They halted in front of an unsmiling Lady Leith.

He laughed inwardly, knowing her formal demeanor was no indicator of her emotions. Since she had decided to forgo the formality of the drawing room to meet Sammie Jo at the earliest possible moment, she wanted to lend a dignity to the proceedings that she felt his new bride deserved. He became his courtly self. "Lady Leith, allow me to present my wife, Samantha Josephine."

Sammie Jo blinked once. She managed an awkward curtsy. "It is a great pleasure to finally meet you, my lady. My husband talks of you frequently."

Bombproofed

Pennywhistle noticed how carefully she enunciated the words, slowly and with barely a hint of her customary twang. She did emphasize the "R" in "pleasure," which marked her as an American.

Lady Leith smiled graciously. "It is a great pleasure to meet you as well. I wish I could say I had heard about you, but your husband has been sadly remiss about writing." She glowered at Pennywhistle briefly, then refocused on Sammie Jo and smiled again. "You must be a remarkable person to have gotten my godson to overcome his phobia about marriage. I have known him when he would rather face a broadside than a parson, a woman, and an altar. *Brava*, my dear!" She moved quickly forward and hugged Sammie Jo unreservedly. "Where did you get married?"

The hug startled Sammie Jo, even though she had been warned; she returned it uncertainly. She perked up as she remembered the ceremony. "Bermuda—the Governor is the brother of Tom's commanding officer, Admiral Cockburn, so he fixed things for us and we bypassed the banns and the waiting period. He and his wife stood as our witnesses. It was a small ceremony, but the governor threw us a lovely party after."

She saw a curious expression flit across Lady Leith's face. Sammie Jo understood, and shook her head forcefully. "Oh, Lord, no, ma'— ... uh... my lady! There ain't no young'un in the oven! It was love pure and simple!"

Lady Leith laughed. "I thought as much from the way you two look at each other!"

The parrot flapped his wings for a few seconds, as if to emphasize everyone's happy emotions. He flew up to the high ceiling, then descended rapidly to the top of a marble fireplace mantel.

Lady Leith looked at the bird, then back at Sammie Jo. "The bird seems fond of you, my dear. My late husband once owned a macaw. But tell me, do you go by Samantha or Samantha Josephine?"

Sammie Jo glanced sideways at Pennywhistle, as if uncertain about revealing a secret, then nodded slightly. "Actually, ma'am—I mean, my lady—my friends call me Sammie Jo."

"Sammie Jo!" Lady Leith said with surprise. "I had heard Americans like to be informal. I would certainly like to be numbered among your friends, so Sammie Jo it is. I want to get to know you better, so let's banish ceremony right now. Please, call me Margaret."

"That's right neighborly of you, Margaret! Honored to oblige!" As Sammie Jo felt more at ease, her customary way of speaking reasserted itself.

Less than five minutes for a first-name basis, thought Pennywhistle. Things were off to an excellent start.

"I expect that you two will want to freshen up after the long journey. I will have a maid ready to assist you, although I suspect"—her voice became knowing and worldly—"that you may prefer privacy. You may have the master bedroom." She sighed sadly. "I have no need of it since my husband passed." For a second, she seemed a thousand miles away. "I miss him—miss his words and his touch. I hope you two have as fine and long a marriage as we had.

"Sammie Jo, I am most curious to find out how you got Tom to commit to something that he considered unthinkable. Let us start tomorrow—just a pleasant chat without a man present to keep us on our best behavior." Her eyes twinkled. "And I would love to know more about America from a native's perspective."

Sammie Jo looked dubious. "You might find parts of my background... uh... uh... kind of peculiar. I know the forest a sight better than I know a drawing room."

BOMBPROOFED

"Nonsense!" exclaimed Lady Leith. "I have already formed a favorable estimation of your character. I merely want to understand the forces that shaped you—and how you," her eyes positively twinkled, "shaped them in return."

Sammie Jo let her breath out and smiled in relief.

"I will have tea, biscuits, and sweetmeats served in the drawing room in an hour. After that, I think a light supper would be in order. Is that is satisfactory to you, Sammie Jo?"

"I would love that, my la—... I mean, Margaret," said Sammie Jo with a mixture of enthusiasm and relief.

"Speaking of food,"—Margaret nodded toward Dale, Gabriel, and Johnny—"you three look famished. Why don't you go see Mrs. Hedges and ask her to rustle up something hearty that brings comfort to weary travelers."

She regarded Johnny with worry. "You look entirely too thin, young man. I think some eggs, sausage, and cod would do you a power of good. How does that sound?"

Johnny's eyes grew as wide as saucers. "That sounds most fine, my lady."

His manner touched her. She smiled briefly, then her face settled into a mask of mock severity. "Now then be off with you, you three! Shoo!"

Lady Leith glared at Pennywhistle. "I know that you hate tea, Tom, but I ordered that strong green stuff from the Japans that you said had some spirit to it. I trust your bride will appreciate its strong taste."

Pennywhistle preferred coffee and had complained about tea being an insipid drink fit only for doddering old men. "Sammie Jo likes things with a distinctive flavor." He looked at his bride. "It has a sharp taste, but it may find favor with you."

"Speaking of beverages, it occurs to me that I have allowed a shocking breech of good taste," said Lady Leith with pretended chagrin, "perhaps caused by the very pleasant shock of my godson and his wife materializing out of thin air. A homecoming deserves a toast, and I have neglected to give you one. I would suggest champagne, but after the rigors of the road I think you might want something more robust. Have you ever tried good Scots whiskey, Sammie Jo?"

Sammie Jo hesitated, not wanting to reveal her lack of breeding. But she saw kindness in Lady Leith's eyes and decided to take a chance with an honest response. "No, Margaret. Only whiskey that I ever had was cheap corn liquor out of an old stone jug. It burned like... like the dickens, and kicked like a mule with a burr up his behind."

Lady Leith looked shocked, then laughed. "'Kicked like a mule'! I have never heard whiskey's effect put so well. You will like Glen Livet, then. It goes down smoothly, a fire that burns with a velvet flame."

"Velvet flame," mused Sammie Jo, "that sounds mighty good."

Even as she spoke, Grimsby came limping in, bearing a silver tray with a Waterford decanter and three small glasses. "I try to anticipate your wishes, my lady."

Lady Leith sighed in wonderment at his prescience. "Once an NCO, always an NCO. Filling in what your commander foolishly left out. I don't know what I would do without you."

Lady Leith unstopped the decanter and poured three glasses. She handed one to Sammie Jo and one to Pennywhistle. Pennywhistle swirled his and inhaled the rising vapors. Sammie Jo merely stared at hers, wondering at the lack of an acidic smell.

Lady Leith raised her glass. "To a long and happy life, blessed with good friends, good fortune, and"—her voice saddened for a second—"good children."

BOMBPROOFED

The three clinked their glasses and took their first sips, though for Sammie Jo it was more of a quick gulp. She blinked in surprise and her first response was as genuine as it was unrefined. "Well holler fire and save the matches! This is prime stuff! Tastes like it came from Jesus's own still. Smoother than a baby's bottom!" She blushed when she realized her tongue had outraced her brain. But her husband and Lady Leith were amused by her appraisal.

"You have just experienced one of the small joys of civilized life, my dear," said Pennywhistle. "But you should savor every drop: remember to sip, not gulp."

Sammie Jo heeded his words and spent the next quarter hour thoroughly relishing the experience. By the time she finished, both she and Lady Leith had a pleasant glow on their faces.

Lady Leith noticed the impatient look on Pennywhistle's face and understood that his devotion to duty had been only slightly quieted by the liquor. "I know, I know, time is precious, Tom. But tonight attend to your bride and forget those old duffers in blue. You need a good night's sleep and a hearty breakfast. Would breakfast at eight suit you? Nothing gets going at the Admiralty before ten."

"Eight would be fine, Margaret. Could your cook manage any stewed tomatoes with that breakfast?"

"She certainly can!" Lady Leith said with a smile in her voice. Many English considered tomatoes poisonous, but a few households had made the exotic fruit welcome.

She carefully appraised Sammie Jo and Pennywhistle holding hands. It was obvious from the stolen glances, merry eyes, and a score of subtle gestures, that they were deeply in love. She remembered her emotions as a newlywed: embracing sensuality eagerly though many proper brides from sheltered backgrounds feared it. She was glad that her godson's bride looked the type to revel in it.

"Sammie Jo, Tom is going to use a contrivance called a cistern shower to freshen up. You know how taken he is with new inventions. Why don't you tag along so he can show you how...everything works."

Sammie Jo knew little of fine manners, but everything about real emotion. She recognized Lady Leith's sly look for exactly what it was and wondered if she had been a virgin on her wedding night. Probably not—that judgment increased Sammie Jo's respect for her.

"Thanks, Margaret. That sounds like a right fine idea. I will meet you in the drawing room in an hour." She looked at Pennywhistle like a cat seeing catnip. "Better make that two hours."

Ten minutes later, Pennywhistle was happily soaping down Sammie Jo's body in the shower. She soaped him, too—carefully, lovingly, and in all the right places. He yanked at the long metal pull. A cascade of blissfully hot water flowed over their bodies. It lasted a wonderful minute and they were soon delightfully clean and refreshed.

They looked at each other through the leftover steam, fire in their eyes. "You told me you should never draw a sword unless you intend to use it," admonished Sammie Jo.

"True enough! Ready for a little erogenous combat?" Giggling like children who had skipped school, they made a mad dash for the bedroom. What followed was pleasure that was definitely not for children.

Chapter Seventeen

Von Steinwehr felt frustrated and irritable. It was well past midnight and he had been slaving away at codebreaking since noon, not to mention having worked at it from sunup to sundown the day before. The ornate turret room in Belvedere Palace had been transformed into a monk's cell of scholarship. The room was so cluttered with books and documents that he could barely walk across the floor, but he had selected every item carefully to assist in solving the puzzle. His eyes were bloodshot from staring at line after line of small print, and his back hurt from the odd positions that he had had to assume shifting among the varied reference materials.

The penmanship on the Clarke letters was tiny, and hours of scrutinizing them had made his eyeballs feel if they were being jabbed by needles. He had tried a myriad of permutations, but was no closer to grasping the key to Mrs. Clarke's code than when he had started. No, that was not quite right—he now knew two hundred solutions that did not work. He lit two more beeswax candles, drank a few gulps of strong but cold black coffee, and steeled himself for a long night.

He had six large volumes laid out in front of him, as well as a score of instructional letters and monographs from a friend who was an expert cryptographer. He had thought to invite the man in on his deliberations, but the potential harvest was too incendiary to share. It was fortunate that he was a linguist, since the books were in French, German, and English. The English book should have been the most likely candidate, considering the nationality of his subjects, but despite the promise of the opening chapter, it had proven to be a dead end. The key that opened the puzzle lock might be in a handwritten monograph or some obscure parchment scribbled by a Benedictine. Yet if there was a will there was a way, and his will was strong.

Just as he would evaluate an opponent in battle, he had formed a mental picture of the letters' authors. Most of the letters were written by Mrs. Clarke, the remainder had been penned as responses by the Duke of York. Mrs. Clarke was intelligent and had a well developed ability to discern what details were important and would have value to the right parties. The Duke of York struck him as an honest, bluff headquarters type with an indiscreet tongue.

The encrypted half of each letter was a series of seemingly random numbers. It looked to be a simple transposition code, part of a family of *petit chiffres*, or "small cyphers"—simple to use, but nearly impossible to break unless you had the key to change numbers back to letters. The key was likely a chart or table giving direct equivalencies. The numbers were in groups of ten. He had figured out that a semicolon after a number indicated a letter that was written twice, and a triple semicolon marked a sentence break. The deciphered half of a single letter would act like a map legend for the remainder.

He strongly doubted that Mrs. Clarke had devised her own code, and while the British Foreign Office employed a complex code that the Russians had been unable to break, it was unlikely the duke would have used it. As a military man, he had occasionally butted heads with the diplomatic service and so would not want to inadvertently give opponents a way

Bombproofed

to pry into his private life. No, the cipher chart had to have come from outside official channels. The more he thought about it, the more he moved away from the idea of a monograph or medieval source and returned to his original thinking: the chart had been lifted whole from some work on codes and cryptography. There were not many such works in print, so he had started a systematic search.

He had agents scouring bookstores in London, Paris and Amsterdam, since those were the publishing capitals of Europe. He'd told them to buy any book about codes, price be damned. The French code breakers had treated the letters as merely a job, just another task to carry out for their masters. *His* commitment was completely personal and he believed that commitment would enable him to accomplish what the smartest cryptographers in the French government had not.

Beyond what was in the plain script that had already proven useful, he suspected what was hidden could provide real financial security once Reichenau was re-established. The secrets could be doled out gradually in return for alliances, territorial guarantees, or even good marriages. Von Steinwehr would filter the information carefully and give Alexander much, but by no means all. He might even return a select few to the British, not for money, but for certain guarantees. The British could be devious, but once they gave their word on something it was as good as gold.

He had made some progress in the last hour. The English book was disappointing, but the first chapter had pointed him in what he believed was the right direction. It furnished valuable, general baseline information that he used as a starting point in his calculations: "ETAON RISHD LFCMU GYMPWYB VKJXQ Z." That was the frequency of use of letters in English, from most to least. The top 12 letters accounted for 80% of words, the top eight for 65%. The most common letter pairs were TH HE AN RE ER IN ON AT ND ST ES EN OF TE ED OR TI HI AS TO. The most frequently doubled letters were LL EE SS OO TT FF RR NN PP CC.

He did a frequency analysis of all five documents. Some numbers appeared far more often than others. He deduced that 8 indicated an "E", 1 a "T", and 9 an "A." He still had 23 letters to go, but given enough weeks he would solve it. Still, he hoped his agents would come through with the right book and speed up the process.

He tried words associated with outré sexual practices to see if any number sequence yielded an intelligible result. He never judged a man by what he did between the sheets, but having some knowledge of his tastes would be useful in guessing key words for which to search. And certainly others, famous others, were named in the messages. Repeating sequences of letters were probably names..

Men were vulnerable when it came to sex, especially if that sex was criminalized by polite society. He recalled that in less civilized times, King Edward the Second had been murdered with a red hot poker up his anus because he had the gall to openly advance his male lovers to positions of command. The Czar was like the Duke of York in a way: he was far too free with boudoir banter. Alexander's conviction that he was God's gift to women would blind him to something that a man with a smaller ego would see quickly. Von Steinwehr's strict fidelity to his wife was not only the right thing to do, it was the smart thing to do.

He looked at the documents again and decided to play a hunch. It was so obvious that he had failed to see it before. Instead of words associated with the practice, he would try a word associated with the outcome: *scandal*. The word contained two "A"s and he would proceed under the mathematical likelihood that they would each be indicated by a nine.

Bombproofed

It took him another hour of tedium, but he thought he had identified the word twice. He now deduced that "C" had to be the number 6. He was making real progress and his joy sent an extra dose of adrenaline coursing through his veins. He was good until dawn and might be able to pin down one more letter of the alphabet before he retired to his bed.

There were two plain-text words written on the bottom of one document in larger letters: Hoylet Framingham. They appeared to have been carelessly scribbled in an entirely different hand, almost as an afterthought. He had thought a Hoylet Framingham must be some mechanical thing like a Spinning Jenny, perhaps a codebreaking engine, or maybe an obscure English colloquialism, of which that peculiar language had many.

Then it hit him. Could it be so simple after all? He had likely missed the forest for the trees. What if those words were neither things nor expressions but one man?

He spent hours checking the printed British army, navy, and diplomatic officer lists that formed part of his array of paper minutiae, but found nothing. He cursed and threw down his pen.

But, wait: what if Framingham was not an officer or diplomat but a writer? The author of the book on ciphers that was the fountainhead of all he sought? It was certainly worth exploring. The name sounded English. He would set his English contacts on the task directly.

He had deployed an extensive network of agents in England to watch for and waylay the brother of the Englishman whom he had killed on the Normandy beach. He had told his men to send word by fast courier when the man arrived in England, but had heard nothing as yet.

There was a loud knocking at the chamber door. He looked at his watch. Almost 4 a.m. He shook his head in disgust. He knew what it meant. It was the immaculately attired Captain Koskov bearing a message from the czar saying he was to return to the Schönbrunn forthwith. Alexander had probably been in another of his long, late-night sessions with the Baroness de Krudener, and she had likely vouchsafed him another mystical insight that he felt compelled to share with von Steinwehr. He heartily wished that the de Krudener woman would go away. Her alleged mystical insights were downright dangerous. They fueled the czar's messianic complex and made him less amenable to the cold reason that von Steinwehr valued.

He sighed deeply, put down his books, and laid the documents aside. He opened the door and accepted the letter bearing the wax seal of the czar. He ripped it open, read it quickly, and nodded to Koskov. "I will join you at the stables in twenty minutes. Have my groomsman saddle up Atropos."

"Very good, Herr Colonel."

At least the ride to the Schönbrunn Palace would give him time to think, and another meeting with Alexander would give him opportunities to mention Reichenau. He had taken many missteps in his codebreaking, but he felt he was finally on the right path. He would solve the puzzle because he had to: his future depended on it.

Chapter Eighteen

"I am Captain Thomas Pennywhistle bearing dispatches from America. It is most urgent that I see the First Lord. I do not have an appointment but trust I am expected. I transmitted a précis of my message via semaphore 46 hours ago. Please inform Viscount Melville of my arrival without delay!" The marine's voice snapped like a whip, though he did not raise it above conversational tones. He held up a heavy canvas package and flourished it twice in the clerk's face: it was instantly recognizable as official.

It might be Sunday but the Admiralty did not consider it a day of rest. The British Navy had seven hundred commissioned ships great and small patrolling the four corners of the globe. They required constant attention and generated mountains of paper work.

Pennywhistle felt better than he had in a long time. Two showers, plenty of good food, and a crisply starched uniform had done wonders for his spirits, though it was Sammie Jo's passion followed by a deep sleep that had put fire and energy into his step.

When he'd arrived, Pennywhistle had noticed four middle-aged naval captains fidgeting on benches in the long corridor outside the clerk's anteroom. Despite their seniority, they resembled schoolboys waiting to be summoned into the headmaster's chambers. Long waits were generally accepted as the price of doing business at the Admiralty, and the sight of senior captains treated as little better than wayward adolescents had determined him on his present course of action. He had walked brusquely past them, ignoring their outraged looks, to push through the door into the clerk's office.

The pasty-faced senior clerk in the high starched collar was the figure of self-importance, the sort of man who seemed to strut even when standing still. He bristled with indignation, then responded with the assurance of long experience. "If you will wait *outside*, sir, I will see if I can arrange a brief audience... for sometime late in the afternoon."

Pennywhistle knew the type well. He sat at the top of the Admiralty's pyramid of 28 minor officials and controlled access to the Board Room, the *sanctum sanctorum* of the highest naval officers. He was a king of a kind, and would not be ousted by a coup staged by some fly-by-night adventurer who did not pay obeisance to his authority. The Marine whipped out his expensive Blancpain pocket watch, glanced at it, then snapped it shut and angrily thrust it back in his pocket—pure theatre, but it might speed things along. Of course this clerk had been notified that Pennywhistle should be accorded top priority, but he evidently could simply not resist the gamesmanship that made him a kind of Horatius at the bridge.

Rather than huffing and puffing and simply blowing the little man down, Pennywhistle decided that, since he needed tact for the interview ahead, he might as well practice some on this little man with a big ego. If he could persuade the clerk to see things his way, he could persuade anyone. Besides, if he were to become a civilian, such wars of wills and words would likely become commonplace, since no one would be bound by oath to obey him.

BOMBPROOFED

He noticed on the man's desk a small flowerpot that contained an arrangement of blossoms such as might be found in a wedding bouquet. Odd, since the fussy little clerk did not seem the sentimental type. His eyes bored into the clerk's and he had a quick mental vision of a pretty young woman in a white gown. He decided to play a hunch.

His attitude, eyes, and voice gentled. "I understand that your daughter married recently. I trust it was a lovely wedding and that you soon will have a grandson." It was a shot in the dark but it felt right.

The clerk blinked rapidly as if he could scarcely believe his ears, yet his face softened. "How on earth did you know that?"

"I am a newlywed myself, and my bride received a bouquet just like that one in the pot." He smiled brightly. "I presume you saved it to remind yourself of an occasion that brought you great joy."

The clerk returned the smile and his gaze became far away and reflective. "Yes, it was a wonderful wedding. I never thought my daughter would find the right man. She is very happy; she and her lieutenant are well nigh inseparable."

"I quite understand her outlook. I experience exquisite pain every minute I am apart from my beloved. I have been married just over a month. I apologize for my earlier attitude; it was my sense of duty speaking, and sometimes that overwhelms a respect for protocol. Could you find it in your heart to advance my appointment so that my wife need feel sadness no longer than is absolutely necessary?"

The clerk looked skeptical, then thoughtful. This was the first officer who had seen him as a man who loved a daughter rather than a faceless clerk who was no more human than an iron gate. The pleasant memory that this upstart had triggered was a true day-brightener. "Give me two minutes,

Captain. I will see what I can do. The Board is in a meeting now, but I may be able to arrange a brief audience. Mind you, I can make no hard and fast promises."

"I understand," replied Pennywhistle. "I thank you for your consideration."

The clerk nodded and disappeared through the tall oak doors. A minute later, Pennywhistle heard excited voices. The clerk reappeared, red-faced and animated. Pennywhistle wondered what the First Lord had said to him. "Lord Melville will see you now, Captain."

"I wish your daughter a long life and healthy children." Where the blazes had that come from? He was talking like a parson rather than a veteran soldier—probably another side effect of his Other World journey.

"Good luck, sir," responded the clerk.

Pennywhistle entered the Board Room and his eyes catalogued every detail in this the heart of British nautical power. He surveyed the men within who were the final arbiters of just how that power was used. They looked like they were in need of a Homer to compose them an epic with a British triumph at the end.

The neoclassical Board Room featured beautifully sculpted alabaster columns and arches crested by a magnificently decorated plaster frieze ceiling awash with quatrefoils and roses. It was in the form of a giant rectangle 90 feet long and 30 feet wide, with a 30-foot depth to the apex of the ceiling. A lush and colorful Persian carpet cushioned any shoes or boots walking on the floor. The whole was meant to impress visitors, and it succeeded admirably. Four large Palladian windows on the south wall admitted generous amounts of sunlight. A strong breeze had chased away the usual morning coal haze.

A clock-like giant wind indicator below a sweeping semicircular arch dominated the west end of the room. The indicator had a fluctuating single arm that was linked to a weather device on the roof and gave second-to-second updates on wind strength and direction, vitally important to a navy which depended on wind for propulsion. A massive bookcase stood on either side of the wind indicator, each shelf filled with works on the most obscure matters nautical. A huge globe stood in front of the port-side bookcase, representing the latest geographic and political information. Maps covered most of the north wall. Four large mahogany bureaux with gigantic pull-out drawers lined the wall below the maps. They contained the Admiralty's extensive and growing library of coastal and harbor charts.

The east wall was covered entirely with a map of the east coast of North America. It was dotted with red- and blue-headed pins, presumably indicating the location of British and American forces. The campaign from which he had returned was likely under discussion. He surveyed the map quickly and decided it contained a number of inaccurate placements that he hoped to correct.

A long, elegant Chippendale table of Honduran mahogany dominated the center of the room. It had been made specifically for the Admiralty, and instead of the usual ball and claw feet clutching pearls of wisdom, these clutched globes. Six concerned faces peered at Pennywhistle from chairs that had been pushed back from it. Each Board member had a large sheaf of papers in front of him that gave every appearance of having been precipitously thrust aside.

Pennywhistle marched up to Lord Melville, came to perfect parade ground attention, and snapped out a crisp salute. Lord Melville returned a more relaxed one.

"Captain Thomas Pennywhistle reporting with dispatches, my lord." His voice was relaxed and resonant. That he felt little tension during such an important event was entirely due to Sammie Jo's tender ministrations. He fought down a smile at the thought of her breasts, and steeled his face into the emotionless mask of command that the Board expected.

"We have awaited your arrival with keen anticipation. It is tantalizing to hear of a victory but frustrating to have no details of it," said Melville cheerfully. The man seemed very down-to-earth. "Your semaphore message caused a sensation. It excited hope not just in *our* weary hearts, but in those of the Duke of York and the PM as well. The duke will want to see you at Horse Guards directly you finish here, and the PM will receive you at five at Number Ten. There is also a fellow from *The Times* who craves a brief audience. And two chaps at the Foreign Office want your attention after the PM is done with you, although they were unwilling to say exactly why. Slippery fellows—can't abide those cloak-and-dagger types. You have a busy day ahead."

The First Lord gratefully accepted the large canvas bag from Pennywhistle and slit it open with a lion-headed penknife. He donned spectacles, laid the contents out in front of him, and opened what looked to be the longest dispatch. He began to read, but looked up briefly a minute later, a kind expression on his face.

"In my eagerness, I quite forgot to extend my hospitality, Captain. Pray sit down and rest. This may take a few minutes." Melville motioned for a servant. "Bring the captain a cup of Darjeeling." The servant nodded, disappeared, then reappeared two minutes later with a fine china cup, steam rising from its contents. It was emblazoned with the family arms of Dundas, the surname of the First Lord.

Pennywhistle accepted gratefully, though a cup of Brazilian coffee would have suited better. He sipped the tea slowly, and found it more robust than the usual insipid infusion served at official functions. He waited as patiently as he could and directed his attention to the American map.

Bombproofed

Many of those pins reflected guesswork rather than recent intelligence. No wonder they were so eager for news.

Melville read quickly, with great concentration. He smiled from time to time and arched his eyebrows occasionally. He sometimes muttered, "Good, good." Thirty minutes later he put the papers down. "I should like to read further, but it seems cruel to keep the rest of the Board in suspense. Could I prevail upon you, sir, to give your own account of the Washington Campaign, favoring us with your personal impressions and observations beyond what the dispatches contain?" He glanced down at a document. "Admiral Cockburn says your role was "considerable and distinguished.""

Pennywhistle's brow constricted in a faint frown, and that was noticed. He detested talking about his achievements like some annoying old buffer years past his prime droning on about his glory days.

"Come, now, don't be so modest," said Melville pleasantly. "Admiral Cockburn is stingy with compliments and he would not have said that if your achievements were not of significance. Feel free to use the map to assist your explanations, Capt—" He paused and smiled. "Forgive me, I should say 'Major.' I have your promotion here, endorsed by the Prince Regent last night."

Pennywhistle felt a certain surge of pride. It was not often one received the public approval of the highest naval officers in the land. Sammie Jo would be proud of him. Damn it—he was thinking about her again. *Duty! Do your duty!*

Pennywhistle rose to his feet and forced a smile onto his face. "Certainly, my lord. It would be my honor to answer any questions the board members may have." He found a long pointer on the table and walked over to the large map. He took a deep breath.

"I and the other four marine exploring officers spent four weeks probing the Maryland coast for the proper spot for a large landing. Based on all of the reports, Benedict, Maryland, was selected." He pointed to it on the map. "The Patuxent had sufficient depth there and no odd shoals or tides; it also featured a wide beach to expedite the landing of troops. It is sixty miles from Washington, D.C., and General Ross and Admiral Cockburn agreed that a quick raid on the enemy capital would succeed if they eliminated their baggage train. We knew we would be outnumbered by approximately three to one, but as a result of the rapid advance, the Americans were caught off guard. Their troops were poorly trained and disorganized, and there was disunity of command at the highest levels."

Sir Sidney Yorke, the First Naval Lord and second-ranking Board member, spoke. "But I gather it was your personal report that caused Admiral Cockburn to choose Benedict?"

Pennywhistle nodded. "That is correct, sir."

Yorke smiled gently. "I thought so."

Pennywhistle continued for the next hour and outlined the campaign as succinctly as he could. He kept things clinical and downplayed his own role. Strangely, his attempt at modesty provoked admiration from his listeners. He rearranged the map pins frequently and pointed out sites where key maneuvers and skirmishes had occurred.

He made no mention of the great change that the campaign had brought to his personal life. He had discovered a half brother—a by-blow of his father's service in the first American War—who had fought gallantly with the US Marines and surrendered his own life to save Pennywhistle's. A jolt of acid raced through his stomach when he thought of John Tracy's tragic death and of possibilities unfulfilled.

BOMBPROOFED

He wondered if anyone noticed the ring on his finger, and could only guess at the shock that would fill their faces if he explained that he had met his new bride when she had tried bushwhacking and had missed killing him by half an inch.

He spoke of Cockburn's admirable cooperation with the army commander, General Ross, and the smashing victory won at Bladensburg that had made possible the capture of Washington. The Admirals all laughed when he said that the so-called battle was referred to as "the Bladensburg Races." In deference to his half brother's memory he added, "A small detachment of US Marines and Navy sailors under Commodore Barney did put up a stout and gallant resistance. Their steadfastness was remarked upon by Admiral Cockburn, and as a tribute he declined to burn the Marine Barracks."

His description of the burning of Washington brought shocked looks and head shakes. It was one thing to capture an enemy capital, quite another to destroy it. That stank of vengeance and barbarism and would not play well with inflammatory elements in the British press. He explained dispassionately how the decision had been arrived at and gave what he thought was a full hearing to all of the arguments involved, making it clear that the torching of Washington had been Cockburn's rather than Ross's idea. Even so, he realized that the tone of his voice made it plain that he disapproved. He added, "The firing was an expression of displeasure with American mis-government and lack of military civility, rather than anger toward the American people. Only government buildings were burned. Civilian edifices were left untouched, although the storm and resident dissidents may have started others. Also the Patent Office was spared, because it contained irreplaceable models belonging to individual inventors. Furthermore, there is one side effect of the campaign that should delight the Clapham

Saints. More than 2,000 slaves were freed by our forces; the greatest mass manumission in the history of America."

He ended his presentation by explaining the preparations Cockburn and Ross were making for a strike at Baltimore. There were mutters of "Good," "Excellent," "About time." Baltimore privateers had been plaguing British coasts and causing insurance rates to skyrocket, so he added a postscript: "Though it is found nowhere in the official dispatches, I should add that the *Dapper James*, the most notorious of Baltimore's maritime marauders, will no longer be a nuisance to our shipping. I witnessed her sinking off Plymouth."

Melville's brows shot up. "You make it sound as if it were the result of accident rather than action. Was that the case? Forgive me, sir, but given your narrative today it is hard for me to believe that you were a passive witness. I should like more detail."

Pennywhistle reluctantly gave an exiguous account that filtered out the horrors of frying flesh and shrieking men. He kept his voice level and steady, as if chronicling the parabola of a scientific experiment with a successful outcome. "I was uncertain as to whether or not the chemistry was correct, but luck was on my side."

"Hmm. Without your novel solution, we would have neither the dispatches nor your personal testimony—is that not so, sir?" Melville prodded.

"That is correct, my lord. But—"

"No buts, Major," interrupted Melville. "Your conduct was as admirable as it was ingenious. Brave officers are easy to find; clever ones are rare. And Admiral Cockburn adds that in addition to your scouting and fighting you found time to recover an army payroll in gold captured by privateers." Melville tapped the table with one strong finger. "I should think that salvage law applies in such matters." He looked

BOMBPROOFED

toward his fellow Board members, who nodded agreement. "The recovery fee is reckoned at 2% of the payroll. Cockburn also remarked that your report mentioned a civilian who had assisted you: one Gabriel Prosser. Would you want him to have a share in the bounty?"

"I would indeed, my lord." Pennywhistle smiled inwardly at the irony. That sum would give Gabriel more ready money than most plantation owners, who were often land rich but cash poor.

"There is truth in the saying that if you want something done, give the task to a busy man. My fellow Board members and I propose to keep you very busy." Melville removed his glasses and laughed unreservedly. The normally taciturn Board members rose from their chairs and surrounded Pennywhistle to shake his hand. Their responses were on the order of "Well done," "Bravo, young man," and "A brilliant coup." One lord slapped him on the back and proclaimed earnestly, "You have brought great glory to our arms. I hope Prinnie understands just how great."

Pennywhistle concluded that the Board was so starved for a victory in an inglorious little war that they had temporarily taken leave of their senses. He feared his report had merely provided fodder for the bitter-enders who wanted to retain captured American territory as the price of any peace.

An admiral's aide took him aside and explained he was expected at the Prince Regent's levee two days hence. He explained it would be an all-male affair that would commence promptly at three. Everyone needed Prinnie sober enough to perform the knighthood ritual properly; if it took place much past four, he would likely be too far into his cups. Three other men were to receive honor, but the aide made it plain that Pennywhistle would be the center of attention.

He extricated himself from the Board half an hour later. His next stop was the nearby Horse Guards, where he underwent a dreary hour of careful cross examination by the Duke of York. The duke seemed an earnest if rather plodding chap, hardly likely to inspire men, but his questions were generally perceptive. He seemed less sanguine about the American War than his Admiralty colleagues. He was concerned that it be clear the torching of Washington had been the Navy's idea.

Next, Pennywhistle spoke for twenty minutes to a reporter from *The Times,* an organ that often functioned as the government's mouthpiece. He kept his account factual and offered no speculations on how the destruction of the enemy capital might affect the peace negotiations in Ghent.

His fourth port of call was Number 10 Downing Street, where he endured a two-hour interview. The prime minister seemed a detail-oriented, methodical type. Liverpool wanted the war ended but felt it was the American negotiators, not the British, who were being stubborn in Ghent. Pennywhistle was distressed to be told in confidence that preparations were underway for a strike at New Orleans, meant to capture the trade of the Mississippi valley.

He then was funneled off for a short talk with two confidential assistants of Lord Castlereagh. The Foreign Office minions described by Melville as "cloak-and-dagger types" went by the names of Smith and Jones, not the most inspired choices for subterfuge.

Smith informed him, somberly, that his brother's body had washed up on a beach near Portsmouth. "The body was rather the worse for wear and was given a respectable, if speedy, Christian burial. I assure you all obsequies were properly observed, and I will of course furnish you the name of the churchyard." He paused, and continued almost reluctantly. "But your brother did not drown. He was shot, then run through with a sword."

"My God!" gasped Pennywhistle.

"What I am about to tell you must remain in the strictest confidence."

"I understand. Recollect, Mr. Smith, that I have been entrusted with important secrets on prior occasions."

"Quite, quite!" said Smith in a voice that indicated he never really trusted anyone. "He was on an important mission on behalf of Lord Castlereagh. It appears things went... badly wrong. We would like you to help us with some materials that he left behind."

Good Lord, thought Pennywhistle. Sammie Jo's instincts had been exactly right. "Could you tell me something about the job that got him killed?"

"It was the recovery of a cache of letters from the French government," replied Jones. "We are not privy to what was in the letters, but the operation was cleared at the highest levels. Only Lord Castlereagh knows the full details, and he is in Vienna at present."

"We made inquiries when the body was found, and turned up a Lieutenant Meriwether Trelawney from the Revenue Service who has proven helpful. He had been chasing smugglers operating out of Cherbourg and believes that he may have seen something through his spyglass: an exceptionally tall man attacking someone matching your brother's description on a beach near Vierville. He had not come forward earlier because he was ashamed; he was into his cups at the time and could not be certain if he actually saw what he thought he saw.

"We do have a number of effects for you that your brother left in his office. They include a red ledger book and two letters that we believe important. Inconveniently, they are written in a code that our best cryptographers have had no success in deciphering. You are welcome to try your luck. We should be most grateful to be informed if you discover... anything."

The red ledger! The one Peter had so desperately wanted him to notice! He cared little for any secrets unearthed save one: his brother's murderer. The ledger and letters might furnish clues to his brother's final activities, and possibly point him in the direction of his brother's killer. The question would then be: What manner of justice would he follow if he identified the killer? The killer might be beyond the reach of the law, since the whole thing reeked of clandestine politics. Would his conduct be about justice, or vengeance? Would the lessons of the Other Side have primacy, or old instincts honed by years of war?

"Could an interview with this Revenue Service officer be arranged?" inquired Pennywhistle.

"It could," replied Smith, "though the challenge would be finding him sober enough to speak lucidly. He retains his present command only due to family influence." Smith scowled slightly. Clearly he disapproved of influence superseding ability.

Pennywhistle suddenly felt drained. He would worry about the ledger tomorrow. All he could think of right now was a hot shower, a warm bed, and a loving Sammie Jo.

Chapter Nineteen

Von Steinwehr stood in the alley off Josef's Platz as the sunlight slowly faded. He looked one last time at the list of those key information brokers whose opinions of him could not be changed. He shook his head in irritation. He had anticipated two who could not be bought off or blackmailed, not four. None of the men were aristocrats; all were what the French called *bourgeoisie*. Nevertheless, these bland, colorless functionaries held the destiny of Europe in their hands. Their highly specialized knowledge of cartography, languages, history, systems of governance, and ethnic populations was indispensable during critical negotiations. If they did not know something, it probably was not worth knowing. Unfortunately, they had proven less susceptible to financial blandishments than most aristocrats of his acquaintance—perhaps because they were not in the habit of living beyond their means.

Fouché had proven to be a sound investment: he had good instincts for ferreting out private and official gossip. A patient listener, he was always available when frustrated diplomats needed a confidante for their indiscreet tongues. His charm was infectious and he was good at quickly evaluating what constituted critical information and what could be dismissed as unimportant. His reports were regular and surprisingly thorough. Most importantly, he had seduced Talleyrand's niece, and their pillow talk had yielded valuable information. She was fully as indiscreet as York and Alexander. Von Steinwehr had assembled dossiers on the men that he had identified as his enemies—schedules, habits, hobbies, weaknesses, and even perversions. He then decided the best point of access.

He had no personal quarrel with Jean La Pierre, though he was about to end his life; all that mattered was the man's unwavering embrace of a principle that opposed the reconstitution of Reichenau, his conviction that there be no repealing of any territorial changes put in place by Napoleon. And Jean La Pierre had the ear of Talleyrand.

Von Steinwehr should have been distressed that he was about to kill a man he had never even met, but his moral firewall was eroding and the manic portion of his nature was assuming a tyrannical rule—something that he was beginning to enjoy.

He had killed many men on battlefields, sheltering under the moral cover of a flag. He told himself that he was again fighting a war, but one in which diplomats formed the soldiery. That made what he was about to do something other than murder.

He checked his Breugeot time piece: 6:10. The man was late. Odd—he had been told Monsieur La Pierre was a man of precise and predictable habits. Such men were generally the most reliable bureaucrats, but it also made them vulnerable to a planned ambush.

He had tried persuasion, bribery, and threats on La Pierre, in that order, but the man had proven resistant to all because he was that rarest of creatures, an incorruptible man. He was a firebrand when it came to telling the truth and treated tranquility as Nature would a vacuum. In better times, he was the kind of man von Steinwehr would have appointed to a ministerial post in Reichenau. La Pierre was unmarried and had no immediate family, likely the sort of

BOMBPROOFED

man who married his country and would grow old, grey, and blind in its service.

Von Steinwehr never involved himself directly in the actions of applying pressure to his enemies, always employing cut outs and go-betweens. In this way his identity remained a mystery. This approach had three benefits. For one, it prevented retaliation. The second was that because they did not *know* who threatened them, they *suspected* many. And thirdly, it rendered them fearful. Dark shadows that might house a poised attacker were more frightening than a clear face.

It was time to send a general message, one of terror that would the opening act in a horrific play. He would be cold and efficient, but wanted the result to suggest mad rage. It had to overpower the inherent drama of the Congress. He wanted La Pierre's death to be remarked upon in the city newspapers and send shivers through the diplomatic community as well as the general public. He needed the city consumed by fear—off balance and on edge. Fear not only made people stupid and pliable, it made them distrustful of any changes to the conservative *status quo ante bellum.*

Yes, the attack must seem the work of a homicidal madman, the sort of person who would have been labeled possessed in the Middle Ages. Superstition and old legends would serve as publicists for his production. And if the killer were eventually brought to justice by someone from Reichenau, that man would be reckoned a hero. Then his modest words of acknowledgment might include a plea for the restoration of a lost realm. Reichenau would be perceived as a breeding ground for heroes—and the world needed heroes. He would be in the position of an arsonist praised for putting out the fire he himself had started. The irony pleased him. He would have to find a pawn to finger as the killer, but plenty of candidates came to mind.

He heard footsteps coming up the hill. He opened his spyglass and confirmed it was La Pierre. He furled the glass, drew a large hunting knife, and waited to strike when the man came round the corner. He had specially chosen this section of the man's route because it was remote from heavy foot traffic.

La Pierre was as forgettable of face as he was of physique, dressed in the chocolate brown coat and wheat-colored trousers that constituted something of a personal trade mark. Von Steinwehr let him walk past, then plunged the dagger into his back, just below the middle of the left kidney. A wound in such a spot was so painful that it paralyzed the vocal cords. He quickly withdrew the knife, then jabbed it into La Pierre's neck just below the skull. La Pierre shuddered like a leaf in the wind; his eyeballs fluttered briefly and turned upwards. He sank to the cobblestones, blood seeping in a dark welter past the blade.

Von Steinwehr dragged the body into the shadows and calmly slit the corpse's throat, letting the blood flow freely. He took a deep breath, swallowed hard, and reminded himself that sometimes distasteful actions were necessary. In five quick, sharp strokes he cut open a flap of skin, severed the liver, and jerked it free. He put it in a small bag, which he would discard at the earliest possible moment. He then stabbed a few times at the site of the excision, to make it look like crude, rather than precise, surgery.

He pinned each of the man's eyes shut and did the same to the mouth. He dipped his finger into the steadily widening river of blood and traced a crude pentagram on the man's chest.

He wrapped a stout rope around the corpse's legs and used his great physical strength to haul the body off the pavement. He entwined the other end of the rope around the top of a nearby fence. The corpse hung, utterly bereft of dignity. He pulled a goat's skull from his bag and placed it beneath the body. Dripping blood soon turned it red.

His handiwork looked the perfect ritual killing, whether by a single madman or a dangerous cult.

He decided on one last gesture. Perhaps it was too theatrical, but it amused his sense of showmanship. It would add to the sense of terror if the killer or cult left a calling card, a frightening sobriquet. The newspapers would fixate on it. He dropped three edelweiss flowers on the ground beneath the corpse. "The Edelweiss Executioner" sounded a fine name for a mad killer.

He dowsed the dead man's hands in oil and lit them, one more bizarre touch that would perplex all Vienna. Then he picked up his canvas bag and walked briskly down the street, fastening a fresh red carnation to his lapel as he went. There was another damned state dinner tonight and he had to allow time to change into his dress uniform and strap on his best set of manners. He had only gotten a block away when he heard shouts. "H*ilfe, hilfe, hilfe!*" The voices sounded frantic. Excellent. One down, three more to go.

The Prussians had proven agreeable to Czar Alexander's suggestion that Reichenau be reconstituted, and Austria was at least neutral. The British and the French continued to oppose it because such an action would give Russia an ally on the Rhine River: Reichenau's east bank had once been France's western boundary. The Russians had been the most brutal occupiers of France in 1814, and Talleyrand would not wish to be seen as receptive to Russian wishes. Talleyrand was as sly as a fox, as slippery as an eel, and as opportunistic as a jackal. He was the ultimate pragmatist, with only one long-term goal: the restoration of France as a key arbiter in the future of Europe. Fortunately, his niece had furnished Fouché, intimate details of his private life that might well cause him to soften his anti-Russian position.

Actually, Talleyrand's vision of Europe was not so different from von Steinwehr's own. He wanted long term stability. While he supported Napoleon's changes to the map of Europe, he was favorably disposed toward leaders from old ruling houses. Perhaps it was best to say that while he liked new fashions, he preferred those wearing them to have a certain type of bloodline.

But Talleyrand wanted Britain's help to block the other powers from establishing a Polish kingdom under Russian influence. Both powers feared that the Polish question presaged further Russian interference in central Europe. And the abolition of Reichenau was a small price to pay for British good will.

Castlereagh was as personally dull as he was principled. But because his core beliefs were unshifting, men like Alexander and Talleyrand afforded him a considerable, if grudging, respect. He also represented the greatest financial power in Europe, and no ship could go anywhere on the high seas without the approval of the British Navy. He was an intellectual immune to a honey trap because he was devoted to his frumpy wife. His personal finances were above reproach, and Fouché had found no skeletons in his background that might expose him to blackmail. But the Clarke letters deciphered would be the fulcrum by which von Steinwehr could leverage Castlereagh: British officials, anxious to prevent scandal, would order a change in Castlereagh's position about the restoration of lost lands. Castlereagh wanted France ringed by less powerful buffer states with no ties to Austria, Prussia, or Russia. If he could privately be made to see that von Steinwehr intended to follow an independent course, Reichenau might be considered as one of those buffer states.

Von Steinwehr would pen a score of letters tonight and dispatch them by fast riders to his agents in Britain. He

Bombproofed

already had planted several in the Russian embassy there, furnishing them with diplomatic immunity.

He realized he was part of a gigantic political game of chess. The game, after all, had been devised as a lesson in the ways of politics for a prince to study. The trouble was, the only piece he cared about, Reichenau, was not even a knight or bishop, but a mere pawn, and pawns were routinely sacrificed.

The men on his list were pawns as well, and if he could remove them as threats it might sufficiently affect the outcome of the game. Their masters relied on them for information, and if that were lacking... those masters might be more amenable to Russian persuasion. Big things often had small beginnings, and these men were the small beginnings.

He felt his plan made him something like a carnival plate twirler who spun wide plates on the top of narrow poles. Everyone waited in suspense for the plates to fall, puzzled by their defiance of the laws of physics. The plate spinner alone knew the right rhythms and subtle motions required to keep them in motion. It was degrading to be a carnival performer, but then the Congress itself was something of a carnival of human nature, containing the sublime and the freakish, the excellent and the outré, and motives mighty and mean. He regarded many in the Congress as aurochs, a European breed of cattle that had died out in the early 17th century. They had become extinct because they could not adapt to changing conditions. He would survive because he could do what aurochs could not: evolve.

A tired Pennywhistle listlessly stripped off his clothes and climbed into bed alongside a soundly sleeping Sammie Jo.

Sleep enfolded him almost immediately, but it did not bring the restorative solace he craved. He was suddenly back in *the dream,* the recurring flashback that had plagued him since his first fight at Trafalgar. That had not happened since his Other World journey, and he had dared to hope that he would never have to endure it again.

He stood on the quarterdeck of *HMS Bellerophon* at Trafalgar, surrounded by choking thunderheads of smoke, ear-splitting booms, frantic shouts, piteous shrieks, and retching sounds as mortally wounded sailors and marines puked away their final moments of life. Bewildered men in the uniforms of marines accosted him. "Orders, sir? Orders? My God! What do we do now, sir?" He regarded them with terror because he had no answer.

But instead of overwhelming him in the old, too familiar terror, the baleful scene began to fade. A deep voice that belonged to a presence that he had simply termed "The Guide" echoed through his mind. "You acted to protect lives. You did nothing wrong. Rid yourself of the hair shirt that your pain requires your soul to wear."

He obeyed the voice, and as he did so he found himself in front of a familiar site: the maze at Hampton Court. It had become a tourist attraction for gentle folk, so intricately designed that many visitors hired guides to navigate its twists and turns. His father and brother had instead trusted his abilities, and he had brought them in and out successfully. He had seen the underlying patterns in its design and applied them to each bend in the path. Once you understood the basic conception of its designer, its seeming randomness actually became predictable.

The Guide spoke again, imperious yet compassionate. "You have the greatest gift of all: free will. While the general patterns of your life will point you in certain directions, the details of your destiny will be written by you alone. You will see three mazes. Unlike the one from your childhood, the underlying designs of all of them have been created by you and will alter as you make choices."

A fog swirled around him, then cleared gradually. The three mazes were concepts of the mind and more figurative than literal, composed of symbols that had significance to him alone.

The first was fronted by a shadowy figure that resembled a magician, with a sword and scalpel lying at his feet. He inferred it represented career: the soldier versus the physician.

The second had a man and woman holding hands at its entrance and represented love: a coffin was on one side of the couple, and children's blocks were on the other. He thought it might mean love would either die prematurely or flourish sufficiently to produce offspring.

The final maze was the most complex. A colorful juggler rotated aloft gold coins in unending motion. An open code book lay at his feet along with a scattering of foreign medals, orders of chivalry, and a Russian flag. In the rear of the maze, he could see the tall spire of a cathedral which dominated the skyline of some overseas city. He sensed this had to do with his brother's fate.

"Tom, wake up! Wake up! You are safe. You are safe!" He felt himself being gripped and shaken and recognized Sammie Jo's voice. He gradually returned to consciousness, following the sounds of her soothing tones.

"You were moaning something fierce, Sugar Plum. I figured it had to be a nightmare."

He looked into her blue eyes and kissed her long and slow. "I have had this nightmare for years; this is the first time it has manifested since you came into my life. But something was different this time. It was much shorter than usual, and my intuition tells me that your love has ensured that this was its final appearance."

True enough, counseled his subconscious, *but should you not let her know of Other Worldly assistance? That affects your destiny as a couple.*

He wanted to tell Sammie Jo about The Guide, but if he did he would have to share all of the details of his other Other World journey. He was keeping secrets again, and a part of him knew it was introducing a slow working poison into their relationship. But, damn it, he was just not ready. "The nightmare was the stuff of old memories, but what followed was entirely new. I am not quite sure what it all means, but I am confident I can puzzle it out."

He described the dream, and the transition to a vision of mazes, then talked at length about his first naval battle. He was soaked in sweat by the time he finished the account of Trafalgar but felt noticeably lighter for sharing his pain.

"I'm damn sorry about the battle stuff, Tom. Much as I have been bothered by what I've done, I ain't been cursed by any of it seeping into my dreams. The maze stuff is a real mystery. The coffin and the couple scare me. But I get a sense you are leaving something out."

Now was not, he decided, the time to increase her fear. "I believe they represent possibilities, symbolically represented variables so that the unexpected may be anticipated and courses of action may be logically planned." *Tell her!* screamed his conscience. *Tell her the whole truth. Tell her about the Other Side. Tell her about The Guide. Trust in the power of love!*

His lips remained silent.

"What happened at the Admiralty, Tom?"

He glossed over his official duties and focused on his chat with Smith and Jones. "You were right about Peter, my dear. He was on some official business and was murdered."

"Fuck!" Sammie Jo burst out. "Sorry, Tom. Any idea who did it?"

"No, but there may be an eyewitness, and I will need to speak to him. I think I recognize the church spire in the last maze. I believe it to be that of St. Stephen's Cathedral in Vienna. Lord Castlereagh was behind my brother's mission and is there now. I know we have just arrived in England, but I have a feeling we might be traveling to the Continent soon."

She began stroking his temples. "We can discuss that later, Sugar Plum. You need some sleep, and you can't get it with your mind racing a mile a minute. Let me suggest a jaunt of another kind; it's a lot simpler and more fun than navigating a maze. Come here." She reached for him and slowly pulled him down on top of her.

He knew he had to tell Sammie Jo about his most significant journey of all: the visit to the Other Side. He would definitely do it today. But it could wait a few hours.

Chapter Twenty

Crack! Crack! Pop! The sounds were familiar and too close for comfort. He jerked awake and instinctively reached to his left. Sammie Jo no longer lay next to him. A flash of panic shot through him. He saw his Ferguson in the corner and barely restrained himself from jumping up and grabbing it.

He cocked his ear toward the source of the sounds. They were coming from behind the townhouse, from the direction of the open fields immediately astern the four-story structure, just the approach brigands would use to stealthily approach the stables. Spartan and Leander were valuable breeding studs.

The reports came from three different weapons: one military, two civilian—a Baker, a fowling piece, and a long rifle. The high rifle bark was distinctively American. Was Sammie Jo defending the house?

There was a discreet rapping at the bedroom door. "Come!" he said without thinking. Gabriel entered, carrying Pennywhistle's civilian clothes—shirt, cravat, waistcoat, tailcoat, and trousers draped carefully over hangers, all carefully and neatly pressed. There was not the least hint of alarm in Gabriel's manner.

Pennywhistle willed his distressed face back to equanimity. "What is going on out back, Gabriel? I thought it might be some nefarious business, but you seem untroubled."

Before Gabriel could reply, happy shouts answered his query. The voices reflected triumph and pride, not fear.

"Oh, don't you worry none about that, sir. It's Mrs. Pennywhistle showing little Johnny all about guns. They are having target practice. The sergeant major heard and decided to join them. Then Lady Leith was curious and came to watch. She went back in and brought out her husband's old hunting piece. They are having a fine time! Like a come-to-meeting, but with guns instead of Bibles."

Pennywhistle breathed a sigh of relief and realized last night's dreams had left him on edge. Gabriel hung up his clothing and helped him into his dressing gown. "What time is it, anyway, Gabriel?" He glanced out the window and noted the sun was well up.

"The clock downstairs done struck 11, sir. Mrs. Pennywhistle said that you had a lot on your mind and was not to be disturbed. She has been up and about for the past four hours, mostly talking to Lady Leith. They were discussing dresses—lots of talk about current fashions. Mrs. Pennywhistle wants to please you, sir. I also heard her say that maybe Johnny could be something more than a page for your new household."

"It does not surprise me, Gabriel. Seneca once said *confide confides cognoscitur*. It means 'one good heart recognizes another.'"

"Well, sir, both Lady Leith and Mrs. Pennywhistle have good hearts. They treat other people real fine." His brow darkened. "Old Masstuh Thomas, he didn't know nothing 'bout a man's dignity 'cept how to steal it!"

Gabriel's words reminded Pennywhistle of the reward. "Gabriel, I have good news for you. It seems we are to be paid a tidy sum for the recovery of the army payroll. It may take some months, but you will soon have sufficient funds to leave my service if you wish, carve out your own destiny as a free man."

"Me? With a pile of money? That would give Old Masstuh Tom a proper fit! But, sir, it don't matter none. I don't want to leave your service. I've hitched my wagon to a rising star and I want to see just how high it goes."

"I am honored that you would say that! I consider our arrangement a partnership much like that between a Scots laird and his chief ghillie. I have never wanted your subservience, but your advice is always welcome. And now, given how tardy I have been in rising, I need you to see to two things: a cup of coffee and the shower cistern to be filled."

Gabriel departed for the kitchen, and soon returned. "I got the coffee right here, sir, brewed just the way you like it; a spoon will stand in it. It will take a little while for the maids to heat up some hot water for the shower."

Pennywhistle accepted a steaming mug and the first blessed sip brought a surge of alert optimism. "The delay is unnecessary, Gabriel. Don't heat the water."

Gabriel looked shocked. "You want a *cold* shower, sir? That don't seem like a good thing; sounds more like a punishment."

Pennywhistle smiled. "Cold showers are hard on the body but splendid for the spirit. It is an unmatchable way to perk yourself up for the day ahead."

Gabriel replied philosophically, "Seems to me, a man who chooses cold water when he can have it hot be knowing a thing or two about mortifyin' the flesh. I'll get the shower ready."

Pennywhistle savored his coffee and contemplated the day ahead. His brother's face flashed into his head, and suddenly he knew.

BOMBPROOFED

The key to translating the ledger and the two Clarke letters given him was a code chart that he and his brother had used as children, chiefly to outfox their mother, an unrepentant eavesdropper. He and Peter had appropriated a cipher as a game that stimulated both their intellects. It came from an obscure book in their father's library, *The Little Code Maker and Pocket Cryptographer* by Hoylet Framingham. He idly wondered what cruel parent would name a child Hoylet, but it was distinctive, and that was why he remembered the author and book. If he could find the book, he knew exactly where the code table lay.

He was familiar with the Clarke *cause célèbre* of 1809 and the parliamentary inquiry that had caused the Duke of York's resignation. The inquiry had ended abruptly because secrets had been coming to light that were best left in the dark. With these letters, the scandal had apparently gained a new and dangerous lease on life. He quickly established the likely chain of the code's use. Peter had boasted that he used that same code key to similarly outfox the King's College masters during his years at Cambridge. He had sown his wild oats there, then trod the straight and narrow zealously for the rest of his life. One of his closest companions during those wild escapades had been James Keaton, who later served as the Duke of York's confidential secretary. He guessed that Keaton had appropriated the code and told Mrs. Clarke and the duke of it so their communications could remain confidential. What had probably started as an innocent lover's correspondence had evidently changed into something much darker when the relationship soured. The trouble was, Framingham's book had been destroyed in a fire caused by a maid's carelessness. The chances of him discovering another copy in a bookstore were slim at best. Still, he had to make the effort. He would be systematic, and if necessary visit every book store in London. Failing that, he knew a few private collectors who might have it. Every approach had to be tried. Hatchard's Book Store, he decided, would be his first port of call. The five-story establishment was patronized by members of the Royal Society and contained many obscure books on all manner of science topics. *The Little Code Maker* had probably had a printing run of fewer than a hundred copies, and because the subject was so arcane it might not have sold well.

Wait a minute! his mind screamed. *The bandits on the road sought a book about codes!* But how the devil could they know about something that he had just deduced? Something very deep was going on here.

But before he could unravel secrets of the past, he had to see to his and Sammie Jo's future: they needed a place of their own. He had no wish to displace his brother's widow from the family home in Berwick. Besides, the old home had very bittersweet memories of their unbalanced mother. A new townhouse erected on one of his godmother's tracts was a possibility, but he was not sure how well Sammie Jo would take to urban life. She seemed entranced by London, but once the newness wore off she might pine for a return to... well... pine trees.

There was one small place that might work: Whistlestop. It had been the family seat in medieval times but had fallen into disrepair. It was a border pele, a small keep and tower combination that stopped just short of being a castle. It was a mere six miles from Scotland, and locals had forted up there when Scottish raiders poured over the border pursuing cattle and English wenches. It was rumored to be haunted by a phalanx of ghosts, but Sammie Jo did not scare easily, and with his experience on the Other Side, he did not scare at all. The land was marginal for farming, but the estate was surrounded by six hundred acres of hardwood forest populated with plenty of stags: Sammie Jo would be able to hunt to her heart's content. It would require the assistance of an architect to modernize the keep, but the result would be both a link to the past and a vision for the future.

And yet, the choice of residence could not be made until he had resolved an even more important issue: his career. He had just been promoted major and if he made the Marines a lifetime commitment he might well finish his days as Commandant of the Corps. Life in the peacetime Marines would be chiefly administrative, filling out an endless supply of forms, requisitions, and memoranda. He would be a glorified paper shuffler and quill wrangler. Adventure, excitement, and danger would have no place in this new world unless you reckoned bureaucratic back biting as combat. His Marine salary was welcome, but with his investments, prize money, and his brother's inheritance he could manage comfortably without it.

He realized that for the investiture he needed a new dress uniform that reflected his elevated rank; then he relaxed. Lady Leith would have already alerted Gieves; they had his measurements on file. She had probably told them in no uncertain terms to put a rush on the order.

He had been on a path to be a physician and surgeon fifteen years ago, though it was a profession considered more suited to the middling orders than to his class. He had a natural aptitude for soldiering, but he had never intended to make it a career. It was odd how a hasty decision could catapult you into an entirely unforeseen path of life: healer and harmer juxtaposed in a strange Cartesian duality. Voltaire's words had always haunted him: "while it is wrong to murder, it is praiseworthy if done in large numbers to the sounds of drums and trumpets."

He liked the Hippocratic Oath, *Primum non nocere*, because he had caused a great deal of harm in his time, and he respected a profession which aspired to cause none. The lesson from the Other World was clear, and medicine might be a form of atonement.

With his title, connections, and a proper degree from Edinburgh it would be easy to establish a thriving practice in Harley Street catering to the unique ailments of the British propertied classes, but that held no fascination for him. He was far more interested in helping people with perplexing cases, no matter what their ability to pay.

He was also the guardian of Carlotta's two sons, and he would have to make sure of their welfare. He had his doubts about public school education since he had been tutored at home, but her older boy seemed to enjoy the rough and tumble competition among the student body at Harrow. His younger brother was a midshipman, but with the inevitable reduction in the size of the navy following Bonaparte's ouster, new provisions might have to be made. Sammie Jo, rather than being resentful of being reminded of an earlier love, respected him for actions that she said "would never occur to most gentlemen."

The internment of his half-brother's heart would have to wait; he could not spare a week to reach St Cuthbert's and return. John Tracy would have understood, since he was soldier. While it was important to honor the dead, a commander's first duty was to provide for the well-being of the living.

Dale needed his help with his discharge, as well as the brokering of a deal to purchase the Black Robin Inn. It would take an entire day at the very least to inspect it and negotiate terms, but that could wait.

Gabriel's cheerful voice burst his bubble of concentration. "Your shower is ready, sir."

Five minutes later he was dancing briskly in exquisite pain as the cold water cascaded onto his shoulders. His

BOMBPROOFED

breath came in short gasps, goose bumps rose, and his skin felt savaged as by a regiment of hornets. Still, each passing second cleared more cobwebs out of his head and he saw the days ahead with a brilliant clarity. When the flow stopped, he knew exactly what to do. He dressed quickly, without Gabriel's assistance. He had sent him down to saddle up Spartan for a ride.

He walked out of the house toward the mews in his charcoal tailcoat, complimented by a buff waistcoat and Oxford grey trousers—the very picture of conservative civilian respectability. His black silk cravat was tied in a simple barrel knot and he wore the broad-brimmed black hat that Sammie Jo had chosen for him in Bermuda.

The open field behind the house had been turned into an improvised gun range.

"Do it again! Do it again!" Johnny gleefully shouted. His leaps of joy merited his name of Johnny Jump up.

Sammie Jo brought her smoking rifle down slowly from her shoulder, laid it carefully on the crude wooden table, and accepted a spyglass from Dale. She peered through it and assessed her target. The red square covering the heart had another hole in it, slightly below and fractionally to the left of Dale's last shot.

The target was a dressmaker's mannequin supplied by Lady Leith. It showed an array of bullet holes in the upper left chest. A large mound of hastily assembled dirt stood behind it to absorb the barrage of lead.

"May I see, ma' am?" said Dale.

"Go right ahead, Sergeant Major—same result as last time, though. You are a right fine shot, but you ain't never gonna outshoot me."

Dale studied the target. "Let me try one more time, ma'am. We have put too many shots in the chest area. Let us see if either of us can manage one right between the eyes."

"Fair enough," said Sammie Jo. "Then let's allow Johnny to do some shooting. I don't think he has fired more than five shots. We got so carried away trying to show him the perfect shot that we plum forgot ourselves and turned it into a shooting match against each other. I think we are both just too damn competitive!"

"Oh, I don't mind, ma'am," Johnny chirped brightly. "I love watching you both shoot. I never seen anything like it. Mr. Hopkins had a horse pistol that he fired at one of my friends. He weren't more than three feet away but his shot was a clean miss. All that stuff you said about a firm grip, a good point, holding your breath and letting it out slow-like, why he didn't have any notion of that. You two are... are..." He struggled for the right word.

"Craftsmen," said Pennywhistle who had come up silently behind. Johnny blinked and spun around. Pennywhistle put his hand on the boy's shoulder. "Had you ever fired a weapon before this morning?"

"No, sir. I was looking at Mrs. Pennywhistle's gun this morning and she asked if I wanted to learn how to fire it. I said I did. She said we might be going on a journey and that you would want anyone along to be able to shoot well enough to stop a bad man." Johnny frowned. "I missed with my first shots, but you see that one in the left shoulder?" Pennywhistle nodded. "That's mine!" he said with great pride.

"Commendable shooting for a first-timer. Such a shot would knock the recipient out of action. You are lucky to have very good teachers."

Sammie Jo fired and her shot went exactly between the eyes, her superior eyesight again proving its value.

Dale fired, put down his Baker, and took up the spyglass. He peered through it and frowned. The shot would have been fatal, but it was a half-inch below the eyes. "You win,

BOMBPROOFED

ma'am." He gave her a friendly smile. "But you do have to promise me a rematch."

"Fine with me, Sergeant Major! Now let's reload and give the boy some real instruction!"

"Just one minute," said Lady Leith in a voice that rippled with mock indignation. "I should like my turn. I have been most patient with you two, and I finally remembered the important thing my husband stressed that had eluded my memory earlier. I believe that is why my previous shot missed. He said, 'Always allow for the arc of the bullet.' In all the excitement here, I quite forgot. I truly am getting old. Now, let me test my theory."

Lady Leith stepped up, sighted the long-barreled piece quickly, and fired. The shot struck the base of the throat, exactly where an officer's gorget would have been. She obviously had remembered her late husband's instructions.

Sammie Jo put her hands on her hips and looked at Lady Leith with delight. "Well, damn, Margaret, you've been holding out on me! Where did you learn to shoot like that?"

"Scotland. My husband loved grouse hunting and I always tagged along. But he has been gone ten years and I have not fired a gun since his passing. It shows what happens when you don't practice. But at my age that might be just a lucky shot, Sammie Jo. I have no idea if I could repeat it."

Sammie Jo looked thoughtful. "I bet you could. I saw something change in your eyes before you fired, like you got all your experience back in a flash. Tom says folks here don't boast about their skill, always downplay it and act real modest. Guess he was right! Get on over here, Tom. Everyone is shooting today; you might as well take a turn."

"Not today, Sammie Jo. I need to get going. That bad business we spoke about last night demands my attention. I can do nothing until I have a certain book. Do you understand?"

"Yes, I do. You got a bee up your bottom that's going to keep stinging until you get what you need. It would be fine if you could just stop for a minute and realize you got plenty of time to enjoy a moment of joy before becoming all grim and driven by duty. But..."—she sighed deeply—"I married you for better or worse and you ain't going to change, so I figure with your compass fixed on a course, it's better to just get out of the way and make the best of it. You ain't perfect but..."—she smiled—"you do pretty well! Just be careful."

He kissed her quickly. "I should be back by dark, earlier if I get lucky."

Gabriel brought Spartan over, neatly brushed and saddled. Pennywhistle mounted easily. "Good shooting, my friends." He waved to everyone, then nudged Spartan to a canter and rode out of the courtyard.

Dale wondered what was going on. He knew Pennywhistle far too well to be fooled by his voice—the cheerier the tone, the higher the worry quotient. Something was definitely up, but it was a waste of time to try to puzzle it out. He would be patient and wait. Pennywhistle would let him know soon enough. He was impressed by how Pennywhistle and his wife were growing closer and it made him wonder about Deborah. He needed to find her, but had not yet acted because he was afraid—afraid that she might have forgotten him. Sometimes happy memories were better than unpleasant reality.

Johnny fired, with Sammie Jo helping him to hold the rifle properly. His round went straight through the mannequin's heart.

"Not bad! Not bad at all," said Sammie Jo with a smile in her voice.

"Not half bad," Johnnie said, grinning up at her.

Chapter Twenty-One

"No, blast it, it's just too sensational. We can't print this! A second murder with the same dreadful *modus operandi* will keep half of the population hiding indoors!" shouted Gustave Shurz, editor of *Weiner Zeitung,* Vienna's oldest and most respected newspaper. "You are my best reporter, Buntz, but the public does *not* need to know this. And you need to stick to the facts. This line here: 'Some fear this dastardly crime may be part of a deeper, more sinister design carried out by an unknown dark society,' is mere speculation and has no business in the article. We have no proof. We should cut the story in half and put it on the back page in the interest of civil order."

"Ah, there you are mistaken, Herr Schurz," countered Karl Buntz in a tactful yet contentious voice. "The cat is already out of the bag and all manner of wild rumors are circulating. I agree that facts are important, but what is being said about them is even more important. With all of the congressional talk of The Rights of Man, one the most basic is that of self protection, and people cannot do that properly if they are not kept informed. Two important diplomats murdered, and nothing of value is taken. Why? I find the scattering of edelweiss blossoms significant, almost as if the killer is taunting us; it reminds me of an artist's signature on a painting. And this is not front page news?"

Buntz did not wait for an answer to a question that was purely rhetorical. "One of the Emperor's aides approached me yesterday and asked if I had any additional details which might assist his intelligence mandarins. He said the emperor is 'very concerned.' People at the highest levels are worried as well: 'Today a diplomat, perhaps a sovereign tomorrow' is a concern I have heard voiced by several well-placed sources. I spent a long morning chasing down leads and finally located an eyewitness who was most forthcoming about details. I know you find them grisly, but—"

Shurz shook the handwritten draft angrily at its author, his face a mixture of rage and incredulity. "*Grisly* is too mild a word! It smacks of something supernatural, something done by a servant of Satan."

It was Buntz's turn to be incredulous. "Supernatural? Really? I think people are capable of sufficiently dark acts without the assistance of the Prince of Darkness."

"I don't believe it's supernatural for an instant," said Schurz with indignation, "but I would wager that some of our readers will. It's not just the middle-class burghers, either. I have heard the Russian czar is involved with mysticism. There are aristocrats and royals who will believe that Satan is acting to disrupt the most important conference in the history of Europe. We may claim to live in an enlightened age, Herr Buntz, but the veneer of civilization is thin. Superstitions accumulated over thousands of years are not dispelled easily. Get people frightened enough, and you can get them to believe almost anything. It was not all that long ago that women were burned as witches."

Buntz fixed Shurz's gaze with a cynical, worldly stare. "All very true, Herr Shurz, and yet…"—he paused portentously—"…would you not agree that the new details will cause our circulation to skyrocket? What could be better than mysterious, bloody killings to sell newspapers? I appreciate

BOMBPROOFED

your occasional outbursts of social responsibility, but I have never known them to overmaster your interest in increasing profits. Surely you can see this is a very hot story?"

Shurz grudgingly nodded.

"Drama sells better than fact, and we have a story on our hands that may become the *cause célèbre* of the decade. People are already talking about the 'Edelweiss Executioner.' Whoever the killer is, he has a public identity now. *Who is he? Why does he act thus? Where will he strike next?* The public has a thousand questions. Forgive my cynicism, sir, but we could not have invented a better story if we had tried. Here is exactly the sort of mystery that would keep a play running for months. We may even be forced to issue special editions to meet the increased demand.

"Allow me to add another consideration," Buntz hastened to add. "Failure to print my story merely puts us behind the other newspapers. We want this story associated with our paper because we were Johnny-on-the spot from the beginning. Unlike our competitors, we have an eyewitness. And..."—he paused as if about to reveal a state secret—"I think I may have a description of the killer."

"Description, description?" Shurz shouted in exasperation. "That is not in the story, Buntz!"

"True, Herr Shurz. Some things should be held back until they can be more tellingly presented. My eyewitness told me he saw someone walking away from the body and that he seemed to be, and I quote, 'almost a giant.'"

"A giant, a giant," muttered Shurz as he considered it. "That could mean very different things to different people. Was your source excitable, given to fantasy and fabulism?"

"No, Herr Shurz. He struck me as a sober, respectable burgher who lacked imagination. I believe his description was accurate."

Shurz pondered. "A dead diplomat hung upside down, eyes and mouth sewn shut, a goat's head nearby. A second dead diplomat found grasping his severed head in his hand, and the only suspect is a giant? I have to admit that is extraordinary. It will certainly sell a great many newspapers!"

Buntz nodded confidently. "Vienna has never seen anything like it. People of every class and calling are clamouring for details, *and* for speculation. And our murderer is not done: I feel it in my bones. You have always trusted my instincts, Herr Shurz, please trust them now!"

Shurz pounded his fist into his open palm and said decisively. "All right, print it. Caution be damned!"

The black horse ahead of von Steinwehr's was truly fast. The stallion's shiny coat and sleek lines showed it was meticulously cared for, and the unusual height of 17 hands gave it an extraordinarily long gait. The horse belonged in competition, not toting around some dull upper-level bureaucrat. Von Steinwehr had misread his man. He had Monsieur du Teil pegged as a quiet, scholarly type. He came to this spot daily at the same time. He usually enjoyed a quiet canter in the woods, but today he was varying his routine. Perhaps he had had a trying morning at the negotiating table. He pushed his mount into a full blown gallop and rode him as skillfully as the finest jockey.

Vienna had plenty of green spaces close to the city center. Von Steinwehr remembered reading that the composer Beethoven had gotten some of his best ideas during solitary walks through the Vienna woods. He had intended to stage his ambush at a glade two hundred yards ahead, taking out his target from behind and using the garrote in his saddlebag, but du Teil rocketed past and kept going.

Bombproofed

Du Teil was an expert on principalities, duchies, and small kingdoms and had penned many learned monographs on their futures. His treatise "The Enlightened State" was considered required reading by all of the more thoughtful power brokers at the conference. His reflections on Reichenau formed a whole chapter and were distinctly hurtful to von Steinwehr's cause. Du Teil called Reichenau "the worst of the Rhineland's petty tyrannies." He referred to von Steinwehr indirectly when he labeled the former ruler "a tin-plated despot of the most arrogant and unfeeling disposition who regarded his subjects as little better than cattle." It was a calumny of the worst sort, and the man was being widely listened to. He had to go.

Von Steinwehr touched his hand to the long cavalry saber in its saddle scabbard. It was a powerful weapon even wielded by a weak arm, and his was strong. If he had to take du Teil at the gallop, a sword was the preferred weapon. But the garrote was exotic; it whispered of intrigue and would excite more terror in the public's imagination.

His own horse was a thoroughbred, but not in the same class as du Teil's for speed. He reined up hard, realizing the excitement of the chase had turned his blood hot but clouded his judgment. His brain needed to control the equation, for that was all the upcoming murder was to him: a cold undertaking having nothing to do with the primal joy of a predator tracking his quarry. He turned his mount's head in a new direction to take advantage of a short cut that put him ahead of his quarry. He positioned himself just behind a large beech tree, five yards from the road. Two horsemen rode by his position, but they passed, and soon the trail in front of him was clear.

He pulled the garrote from his saddlebag. Attached to its two wooden handles were not one but two coils of piano wire, each having a knot in the center. If a man tried to loosen one coil, it had the effect of tightening its companion. The knot in the center was designed to crush the larynx if the assassin had sufficient strength to pull it tightly enough. He had the strength.

Du Teil materialized. Horse and rider walked along slowly, relaxing from their earlier exertions. Du Teil touched his top hat in greeting as he rode past. Von Steinwehr returned the salutation. He would not need the sword after all.

The man was unintentionally cooperating. His reward would be a quick death. Von Steinwehr had no interest in prolonging agony: those who reveled in the pain of others were twisted men and, more importantly, inefficient ones. He waited until du Teil had trotted a few feet ahead before he moved in behind and deployed his weapon.

Du Teil turned his head slightly when the twin coils dropped from the sky and entwined themselves around his neck. They did not tighten properly because du Teil had idly been reaching up to scratch his neck. The wire cut deeply into his fingers, but he was still able to breathe, and a muted scream of terror rose from his throat.

Of all the damned bad luck, thought von Steinwehr. He could not allow any noise! He put all of his frustration into a gigantic convulsive jerk of the two handles. What happened next astonished him. The man's head simply popped off his neck, flew a foot in the air, and plopped unceremoniously on the ground. The horse reacted to the smell of spurting blood by neighing loudly, but it was too tired to bolt after the earlier vigorous ride. The body of its rider slumped to the ground. The relaxation of the pressure from the reins allowed the horse to follow his natural instincts and begin grazing on the long grass.

Von Steinwehr jumped from his horse and quickly retrieved the head, holding it by the hair and feeling, for a bizarre moment, like Perseus with the head of Medusa, prepared to turn his enemies to stone. Du Teil wore a permanent look of puzzlement. Was that an eye blink? Von Steinwehr gasped. No, merely a muscle spasm.

He took control of du Teil's horse and secured him to a large oak tree with enough slack to the reins that he could continue grazing on the verdant herbage. Du Teil's head he placed in the tree's crotch, where it was prominently visible above the saddle. But his tableau was not complete. He reached into his saddle bag and extracted three edelweiss blossoms. He stuffed one in the mouth and one in each ear.

Another murder of a diplomat, and this time with an unusual weapon. The play he had written in his mind was proceeding. But he would eventually need to give the hounds a hare to chase. Von Steinwehr needed a dupe who could plausibly be connected to the murders, one whom he himself could capture.

A young hussar officer on the Austrian staff, Captain Emil Von Danniken, would fit the bill. It would truly unsettle things if the villain turned out to be a servant of the emperor hosting the Congress! And Von Danniken was headed for a bad end—he provided such good raw material.

Von Danniken enjoyed rough sex, to judge from the facial bruises of some of his lady friends. Those bruises had occasioned unwelcome gossip, and he had heard rumors that Von Danniken had been counseled by his commanding officer to restrain his immoderate appetites, or at least confine his attentions to whores. The hussar had a reputation as a brutal hothead. Probably useful in a grand charge, but a distinct liability once the heat of battle had passed. He was ill suited to the staff position that he presently occupied. He had made a lot of powerful enemies, but he came from an old family and so remained untouched.

Von Steinwehr had already started to cultivate the acquaintance of the hussar at various official functions. He wanted to get an idea of Von Danniken's habits and schedule, so that future murders could take place when Von Danniken was alone, or with a trollop. The word of a whore was a poor alibi.

Lost in a reverie, Von Steinwehr was alerted by the sounds of approaching riders. He mounted his horse quickly and galloped away. People suddenly shocked often had difficulty recalling precise details, and the descriptions they gave were often close to useless: "Yes, Constable, we saw a tall man on a brown horse riding away. At least I think it was a brown horse. No, constable, I don't remember the color of his clothing."

He slowed his horse to a canter after putting 200 yards and several turns in the path between himself and the staged murder, and fixed a fresh red carnation to his lapel. Just then the screaming started; evidently one of the riders was a woman. Excellent! Only one more death to go, he reflected, with a feeling almost of regret.

Chapter Twenty-Two

Dale had not seen Deborah for nine years and feared that age might have been unkind. He wanted her to forever remain the perfect vision that she had been before he left for Trafalgar. Her oval face, chestnut hair, and trim form had been attractive enough, but she could easily pass unnoticed in a crowd. She lacked those attributes that typically attracted men in his Service: large bosom, smouldering eyes, saucy tongue, and come-hither manner. What she had was a character as full of iron as his own.

Her earlier publication had brought her into close contact with sailors and marines, but they soon realized that she was not the kind of woman who would ever consider a quick fling. There was nothing casual about her. She was plain-spoken, direct, and capable—a woman with whom you could build a life. She carried an air of deep determination, giving the impression of someone resolved to jump an impossibly wide canyon and about to try.

He panned his spyglass slowly across the front of her small print shop, 200 yards away. From his post on the second floor of The Two Roses Inn, he had a clear view of the comings and goings in Watling Lane. He told himself he was there to conduct a proper reconnaissance, to establish her identity and then ensure she was in no immediate danger. Though he agreed with most of what she published, he felt it was but a matter of time before her operation was shut down by the government as a threat to established order. He should have marched boldly into her shop, but he had not yet worked up the courage.

He had been watching for two hours and had not yet been rewarded with a view of Deborah. He had seen many men who looked to be merchants come and go: her publication was popular with prosperous men who were as yet unrepresented in Parliament.

Then he saw a sight that made his heart freeze: a well made boy of ten years who carried a tray full of type. His face was Dale's at that same age. No wonder Deborah had left Portsmouth after his apparent death. He dropped the glass in shock and delight. He had a son! A son! My God!

Had Deborah told him about his father? Probably not. Deborah had likely proceeded with the cold logic that almost constituted her calling card. In London, she could easily pass off a child as the product of a deceased father that she had married. No one was likely to check the records in Portsmouth.

He picked up the glass and watched the boy carefully. The lad deserved a real and legal father, and Deborah deserved a real family. The Black Robin might be just the place to raise one.

He had feared one person was in peril, but now it might be two. He cudgeled his thoughts and considered who could help him. Lady Leith was fond of him, a rebel, and had important friends in the government. He would speak to her as soon as possible. He furled his glass and headed briskly down the stairs and out the door.

Pennywhistle knew that he was being watched. His intuition snapped alert as soon as he crossed the threshold of the bookstore. The prickling of skin, the rise of the hair on his arms, and the subtle current of electricity which coursed through his body were signals that only appeared when something was wrong. As he walked among the shelves, he glanced behind twice and saw nothing suspicious. The third time, the man was just a fraction of a second too slow to duck around a corner. That split second was enough to fix a clear image in Pennywhistle's mind.

The man's clothes were of excellent quality, the attire of a prosperous squire who would be in his *milieu* in any of the finest gentlemen's clubs in London. His dark grey riding cloak was of superfine broadcloth and looked to be a confection of Hawkes; the wide brimmed beaver hat which shielded most of his face probably came from Lock & Company. His jockey boots could only have come from James Hoby, Pennywhistle's own boot maker. He would make inquiries with those tradesmen later. The other thing that stood out was the man's height. He was nearly as tall as Pennywhistle, and few men literally measured up to him. The man had a similar rangy, whipcord build.

Hatchard had evolved a capricious, unsystematic cataloguing system for the books he sold, and Pennywhistle guessed there were four categories where the book he sought might reside. He decided to be about his business and ignore the tail for the time being. It took him an hour to work through the books in the military affairs section, since they were grouped neither by dates, events, nor author. He thumbed through row after row filled with hundreds of titles. Occasionally he checked his peripheral vision and again saw his minder. He decided to label him Grey Cloak.

He ascended one stairway and walked to the section that dealt with calligraphy. It took him half an hour to determine that that was a dead end as well. Every few minutes he checked on his shadow. He did not see him every time he looked, but often enough to conclude that he was a persistent fellow.

His next destination was the diplomatic section. An hour of fruitless searching brought nothing except a nagging feeling that he was on a wild goose chase. He wished all book stores had a uniform system, but each appeared to have its own methods unrelated to that of any of its competitors. It was English eccentricity taken to an exasperating extreme.

He had one last inspiration, but it was a long shot: useful arts. Codebreaking was certainly that. He strolled casually along the aisles until he found the section, and began reading titles, although he was primarily looking for the well-remembered shape of the book. Eureka! The thin volume was sandwiched between two fat ones, and in his growing despair he had nearly missed it. He plucked it forth and thumbed through the book to make sure it was intact. He turned to page 84 and saw that it was just as he remembered it. The chart was there. He had the key.

He swept the aisles with his eyes but his minder seemed to have retreated. Odd—the man had been the picture of patience, and such men did not suddenly give up. He would have to be on his guard.

He paid for the book and walked briskly into the afternoon sun. He was so excited that he opened the book immediately in an effort to commit the chart to memory. It was because his mind was so engaged that he did not see the blow coming.

A heavy cane hit his shoulders hard from behind, knocked the wind out of him, and sent him plunging to the cobblestones. The world spun and he saw quick flashes of light, but he did not quite lose consciousness. The book lay perhaps two feet away; he tried to extend a hand to it, but his muscles refused to obey. A long arm reached down and plucked it up. Boots moved quickly away, and he knew that they were the ones from Hoby's.

Bombproofed

Damn it, get up! Don't let him get away with your prize. He shook his head painfully, hauled himself to a sitting position, and focused his vision on Grey Cloak walking away, fast enough to disappear swiftly but not fast enough to arouse suspicion.

No permanent damage, a quick check of his body told him—just a few bruises and miscellaneous lances of pain. He rocketed to his feet, shook his head to dissipate the dizziness, and rotated his arms in circles to restore circulation. He broke into a slow trot that changed into a run as all of his body departments informed his brain that they were intact and functional. His face flushed crimson, and his anger at his own foolishness caused him to put on a sprint of speed that closed the distance to Grey Cloak quickly.

Grey Cloak turned on him without warning when he was three feet away. He held a cane in one hand and quickly pulled the top off, extracting a long, narrow sword. He moved it slowly side to side, daring Pennywhistle to advance. His chiseled face spoke of hard service and his expression showed challenge, not fear. His stance was that of an expert swordsman.

Pennywhistle cursed himself for going about unarmed. He would have given a king's ransom for his cutlass at that moment.

He still had his boot dirk, though, which was lethal at close range. Engaging meant he would take damage from the sword's longer reach. Surprise was his best weapon—his opponent held himself like he expected a gentleman's duel.

He shouted something completely ungentlemanly at the top of his lungs as he launched himself into the air, aiming his arms at the man's throat. He felt a sharp pain in his back. The flashing sword cut a diagonal trench, but his frock coat absorbed enough of the force to prevent the blow from incapacitating him. His mass of one hundred eighty pounds crashed into his opponent and slammed him hard into the ground.

Grey Cloak was fully as strong as he and grabbed him with a grip like a gorilla's. They rolled over and over several times, but Pennywhistle could not quite reach his dirk. Grey Cloak ended up straddling a prone Pennywhistle and punched him twice in the face. His legs pinning Pennywhistle's arms, he wrapped two immense hands around his throat and started to squeeze.

Pennywhistle saw twirling pinwheels and knew he had only a few seconds before he lost consciousness. He poured every ounce of effort into his right arm and yanked it free. He shot his hand down and felt the dirk's hilt slide firmly into his grip. He blasted it skyward in a fast arc and stabbed with all his might. It penetrated the man's ribcage and continued inward.

The man roared like a bull being gelded. Blood spurted everywhere as the man's heart continued to pump, obedient to the demands of adrenaline. Pennywhistle's vision cleared; he gave a convulsive jerk and pushed the man off. Grey Cloak spasmed for a few moments as the spreading blood enveloped him, and then he breathed no more.

Pennywhistle rose to his feet, covered in blood. He felt a lance of pain in his back and put his hand over it. It came away bright red. His first thought was the damned man had just ruined a good frock coat, but his second was more germane to the situation. Dead men told no tales and yielded no useful leads; he wished he had not killed the man, but he'd had very little choice in the matter. He recovered the book, then examined the body. It yielded nothing of interest.

As he massaged his back he noticed a landau waiting a hundred yards away. The driver glanced nervously from left to right as if awaiting a passenger. It was a gentleman's vehicle, not an ordinary hansom looking for a fare.

BOMBPROOFED

Unfurling his six-inch pocket Ramdsen, Pennywhistle examined the driver. The man was sweating profusely. Of course! His opponent had prearranged an escape route and transportation.

He glanced at the body and an insane idea hit. He stripped off the man's cloak and grabbed his hat. The cloak was a good fit, but the hat a bad one, being one size too large. He quickly put two silk handkerchiefs into the lining to compensate and hoped the driver was too worried to notice anything amiss. He picked up the sword and reinserted it into its cane sheath, then pulled the hat down low to conceal his face.

He hunched over, one hand holding his stomach as if in great pain. He shambled forward. The coachman spotted him and waved him forward urgently. He jumped down and flung open the door.

The coachman's face turned white when he saw blood dripping from under the grey cloak. Pennywhistle kept his head down and emitted some vague grunts that suggested he was in great agony. When he got himself settled in the coach, he simply waved his hand violently forward, as if too beset by pain to form words. The fearful coachman spoke in what sounded like German. One word Pennywhistle could make out: "embassy." The coachman jumped back into his seat. Pennywhistle heard him shout "Haa!" Then his whip cracked, and the carriage lurched forward. Pennywhistle rolled into one of the long seats, which quickly became soaked in blood. He breathed deeply to slow his pulse, and concentrated on blocking the pain in his back.

An embassy? Did Grey Cloak's efforts have official backing? Pennywhistle wondered what kind of a conspiracy he was up against. He breathed deeply three times to calm himself. It worked on his muscles but not on his mind; his thoughts continued to race.

Chapter Twenty-Three

The carriage ride took twenty minutes. The driver paid him no mind, since navigating heavy traffic at high speed absorbed his concentration. Pennywhistle ripped out several oblong pieces of the cloak's silk lining and used them as bandages to stanch his bleeding. His fingers told him that the gash was long but not deep. It would have to be sutured, but he could function if he steeled his will. He sat up after a few minutes and passed a hand over the improvised bandages, pleased to find that they had slowed the blood flow to a trickle.

The carriage raced past Green Park and continued west along St James Street into an area of gentleman's clubs, passed the imposing Palladian block of Brooks, to which he belonged. He seldom patronized the place since he had no interest in high-stakes gambling, but his brother had said it was useful to have a place to meet "the right people." The carriage took a right at King Street and continued three blocks to St James Square where many foreign embassies were located. He felt the carriage reducing speed. It plodded past the Prussian Embassy and continued toward a grander structure that resembled a giant brown hatbox. Pennywhistle wondered if Grey Cloak had occupied an official diplomatic position that would have protected him from arrest. The way he'd fought and held his sword suggested that he had served as an officer in someone's armed forces. The carriage slowed

BOMBPROOFED

as they reached the Russian Embassy. It exited the street and pulled into an alley, probably headed for a rear entrance.

What would the Russians want with the code book? British interests at the Congress might well be opposed to those of the Russians, he reasoned, so something in the book would decrypt a message that benefited the czar. Apparently, Alexander's minions considered that message important enough to warrant murder.

The carriage ground to a halt. Pennywhistle focused his fading energy on making a fast getaway. He could hardly go inside the Embassy and begin asking—or answering—questions. He pulled the hat down low again, grabbed his stomach, and groaned loudly. The carriage door opened slowly and an equerry addressed him in what he guessed was Russian, a guttural language that sounded like someone speaking English backward. He did not understand the man's words, but the concern in the voice seemed genuine.

He jabbed a quick right to the equerry's nose, which sent him reeling back. He kicked the door open and leaped out almost into the arms of two very surprised Russian grenadiers. He kicked one in the shin and elbowed the second in the jaw. He broke into his best effort at a run. He had nearly made it to the street when a shot rang out. It came nowhere close but served notice that the Russians meant business. He turned onto King Street. He only had to make it three blocks to Brooks.

His pain limited his pace to that of a moderate walk. He looked behind and realized he was leaving bloody footprints for his pursuers—he should have cleaned his boots in the carriage. His breath was coming harder now and he felt lightheaded. He reluctantly admitted to himself that he was hurt worse than he had first supposed. He slowed his pace to that of an old man and the pain abated. Only two blocks to go. He looked behind and saw his pursuers: tall men with round Slavic faces dressed in the kind of attire that would blend in with the gentleman's clubs in the area. They flourished silver-headed walking sticks that looked expensive and were stouter than the ones used by Englishmen. He tried to extract Grey Cloak's sword but it jammed; the tip of the old blade had probably been slightly bent during its last use, and in his haste he had neglected to clean it. He made it another block and then the searing pain forced him to stop to catch his breath and let the creeping darkness clear from his vision. He leaned against a post like a gentleman recovering from too many shots of whiskey and looked back as surreptitiously as he could.

The two Russians were still coming. They looked formidable, if thick-headed: if Grey Cloak had been a rapier, these men were bludgeons. They would strike quickly, grab the book, and run. Once on the Embassy grounds, they would be on foreign soil.

He staggered on, but they were closing faster than he could advance. He needed a *ruse de guerre.*

There was a small alley twenty yards ahead which would serve. Alleys were often packed with all sorts of discarded oddments that might provide camouflage. He glanced behind. The two men had picked up their pace but not enough to call attention to themselves.

He slogged to the alley entrance, stopped briefly to catch his breath, then ducked in. Quickly scanning the narrow lane, he saw what he wanted—a pile of rags, awaiting the weekly call of the ragman. They would eventually be turned into printing paper, but for now they constituted a refuge.

He found two five-foot strips of discarded thatching that had probably come from a Tudor building at the alley's far end. He took off the bloody cloak and wrapped it around the bundles, then leaned his scarecrow against the far wall and placed the hat atop a rotten melon.

BOMBPROOFED

Viewed from behind, it gave a fair approximation of a man with a bad wound doubled over in pain, but the illusion would only fool his pursuers for a few seconds. He took a deep breath and burrowed into the adjacent heap of rags. He could hardly breathe from the alley odors of dead fish, dog droppings, and decaying vegetation. Dirk in hand, he waited with anything but patience.

He heard boots a minute later and some words that he judged to be the Russian equivalent of "We have him." They pointed their heavy walking sticks and advanced down the alley, eyes on the decoy. The derisive laughter of the overconfident accompanied their strides.

"Aaaahhhh!" A wordless, animal cry erupted from the first Russian as Pennywhistle plunged the dirk into his foot with such force that it pinned his boot to the pavement. Pennywhistle sprang from his crouch, snapping a hard jab into the man's testicles as he rose. The man fell forward, clutching his groin and mewling in agony. Pennywhistle silenced him with a chop to the back of his neck, even as his vision darkened in time to the pulsing of his heart.

The second man struck out with his cane. Pennywhistle sidestepped and chopped hard at the man's left wrist, causing him to drop the weapon. He raked the Russian's eyes with the townhouse key, then grabbed the man's left wrist with his right hand, locking it in place. Then he gripped his opponent's index and middle fingers with his left hand and bent them violently back, simultaneously shooting his left leg behind his opponent's and kicking upwards. The man flew off his feet and slammed hard into the cobblestones.

Pennywhistle's breath came in hard rasps and he barely had enough energy to stand. The pain in his back was becoming unbearable; his exertions had probably torn the wound wider and deeper. He tried to mentally stand apart from it; pain was a thing of the mind and such things could be managed. He stumbled out of the alley like a drunk at the end of a bender, but he could see Brooks a block ahead—the sight spurred an unexpected reserve of energy.

He ignored the disapproving stares of those who passed him and ploughed steadily on, just putting one boot ahead of the other. His head swam and images became hazy. He knew the warning signs—he was about to pass out. He lurched across the street, nearly getting struck by two hansoms as he did so. Both drivers cursed what they saw as a drunken derelict. He summoned his last ounce of energy and made it to Brook's door. He banged on it heavily.

Dodson, the club's legendary majordomo and *chargé d'affaires,* answered the door. He looked at the dirty figure with distaste. "Here, now. Clear off! Clear off, you! This is a gentleman's establishment! Be gone; we don't want ruffians soiling our doorstep."

Pennywhistle steeled his gaze and shot fire into Dodson's eyes. His voice was a hoarse whisper but still bristled with the crack of command. "I am a member—Major Thomas Pennywhistle. I've been stabbed. Get Lord Livermore, on the double! Snap to it, damn it."

Dodson responded immediately, too well schooled to the voice of authority to ignore this one. The man might be a stinking mess but he could be telling the truth. His accent was certainly that of a gentleman. "Wait here, sir."

Dodson slipped away and returned a minute later with the club's president. Livermore's patrician face lit with shock and his beetling eyebrows shot skyward. "Pennywhistle, by God! You look like something the cat dragged in then threw up. Damn me, I read about you in the *Times* this morning! Come inside! Come inside!"

Pennywhistle stumbled forward. "Hurt bad. Need help." He saw two Lord Livermores.

BOMBPROOFED

Livermore yelled for several gentlemen and together they carried him inside and upstairs to one of the club's bedrooms. Pennywhistle was barely conscious. Still, his second death looked likely to be postponed. He sighed heavily and thought of Castlereagh in Vienna. The room swirled, the last trace of color fled his face, and everything went black.

Chapter Twenty-Four

"The outfit becomes you, my dear," said a delighted Lady Leith. "The jaunty look suits you, although I am certain that some old prunes will find it startling. It is stylish as well as practical. Who knows, you may establish a new fashion trend. We should go for a ride in Hyde Park and test people's reactions."

Sammie Jo smiled in relief. Señora Castillo, the dress maker, had said it was a Spanish riding habit. The style had developed during the Peninsular War to make it easier for women to ride as men did, yet remain modest and feminine. The war in Spain had been brutal, and women had fought alongside male partisans to rid the country of Napoleon's soldiers. It was little seen in London but well known in Madrid. The bottom half of the habit resembled something worn by Turkish janissaries; military-inspired clothing was very popular with women just now. The black trouser legs were exceptionally wide and billowed like harem pantaloons; when the legs were brought together they merged to give the appearance of a long skirt.

Sammie Jo wore a short black top above the trousers. It was closely fitted in the manner of the Spencer Jacket popularized by regiments of British Light Dragoons. Beneath the jacket, she sported a white blouse with a jabot, and a purple sash circled her waist. A pair of black leather boots extended to mid calf. A stiff-brimmed circular black hat with red beads surrounding the low crown completed the outfit.

Sammie Jo decided she would model it for Thomas this evening, along with two of the dresses. The formal evening gown she would not reveal until just before they departed for the Palace of St. James. Castillo and her legions of assistants had performed prodigies of labor in getting the dresses ready in less than 24 hours.

Here came the Señora with the important dress, the one she would wear at the Prince Regent's Ball. She gasped in awe. She would be a fairy princess wearing it! "Lady Pennywhistle," she said under her breath. At their finest, those Baltimore harpies who had mocked her would look like broken-down washerwomen by comparison.

"What do you think of it, my lady?" said Señora Castillo. Sammie Jo knew she was being flattered by the premature use of the title, but she enjoyed it nonetheless.

"I love it! I love it! What do you think, Margaret?"

"You will the belle of the ball, of that I am sure. I warn you, my dear, that every eye will be fixed upon you. The women will be jealous and the men will be fascinated. Your husband is supposed to be the object of attention, but it is you who will be talked about. Still, we cannot be absolutely sure how brightly you will sparkle until you try the dress on."

"Coming right up!" Sammie Jo took the outfit from the well pleased señora and headed into the dressing area.

Lady Leith was saving a surprise for Sammie Jo. Lovely though the dress was, it lacked one thing to complete it. Her surprise had been a gift from her husband, but he would approve of her passing it on to someone she considered as a daughter-in-law. She loved having Sammie Jo, Thomas, and his entourage at her home. She even enjoyed the parrot's exclamations. She had been terribly lonely since her husband had passed, and had no one upon whom to shower the attentions of her generous heart. It had been a long time since she had felt both wanted and needed.

Sammie Jo's honesty and directness touched her. Though she was as tough as a pine knot and could handle herself in the woods, traversing the minefields of British society was another matter entirely. There were a thousand things of which she was unaware that could damage her and her husband's future. She could detonate a social land mine without even being aware that it had exploded.

"How do I look?" said Sammie Jo euphorically, returning from the dressing chamber.

Lady Leith's eyes widened. "Perfect! Turn around so that I may see the train."

The train had occasioned quite a bit of discussion. Sammie Jo wanted the train short to allow ease of movement, while Lady Leith had argued for a longer one to add to the dignity of the dress. Castillo had suggested a compromise: a medium-length train but with more ornamentation. As Sammie Jo completed her turn, Lady Leith knew that Castillo had been right. Reluctantly, Castillo had also added a refinement suggested by the practical American lady and approved by the Dowager Countess. The dress had two lace-trimmed slits at the bottom, each only about three inches long. They would facilitate walking, but also expose a bit of ankle. Castillo hoped no one would be scandalized by it, but the two ladies seemed to find the whole thing vastly amusing. She had to admit the American lady had beautifully shaped legs and a graceful stride that showed off their athleticism.

Sammie Jo seemed to glow, a living jewel in a setting of silken gold. The silk had a subtle floral pattern that added panache to the dress. The soft fabric shimmered, complementing her honey-blonde hair, tanned skin, and cornflower-blue eyes. A pale complexion was preferred by the elite, but Sammie Jo's tan set off her blonde hair more strikingly than pallid skin would have.

Her shoulders were bare—another unwritten rule for Court dresses, along with trains. Her scooped neckline was modest enough, yet left no doubt of the prominent bosom beneath. Three gold bands of expensive French lace formed a "V" that ran from her bust line to the high waist of the dress. The sleeve tops were puffy and covered with thin lace that extended to the elbow. She wore long white gloves, yet another Court requirement, and on her long arms they were elegance personified.

Her hair was tucked under a white muslin turban. It had a red rosette in front, and a single ostrich feather draped itself gently over the right side. Just enough hair showed at the top and sides to perfectly frame her strong-featured face. Her embroidered blue silk slippers resembled those of a ballerina. Though they had only one-inch heels, in them she stood slightly over six feet. "You are a goddess, Sammie Jo. The Prince Regent may not be able to restrain himself. But I think one quelling glance from your eyes will chill his blood faster than the slap I used."

"Tom warned me twice about that. I'm prepared!"

Both women laughed.

"My dear, your appearance is perfect in every way, save one. You lack jewelry. The current styles do more than frame a lady's face and décolletage, they are intended to showcase a necklace and earrings. I believe I have just the items to complete your attire, and I would like to gift them to you for your very own." She walked over to the small table and picked up her purse to draw out stunning examples of the jeweler's art. She fastened the necklace around Sammie Jo's neck and a pair of screw-on back earrings to her graceful earlobes. Sammie Jo looked in the mirror, and was speechless.

The necklace contained three large emeralds and two smaller ones. The larger stones were set in small gold circles and placed at the bottom and sides of the necklace to form a sparkling "V." The smaller stones were positioned on either side of the rear clasps. It was simple, elegant, and stunning.

Each earring contained a single ruby.

Lady Leith stood back and her eyes grew wistful. "This combination was my husband's favorite. I have always treasured it, but it looks far better on you than it did on me."

"Oh, Margaret, I can't accept these! These are the most beautiful things that I have ever seen, but I could never rob you of a link to someone loved and lost. I..."

Lady Leith's eye's brimmed. "Nonsense, my dear. My husband would have liked you, and it is time to pass the torch. Look closely at the emeralds. They are exactly the same color as your husband's eyes."

"You're right about that." Sammie Jo slowly caressed the emeralds. "Thank you—thank you so much."

"You can thank me best by wearing these proudly and showing all those old buffaloes at Court what style and grace really mean."

Sammie Jo heard shouting at the shop's front door and wondered who was disturbing one of the most splendid days of her life. She looked at Lady Leith in consternation, and they both marched out of the fitting salon and into the business end of the store. They saw an out-of-breath little man dressed in the livery of some great lord, talking rapidly to the shop's senior assistant.

"Lady Leith—I said—Is she here? Is she here? It is urgent!" panted the man.

"I am Lady Leith. Who dares cause such an unearthly commotion?"

"I beg your pardon, my lady." He touched his hat in deference. "I am sent by Lord Livermore. Brabington is my

BOMBPROOFED

name. Major Pennywhistle said you and his wife would probably be here. He's been hurt, attacked by someone. He is at Brooks, and Lord Livermore said you should send someone along."

"Send someone? Are you out of your head?" demanded an indignant Sammie Jo. "I'll go myself, faster than a greased otter over a waterfall. How bad is he?"

The fire in her eyes and voice frightened Brabington. He struggled to compose a reply.

"Come on, you pasty-face pipsqueak!" She grabbed him by the collar and abandoned any trace of her new-found refinement. "Speak up!"

"Ma'am, I... uh... well, I... uh..." Brabington stuttered. "It is my understanding that he had to be carried inside Brooks, but a physician is attending to him at this very moment. He is in good hands, ma'am."

Lady Leith took charge and addressed herself to Brabington. "Major Pennywhistle's man Gabriel is outside with our carriage. Alert him as to what has occurred and tell him that we will be out shortly. I want *you* to proceed to my townhouse at number 7, Portland Street, and convey your message to Grimsby, my butler. Tell him to summon the family physician and proceed forthwith to Brooks. Tell him to bring Sergeant Major Dale along as well. Have you got that?"

"I do, my lady—you may rely upon me." With that, he touched his hat deferentially and shot out of the store like a mouse chased by a cat.

"How fast can we get there, Margaret?" said Sammie Jo, her anxiety making her lilting voice sound strained.

"In fifteen minutes, but no women are allowed in the club."

"Fuck that!"

"I thought that might be your answer! I'm coming, too. But you can't go like that. How fast can you change?"

Sammie Jo dashed back into the dressing room and reappeared two minutes later in the riding habit, tapping a riding crop impatiently against her side. She and Lady Leith raced out of the shop. Gabriel had the carriage ready. Since he already had wide knowledge of horses, he had wanted to increase his usefulness by training as a coachman. The coach was a large four-wheeled affair pulled by four horses and seating six. It was colored blue and gold and had the Leith Arms painted on the doors.

"We need to get to Brooks posthaste!" exclaimed Lady Leith. Then it hit her—Gabriel had no idea how to do so.

"My lady, I'd love to oblige, but..."

"Never mind," said Lady Leith decisively. "Get inside, Sammie Jo." She jumped up on the coachman's seat. "Move over, Gabriel—I'm driving!" She grabbed his whip, cracked it hard, and the horses shot forward.

Chapter Twenty-Five

"*Waaaah! Waaaah! Waaaah!*" Gabriel blew the long carriage horn in staccato bursts at five-second intervals. The discordant blasts were unlike the clarion sound an experienced coachman would have produced, but they accomplished the instrument's mission of telling everyone to get out of the way. "Move! Move! Move!" Gabriel alternated shouting with blowing. He was not sure if perhaps his strong, deep voice worked better than the horn.

Lady Leith's carriage careened through the side streets of London, swaying so violently that it frequently seemed on the verge of capsizing. When they encountered a jam of foot, wagon, carriage, and cart traffic, Lady Leith reined in the horses and weaved expertly through the muddle. There were some near misses, and shouts of confusion, anger, and consternation followed the carriage. Street urchins hurled rotten vegetables at them and several dogs commenced a chase.

Gabriel noted Lady Leith's face seemed to have shed decades. Her expression was wild with youthful glee and she wore a grin. "I have not had so much fun in years!" she yelled as she cracked the whip.

Sammie Jo stuck her head out of the carriage window and watched the unfamiliar city fly by. Some of the buildings were of fine Portland stone or Flemish brick, new and grand. Others were decayed and seedy. Haberdasheries, poultry shops, and the stalls of fishmongers were hard by nobleman's mansions, in no particular order, and, like so much of London, appeared to be the result of chance rather than planning.

She would normally have relished a wild ride, but worry over her husband's injuries furrowed her brow and constricted her chest. Who would want to harm him, and why? He was home now, not in enemy country! A rotten apple flew through the carriage window, just missing her head. She angrily picked it up and threw it back at the costermonger who'd tossed it. It hit him square in the face and, in spite of her worry, she laughed.

When the carriage hit Pall Mall, a much wider thoroughfare, the vehicle accelerated to 13 miles an hour. The four horses pulled for all they were worth and flecks of white formed at the corners of their mouths. They roared round the corner onto St. James, an area of expensive gentlemen's clubs where no dilapidated buildings were allowed. Quite a number of cabinet ministers lived in the area as well. Sammie Jo was impressed and wished she had paid more attention to her husband's discourse on architectural styles. She wondered which of the buildings was Brooks. As if to answer her, Lady Leith pulled back hard on the reins and bellowed "Whoa!" like a cavalry sergeant. The carriage jerked to an abrupt halt.

Brooks occupied an entire street corner. It was a neoclassical cube composed of four stories of sand-colored stone, with large white Ionic columns and huge bow windows on the first floor. Sammie Jo watched a short man in a black tailcoat slowly descend the steps in front. Every step seemed an exercise in either dignity or constipation. His unflappable expression suggested that a hurtling carriage grinding precipitously to halt was an everyday occurrence. At the same time, she saw a grey horse with a lone rider in scarlet come bounding up to the entrance steps. The rider reined the horse to a halt and quickly dismounted. It was Dale! Thank God!

"May I help you, ma'am?" said the doorman to Lady Leith. His manner was genteel yet faintly condescending. His eyes then noted the Leith arms on the carriage door and he stood just a little straighter; coaches with armorial bearings were always taken more seriously than those that lacked them.

Lady Leith's eyes grew imperious, matching the tone of her voice. "You are Dodson, are you not?"

"I am indeed, ma'am. How might I assist you?"

"I am Lady Leith and I recognized you from my late husband's description; he was a member for many years. I was sent an urgent message from the club president to come at once. Major Pennywhistle, my godson, is inside and badly injured. His wife is with me. Please convey us to him immediately."

"I am sorry, milady, but no women are allowed in the club, and I have not received any instructions to the contrary from Lord Livermore. Is there someone else you could send? Perhaps the sergeant major."

Sammie Jo flung open the carriage door, jumped onto the marble steps, and marched straight up to Dodson. The air near her shimmered with anger and she brandished the riding crop menacingly.

Gabriel followed at a discreet distance.

Dodson stared in shock as the amazon advanced on him. She was beautiful, but the furious expression on her face caused him to shiver slightly. She was dressed in a stunning black outfit, the like of which he had never seen. He prided himself on never being surprised, but he was now.

"What the hell is wrong with you, you jackass? My husband's lying deathly ill inside and needs my help!"

Sammie Jo moved closer and towered over him. "We ain't got a month of Sundays! You either take us there direct or..." —in a flash, she extracted her husband's spare dirk from a red and gold reticule that hung from her right arm and flourished it boldly—"I turn you into a gelding!" She thrust it directly at his groin and stopped only a quarter inch from its destination.

Dodson froze. The woman was insane.

"Easy now, ma'am, easy," came the calm voice of Dale as he put a restraining hand on Sammie Jo's wrist. "No need to be hasty. I am sure Dodson here will see reason."

Dale looked at Dodson and his voice changed to that of a seasoned NCO speaking to a new recruit. His tones became patient, almost silky: yet full of menace. "Mrs. Pennywhistle made a request, as did Lady Leith. I would advise you to honor them, sir, both for the continued retention of your masculinity as well as your current employment. Major Pennywhistle is the man of the hour and I am sure that you are a patriot. Why would you deny a wounded hero the comfort of loved ones?"

Gabriel and Lady Leith moved alongside Sammie Jo and Dale, and four pairs of eyes bored into Dodson's. Dale released his grip on Sammie Jo's wrist and the dirk edged a fraction of an inch closer to Dodson's privates.

"Yes, yes, yes," Dodson said, in a voice that sounded several octaves higher than its usual baritone. "I will take you all there. Follow me."

"Where is Grimsby?" Lady Leith queried Dale.

"Dr. Hewes was not in his surgery, and Grimsby went to fetch him from a house call in Piccadilly. I am sure he will be here shortly."

The four of them followed Dodson up the steps. He opened the large doors into the main foyer. The quartet stepped through and waited for directions. "He is in one of

BOMBPROOFED

the guest bedrooms on the third floor, my lady," said Dodson meekly.

Sammie Jo gazed about and gasped. *No wonder gentlemen spend so much time in these places*. A magnificent winding marble staircase yawned at the far end of a vast foyer. There were spacious landings on each of the four floors; every one featured a toga-clad bust on a plinth in front of a portrait that she guessed represented a past club president. The wallpaper was pear green and maroon, reflecting the general color scheme.

Lady Leith recalled what she had been told about the place by her husband. There were four huge rooms on the ground floor: one for dining, one for lounging and reading, and the last two, much the largest, were for gambling.

A few well-heeled members strolling by froze at the sight of Sammie Jo. Gentlemen of refinement and wealth though they were, they looked at her like thunderstruck schoolboys.

Lady Leith spoke to the transfixed gentlemen. Her tone was commanding yet compassionate. She understood her audience and addressed them like long-lost relatives ."Most of you know who I am and many remember my late husband. I beg your leave to walk your premises on an errand of mercy. I respect your rules, but I also appeal to your humanity.

"You may have heard that a gravely wounded man was brought in: it this fine lady's husband, my godson. You have all seen excerpts of Major Pennywhistle's dispatches on *The Times'* front page, and it is my belief that he was attacked by men who are no friends of this kingdom. He lies abed upstairs and we have come to escort him home. I appeal to all those who love Britannia to speed us on our way."

Her speech was magic. Disapproving glances changed to ones of concern. Sammie Jo had thought she understood men, but realized she was a complete amateur compared to

Lady Leith. Appealing to men's honor could be even more effective than charming or threatening them—so long as the men were indeed honorable.

A small delegation of supplicants advanced on Lady Leith. A spare man, who appeared to be their leader, spoke. "I am Sir John Summers, my lady, and was pleased to read of your godson's exploits. I have only met him a few times, since he is an infrequent visitor here, but have always found him agreeable, though he repeatedly declined my requests for a game of whist. It distresses me that he has been wounded and it would please me if I and my friends could assist you in some small way. Let it never be said that we at Brooks are not ardent patriots."

Lady Leith smiled ever so pleasantly. Sammie Jo was impressed. You really could get more flies with honey than vinegar, a lesson that she had never quite learned.

"I thank you, Sir John. His wife and I must speak to the physician in attendance to make certain his life is in no danger and to learn whether or not he can safely be moved. Your kind hearts and broad backs would be most welcome if he is up to being transferred to my carriage."

Sammie Jo in turn smiled coyly toward the younger men. Their eyes were chivalrous, but bulging breeches betrayed a different intent. She knew a man's little general often planned most of his strategy. All to the good, if lust guaranteed their help.

"I will show you the way," said Sir John. Six gentlemen followed as escorts.

Sammie Jo found Pennywhistle sitting up in bed sipping a cup of steaming coffee. His back was to her and he was talking animatedly with a ruddy-cheeked older gentleman, who looked to be a physician, judging by the distinctive bag next to him. Her husband sounded composed, but that could be misleading, since he seldom gave voice to pain.

BOMBPROOFED

An uncertain half smile of relief crossed her lips—a full one would not be justified until she knew more. She was about to dash to his bedside when Lady Leith restrained her with a gentle touch on the shoulder. "Just listen for a moment," she said. The rest of the party followed the suggestion as well.

Pennywhistle's blood-soaked shirt lay crumpled on a side chair. The young gentlemen noticed it and exchanged glances of admiration. It must have been quite a fight!

"I counsel bed rest for the next few days," said the physician gravely, "and after that no heavy activity for a week. No fencing practice—violent motions could pop the stitches. I advise drinking plenty of tea, a good purge, and a bleed at least once a day. Several drops of honey in the tea would be invigorating. And I recommend Hopson's New Patent Pills once a day."

The doctor noted Sammie Jo's arrival with a quick nod, then continued, "I would also recommend a respite from..."—he groped for the right words—"...the joys of love, for a week or two. That can place undue strain on a constitution weakened by wounds or illness. The body must devote all of its energies to healing."

Sammie Jo made a face that was half sneer, half glower. She doubted her husband would follow many of the prescriptions. He disliked tea and opined that bleeds and purges weakened the body's ability to heal. He had studied medicine years ago, and, rather than trusting physicians, his knowledge made him suspicious of them. He understood how little they really knew.

"Have your wife check the stitches from time to time for any signs of suppuration. I will call upon you to check them myself, the day after tomorrow. The wound should heal fully in a few weeks and you will have another scar to add to your already considerable collection."

Phelps spoke in the voice of scholarly concern. "I know your investiture is tomorrow, but I think the ceremony should be postponed. I feel certain that the Prince Regent would understand and would be agreeable to other arrangements. Well, that is all for now. You have visitors, and I am sure their felicitations will boost your spirits. I know you can walk, but I would strongly advise a stretcher."

He shook Pennywhistle's hand, picked up his bag, and discreetly exited the room, knowing the presence of loved ones would do his patient more good than his continued attendance.

"I declare, Tom Pennywhistle, I can't let you out of my sight for even a single day without you getting into trouble."

Pennywhistle's customary alertness had temporarily failed him. He turned in surprised joy when he heard Sammie Jo's voice.

She thought he looked gaunt and pale, but nonetheless he greeted her heartily. "Thought you'd never get here. Some unfriendly chaps decided to pick a fight and I could not move fast enough to get out of the way." The contrast between his appearance and voice told her that he was in a bad way.

She ran to the bed and threw her arms around him. She hugged him as tightly as a nun embracing a reliquary chest filled with saint's bones. "Owww..." he muttered. "Sorry, the cut is a little tender."

"Damn, Tom, I just wasn't thinking. I been so worried..."

He put a finger softly to her lips. "No—love is the best medicine of all, even if slightly painful. Just the sight of you is worth a regiment of doctors and a battalion of pills." He hugged her gently and whispered, "I got the book. That's what's what they were after."

He kissed her deeply and felt the healing power of her love begin to flow through him. He had never met anyone as vibrantly alive as Sammie Jo.

Bombproofed

The fire in the kiss caused Sir John to blush. He felt he should not look but could not help himself. He had only known the rehearsed motions of courtesans and had never experienced anything close to passionate love. There was a fierce power in the kiss, something beyond the authority of mere lust. He shuddered inwardly when he thought of the arranged marriage that awaited him in a few weeks.

Pennywhistle let go of Sammie Jo reluctantly. He took a deep breath and pulled himself slowly to his feet. He grimaced for a second as pain battered the doors of consciousness, but he ignored it and stood fully erect. He forced a smile onto his face, which fooled the young gentlemen but alarmed Lady Leith, Gabriel, and Dale. They knew that false smile far too well; its width was directly proportional to the pain that it masked.

He addressed the young gentlemen in his friendliest manner. "Good sirs, I thank you and the club for your hospitality. I presume you are waiting to be stretcher bearers, but I assure you that will not be necessary. I plan on departing under my own sail—I do not require a set of oars."

Sir John spoke on behalf of his friends. "Are you sure of that, Major? It would be an honor for us to carry a hero to his carriage." His friends smiled or nodded agreement.

"Quite sure, Sir John. I promise you a game of whist when I am better. You are mistaken, however, if you think me a hero. I have been blessed with good fortune, good superiors, and good assignments. I would caution you against believing too much of what is being said about me in the newspapers. It is mostly stuff and nonsense calculated to increase circulations."

Sir John gave a knowing smile. "Of course, Major." It was clear he believed not a word about Pennywhistle's ordinariness and instead regarded his modesty as becoming of a real hero. "We will take our leave of you now, sir. But please, if you need anything in the next few days, do not hesitate to let me know. One thing—and forgive my impertinence in asking—but we are all curious: are you going to attend the Prince Regent's levee tomorrow afternoon?"

Pennywhistle groaned inwardly at the thought, but spoke confidently. "I assure you I will be there, Sir John. I have no doubt people downstairs are already wagering on whether I will attend, but I would strongly advise you not to bet against me. My wife is to be a lady, and no power on Olympus will delay that outcome."

Sir John replied gallantly, "With such a lovely wife, it surprises me not at all that you would make such Herculean efforts. Now—Major, ladies—we will take our leave of you." They all bowed deeply and almost in unison.

Sammie Jo suppressed a chuckle. It began to dawn on her that the newspapers had created a public Tom Pennywhistle that might be different from the private one. He would be different things to different people: each newspaper reader would see something which conformed to his expectations.

"Thank you for your concern and kindness," said Sammie Jo. She spoke slowly and enunciated carefully, hoping her backwoods accent was not too much in evidence.

As soon as they were gone, Pennywhistle slumped slightly. Sammie Jo and Gabriel moved to him and supported him under each arm. He leaned heavily on them. "Now don't try to be the hero from the newspapers, Tom." said Sammie Jo."Tell me honest—can you make it to the carriage?"

He looked her deeply in the eyes. "I have never seen any woman look as splendid as you do right now. The heat you are generating could bring a dead man back to life. Damn right, I can make it to the carriage." He tried to smile, but it did not quite come off. "Anyway, we need to get out of here. I have some urgent reading to do when I get home. I—"

"Shush! Don't even think about that, Sugar Plum. I don't want you frying your brain with a puzzle when you should be sleeping. But I ain't gonna argue right now. Ready?" she said.

"Ship shape and Bristol fashion, ready to depart the harbor!" He again tried to laugh but a spike of pain cut it off. He put one foot tentatively in front of the other for a few steps. Sammie Jo and Gabriel took as much weight off his feet as they could, and after four yards the trio had developed a rhythm to navigate the long, winding stairway. He kept his face impassive, but Sammie Jo knew that he did so with great effort.

He muttered to her half way down, "I'm damned if I'm going to drink tea and cancel my fencing appointment! Bloody quack—told me the night air was bad, too, and that all the windows should be shut. Keep 'em open tonight and let the breeze in!"

It took them twenty minutes to reach the bottom of the stairs. They had to stop a few times when his pain became too great, although he gave no verbal exclamation. A crowd gathered in the foyer to watch.

The men were riveted by three things: an injured hero being heroic; the spectacle of women traversing sacred ground; and a remarkably beautiful female sporting an extraordinary outfit. The older men were focused on the first two, but the younger crowd was mesmerized by the third.

The young blades were used to polite women—dainty steps, studied shyness, and demure bust-lines were their hallmarks. They had never seen an Amazon whose stride radiated power, hips undulating gracefully and chest outthrust. They all wondered where Pennywhistle had found such an incredible creature.

Sammie Jo and Gabriel bundled Pennywhistle into the carriage. Pennywhistle's eyelids drooped and he was asleep as soon as they laid him on the long cushion. Sammie Jo looked at him and knew her kind of care would serve much better than that prescribed by the doctor.

She was eager to get him home, but reminded herself that it was time to start comporting herself like a lady. She wanted to do her man honor and show that, while untutored, she understood the importance of gratitude.

She told Lady Leith to wait and marched back inside. Lord Livermore and a crowd still stood in the foyer. All eyes focused on her and she felt fear for a moment.

She knew that she should try to imitate Lady Leith's diction and phrasing, but an inner voice proclaimed that a simple message honestly delivered counted for much more than the manner of its presentation. *Just tell the truth!* She remembered her husband's admonition that the only speeches that the British liked were short ones.

"My lords and gentlemen: I thank you for saving my husband's life. I will never forget your kindness and I owe you a debt. I am new to this country, as you can tell from my speech, but I am learning that the British have hearts as generous as they are brave. I thank you for welcoming me into your fine club." She concluded with a curtsey, something she had been practicing for the Prince Regent's Ball.

There was a long silence. She worried that she had done something badly wrong. Then one man started to clap, and then another and another. The crowd erupted in clapping and there were loud shouts of "Brava! Brava!"

She flashed them a smile that reflected the genuine warmth of a personal triumph: she had acted as a lady and no one had seen through her pretensions. She could not help noticing that their approval was best reflected in their nether regions. Playing the lady had not affected her appeal to the opposite sex.

She made one final curtsy in acknowledgment, then walked out the door, making sure her stride was slow and graceful. It was, but it accentuated the natural roll of her broad hips and the bewitching sway of her muscular buttocks. Though she meant her deportment to be genteel, it had the opposite effect.

"Remarkable woman!" exclaimed the Earl of March, whose affinity for eccentricity was well known. "Damned odd accent, but bloody good sentiments spoken well and honestly. Where did she get that outrageous outfit? Have to admit it looked splendid."

"No idea, but..."—Livermore took out a green silk handkerchief and slowly mopped the beads of perspiration from his forehead—"if my wife finds out, she will surely demand something similar. Dare say all the ladies at Court will, too. I fear all manner of women will soon be demanding entrance into our club as well. Can't allow that. Must make that very clear. Will have to put it about that we made a one-time exception for a national hero."

Both nodded in agreement about the preservation of male privilege. Sir John moved closer and spoke quietly to Livermore, voicing the spirit of the crowd. "My Lord, is it just me, or has the temperature risen twenty degrees?"

Livermore flashed a half-smile of acknowledgment. "It most assuredly is not just you! I need a drink!"

Chapter Twenty-Six

Boooooom! The explosion on the Viennese street was spectacular: plenty of flame, thunder, and cobble stone shaking. Bits of carriage, upholstery, wood, and Count Blois flew forward. The footman died, but the coachman was thrown clear, although bleeding badly from a large wooden splinter in the arm. The bleeding horses reared, bucked, and soon shattered the damaged yoke that held them. They broke free and dashed madly down the street. Von Steinwehr felt bad about the horses.

The little stand selling apples that the count stopped at every day had been smashed, but its two owners were alive—blackened with soot and speechless, but nonetheless breathing. People milled about in confusion. Von Steinwehr wondered if he was overdoing it with the edelweiss flowers that he had glued to the bottom of the portmanteau containing the bomb, but the local constabulary might miss them unless they were spectacularly obvious.

Von Steinwehr's expression of satisfaction changed to one of alarm as he realized that he had been a fool to attempt a daylight killing in a public place. He had weighed the risks carefully but, like many people who were compulsive planners, he had neglected to allow for the random element, chance inserting a wholly unexpected obstacle in his well conceived design.

Bombproofed

The stubby constable had no business being where he was. Von Steinwehr knew the patrol times of the local *gendarmerie* and this man was not following routine. Some sixth sense had caused him to look in von Steinwehr's direction at exactly the right moment. Von Steinwehr's face was shielded by a broad-brimmed hat and he wore civilian clothing, hidden by a royal blue cloak, but, his great height could never be concealed.

The constable made quick deductions and blew his whistle to summon help. He stopped half a minute later and yelled in von Steinwehr's direction, "Halt, halt!"

Von Steinwehr should have watched the results of his handiwork through a spyglass. He did the only sensible thing: he ran. He could have killed the constable, but a crowd had begun to form. Five burly members of the city watch gathered close to the constable, obeying his summons. Only a fool challenged six-to-one odds.

He ran uphill toward a narrow, twisting lane from which several small alleys branched off: his pursuers could easily take a wrong direction. The lane led to one of the city's many promenades, where he had left his horse. He was an idiot not to have come on horseback in the first place, yet it had been satisfying to have a front row seat for the little drama of destruction that he had orchestrated.

He ducked into the lane and peered round the corner. He breathed heavily and willed his racing heart to slow down. He glanced down the hill and saw the constable and his men closing fast on his position. Then the mania exerted its influence and logic departed. His fevered brain told him the men could not possibly catch him and he permitted himself a few moments to consider how his dreams were playing out.

Blois was his final victim. All of the experts who had opposed the restoration of Reichenau were dead. He just needed the code key to complete his plans and bring

Alexander into his corner once and for all. Vanity had almost undone him, but in the manic stage of his disorder he was prone to high energy, racing thoughts, and an overwhelming confidence that every enterprise he undertook would be completely successful.

He was also given to obsessions, and that had worked to his advantage in the preparation of the bomb that had dispatched Blois. He considered it a minor mechanical triumph and had chosen a new method of death because the newspapers would fixate upon something dramatic. He had devoted two full nights to linking the fuse, a flint and striker, and the clock's chiming gears. He concealed the device in an expensive portmanteau marked with seals indicating the House of Hapsburg.

The explosion had been preceded by five chimes that were the first notes of "Pop goes the Weasel": probably the last sounds that Blois had heard. Another detail the newspapers would publicize.

He heard the constable's strident whistle again, much closer this time. It shattered his daydreaming and he broke into a run. His manic energy speeded his pace even as it excited his memories of the day leading up to this present moment.

He had employed an actor to deliver the bombs, though the actor believed the cargo perfectly innocent. The actor had represented himself as a certain Captain von Danniken, whom he closely resembled. He styled himself as a personal representative of the emperor. He had said the documents within were of great importance and must be handled with the utmost discretion and care.

Blois's men never argued with a fancy uniform and knew that the count often dealt with confidential materials; this cargo did not seem out of the ordinary.

Bombproofed

Count Blois was a man of precise habits who had departed the palace at precisely noon, exactly as expected. Routine was the lifeblood of bureaucrats, and he had used that in setting the bomb's timer.

He had watched for Blois from the palace steps, 200 feet away from the carriage. The count was a short, dapper man who walked with a purposeful air—a sunny, charming individual who loved many things about life. Reichenau's rebirth was not one of them. The count owed his title to Napoleon, but had adroitly switched loyalties like his mentor Talleyrand when the Bourbons returned. He might serve a new sovereign, but he was still guided by his old master's ideals of a more united Germany.

Von Steinwehr knew the route the carriage would take because he had spent two weeks observing his mark. He had ridden on ahead to be close to the expected site of the explosion. Detonation had occurred at the edge of the Ringstrasse Marketplatz.

He was glad his calculations had been exact enough that the injuries to the horses would not be fatal. He found the equines attractive because they displayed simple emotions easily understood, and lacked any hint of the guile and double-dealing which cursed humans. He was seriously considering turning Reichenau into the horse breeding capital of Germany.

He felt confidence in his plans, but wondered for the hundredth time if he was losing his humanity. He was getting so caught up in executing the campaign and rejoicing in his successes, that he fretted he was losing sight of the point of the whole thing.

His victims seemed less and less human each time, more like lemmings just needing to be helped over a cliff. He did not see himself as a monster, but each murder skewed one's moral compass a little further toward darkness and made it more and more difficult to resume the path of light.

He wanted to be a proper sovereign for his people and hoped the black taint that he wore like a cloak could be just as easily cast aside. He would be a good and righteous ruler: firm but just, with more emphasis on the just than the firm.

He thought of the bright, smiling faces of his children and the vision reassured him. They were the greatest blessing of all and deserved a good life and a joyous future.

He saw his wife's blue eyes and red hair in his mind and sighed quietly. She shared his dynastic ambitions but was no Lady MacBeth. She would never sleepwalk in an agony of despair—she was more likely to spend the night hours helping him choose administrators for his country. Yes, "country" sounded far better than "palatinate."

He reminded himself that the originators of many great dynasties had committed dark deeds in order to establish them. They, too, had put family first. Look at the family tree of any great royal or house and you invariably discovered that the originator was clever, vicious, and expedient. Founding a dynasty was a bloody business that sometimes required conscience to swallow a mental opiate.

The founder of the House of Hapsburg, Radbot of Kiettegau, had been an extremely rough character who carried out more than a few assassinations and had executed them with less finesse than von Steinwehr. Like the Hapsburgs, von Steinwehr would later hire legions of "historians" to frame his deeds in a virtuous light.

He had done things right: ritual killings, and now bombs. The papers were eating it up. People were constantly talking about his alter ego's identity, goals, and who would die next. It gratified him to see how correctly he had predicted people's reactions because it fueled his sense of superiority over the unthinking masses. He was clearly born to rule.

Bombproofed

He chaffed at having to serve Alexander. He was tired of being a lackey to a master who was ruled by vanity and an insatiable sexuality. He hated pretending that he was slower than his master and feigning amazement when his master came to conclusions that he had reached months ago.

Alexander had vague, grandiose dreams while von Steinwehr had specific, well ordered plans. He also had an iron determination that Alexander lacked. Once he set himself on a course, nothing could sway him from its execution. Alexander was a prisoner of his passions and changed his mind with the frequency of a compass exposed to magnets.

And yet von Steinwehr knew the current mania was triggering in him exactly the sort of dreaming that he hated in Alexander. Logic was always a casualty when the mania was at its height, and Irony reigned supreme.

His flattery of Alexander was succeeding. Von Steinwehr told him that when he ruled Reichenau he would remain his firm and steadfast ally. It was always useful for a small state to have a large one as its patron.

Alexander's outsized ego naturally wanted to believe that he inspired in his minions loyalty that would continue even when they ruled in their own right. Von Steinwehr had no intention of keeping Reichenau a client state beyond the first few years; he planned to forge an independent foreign policy once he was fully established.

The shouts behind him were fading. The manic energy had proved to be his savior, allowing him to outpace his enemies. He reached his horse and put the spurs to her. About the only thing that the Watch could say later was that the man they had chased had been very tall.

Now all he needed was the code book, though the red ledger would be a bonus. He wondered if his hirelings had spotted Thomas Pennywhistle yet. He had no rational way to know what the man looked like, yet his face kept popping up in his dreams. He hated the mania yet trusted it. It brought him visions and dared him to embrace power. Men were usually corrupted by power, but his wife had assured him he was uniquely equipped to use it wisely. He trusted her implicitly.

He fastened a fresh red carnation to his lapel in triumph.

Chapter Twenty-Seven

Sammie Jo gently stroked her husband's hair as he slept. The carriage moved slowly to provide as much comfort as possible for its injured occupant. The prospect of being a lady pleased her, but it meant nothing if attending the ceremony slowed his recovery. But her husband had made a promise, and he would stop at nothing to carry it out. Rather than trying to out-think him, she would have to to nurse him back to a semblance of functionality.

The best medicines were love and rest, but she also had in mind a nostrum that was better than any patent pills or special teas. It was an old Indian remedy made from the bark of the willow tree, ground into a fine white powder, which could be mixed with almost anything. Her father had given it to her for headaches, cuts, and bruises; it reduced swelling and pain. She always kept a pouch of the stuff with her when she went hunting, and she had a sizable quantity in her possibles bag. Thank goodness that she had insisted on bringing all of her hunting paraphernalia to England.

Dr. Hewes, Lady Leith's physician, would probably decry it as backwoods folk medicine, but she did not care. She could mix it in with his coffee, adding a lot of cream and sugar to mask the bitter taste. Unlike the opium in laudanum balls, this substance was not addictive, and one could never develop a tolerance for it that would result in needing increasingly large doses. She had no way of knowing that its active ingredient was salicylic acid; later generations would refine it into aspirin.

Her husband woke up when the carriage reached Lady Leith's townhouse. "We are here," Sammie Jo said. "Let us help you, don't try to be brave."

"Yes, fine, good," he said quietly, the fatigue in his voice evident. "I feel like an old dishrag that has washed too many pans. Can you get some hot water going for the cistern? It would help revive me."

"Sounds like a fine idea, Tom, but I may have to join you. Not sure you can stand on your own. Course, I don't mind that one little bit."

Dale and Gabriel exited the carriage first and Sammie Jo gently helped her husband out and into their arms. He again refused the offer of a stretcher but accepted the use of their shoulders so he could walk after a fashion.

Lady Leith spoke to Sammie Jo after Pennywhistle was out of earshot. "Your plan for his recovery makes perfect sense. A warm loving presence is the only thing that will prevent him from jumping up and dashing about prematurely. And you say this powder has always worked for you? Good. I agree that opening the windows and letting in some fresh air is far better than a sealed room. I will have his best nightshirt laid out but... perhaps he won't need it?"

Sammie Jo replied without embarrassment. "The best nightshirt for a man is a good woman. Ain't no better way to heal a man then pleasuring him, then spooning all through the night."

Lady Leith smiled with approval. "I cannot tell you how many ladies view womanly desires as a curse. And it stuns me that the usual gentlewoman has no idea of how to pleasure a man; most never think to ask their husband what he likes. The idea that a woman should just lie back and be passive is pernicious nonsense. My husband and I enjoyed a fine life in the bedroom and I wish you and Tom the same."

Her expression turned serious. "You wear the glow of love well, Sammie Jo. It is both ineffable and easily recognized. Women will gossip about you because of it, even if you say nothing. They envy that which they cannot have because they do not really understand it. Pay them no mind, smile sweetly, and just say, "My husband and I are very happy."

"Thanks, Margaret. That's good advice. I don't want to say anything stupid tomorrow night."

"You think he will be fit enough for the investiture?" asked Lady Leith with concern.

"It don't matter, Margaret. You and I might try to argue him out of it, but, in the end, he will go, ready or not. Our job is to heal him as much as we can in the time we have available. If you could have the cook get a good pot of coffee going, I'd be much obliged."

"On my way," said Lady Leith.

It took fifteen minutes for Dale and Gabriel to get Pennywhistle to the bedroom. He slipped in and out of consciousness and his feet seemed to move independently of his brain. They laid him on the bed and he was sound asleep as soon as his head touched the pillow.

"I'll take it from here, boys, thanks!" said Sammie Jo. "The hot water should be just about ready. You know how keen he is on being clean. He once told me the thing that struck him as most horrid in battlefield surgery stations was the sheer amount of dirt and filth. Gabriel, can you see to it that a footstool is placed in the shower?"

"Of course, ma'am. I will get right on it, don't you worry none." He was gone in a flash.

She stripped off Pennywhistle's clothing and shuddered when she saw the sword cut; it was far deeper than she had expected. She shook her head as her tightened lips disapproved: typical of him to make light of his wounds. She examined the stitches and they looked expertly done. She checked for pus and found none.

There was a discreet rapping at the door. Sammie Jo covered her husband with a quilt and answered it. It was Lady Leith bearing a silver samovar of steaming coffee. "I wanted to deliver this personally," said Lady Leith, "and I am curious about this special powder."

"Thanks, he is going to need some coffee to wake him enough to make it to the shower," said Sammie Jo. "The wound is a damned sight worse than I thought and has to be causing a lot of pain." She reached down on the table and produced a blue china cup filled with a dusky white powder.

Lady Leith looked at it. "How soon until you see some effect?"

"I'd say real soon, within an hour. Some folks notice effects in a quarter of that time."

"How much are you going to give him?"

"Normally I'd give him two teaspoons but with that wound, I'd say four would be better. I think we will need to use up all of the stuff in that fancy contraption you hold." Sammie Jo accepted the samovar then turned the spigot so some of its contents flowed into a large mug. She dumped the powder in and stirred it energetically with a spoon. She plopped in three cubes of sugar and poured in fresh cream. "That should do it."

"I will instruct the servants to stay off your floor, but do not hesitate to ring if you require anything."

"Thanks, Margaret. He will probably be hungry later on, but for now I want him to rest. I can get him into the shower without any help. I am just going to have him sit and will scrub him good and clean of any blood or gristle. Once back in here, well..." She left the sentence unfinished. Lady Leith nodded in approval.

BOMBPROOFED

"Good luck, Sammie Jo," Lady Leith said as she closed the door. "I will keep my fingers crossed."

Sammie Jo hoisted her husband upright. "C'mon, Tom— good steaming coffee: strong but with a lot of sweetness added in for your pain. And it has a special ingredient."

Pennywhistle's nose twitched as the welcome aroma lured him to consciousness. His eyes blinked open. "Sorry I was out there for just a bit." She put the mug to his lips. He sipped it gratefully and smiled. "Ambrosia!" he said. "But why all the cream and sugar?" Then his face clouded slightly. "Concealing the extra ingredient?"

"It's powder from willow bark, a country remedy that I used a heap back home for bangs and bruises. Drink your coffee and give it a chance to work."

"I have heard of your medicine; used by the Pisacatawy Indians I believe," he murmured. Pennywhistle felt life returning as the sacred substance coursed down his throat. "I'd like another!" Sammie Jo poured some, but this time he sipped it slowly, savoring its blissful message. His eyes continued to brighten.

She provocatively stripped off her clothing and watched his reaction. Even in his fatigued state his ardor was obvious. She needed that energy to get him into the shower. He took her hand and pulled her down toward him.

"No! Not just yet: let's get you cleaned up first."

She helped him to his feet and gripped him firmly under his armpit. "Lean on me, Tom."

"I already do, in so many ways." He winced as the pain hit. She saw his grimace and simply said, "C'mon!"

They hobbled clumsily out the door and down the hall. "Sit down," she told him, pointing to the footstool when they got inside the wide stall. He did so gratefully: even the short walk had tired him. She began to scrub him with a long brush brimming with sandalwood-scented soap, being careful to avoid the stitches. Her strokes were strong yet laced with affection. After a full five minutes she quietly said, "Ready?"

He nodded.

She yanked on the metal pull and a welcome torrent of delightfully hot water splashed over both of them. She sat down next to him and hugged him as the water washed away dirt, pain, and everything but their love for each other. When the idyll ended she saw much less ache in his face.

She got to her feet and grabbed a large, luxurious cotton towel from the rack. She toweled herself dry vigorously then applied the towel to her husband much more gently. She helped him to his feet, noticing he did not lean on her as heavily as before.

He blinked in surprise and managed a half smile. "I do believe that medicine of yours is working. The pain is fading except for an occasional twinge."

They headed back to the bedroom but this time his stride, while slow, was more confident. She unslung her arm from under his and laid him gently on the bed.

"There is one more kind of medicine you need and I got it right here. It's the oldest and best of all but we will have to be careful: I don't want to rupture those stitches. You are going to have to be like a ship in drydock."

She proceeded to wrap his back and chest in a protective carapace of fresh linen, giving him the appearance of a mummy-in-progress, then laid four soft pillows on the bed, braced them in place with the cherry wood bed steps from the sides of the four-poster, and told him to lie down. "This will be your velvet vice," she said with a wicked grin. Bemused, and moving slowly, he shifted position. It was a surprisingly comfortable arrangement, and he felt tensed muscles begin to relax.

BOMBPROOFED

"Now this ain't going to be our usual violent thing. Just lie back, relax, and let me tend to things."

She fondled his manhood gently and it came quickly to the parade attention. She eased herself on to him as smoothly as a silken glove and her motions were long and slow. He moved little in the next five minutes but felt great refreshment nonetheless. She let out a loud cry of ecstasy in the end, but in his fatigued state all that issued forth from him was a long "Ahhhhhh" of satisfaction and a lopsided grin.

He started to say something, but she put a finger to his lips. "Now just sleep. I will be here when you wake up."

"Thank you. You are..." His eyelids grew heavy and he slowly closed them. She stroked his hair twice and he fell fast asleep. She curled up close to him and willed the love and heat from her body to heal him. He murmured once and turned contentedly on his side.

He slept peacefully for the next ten hours. She got up once during the night, plucked the book from his clothing, and hid it carefully. She would permit no concern to oppress his mind for a full day, no matter how loudly he protested. She crawled back into bed and burrowed blissfully under his arm.

She considered herself a huntress, but being a nurse certainly had its compensations.

Chapter Twenty-Eight

The phaeton maneuvered smartly, and under normal circumstances Pennywhistle would have enjoined more speed, but right now a sedate rate of travel was all his back would bear. Named after the mythical Phaeton who had attempted to drive the chariot of the sun and in so doing nearly set the Earth on fire, the lightly sprung open carriage possessed four huge wheels and was dangerous to pilot. With two swift horses pulling it, there was no faster vehicle, and so it became the choice of attention-seeking young bucks with more daring than sense. Gabriel guided the horses expertly. Had he himself driven, the pull of the reins would have ruptured the sutures in his back.

He was on his way to an event that he absolutely could not miss. St. James's Palace now lay only a few blocks away. He quickly checked his Blancpain. Thank God he would make the ceremony—but just barely.

The pain in his lower back felt like dozens of fullers were pounding lumps out of coarse wool. He had refused Lady Leith's offers of laudanum balls because he needed to be clear-headed for his investiture, but he had consented to extra doses of his wife's seemingly magical powder.

The Guide from the Other Side accompanied him, having manifested just after he awoke. The presence showed him how the pain could be quarantined, but warned that that was purely a temporary expedient. A physical penalty would soon

BOMBPROOFED

be exacted for disobeying the verdict of Mother Nature. *Just get me through the day*, he instructed it.

"God damn it! No way in Hell you are going, Tom!" His mind flashed back to the long and tempestuous argument with Sammie Jo that was the reason he was running late. It had been followed by a much shorter one along similar lines with Lady Leith.

"You need at least a week of bed rest before you can even think of leaving this house! Are you that eager to meet death?" Sammie Jo had yelled at him. Though her voiced rippled with anger, he knew that fear for his welfare was its cause.

The expression on her face finally changed to the resigned one worn by a man on a Forlorn Hope. "Well, I had to try—couldn't live with myself if I didn't make the effort! Do try to be careful!"

"Funny you should use the term *meet death*, Hawkeye. I actually have embraced the Grim Reaper. And it is partly because of you that I returned from his grip."

"That's crazy talk, Sugar." Her anger subsided as fears for his sanity consumed her. "It must be the pain speaking. Now get out of them breeches and climb back into bed."

Pennywhistle looked chagrined. "I am afraid that I have kept a secret from you. I did not do so out of distrust but because what happened is nearly impossible to put into words. Shakespeare himself would have had trouble finding the right phrases. Even now, I am just beginning to grasp the long-term implications."

Sammie Jo looked exasperated. "You're not a man who finds himself at a loss for words, Tom, not when you want 'em. And this morning I found out something real important you had not bothered to tell me! That you had been in a big fight at Lady Cockburn's! She called on Lady Leith to find out what had happened at Brooks and spilled the beans! What the hell were you thinking?"

"I thought at the time that you had had enough excitement for one day," Pennywhistle said lamely.

"God damn it, Tom! I maybe many things, but I ain't no weak sister! When you hold things back, I feel like you don't trust me. I had enough of that from my Pa!"

He sat down on the bed and put his arm around her. "I am sorry. I was a fool to underestimate you. I will tell you the whole story of my bout with death. But I warn you, you will see existence differently when I am done."

Sammie Jo's expression turned cynical, yet she knew her husband was a deep man and not prone to fantastic stories. If he had been trying to spare her, he probably had a good reason for doing so.

"I'm all ears, Tom. You know that whatever you say, I will listen."

"Just before I rendezvoused with you at Benedict, my horse stepped on... a bomb. Dale and the others thought me dead because I had no heartbeat and no breath issued from my lips. But death was actually just the beginning. Instead of a brick wall, I found a doorway. The 'sleep of death' turned out to be a misnomer, because what lies on the Other Side is no dream but a vigorous reality. It is a realm permeated with compassion; a place outside of time where fear can gain no foothold, secrecy is set aside, and lost loved ones are no longer lost."

"Moses and Jehovah!" Sammie Jo's expression was a mixture of awe and alarm.

"What is it?"

" It's your eyes! When you started talking about the Other Side, it was like someone lit a miner's lamp behind each eyeball, 'ceptin' the light shining out don't come from any candle I ever seen."

Bombproofed

It took five minutes to settle her down and an hour to tell her the tale. She preferred blunt honesty, so he held nothing back.

Her eyes reflected her varied emotions as his story progressed: curiosity, disbelief, uncertainty, terror, wonderment, and finally acceptance. When he finished, she took several deep breaths to calm herself—her view of the world had indeed been turned upside down.

"Coming from anyone else, I'd say that's the biggest load of horse shit that I have ever heard. But from you, I know that it's God's gospel truth." Her brows knitted and her eyes narrowed as she struggled to understand. "You've mentioned Carlotta a few times, but only in passing. I wanted to believe that your caring for her orphans was a tribute to your concern for the downtrodden rather than an offering to her heart. Did you love her?" Her expression turned fearful, as if she really did not want to hear an answer.

Pennywhistle stroked her hair. "Yes, I did, and I thought that I would never know love again." He saw tears in her eyes and gently wiped them away. "Until I met you! You made me whole again. I was too stupid to know that at first, and needed your forthright ways to make me understand. You need never worry about Carlotta—she gave our marriage her highest endorsement."

Sammie Jo kissed him hard.

"Still think I am crazy, Hawkeye?"

"Maybe just a little for falling in love with a forest filly like me." She smiled wryly. "But that kind of lunacy I welcome. So you ain't afeared of death no more?"

"No, but I still have a healthy respect for it. Let's just say my visit to the Other Side has increased my appreciation of life and its singular joys, you chief among them. That is why I want to attend the ceremony and take you to the ball tonight. You are already a lady in my mind, in all the ways that matter. I am determined that you shall have the formal recognition that is your due."

"That is a wonderful thing to say, Tom, but your pain is a lot more important than giving me some fancy title. You shouldn't go."

"Nonsense, my dear. My life is in no real danger at present and I have an ace in the hole."

"What do you mean?"

He explained about The Guide.

"That is just too strange, Tom. Coming back from the dead and having some... some... *thing* follow you. I feel like I'm hearing one of those scary campfire stories my brother used to tell."

"I assure you, Hawkeye, The Guide is benign. With his help and yours I can make it through this long day. Please, my dear, trust me. I need you to help me make the ceremony on time."

"I will help on the condition that you get back here fast as you can once the ceremony is done and get some bed rest. After that we will have to see if you are up for the ball tonight."

"I can live with that," said Pennywhistle.

"I trust you, but that don't extend to that Guide of yours. And just to be sure you don't get carried away thinking that you are stronger than you are, I hid your special book. You ain't getting it back until you spend a respectable amount of time in bed."

"Damn it, that's blackmail."

"I prefer the term 'leverage.' You always told me that a good commander should have an alternate plan."

"Looks like I taught you too well. "

"And you taught me that a good commander is always mindful of the lives of his men. I have just one man that I care about."

"Oh, very well" sighed Pennywhistle. Now summon Gabriel and help me get into my new uniform. You did say Gieve's delivered it yesterday?"

"Stop fretting, Tom, you sound like an old pea hen. Yes, Gieves came through. Got to admit the coat sure is fancy—it has them big epaulettes with the giant star on them. Though I don't get why it has breeches instead of trousers."

"Breeches are still worn at Court because of tradition."

"Damn, that silly tradition stuff—don't seem to be no end to its reach. All right, then: let's get you saddled up, good sir knight!"

It took Pennywhistle an hour to dress. Most of the time was spent with Lady Leith fussing over how his black silk cravat should be tied. There was a bewildering variety of knots, each making a slightly different fashion statement. She asked Sammie Jo's opinion about each one and they finally agreed that an oriental knot was the most becoming.

Their fussing annoyed Pennywhistle, but he realized that Lady Leith knew better than anyone how to create exactly the right impression at Court. He had seldom worried about his reputation, but now that he was part of a couple and thinking of starting a family, he was coming to see things differently. It bothered him that he was now thinking more like his brother.

"He sure looks fine, don't he Margaret?" said Sammie Jo with pride.

"Nothing like an exceptional uniform on an exceptional specimen of manhood," said Lady Leith. She saw the expression of distaste on Pennywhistle's face. "You'd better get used to compliments, Tom. And don't worry, the phaeton is ready. Glad to see you had enough sense to let Gabriel drive you. You won't be late."

She and Sammie Jo gave him a hearty sendoff, accompanied by stern warnings to limit exertions and return at the earliest opportunity.

Once the phaeton was out of sight, Lady Leith spoke. "I wish we could keep a watch over him."

Sammie Jo chuckled slyly. "I have a plan, Margaret, but I need your help. I got the idea from a play Tom mentioned—*As You Like It*. He said a woman named Rosalind dresses up like a man in order to go where a woman could not. That's what I aim to do. I will see Tom get his knighthood if it's the last thing that I ever do."

"Bless my heart, Sammie Jo, you are a devil! We are much alike!"

"You told me two things, Margaret, and I stitched them together: that I was of a similar height and build to your late husband, and that out of love you still kept his uniforms dusted and the buttons polished."

"Very clever, Sammie Jo! I think the disguise will work. But we will have to do something about your hair, face, and voice. Not to mention the fact that without a formal invitation it will be difficult to gain entrance to St James's."

She tapped her toe as she considered, and her face gradually brightened. "I believe I have answers to all of your problems. It will mean calling in a favor from an old acquaintance, but a hand written note on my stationary should do the trick. One of the advantages of being a societal dragon is that people will do anything to avoid your flames."

She carefully studied Sammie Jo's face. "We shall have to make you an old-fashioned hussar who still ties his hair in a queue. I think one of my old wigs will serve as a source for a dashing handlebar mustache. Makeup will imitate sword scars, and a scarf round the neck concealing a recent injury will explain why you cannot speak. Yes, it can all be done, but we shall have to act quickly."

"Thanks, Margaret. I wish you could come, too."

"One thing, Sammie Jo. Can you ride a fast horse? Ride it like a hussar would?"

"Damn right I can."

"Good! Reginald my groomsman will accompany you and guide you to the palace."

Pennywhistle was only a block from the palace when an officer clad in the blue and grey of the 16th Light Dragoons thundered by, preceded by a servant on a fast grey mare. He rode like a man possessed and Pennywhistle wondered about the object of his urgency. There was something familiar about both the horse and the rider.

CHAPTER TWENTY-NINE

Forty minutes later, Pennywhistle stood inside the heart of St James's Palace, having been guided to his present spot by obsequious lackeys, all eager to say that they had spoken to the man the tabloid *Anti Gallician* had designated as "The Wizard of Washington."

"Major Pennywhistle, His Royal Highness The Prince Regent will be ready for you in two minutes," said an older equerry in an condescending voice suggesting that he had done this often and that the present honoree was nothing special. "There will be trumpets and the Lord Chamberlain's Herald will announce you. Could you please position yourself over there?" He pointed to a small waiting area five paces from the door to the Throne Room.

Pennywhistle would not give the superior little man the satisfaction of betraying excitement. He responded in flat, even tones, "I understand. I have seen this particular play three times already." He nonchalantly opened his watchcase and noted the time as 3:15—things were running ahead of schedule. "Two minutes. I shall hold you to that." The political investitures preceding him had likely been introductory acts, since he was the man of the hour.

Instead of being gratified, he felt annoyed. He disliked being used as a prop for the government propaganda machine. Still, the ceremony was part of his military duties

BOMBPROOFED

and he could not avoid it without staining the honor of the Pennywhistle name. Though the Other Side had taught him that earthly honors were of marginal importance, he had to think of children yet to come and the legacy that he would bequeath to them.

The pain was building again as the effect of Sammie Jo's medication wore off. He decided that he could use the pain as a force to counter the fatigue that made his limbs feel like lead. News of the attack on him had circulated, adding to his already heroic reputation. He hoped he could use it as an excuse to depart quickly after the ceremony had finished. He would say that he was fatigued by his recent spot of unpleasantness.

He had no idea if he could make the ball this evening, but he hated to cheat Sammie Jo of an event that she would remember for the rest of her life. Then he reassured himself that a few hours of solid sleep would do the trick. Years of campaigning had taught him to make do with very little.

Eight trumpeters clad in yellow and black blew a loud fanfare announcing the Prince Regent's summons. Pennywhistle stepped toward the tall archway marking the entrance to the Throne Room. The Chief Herald gave a stentorian bellow: "Major Thomas Pennywhistle."

Pennywhistle squared his shoulders, took a deep breath, and summoned his best expression of grave dignity. He entered the Throne Room with a stately step that was roughly half the standard battlefield step of 75 paces to the minute. The dignified gait gave the audience plenty of time to gape and stare, although they were much too genteel to make it obvious. The factions at court reminded him of galaxies whirling through space, each with its own little planetary clusters whose orbits occasionally coalesced, often collided, and were sometimes crossed by comets like himself.

Command had taught Pennywhistle that you were never more alone than when in a crowd. Many would have been intimidated by the assemblage of the great and mighty but he was not, because inner solitude was an old friend. His father, who had commanded the 23rd Foot, had once told him that "He who would inspire and lead his race must be defended from traveling with the souls of other men, from living, breathing, reading, and writing in the daily, time-worn yoke of their opinions."

Leadership was not about preserving routine, as so many in the crowd were doing just now, but about reaching deep inside one's thoughts to ask the questions that upset one's equanimity. The answers could never be described as commonplace or usual, but were indispensable to being a real leader who would not allow those in his charge to behave as superior lemmings.

He had to admit his surroundings were impressive. The ornate gold throne stood on a small dais under a magnificent maroon and gold canopy at the end of the double-cube room. It looked miles away but the distance was actually just 80 feet. The 30-foot-high red and gold walls were covered with huge portraits, and the 40-foot-wide carpet was a lustrous burgundy. The ceiling was bone white with gold filigree work on the wide border just beneath it.

His peripheral vision detected a tall hussar officer with an impressive medley of scars on his face. It was the same officer of the 16th Light Dragoons who had shot past his carriage earlier. The contours of the face looked familiar. It took a minute for everything to register. When it did, he nearly lost his composure.

He could not decide whether to swear, laugh, or quake at the risk Sammie Jo had taken. He marveled at her ingenuity and wondered how she had gained entrance... Of course! Lady Leith! Her connections were as vast as they were impressive, and she had probably instructed Sammie Jo on how to bluff her way in by using a written note and pantomiming.

His wife's determination to see the ceremony secretly pleased Pennywhistle. It was leadership of the kind that he had considered a few moments before: unconventional thinking so bold that her imposture might just go undetected because not a one of those watching could even conceive of such a thing. Her beauty could not be entirely hidden, but Lady Leith had done a fine job of misdirection through the adroit use of makeup. Thank God Sammie Jo's usually lively face remained sedate, though he detected a hint of amusement in her eyes.

Three men in red robes stood to the left of the throne, and the Lord Chamberlain stood to the right. One of his assistants held the ceremonial sword of state. Pennywhistle had never met the Prince Regent before, but the man matched the description given by the prince's worst detractors, and he was the least impressive ornament in the room. Pennywhistle looked carefully at his eyes, to see if they had much of a glaze. Good, they did not. The prince was at least reasonably sober.

Pennywhistle stopped ten feet away from the throne as he had been instructed to do. The whole thing felt anticlimactic and comical, though it was supposed to be one of the defining moments of his life. Mostly he felt an eagerness to get the whole thing done quickly so he could return home and study the code book. Then he remembered in frustration that Sammie Jo had hidden it. She had probably been right to do so, because sometimes his capacity to obsess exceeded his capacity to attend to his physical needs.

He was proud of the service he had given but needed neither public encomiums nor ostentatious displays to tell him so. Real pride came from within, never from without.

The only praise that mattered was that given by men like General Ross and Admiral Cockburn who had been through the fire.

He kept his expression neutral but felt contempt for the man on the throne whose character was as far from the heroism of the Black Prince as a butter knife was from a dagger. The most perilous things that *he* had ever faced were jilted mistresses and unpaid jewelers. The closest he had come to war was gazing upon the heroic battle paintings that the Prince Regent so favored.

The prince was the picture of the aging roué, but he at least looked cheerful. His once handsome face had muddy eyes set in flabby cheeks and a wide, almost feminine, mouth. Mercifully, he had not been cursed with the pop eyes of his brothers. His hair was thinning, and his elaborate curls were dyed to conceal the onrush of middle age. His obese form was clad in the scarlet uniform of a British field marshal and blazed with the insignia of the Order of the Garter. He was entitled to the uniform as a sovereign, yet Pennywhistle found it distasteful since it had been in no way earned.

In a few weeks Pennywhistle would to have to undergo another ceremony at Westminster Abbey, the ritualistic introduction into the Order of the Bath. That would involve more arcane words, odd oaths, and formal nonsense. He banished the thought of that and used his pain to focus on his next steps.

"Your Royal Highness, Major Thomas Pennywhistle," the Lord Chamberlain loudly announced. An equerry handed the Lord Chamberlain a sword on a large red pillow. The Chamberlain advanced toward the Prince Regent and Prinnie grasped the sword.

Pennywhistle advanced a few paces, faced the sovereign, and bowed slightly. He continued a few more paces, halted,

Bombproofed

and knelt carefully on an ornate red and gold stool in front of the throne. He bowed his head slightly. He saw Prinnie's feet move toward him.

He felt a slight pressure from the sword first on his right shoulder and then on his left. "I dub thee knight," said Prinnie in a solid base voice with no slurring of words. "Arise, Sir Thomas!"

He did as ordered. Prinnie put the sword down and offered his hand. Pennywhistle met his eyes firmly but briefly. One was never supposed to have an extended chat of the eyes with one's sovereign. The handshake was expected, but Prinnie's grip was unexpectedly enthusiastic and he smiled at Pennywhistle with real zest. "Congratulations, Sir Thomas, it is a great pleasure to meet you. You have brought most welcome news, and recovering that stolen payroll was excellent work. I should be most eager to hear more details of your recent service later this evening."

"I am pleased that I have brought your Royal Highness good cheer. It would be my honor to give you the full particulars at your convenience." *Damn it, that meant he was on the hook for the evening ball.*

"I understand you were attacked recently, Sir Thomas. It is a terrible thing to have happen to someone who has done so much for his country. Makes me want to thrash the bounders myself."

The Prince Regent loved to speak authoritatively of his part in battles that he had never come close to; he was a formidable warrior in his own drunken imagination. His generals simply humored him and congratulated him on his fighting spirit.

"Very gallant sentiments, Your Royal Highness, and I thank you for them." Pennywhistle bowed deeply and backed away slowly. At a discreet distance he turned to face three red-robed knights. One placed a long pinkish-red ribbon over his right shoulder, and the second affixed a large silver star to the left-hand side of his coat. A third knight draped the long crimson robe of the Order over his shoulders and asked him to raise his right hand. He repeated clearly the words of oath that the third knight mumbled.

Two parchment pieces of paper with all manner of heraldic designs were thrust in front of his face. They both began "Know all and singular by these presents..." Someone offered him a portable writing desk and a quill and he signed the documents quickly. Even knights had to complete paperwork.

Each knight shook his hand and said, "Congratulations, Sir Thomas, and welcome to the Order." He thanked them and then the cloak was removed—evidently just a loaner. The lead knight made a motion for him to turn and face the crowd on the right. The knight then bellowed, "Your Royal Highness, my lords, ladies, and gentlemen, it is my honor to present to you Sir Thomas Pennywhistle."

To his surprise, he saw bright smiling faces, not the cynical ones that he expected from Court habitués. He did not care what these people thought, but reminded himself that future children might benefit from their favorable estimation.

Sammie Jo's smile was so broad that it worried him; he was afraid her joy would sabotage her assumed identity. She needed to get out of there as fast as possible. He caught her eye then rubbed his chin three times and stroked the hair on his temples twice. It was a danger signal they had worked out in Maryland. She gave the expected countersign: brushing her left hand twice across her lips.

She unobtrusively began moving to the rear of the crowd and safety.

He had a receiving line to endure, a thirty-minute charade of handshakes and self-serving compliments from

BOMBPROOFED

men who wanted to be his bosom companions though he was meeting most of them for the first time.

He shoved a mental ramrod up his backside and plastered a suitable smile on his face. The pain was growing worse and he was so, so tired.

Chapter Thirty

Most of the receiving line was a blur, and he was grateful that he had acquiesced to Lady Leith's suggestion that Gabriel drive him. Once inside Lady Leith's door, he stormed up to the master bedroom and confronted his wife.

"I don't know whether I should kiss you or horsewhip you with my tongue." Satisfaction and distress warred for control of his face. "I admit I am pleased that you made it to the investiture, but I shudder to think of the scandal that would have ensued if you had been caught!"

"Since when did you give a damn about doing things right and proper?" said Sammie Jo with a mixture of defiance and amusement. "Someone had to keep an eye on you. I decided to act first and apologize later. Besides, I got away with it, and you always say it is a waste of time to worry about what might have been! And,"—her tone softened—"I was right proud to see you get something that you've earned many times over."

Pennywhistle sighed. He could rail at her all he liked but nothing could change her essential nature. She would always think independently and follow a different drummer, rather like him. The best he could do would be to occasionally change the rhythm of the drum beat.

"You're looking peaked, Tom, and a little unsteady on your feet. You need some of my potion and a lot of sleep." Lady Leith's tut-tutting over him was apparently infectious.

He opened his mouth to protest, but stopped because he knew she was right. "I am too tired to argue, but we *are* going to the ball tonight."

"We don't have to go, Tom."

"Actually, we do, my dear... I mean, 'my lady.' This ball will be a rite of passage and is far more significant for you than my knighthood is for me. It will be like a debutante's coming out, but on a far grander scale. You will be leaving behind the abused country girl and showing the world the forthright woman who charms with her honesty. You will make the Court ladies look like washed-up hags who were sent for and could not come. I have long fantasized about seeing you dressed with an elegance that befits your beauty, and from what you have told me about your ball gown, I believe that I will have my wish gratified tonight."

"Oh, Tom, you do have a silver tongue sometimes! I do so want to go! I'm a little bit intimidated, though!

Pennywhistle laughed. "You just impersonated a hussar and outwitted some of the greatest men in the land, and you are worried what a few jealous old ladies will think of you? That's like saying you faced down a lion but are worried about the mouse at your feet. No, you will be fine, and I shall be most proud to claim you as my lady."

She blushed.

"There is also a more mercenary reason to go: The Prince Regent. I made a good impression on him and he wishes to speak to me further about the Washington Campaign. I have an idea how to wring an advantage from such a talk that could assist the search for my brother's killer. Speaking of that, could I persuade you to return the Code Book?"

"Not on your life," said Sammie Jo with fire. "I give that to you and you will be off and running. You won't get a lick of sleep. I'll make you a bargain. I will return it to you if—and only if—you turn in right now and get a few hours' shut eye.

Then when we get home you will hit the hay directly and sleep until tomorrow afternoon."

"You drive a hard bargain, my dear."

"No, a soft one, since it involves a comfortable pillow and a deep featherbed. Do we have a deal, good sir knight?"

"We do, Lady Pennywhistle."

He kissed her hard to seal the bargain and felt the usual stirrings in his loins, but he was too tired to explore them any further. She calmly proceeded to undress him and tuck him into bed as if he were an unruly child who had reluctantly yielded to the wisdom of his mother. Less than a minute after his head met the pillow a profound sleep took him.

He had the dream about the juggler, gold coins, and the code book again. This time, however, the background scenery was closer and clearer. The cathedral was definitely St. Stephen's in Vienna, but, illogically, the Russian flag was flying over the Schönbrunn. The palace was much bigger than the last time.

The face of the juggler had previously been hidden by shadows but now it was fully visible. It was replete with scars and burn marks: not a face you wanted to meet on a dark night, and never on a clear day. The face was moving toward him menacingly when he heard a voice calling him.

"Tom! Tom! Wake up! Wake up! You're having a nightmare!" cried Sammie Jo.

His eyes flew open and saw the worry on her face. "I am all right! I am all right!" he exclaimed.

"No, you are not!" retorted Sammie Jo with less of her usual fire. "You only slept four hours. Are you still determined to attend the ball tonight?"

"I am."

"Well," she said with a smile in her voice, "I know it ain't right, but I sure am glad you said that!"

BOMBPROOFED

"Then let the process begin!" said Pennywhistle in a jesting voice..

The process became "all hands on deck," with Sammie Jo, Lady Leith, Gabriel, Johnny and every servant carrying out his or her part with military efficiency.

Gabriel brushed and polished Pennywhistle's new uniform and helped him dress. Dale assisted in making sure his appearance satisfied military protocol.

Lady Leith and a small army of maids fussed over every detail of Sammie Jo's dress and hair. The metamorphosis was complete ninety minutes later. Pennywhistle looked a new man, though he did not feel like one.

He had dressed separately from Sammie Jo, and she had only given him a general idea of her outfit. When she walked out in her magnificent gown, stunning necklace, and dazzling earrings, he gasped. She was Diana fresh from Olympus. "'Her beauty doth hang upon the night like a rich jewel in an Ethiop's ear.' I have to employ Shakespeare because my own words would be as a blind man trying to describe stars. You look... wonderful!"

Sammie Jo's smile lit up the room more brightly than a dozen chandeliers. "You look mighty fine yourself, Sugar Plum. I think every woman there is going to die of envy!"

He did not care that he hurt. And he could sleep later. He wanted Sammie Jo to have the best night of her life and would use every ounce of his willpower to make it so.

Chapter Thirty-One

The Palace of St. James loomed a hundred yards ahead. Sammie Jo thought that the Tudor gatehouse with its twin crenellated towers and large clock appeared worn and gone to seed: the residence of royals down on their luck. Her husband explained that the House of Hanover had long since taken up residence in better accommodations and that this subsidiary possession was now used mostly for official ceremonies, such as the presentation of credentials by newly arrived ambassadors.

Normally the ball would have been held at Carleton House, but it was undergoing an extended bout of reconstruction since the Prince Regent took considerable joy in being an interior designer and frequently made changes to his chief residence.

The coach slowed almost to a stop and Gabriel maneuvered into line behind others moving through the main gate. Some liveried royal servants stood and directed traffic, while others passed slowly down the growing line, stopping occasionally to check invitations. That was strictly pro forma since it was highly unlikely that anyone in a fine carriage was a party crasher.

Sammie Jo did a quick mental review of the book Lady Leith had given her to read, *The Manners, Etiquette, and Courtesies of the Aristocracy Written by One of Their Own*. Its title page proclaimed that it contained "full directions for correct manners, dress, deportment, and conversation." Its polite injunctions had filled her head to bursting, though she had only been able to read half of it. She felt droplets of sweat on her forehead as they passed under the second archway of the palace.

The carriage stopped at a flight of steps that constituted the main debarkation point. Her breath caught at the colorful assemblage of people, who made peacocks seem drab. The military men were clad in blue and scarlet uniforms overflowing with the gold lace of high rank, the civilians were in blue-, bottle-green-, grey-, buff-, snuff-, and cranberry-colored tailcoats, and the Court functionaries were in ornate liveries of red and gold. The men moved freely about, shaking hands, laughing politely, and engaging in stilted conversations. She sensed that this was not really about good fellowship, but that dominant males were jockeying for position and measuring the size of each other's ... reputations.

Yet if the men dazzled, the ladies blinded. She saw dresses in every color of the rainbow and jewels of every shade, size, and description. Indeed, the sheer number of emeralds, rubies, sapphires, and diamonds almost made her think the Crown Jewels had been looted. A few sported daring amounts of décolletage, probably to please the rakish attentions of the Prince Regent. Since married women were preferred by royalty for assignations, she wondered if they were here for a ball or an audition. Some wore outlandishly large turbans. Only a few women were beautiful, but the clothing made even a plain woman look like a queen. This was the world of *Pride and Prejudice* amplified tenfold by the wealth and power in evidence. She had once traded a bundle of fur pelts for a copy, but had never really understood the concern with manners and status it described until now.

Footmen opened the carriage door and helped Lady Leith out first since she was a dowager countess. Pennywhistle followed, then extended his hand to his wife. "Show time," he whispered quietly.

Pennywhistle was immediately ambushed by a crowd of well wishers. Some he knew well, others only slightly, but most not at all. They had clearly read the newspapers and heard of the Brooks episode. They congratulated him on both his exploits and his survival. But their attention quickly turned to Sammie Jo, standing just out of earshot. Battles came and went, but a beautiful woman of stately proportions was an extraordinary event. "Stunning," "Lovely creature," "Magnificent woman," "Breath-taking," "A goddess," and "Delightfully unexpected," were but a few of the compliments that he received on her behalf. He was called a lucky man more times than he could count. The question of the hour became: "How did you meet her?"

He answered with a story that had all the right elements of a good drama: an orphaned damsel distressed by bullies, brigands, and battles, all playing out on an exotic landscape. Only about half of it was true, but it put Sammie Jo in the best light, portraying her as a plucky woman whose beauty was the perfect reflection of her character. His listeners nodded in approval.

"Forgive me. The recent attack has caused my manners to desert me. Allow me to introduce you all to Lady Pennywhistle." He motioned to Sammie Jo, who dutifully responded with the stock phrase that Lady Leith had said worked in almost any situation: "I am honored to meet you." She followed it with a short curtsey.

Sammie Jo saw in their worshipping eyes that she had them spellbound. More than a few looked as if they were about to pledge their undying love. Had she offered her hand, gentlemen would have fought each other to press their lips to it. They probably would lay down their lives for her honor if they believed it impugned. The magic of the evening had cast its spell upon her and she felt herself to be a princess of the blood royal. Her customary cynicism had vanished, and the abused little girl from the backwoods had been replaced by a confident woman fully worthy of her husband. Tonight, she was Cinderella! Yet there was a wonderful difference. After midnight, she would still be a lady, and her handsome prince would need no glass slipper to find her.

"Well, blow me down, Pennywhistle, if that isn't the most extraordinary tale I ever heard." Lord Upton echoed the sentiments of the crowd of the crowd perfectly. "Have you two begun accepting invitations for the season yet? I assume you will be living in London."

"No, my lord, nothing has been decided yet. It has been very hectic since we got back and we have had little time to sort things out. I assure you it would give us great pleasure to call upon you and your wife." Actually, he found Upton hopelessly reactionary, but it was unwise to tweak the nose of someone so well connected.

A tall, dour gentleman shook Pennywhistle's hand vigorously, and his countenance broke into a rare smile. "Pennywhistle! You have the most amazing luck!" said Harris Bigg-Wither. "Would that I might meet someone as naturally lovely as your wife, and as obviously devoted! The women I meet think only of my estate and care nothing for the sensibilities of my heart. Perhaps I, too, shall have to go to America for a bride," he said, tipping hi shat to Sammie Jo. The man's manners were as ungainly as his name. He took perverse delight in bewailing his problems in love, recounting to all and sundry how, twelve years before, he had proposed to Jane Austen, and been refused.

"Yours is indeed a sad state of affairs, but they say all things come to he who waits. Now if you will be so good as to excuse me, I know my wife is eager to dance, so I shall take my leave," said Pennywhistle smoothly. It was time to go, before Bigg-Wither begin rattling on about his courtship misfortunes, which were brought on by a prickly nature that he was unable to see.

Pennywhistle gave a quick bow to the small crowd, then took Sammie Jo by the arm and led her slowly up the stairs. Lady Leith followed a few steps behind—incorrect by protocol, but completely correct emotionally because right now two were company and three a crowd.

Fifteen steps brought them to the palace forecourt. "It is... breathtaking!" exclaimed Sammie Jo. "The inside of this place is a lot more impressive than the outside."

The forecourt was a massive square with a white marble floor and a gold-bordered ceiling that seemed to reach to the sky. Blue and gold Corinthian columns on dark blue marble bases supported the ceiling, which was decorated with paintings that Sammie Jo gathered represented tales from Greek mythology. She wished she knew something about art since she gathered these had been done by famous artists. Her husband had said something about Rubens, whoever he was.

Two wide stairways luxuriously carpeted in red and gold encircled the room and led to the ballroom on the second floor. There were numerous marble busts of people in ancient garb on plinths in small alcoves. Four massive chandeliers illuminated the room along with six smaller ones. The candles were probably of spermaceti since they gave plenty of light and no smoke. The annual budget for candles probably exceeded the total yearly revenue of her home state of Maryland.

Bombproofed

Even the stairway banisters were works of art. The tops were made of polished ebony, but the intricate filigree work which formed the sides looked to be real gold. She ran one hand along the gold in an effort to make sure she was not dreaming.

"Is it what you expected, my dear?" said Pennywhistle gently.

"Oh, yes, Tom, it's like a fairy tale come to life, and it makes the Baltimore mansions I always envied look like... well, squatter's shacks."

Pennywhistle laughed quietly, then noticed a man in a Russian officer's uniform watching him closely. The facial expression of a captain of hussars reminded him of a hawk that had just spotted a dove. After his experience outside the Russian Embassy, the man's presence did not feel coincidental.

The pain in his back was becoming severe. He estimated that he had about two hours before his distress would compel him to seek a bed. He hated to cheat Sammie Jo out of an extended round of dancing, but about all he could manage tonight would be to metaphorically show the flag.

Lady Leith and Sammie Jo saw the suppressed agony on his face and both sized up the situation correctly.

Lady Leith spoke with decision. "Let me guide you both and make the introductions. I know most of these people and while my opinion of a great many of their characters is low, I know which ones count socially and which ones do not. Sammie Jo, your best bet is to play the woman of mystery. These people are jaded and welcome the unexpected."

The introductions Lady Leith brokered took an hour. Pennywhistle lost track of the hands that he shook, and the faces blurred together. He noted a few expressions of envy, jealousy and resentment, but they were in the distinct minority. Most people were sincere enough, although in many cases that sincerity was clearly aided by alcohol. He accumulated enough calling cards to wallpaper a drawing room, and enough dinner invitations to keep him fed for the next six months. Apparently one of the perquisites of being a hero was a substantial reduction in one's culinary expenses.

The short conversations in which he was engaged covered the gamut: "Great honor," "Congratulations," "Splendid work," "Well done, young man," "Wonderful that we have heroes left," "Thumping good thing you did against the damn Yankees," "...business proposition we should discuss," "You must stand for Parliament," "Look forward to calling upon you." He smiled as pleasantly as he could and cranked out what he thought were appropriately gallant and modest responses. They apparently worked, for no one seemed offended. The pain is his back flared and it was with difficulty that he restrained himself from consulting his watch.

He unobtrusively listened to the responses that Sammie Jo provoked. "We must talk," "Lovely dress," "Charming outfit," "Newlyweds—how quaint," "You look wonderful," and "You must be so proud" were typical comments.

"Where are you from, dear? Do I know your family?" were the two most commonly asked questions. They came from the older women and arose from snobbery; it was important that everyone have a societal niche and they simply could not classify her. A few had heard that she hailed from America, and some wondered if she came from a great family whose cadet branch had emigrated after America gained its independence. Most could not place her accent. The English had many regional dialects and often people living thirty miles apart had very different ways of speaking.

Most remaining questions were asked by the younger women and were on the order of "How did you meet your husband?" and "Who is your mantua maker?" Sammie Jo gave short answers that were poised because they were unspontaneous, having been carefully rehearsed with Lady Leith the day before.

She felt sorry for many of the unmarried women. They were facing spinsterhood and wondered what magic formula she had used to ensnare a man well known for his aversion to marriage. After nearly two decades of war, there was a shortage of marriageable men of breeding, and handsome ones were as rare as fireflies in a fishbowl. Even dumpy older men with pinched faces, sharp noses, and scarecrow physiques were fair game if they possessed decent incomes. For desperate women, tonight's ball was not a party but a hunting expedition.

By the time Pennywhistle had shaken the last hand and accepted the last calling card, he noticed Sammie Jo was surrounded by a small but approving crowd of women who seemed to be hanging upon her every word. Most were young, but at least three were beyond fifty. She was talking slowly and carefully yet with animation. He could see in her eyes that she was working hard to restrain her predilection for colorful language.

Waiters came up to Sammie Jo's group and offered silver trays full of crystal glasses filled to the brim with champagne. Most of the group accepted one, including Sammie Jo. The orchestra which had been playing unobtrusively in the background, now transitioned to the first dance music of the evening. It was a waltz: new to England and considered somewhat risqué. People took their places on the dance floor and commenced twirling with delight.

Pennywhistle's back throbbed, but he was determined to give Sammie Jo at least one dance. He walked over to her group. "Forgive me, ladies, but I should like to borrow my wife for this dance." He extended his hand to Sammie Jo, which she accepted with a smile that was not entirely genuine.

"Are you sure you are up for this, Tom?"

"I am not an invalid yet, my dear. I will manage."

Unlike most of the crowd, Pennywhistle was familiar with the waltz from his time in the Adriatic. His steps were fluid, graceful, and rhythmic, and Sammie Jo responded perfectly to his lead, her years of hunting giving her movements an almost leonine grace.

They were the most handsome couple on the floor and gradually all eyes focused on them. "I feel like I am a bug under a magnifying glass," whispered Sammie Jo.

"Don't worry, my dear," Pennywhistle whispered back. "You are making a lovely impression. Most are just wondering where we learned to dance so well. What they don't understand is that no dance instructor can teach the love that guides our movements."

The world of the great and mighty disappeared as Sammie Jo relaxed and her universe became her husband. Because of her height, he did not look down at her; their joyful eyes met on the same level and were reflections of tempestuous souls made content because each had found its equal. As they whirled gloriously, it struck her that the real beauty of the evening was not the exquisite clothing and expensive jewelry everywhere in evidence, but the hidden finery of two hearts beating as one.

Sammie Jo wished the dance would never end. When it did, her husband offered another. "No, Tom," she said reluctantly, "let's not push things. I know you have some politicking left to do."

The room buzzed with general conversation. Those who were not dancing broke up into little groups. The earlier coterie of women quickly reformed around Sammie Jo, and he heard gasps of awe as she recited a tall tale, reveling in pulling the legs of the august and sophisticated: "The mosquitoes in Maryland bark before they bite, and often they rear up on their hind legs like little dragons, though one of them is large enough to fill your hand, and a dozen can block a road." Pennywhistle was soon trapped by two old generals who earnestly sought his opinion about the situation in America.

The Prince Regent circulated among his guests, his complexion now considerably more ruddy thanks to multiple glasses of champagne. He was laughing, talking gaily, and seeking partners for a late-night game of whist at Carleton House. He was unpretentious, personable, and genuinely concerned that his guests have a good time.

Pennywhistle wanted to speak to him but did not want to be inveigled into a game since he detested cards. Not to mention the fact the Prince Regent was an inept player who frequently resorted to cheating to win rubbers. Normally cheating at cards could smash a man in polite society, but none of those rules applied to the Prince Regent. As with so many social conventions, he was a law unto himself.

He had his admirers, opportunistic women, sycophants seeking jobs, puffed up architects, and assorted courtiers who were simply attracted to power. His detractors included evangelicals, unpaid royal vendors, hardcore Whigs, and military men who resented his appropriating their deeds for his own. None of these groups was in attendance tonight.

Pennywhistle might not like the prince but understood that he would someday be George IV and had to be dealt with on that basis.

Pennywhistle accepted a glass of champagne from a passing waiter, not so much for taste as for its value as a pain killer. He gulped rather than sipped it. He caught Sammie Jo's eye and winked at her. She bobbed her head in acknowledgment but kept talking. She appeared engaged in a phenomenon that no man could ever puzzle out: feminine chatter. She claimed no facility with it, but was evidently doing well.

"I think your godson's wife is acquitting herself splendidly, don't you, Margaret?" said Lady St. Vincent to Lady Leith.

"Yes! She is talking to those women like a seasoned old trooper," replied Lady Leith. "Give her a few years and she will be a force to be reckoned with."

Pennywhistle caught Sammie Jo's eye again and the unspoken message was clear: "I need your help." The pain in his back was mounting. Her acknowledgment via a subtle shift of posture said, "Just a minute or two."

The Russian officer who had piqued Pennywhistle's interest was introduced to him by one of the old generals. He was Rittmeister Frederick von Gilsa, a Prussian in the Russian Service. He stood six feet tall, looked tough and fit, and appeared to be roughly Pennywhistle's own age. He spoke English well enough, if with a heavy accent. They exchanged a few insignificant words, but their eyes locked and he acquired a wealth of unvoiced information. This was a man of direct and forceful action not courtly maneuvering. Pennywhistle's intuition said that he had come specifically to observe him. He would see this man again, and soon. He doubted the meeting would be pleasant.

He quickly lost himself in his analysis and blinked in surprise when Sammie Jo tapped his arm. "Tom, are you all right? You look a million miles away."

"Fine, my dear. I need you for a charm assault. I see the Prince Regent is glad-handing the crowd and he is headed our way. He is rapidly becoming three sheets to the wind and I require a favor. He loves beautiful women. You don't have to say or do much save smile at his clumsy compliments. I need you to be..."

BOMBPROOFED

"An object of decoration and desire?" she replied with amusement.

"Precisely," he replied with a hint of chagrin in his voice. "You know how I feel about you, but this is a case of giving a rake a glimpse of exactly what he expects. Let him kiss your hand and babble compliments. I need him off balance and distracted. Just follow my lead."

"Does this have anything to do with Vienna?"

"It does indeed. Ah, here he comes—get ready." He linked her arm with his and knew from her touch this was truly a joint effort.

"Well, finally! The man of the hour!" the Prince Regent positively gushed. He grabbed Pennywhistle's hand and pumped it vigorously. "And this lovely creature must be Lady Pennywhistle."

Sammie Jo extended her hand, and instead of barely touching his lips to it, Prinnie slobbered, then rose to his full height and rocked on his toes to make himself look taller. Even so, she towered over his portly frame by at least five inches. She locked eyes with his, and her brief gaze returned the expected verdict. Prinnie quickly dropped his eyes from her face to her ample bosom. "It is a pleasure to meet you, my lady. I don't mind telling you that you have caused a sensation here tonight. You are quite an extraordinary creature—yes, indeed. You are a breath of fresh air." He patted her hand contentedly and again fixed his eyes on her bosom. "Yes, indeed, a breath of fresh air."

"It is a pleasure to meet your Royal Highness," she said cheerfully. She pictured his flabby, bloated physique without his well-cut uniform and it amused her, utterly banishing any fear of royalty. He was drunk enough to manipulate—time to test the waters and help her husband.

"I have heard so much about you, your Royal Highness. How you were a brave soldier and a fine ruler, but no one told me how handsome you are!" she cooed.

"Well, damn me, my dear.,you are an unusually bold and perceptive lady. Wish we had more like you at Court. You and your husband must join me very soon for dinner at Carleton House. It would be a great pleasure to know you... to know you both so much better." He continued to stare at her bosom.

Pennywhistle flashed a quick glance at his wife. *Proceed*, it said.

"I understand that you fought in the Washington Campaign. Did you first meet my husband there?" She was gambling that he was just drunk enough to allow his alternate martial personality to surface.

"Well, damn me, my dear lady, ain't you incredible! How did you know?"

"My husband spoke of you as a great warrior. I just assumed that you would be where the fighting was thickest." She saw him smile in satisfaction and his muddy eyes acquired flecks of color.

"Yes it was a rough campaign, wasn't it, Tom?" He threw his arm enthusiastically around Pennywhistle's waist as if they were old companions.

"It certainly was, Your Royal Highness. I was lucky to have you there. I lost track of how many times you saved my life." He was shamelessly overacting but it was having the right effect. The Prince was so eager to be a soldier that fantasy smothered reality—pathetic, but useful.

"Yes, damn me, very rough, very bloody, but we gained great honor."

Pennywhistle kept his expression friendly, though he disliked what he was doing. "I wonder if you could do an old companion a great favor, Your Royal Highness," said Pennywhistle in his warmest manner.

"Ask freely—you are the hero of the hour and a friend. If it is in my power to grant it, I shall do so most happily."

"I have seen much of war, but would very much like to assist in the business of peace, even if in a small way. I have heard that Lord Castlereagh has not yet found an assistant naval attaché for the talks in Vienna. I should very much like to be that man. I believe a marine's viewpoint would be most welcome, since I am conversant with warfare both at sea and on land. I have not yet received a new assignment since my return, and I believe my superiors would be agreeable."

The Prince Regent laughed loudly and slapped his thigh. "Well, damn me, ain't that extraordinary! The most patriotic thing I ever heard of! You are just back from a war and already champing at the bit to serve your country. Would that every officer had your zeal!" He calmed down and continued, "That is easily arranged. I will speak to Lord Liverpool tomorrow. But are you sure you are up to it? I would not want one of Britain's heroes to be cheated of the chance to recover fully and enjoy the good wishes of his grateful countrymen."

"I assure Your Royal Highness, the wound was trifling." The shooting pain in his back strongly disagreed. "I am ready to depart at the earliest possible moment, and my wife has never seen the Continent. It would be a wonderful adventure for her."

"I would so love to see the Continent," gushed Sammie Jo.

"It would delight me to bring pleasure to such a fine lady. You may consider it done. Call upon the Foreign Office the day after tomorrow and they will have your credentials ready."

"Thank you. It is most gracious of Your Royal Highness," said Pennywhistle with cynical sincerity. "But then graciousness is one of your most sterling qualities." Sammie Jo barely stifled a laugh and managed to turn it into a sweet smile.

The appointment would grant him official backing for any inquiries that he might make about matters related to his brother's death. Any foreigners puzzled about the appearance of a new man on the diplomatic roster would be referred to his distinguished record, which included a sterling performance at Trafalgar, the greatest naval battle of the age.

Diplomatic accreditation would provide access to even the most secret information and would secure entrée to the balls, parties, and entertainments where much of the real business of the Congress was carried out. He would have plenty of official latitude to do all the unofficial poking about that he wished. The reason for his brother's murder might not lie within the British Embassy, but it was a fine starting point.

Then Pennywhistle heard the words he dreaded. "We are having a friendly game of whist around two tonight at Carleton House. Wonder if you'd like to come. Plenty of people would like to meet you and I am sure you play cards just as well as you fight. Ha, ha, ha!" The Prince winked.

Pennywhistle was about to reply, having no idea what would issue from his mouth, when Sammie Jo saved him.

She cooed and smiled alluringly. "Your Royal Highness, I must protest. My husband is far too modest to tell you that his wound troubles him and that his doctor has counseled rest, but I am not bound by anything except wifely concern. I would take it as a great personal favor if you might postpone the invitation for... another time." She shot him a look that said she might be very grateful in several ways.

"Of course, of course. Forgive me for thinking of meself. Very happy to oblige you, dear lady." He gave her a look that said he understood future possibilities.

Some equerries accosted the Prince and whispered in his ear. He frowned. "Oh, damn it—I have to go. Some blasted official duty. So much more pleasant to pass the time with you two." He bent forward and Sammie Jo extended her hand. "Look forward to getting to know you better, milady." He again slobbered over her hand.

He addressed Pennywhistle one last time. "Look forward to speaking with you again, Sir Thomas. We veterans need to talk to others who understand! Ha, ha, ha!" A grizzled old equerry gently guided him toward two distinguished looking gentlemen staring expectantly in his direction.

Sammie Jo looked quickly to both sides to make sure no one was within earshot and spoke *sotto voce*. "What a goddamned letch! Man's as windy as a sack of farts, and so full of shit that his eyes are brown!"

Pennywhistle laughed heartily and did not care who heard—it greatly relieved the pain. "That is the most honest and accurate appraisal that I have ever heard of the man. Most here are so worried about keeping him happy that they cannot even allow themselves to think the truth, let alone give it voice."A lance of pain cut off a second laugh.

Her look instantly changed to one of great concern. "How bad is it, Tom?"

He smiled pleasantly as he whispered to Sammie Jo, "I need to get out of here. I fear I have popped several stitches and I cannot let anyone see blood. Give me a hand and make it look loving and easy. I need your power, literally and figuratively."

She shot her arm under his and he felt her great strength lift him even as his own began to flag. "Walk slowly," he whispered to her. "We must give the appearance of a dutiful wife helping a beloved husband who celebrated a bit too grandly. No one will pay such a sight any mind. Just get me it to the carriage."

"I love you," she said with a fire that calmed his agitated spirit even as it warmed his heart. "I will never let go until you say the word."

Because pain had to be obeyed, it created bridges that could be built no other way. What flashed invisibly between Pennywhistle and his bride settled things for a lifetime. Any doubts and fears about their unusual pairing were permanently exiled in that instant of understanding.

They reached the edge of the ball room. "Is it worse?" she said.

"I've been better," he replied, forcing what he hoped was cheer into his voice, though it came out as a whisper that he barely recognized. "I can make it. Keep going. It's not that far. Just get me into the carriage. I need a little sleep, that's all. Don't worry about Lady Leith. She will be fine."

By the time they reached the bottom of the grand staircase, she was supporting him entirely. She smiled pleasantly at a variety of well wishers and even managed to wave at one. She summoned a page who communicated her message quickly to Gabriel.

Gabriel pulled the carriage round, quickly dismounted, and helped Sammie Jo bundle Pennywhistle inside. "How bad is he?" said a shocked Gabriel.

"He just told me that it weren't nothing, and that means its god awful! Get up in that seat and lay the whip on with everything you've got. We need to get him home faster than grass through a goose!"

Gabriel did as instructed and the carriage shot out of the courtyard. Johnny crawled inside from his backboard perch —he had been detailed to keep street urchins away. "My lady, Sir Thomas looks pale as a ghost, but... but... how can that be?" His boy's mind would simply not credit the obvious evidence of his own eyes—heroes never sweated, agonized, or bled.

"Damn it, Johnny!" Sammie Jo's voice snapped with authority. "I need you to grow up quick and be a man! Help me—off with his coat. I need to see how bad the bleeding is." Johnny responded instinctively, and the two of them pried off the heavy scarlet coat and silk shirt. The wound made Johnny avert his eyes.

Three stitches had popped and blood was leaking faster with each passing second. She reached into her reticule and extracted a vial of her powder. "Johnny, did the cook give you anything to drink?"

"Just some cold tea, milady."

"Don't care if its horse pee." Her voice rippled with anxiety. "I need something liquid to get medicine into him."

Johnny produced a small bota. She seized it, mixed the powder with its contents, and forced some down Pennywhistle's throat. He gasped, but drank. She took some silk handkerchiefs from her purse and pressed them against the wound. She and Johnny then manhandled Pennywhistle back into his heavy coat.

Suddenly the carriage started to slow. She thrust her head out the window and saw a roadblock two hundred yards ahead. The skin on her cheeks tightened and her jaw clenched. A wagon lay on its side and three large men stood beside it. It was supposed to look like an overburdened wagon had simply taken a corner at too a high speed and suffered the punishment of basic physics.

"Damnation! If it ain't ants, its bedbugs!" she muttered in alarm. The scene was far too neat and orderly for there to have been an accident—there were no boxes or bales of goods strewn randomly in the street. The wagon balanced precariously on wheels whose rims appeared unbent; not a single spoke was missing or damaged. It was exactly at right angles to the street—a little too exactly, as if it had been carefully positioned rather smashed into place.

The men next to it looked neither frustrated nor angry, as they should have been. The odds that a random accident would occur at the only choke point on their route home were low. Her husband was unconscious from pain. It was up to her.

Three miles away, Grimsby and Dale sipped ales in the butler's pantry and speculated on how the ball was proceeding.

"Its been a good and memorable day, but I think the knighthood should have been granted a long time ago," said Dale.

"Probably so," responded Grimsby, "but from what you have told me, the major is neither interested in nor good at self promotion. I know of several far less worthy individuals who lobbied for knighthoods and succeeded mostly because their energy in buttonholing the right ministers far exceeded the energy that they expended upon the battlefield."

Dale shook his head. "It is often so. Snobbery is a curious thing, and good men generally fail to understand its appeal. Too often the gentlemen who talk volleys of charm advance long before individuals like the major, who have endured volleys of bullets. Those stuffed shirts at court need a title because inside they are hollow. No award, title, or rank can make a man a hero if he does not possess capability at his deepest core. As we marines know, you may salute a rank, but respect must be earned."

Thummmppp!

Dale's ears perked up and his expression became the face of battle. "Did you hear that, Grimsby? Sounded like it was coming from the roof."

There was a second loud *clunk*.

Grimsby nodded. "I did. Whatever caused that, it was no bird or squirrel. I think we should take a look, don't you?"

"Definitely—after what happened to the major the other day, there is no sense taking any chances."

There were two more thuds on the roof. "That's no animal; that's enemy action!" said Dale.

"I'll get the Purdey," said Grimsby.

"I'll get the Baker," responded Dale.

Grimsby limped as quickly as his wooden leg would permit—the frustration that he was not his old battle-worthy self evident on his strained face.

Once he had the shotgun in hand, he rang for all the servants. "Burglars," he told them. "Stay in the kitchen until I tell you otherwise."

They trusted Grimsby and complied readily. News of the attack on Sir Thomas had spread quickly through the servant's hall, and most connected it to the present excitement.

Sammie Jo poured one more draft of the wine and powder mix into Pennywhistle. He revived enough to drink the final dose quickly. He blinked, and light returned to his green eyes. "Roadblock ahead!" said Sammie Jo with as much forced calm as she could summon.

The undercurrent of tension in her voice told him everything. "How far?" rasped Pennywhistle.

"A hundred yards."

He shook his head, trying to retain his tenuous grip on consciousness. "Tell Gabriel to stop. Immediately!"

She yelled out the window and the urgency in her voice commanded Gabriel's instant obedience. From the way he said "Yes, ma'am!" it was clear that he, too, saw that something was wrong.

The trio at the wagon saw the carriage grind to a halt and drew pistols from under their dusters. They glanced at each other and muttered something in German. They were supposed to look like stout-hearted yeoman from the country, come to the city to sell their produce, but their disguises did not quite come off. Their high cheek-boned, pig-eyed faces were not the ruddy, angular faces of good English farmers.

Sammie Jo noticed something was also off about their clothing. Their dusters were of quality broadcloth, not coarse wool cut from cheap bolts. Their overalls were unblemished by any barnyard stains and displayed no patches from heavy labor in the fields. Their round, wide-brimmed, floppy hats were correct enough, but it was the quality of their footwear that truly gave them away. Farmers wore work boots, not polished black leather shoes. And farmers had no need of guns.

The trio hesitated. They had been told to make things look like a robbery. They were supposed to avoid violence if at all possible and rely on fear to compel obedience. They had been instructed to take what they liked, and that it was only a code book and a red ledger that their master coveted.

Sammie Jo called them Black Hat, Brown Hat, and Grey Hat and noted that their pistols were only good at very close range.

Pennywhistle hurt like the devil, but was now fully conscious. "The wheels are intact, you say?" She nodded.

"Good. Help me to the window." She did as asked. He fought down the pain and assessed the angles. Yes, it could be done. They would need plenty of speed and just the right point of impact.

Johnny popped through the opposite window, carrying something very long in a leather case. "My lady, I brought

Widowmaker. I know you don't like to be without it, so I strapped it to the luggage board... Can't ever be too careful!"

Sammie Jo's face lit up like a fire in the night. "Bless you, Johnny. This will help even the odds." She withdrew the weapon and quickly checked to make sure the flint and priming were still good.

The Teutonic Trio advanced uncertainly toward the carriage.

Pennywhistle explained his plan, and Sammie Jo instinctively grasped the mathematics of it. "It is a matter of the angle of incidence equaling the angle of reflection, and force equaling mass times acceleration."

"Damn," she said. "Hate to waste a perfectly good dress but..."

She pulled up the bottom of her golden gown and produced a hunting knife from underneath. She must have had it strapped to her leg.

He started to laugh but the pain caused his laughter to die in infancy. *Once a hunter, always a hunter.* She calmly slit the side of the dress.

"Got to be able to move!"

Pennywhistle nodded.

She kissed him quickly. "We will be all right, Tom. I will get you home."

"You were always one to run with the big dogs and not hide under the porch," he said quietly. The pain was trying to drag him back to unconsciousness but her will was infectious and he held on. "Aim for the pack leader."

She flashed him a look of mock exasperation which said *Obviously.*

"Kill the brave ones, then the cowards will run away and take the rest of the men with them, right, Tom?"

He nodded.

"Can I have the knife, my lady? Maybe I can help too!" Johnny assumed his fiercest expression, feeling himself a dangerous pirate.

His sincerity touched her and she gave him the knife.

"Your post will be on the luggage board. If anyone tries to jump on, stab low and hard."

She slammed open the door, jumped down to the pavement, and a second later rocketed onto the driver's board beside a very surprised Gabriel.

"We are going to barrel through that block like it was made out of paper, Gabriel. We will need every ounce of speed that we can get out of these old nags, so pour on that whip like the Earl of Hell is right behind us. We need to hit the wagon exactly there." She pointed at a spot a foot ahead of the front wheel. Understand, Gabriel?"

"Yes, ma'am!" He smiled. "Ramming speed!"

The Teutonic Trio stopped seventy yards away, assessing the situation. Sammie Jo braced her feet securely against the foot rim and pushed her back hard against the rear board of the long seat. She brought the long rifle to the point.

She nodded at Gabriel, who cracked the whip, shouting, "Ha'ah, ha'ah!" The horses leapt forward and dashed toward the wagon.

The men jumped aside as the carriage raced at them. Gabriel noted them raising their pistols but focused his attention on the point of upcoming impact: being a fast moving target was his best guarantee of safety.

He heard a *pop* and felt something whiz past his face—a second later he heard a sharp *crack*.

Sammie Jo's round slammed Black Hat between the eyes, blasting him six inches off his feet and a foot to his rear. His mates looked stunned, as if no one had told them anyone would resist. Her eyes blazed with satisfaction. She wished she had the means to reload.

Bombproofed

The carriage thundered into the wagon, the stout pine yoke of the horses absorbing the impact. Pennywhistle's theory was right and Gabriel's aim was true. The stout wagon spun on its wheels, the centrifugal force causing the wagon to rotate away from the carriage like a turnstile. The carriage shot through the gap into the empty street beyond.

The two remaining bandits recovered quickly and jumped onto the luggage board. They grabbed at Johnny as the carriage tore down the street. He dodged and stabbed one of the men in the stomach, but the man's heavy duster absorbed most of the blow. He jumped up onto the roof. They drew their own knives and jabbed at him. They missed but kept their knives anchored in the roof so they could use them as handholds. They were going to swing out and jump onto the foot rests below each door.

Johnny yelled at Sammie Jo, "Ma'am, behind!" He swung down from the roof and jumped inside.

Sammie Jo looked astern in alarm. Damn, they were not out of the woods yet. She needed a weapon—of course!

"Gabriel, give me your whip!" She wished she had her long bullwhip, but this one had enough length to reach Brown Hat's hands. She wanted to hurt them, hurt them bad. No, that was not true. She wanted them dead. She might be dressed as a lady and trying to ape the right manners, but the killer instinct that formed the core of her soul was in the ascendant.

She snapped the whip down hard on Brown Hat's left wrist and he yowled in pain. She cracked it at Grey Hat on the opposite side but it's tail came up a foot short of his wrist.

"Yaaah!" screeched Grey Hat as he abruptly snapped a bloody hand back from inside the coach. *Johnny and the knife!* thought Sammie Jo.

Brown Hat and Grey Hat retreated to the luggage board and clung frantically to the top rail as the carriage rocketed along at a breathtaking speed.

Pennywhistle knew that Sammie Jo and Johnny had only bought a short respite. He was close to surrendering to the Sandman, but could summon the strength for one last effort. Time to see if the dress sword lent him by Lady Leith had any real bottom to it.

Brown Hat leaped from the luggage board, flew through the air for a split second, and grasped the right door for dear life. Pennywhistle's eyes locked with his. He saw fear and uncertainty, which he returned with emerald fire.

Now! He shoved the sword two-handedly toward the man's right eye, putting his shoulder and every ounce of his flagging energy into the thrust. It penetrated the retina, continued through the brain, and shot out the back of the head. The man started to scream but stopped abruptly as his brain ceased to function.

Pennywhistle yanked back hard with his remaining strength. The sword wrenched free and flew inside. Pennywhistle sighed heavily, then lapsed into an unwanted sleep.

Grey Hat watched in horror as his mate splattered onto the cobblestones. They had been friends a long time. It was personal now, not about his master or any damned books. He would get inside the coach no matter what. He took a deep breath and jumped.

His hands locked firmly onto the left side of the speeding coach. He saw a boy and a passed-out man in scarlet inside. That scarlet man had been the target in the first place. He would simply crawl inside, search him, then kill him.

Sammie Jo felt panic. She could not reach Gray Hat before he got inside. If she had felt much trust in God, she would have started to pray.

Bombproofed

As if to mock her lack of faith, something red and black shot out of an adjoining lane. She had the quick impression of a man in a scarlet coat, yellow and gold sash, and plumed Roman centurion's helmet. He stood in his spurs atop a black speeding stallion and held a long saber vertically, poised to strike. The horse was at least 17 hands high, considerably larger than the usual thoroughbred.

Man and horse sprinted alongside the carriage, the rider's right wrist now level with Grey Hat's 's ear. The rider snapped his wrist and a 40-inch pattern '96 heavy cavalry saber flowed like a fast blur out and down in a quarter circle.

The wide, finely honed edge then flew forward and up in a deadly trajectory; the horses gallop adding greatly to its force. Grey Hat's head flew off like a speeding comet. The body's hands clung to the coach for a few seconds. Then its grip relaxed and it dropped below the carriage, swiftly run over by the rear wheels.

The black stallion slowed and the man on horseback signaled to Sammie Jo. She recognized that he was some sort of cavalryman, definitely an officer. She knew nothing about cavalry regiments—which were the smart ones and which were the ordinary—but his uniform was beautifully cut and flattered his trim form. He looked like a military print given life, yet his actions proved he that was no bandbox soldier.

He motioned for the carriage to stop, smiling pleasantly, almost as if someone else had done the grisly deed of a few seconds before. Gabriel looked suspicious, but Sammie Jo returned his smile, almost against her will. She instinctively knew that she had acquired a friend, though she had no idea who he was and why he had intervened.

Gabriel halted the carriage. Sammie Jo still clutched the whip, just in case her instincts had been wrong.

The cavalryman trotted up and touched his helmet in salute. "Good evening, ma'am. I saw a woman in distress and thought I might be able to help. I have never been able to resist *demoiselles* and danger!" His speech was as confident as it was insouciant.

Sammie Jo stared at him for a few seconds. She could read nothing in his face except an eagerness to be helpful. He was not handsome, yet his face had character, and she guessed that many women found him quite attractive. The grey eyes sparkled but the crow's feet and worry lines around them suggested that he had at some point seen some hard service. His skill with a sword confirmed that.

"Who the hell are you?" she finally burst out, completely forgetting her resolve to restrain her language.

"Ha, ha, ha!" he burst out in laughter that was as heartfelt as it was ungentlemanly. He preferred forthright language, which he found rare in ladies of quality.

"Lord Steven Thynne, ma'am, Captain, 1st Life Guards, at your service. You handled the whip smartly back there. Never seen a woman do that! Allow me to compliment you on your resourcefulness and ask the obvious question: whom have I the honor of addressing?"

Sammie Jo rallied. She breathed deeply for a few seconds and tried to remember her newfound training as a lady. "I am Samantha, Lady Pennywhistle. I am dam... exceedingly grateful for your intervention."

His face blanched as if he had seen a ghost. "My God, did I hear that right? Lady *Pennywhistle*? Is your husband Thomas Pennywhistle?"

"Yes, he is!" she said proudly.

Thynne burst into laughter. "Will wonders never cease! Tom Pennywhistle married! Extraordinary! Never thought I'd see the day. And to an American! An incredible turn of events!" He shook his head in wonder.

"Pardon me, sir," said Sammie Jo with what she hoped was sufficient dignity, "how do you know my husband?"

"We enjoyed a unique association in Spain, my lady. I was on my way to the ball to speak to him but was unavoidably delayed by... uh... uh... other considerations that took longer to settle than I anticipated. But it looks like fate worked things out in advance since it placed me in exactly the right place at just the right time."

Sammie Jo noticed the faintest outline of a woman's lips on the gold of his collar. She perfectly understood what "the other considerations" were.

"I count your husband one of the most stalwart fellows that I have ever met." His face suddenly looked worried. "Forgive my stupidity, my lady. He must be in great distress if so fine a woman is defending the carriage."

"He lies unconscious inside. It is imperative that we get him to safety as soon as possible."

Thynne's face assumed a resolve that made steel seem paper. "He is my friend and will always be thus. I pledge my sword to his service and give you my most solemn word: none shall lay a finger on him this night."

"Thank you!" Sammie Jo leaped down from her perch and raced to the door. Her heart jumped when she saw her husband was awake, although as pale as milk. She flung the door open and jumped inside. She put her hands on his face tenderly and kissed him gently.

"I gather we are safe. What happened?" he asked weakly. She told him breathlessly.

He perked up at the name of the cavalryman. "My God, Steven Thynne! Of all the odd things! He rescued me in Spain and now it looks as if he has done it again."

It pleased her that he had such a friend. One of the first things that impressed her when they had met was the loyalty that he inspired in subordinates and colleagues. It was a quiet, unpretentious undercurrent that did not manifest in extravagant words and frivolous chatter but surfaced in swift action and brave deeds.

"He will escort us home, Tom."

"Then you may relax, my dear—we could not be in better hands." He turned thoughtful. "He might be just the man I need right now, for a variety of reasons. He has contacts not open to me. We definitely need to talk. I seem to recall he spent some time at a German university."

She put a hand firmly to his lips. "Hush, Sugar Plum: stop talking. You need rest. You have had enough excitement for one day."

"You are probably right. The best idea..." The pleasant abyss of sleep yawned before his fading consciousness.

Finally! Thought Sammie Jo.

Chapter Thirty-Two

"Boom! Boom! Crack!"

Pennywhistle drifted in and out of consciousness as Gabriel and Lord Steven helped him toward the townhouse, but wakefulness prevailed when he heard gunfire. The acoustic signatures were distinctive: a double barreled Purdey and a Baker. The faces of the weapons' owners flashed into his mind and he cocked his head toward the source of the reports, the library. Intruders after the book!

Sammie Jo saw his intention in his pinched cheeks and weary eyes. "Not on your life, Sugar. I'll handle this." She turned to Gabriel and Steven. "Get him inside and don't listen to anything he says about my needing help."

They nodded.

"The book..." Pennywhistle croaked.

"Safe, Sugar Plum. I hid it well."

"Good, good," said Pennywhistle weakly.

Sammie Jo raced inside and bolted up the stairs to the first floor, though in her American mind it should have been numbered the second. She could smell brimstone as she darted into the library.

Dale and Grimsby were on their knees, methodically searching the bodies of two dead burglars. Dale rose when he saw Sammie Jo. "Sorry that we have not had a chance to clean up the mess, my lady. These two chaps made the mistake of disputing our presence and we had to explain to them the errors of their ways. Ex-army I would say by the way they held their weapons."

He pointed to a section of the large bookshelves denuded of books. "They seemed to be after something specific, though it does not make sense to me why they would focus their attentions on the library."

Sammie Jo made a face. "I know just what they were after. My husband and I were attacked tonight after the ball. He is badly injured and being helped to bed as we speak."

Dale and Grimsby winced at the unwelcome news.

"This break-in was part of a concerted effort against us. I am pretty sure it is the same group behind the attack at the bookstore and Russian Embassy. They are persistent bast... uh... blackguards. I think we have seen the last of them for tonight, but I can't be certain. I would take it as a great favor if you two could mount a guard tonight in case they have friends."

"Of course!" chorused Dale and Grimsby.

"He shall be as safe tonight as if he were residing in Stonehouse Barracks," added Dale.

Pennywhistle slept long and deeply. When he awoke he judged it to be late afternoon by the length of the sun's rays. He hurt, but nothing like before. He put his hand to his back and realized the stitches had been redone. Sammie Jo sat in a *chinoiserie* chair next to his bed. When she saw his eyes open she let go of the death grip on his hand and stroked his cheek gently.

"The sight of your face is the best medicine a man could wish for," said Pennywhistle. "I hope you have not been in that chair all night."

"No, just since dawn. I slept in the other room on the advice of Doctor Hewes, though I hated doing so. He warned me about putting your stitches in jeopardy, so no bedroom

BOMBPROOFED

delights for at least a week. You know how we are, Tom; put us within ten feet of each other and we turn into rabbits."

"True enough, but a week without you sounds more like torture than good medicine."

Sammie Jo's mouth twisted like she had bitten a rotten rhubarb stalk. "That's not the worst of it. He said that for a full recovery, you will need to be dry-docked for a month."

"A month! A month! Nonsense! Nonsense! I am ready to fight right now!" He tried to sit up.

She gripped his shoulders and gently forced him down.

"You should never have left your bed after we got you back from Brooks. You are your own worst enemy, thinking that you are a man of steel rather than one of flesh and blood. You beat death once, and now it seems like you are baiting him. I want you back hale and hearty. Besides, bed rest will give you plenty of time to solve your code mystery. Show some sense and give recovery a fighting chance."

She saw the look of alarm on his face. "Don't worry, Sugar Plum. The book is safe. Those burglars never had a chance thanks to Dale and Grimsby. The book has been in the bedroom the whole time, just a few feet away from your bed."

"What do you mean, Hawkeye?"

"I thought I would sit on the book, and that's exactly what I am doing. I found that the seat was loose in this chair: there's just enough space between the seat and support to slip in a slim volume. All the swirly Chinese designs on it reminded me of code stuff."

"Very clever of you," said Pennywhistle wearily. "I should like to get started straightaway, but I believe my body has other ideas." His eyelids seemed like falling boulders and he yawned heavily.

"Then listen to it for once instead of your head. You need rest and lots of it. Now get some sleep."

"Yes, yes quite righ..." He had not finished the sentence before his head flopped back on the pillow.

He slept most of the next five days, waking only to eat, visit the water closet, and converse briefly with Sammie Jo. Yet his mind remained active and his dreams told him just what he needed to do, and just how to do it.

At the end of the sixth day of his convalescence he felt noticeably stronger, but Sammie Jo would not hear of him leaving his bed.

She and Lady Leith hatched a quiet conspiracy among friends and servants to make sure he rested and avoided anything physical that might tax his strength. Someone seemed to check on him, albeit discreetly, every hour or so. It was supposed to be random but it was so well organized that he began to amuse himself by timing visits with his watch.

The servants were attentive, although their well meant kindness became overbearing at times. They brought him his meals, set his bed tray, laid out the chafing dishes and utensils and always inquired if he needed anything further.

The hardest part was Sammie Jo's enforced absence from his bed. It made him realize how accustomed he had grown to her presence not just in his bed but in his life.

During the seventh, eighth, and ninth days of his confinement, she sat on his bed and talked with him for hours, completely unguarded conversation about matters both trivial and profound. Each came to understand the other a little better.

She read to him sometimes, from books that he recommended. Gibbon was his favorite. He told her that he marveled not at the existence of the Roman Empire but that it had survived so long. He wondered if the immense size and complexity that had been one of the causes for its downfall might not be a warning to the burgeoning British Empire. She did not grasp all of Gibbon's wisdom, but agreed with his skepticism about organized religion and felt an affinity for the history-changing rebels that he brought to life. She particularly liked the story of the Empress Theodora, one of the most powerful women of history who had started life as a prostitute. When she read "the generality of princes if stripped of their purple and cast naked into the world would immediately sink to the lowest level of society without a hope of emerging from their obscurity," she burst into laughter and exclaimed, "He must have met Prinnie!"

Reading to a spouse was a surprisingly intimate activity. She enjoyed learning about a greater world and understood that her voice relaxed her husband, speeding his healing. She believed herself embarked on a personal *Gulliver's Travels* and sometimes felt just as marooned as the protagonist of *Robinson Crusoe*. She was several times tempted to break her pledge, but reason always staged a late comeback and her promise was kept.

When she was not in the room, he focused his energies on his big project: breaking the code and deciphering his brother's ledger and letters. His mind craved gainful employment even more than his fit body craved exercise. *The Little Code Breaker and Pocket Cryptographer* became his constant companion. The book was a mere hundred pages long, and after reading it through a dozen times he almost had it memorized. Still, he was missing something.

He had his brother's ledger and the letters spread out on the bed and glanced back and forth between them and the book. The solution lay somewhere in front of him. Why could he not see it? He was frustrated beyond measure because he knew he was at exactly the right door and only lacked the proper key to unlock the mysteries of the room within.

One of the ten tables in the book held that key, but the one that he thought would work turned out to be a dead end. The other nine were variants of the one he and his brother had used long ago, but those variations constituted the difference between a ditch and a canyon.

He was experienced enough to know that a glorious Eureka instant of understanding could only be purchased at the price of weeks of work and deep thought. Good luck most often comes to the prepared mind. It was a matter of sift, categorize, guess, test, hypothesize, test, fail, then start again.

Rather than being discouraged each time he failed, he told himself he was like a pilot plotting the main channel through a winding river; careful to chart each sandbar.

He had one advantage over everyone else: he was familiar with his brother's manner of speech and his mode of writing. His brother's prose was as distinctive as the man, infused with the mathematical intelligence of an architect. He could hear the equivalents of square roots, prime numbers, and The Golden Mean in the meter of his sibling's penned discourse.

As near as he could make out, the ledger was some form of diary, a strange thing for a man of secrets to possess, and probably why it was written in code. If he could correctly identify even one phrase his brother regularly used, it would be a doorway into the attic of secrets. He started with Table One and started to methodically apply the codes.

Days later, after finishing Table Five, he shook his head in frustration.

Assuming a one to one correspondence between letters and numbers, he needed to find a regularly repeated sequence of between 10 and 26 numbers amidst the unbroken sea that confronted him. This last day of meticulous scrutiny had yielded nothing but eye strain and frustration. What phrase of his brother's could he apply to this chaos of numbers?

BOMBPROOFED

Peter had been a committed Tory and admired Edmund Burke. Peter loved Burke's observation, paraphrased from Plato, that "all that evil needs to succeed is for good men to do nothing" and had coined his own corollary: "good men who do nothing good are good for nothing." Either one would be a long string of patterned numbers, and his eyes and intuition had seen nothing that echoed those phrases yet. "Brag and bounce," was another expression Peter had employed. He had been a cynical man, the essence of a conservative, quick to disparage new ideas and even quicker to consign them to the dustbin of ill-informed speculation. That phrase was short enough to be used more frequently than his corollary to Burke. Pennywhistle sighed and put the ledger away, then rubbed his eyes.

Another day's searching served no purpose other than to ratchet up Pennywhistle's rising level of frustration. He grew angry and narrowly restrained himself from ripping up both book and correspondence and chucking them into the fireplace. It was like traveling an unmapped, winding road in a dense fog. He knew a large building lay just ahead, knew its general shape, but he needed the breeze of insight for a brief second to discern its exact configuration.

Strangely, it was the anger that rescued him. "Confound it!" he exclaimed with asperity as he crumpled up his last set of calculations. It hit him that he sounded exactly like his judgmental brother because he had just spoken his actual favorite phrase.

He froze. It could not be. He counted the letters in his mind. It would be almost too easy. And yet, given his brother's passion for perfection, it might just be exactly right.

He fought down the rising excitement and forced himself to think logically. Then he remembered two sketches at the beginning of the ledger and flipped back to study them: a five pointed star at the top of the first page and one at the bottom.

The pentacle was a medieval symbol of wisdom that Sir Gawain had carried on his shield. The five points of the first star represented the five senses. Those of the second represented the five fingers of the Hand of Destiny. Next to the first star was a sword that he recognized as his brother's idea of Excalibur, from a childhood fascination with King Arthur. Accompanying the second star was Arthur's other sword, the one almost never spoken of: Clarent, the sword of peace. Perhaps the stars and swords represented a puzzle, both a guidepost and a warning. He stroked his chin pensively. The sum of the points was ten. Could that number be telling him the Tenth Table was the key? The key to both war and peace?

Yes, damn it, that had to be it! A decimal cypher! The tenth table was the key in such cases, and meaningful phrases were in blocks of ten numbers, starting with the very first number.

Suddenly, another sketch in the ledger made sense. It was *Il Balzana*; a shield whose top half was white and bottom half was black. A symbol of the city of Sienna, its colors played a prominent role in *Il Palio*, the city's famous horse race. A white flag signaled the start of the race, a black flag its finish. He and his brother had witnessed that race when their father had taken them on the Grand Tour as children. Those flags could also be start/stop symbols in a cipher. Of course! The cipher was like a series of switches: on, off, on, off. Every other set of ten was gibberish designed to confuse. That flag was a clue that no one else but himself would have understood. For all their estrangement, his brother had clearly kept him in mind as a man to entrust with secrets.

Bombproofed

He breathlessly took the first entry in the ledger and made slash marks after every ten numbers, disregarding every second set.

Half an hour later, he threw down the ledger, hit a fist against his palm, and exclaimed, "Yes!" in triumph. He had what he needed. Now it was just a matter of time and applying the frequencies of letters in the English language, aided by his knowledge of his brother's cadences of speech and thought. He began to write his transcriptions in a journal. One grouping of ten numbers snared his eye: the second and fifth numbers were the same, as were the third and seventh. "*Confound it*," he murmured. The key turned in the lock.

*****

As the days passed and his brother's secrets became clear, he acquired a newfound respect for a man that he had entirely misread. Peter had been involved in some very dangerous business and had done great service for his country. *Why was I so damn pig-headed? Two simple words would have fixed things: "I'm sorry."*

But The Guide instructed him that regret was a heavy, pointless burden. To honor his brother's memory by solving his murder he needed to clear his conscience by forgiving himself.

He let nothing disturb his concentration for the rest of the day and long into the night. Every time a servant knocked he yelled, "Go away!" The final time he added Sammie Jo's favorite expletive to his request. He did not care if he sounded uncivilized; this was far too important.

Sammie Jo knew better than to disturb him when what she called "the tyranny of the mind" came upon him.

His expression changed frequently as he worked. Satisfaction, puzzlement, alarm, disbelief, certitude and doubt each enjoyed fleeting moments of control. He found out not just the nature of the mission that had gotten his brother killed but also who stood to profit from possession of the wayward letters.

By the time he got round to translating the two letters in the wee hours of the following morning, he had enough background information from his brother's private thoughts to know that what Mrs. Clarke had written was explosive, specific enough to wreck quite a few careers and possibly bring down the present government. And these were but two of probably five and twenty letters.

One entire letter was a list of twenty gentlemen, many of whose names he recognized. Alongside each was a listing of his private peccadilloes; those included everything from a love for men to pedophilia, as well as bribery, treasonous correspondence, and even murder. Two were from the greatest families in England while others were members of Parliament. Several cabinet officials made the dubious list, as did three members of the royal family.

The material would be very useful to a foreign government determined to disrupt British plans in Vienna. It perfectly explained all of the attacks against him since he had landed in England. Whatever parties held the letters could not translate them—they had guessed that he might have the book that would allow them to do so.

Cui bono? He asked himself the classic lawyer's question. Who benefits?

He thought of von Gilsa at the ball, a Prussian in the Russian Service. He had undoubtedly been detailed as a minder and had probably helped coordinate the attack on the carriage. All of the men killed in the carriage attacks had been identified as Germans who sometimes freelanced for the Russians. Grey Cloak had later been identified as one Lieutenant Karl von Grosse, late of the Russian Embassy.

Bombproofed

The Russians had motives to want to disrupt British efforts. Their expansion in the East was bringing them into unwanted contact with British possessions in India; that tension was already being called "The Great Game." They had no interest in stopping the persecutions of Jews, and even less in ending the trafficking of slaves. Free trade and freedom of the seas occupied no place in their thinking. They wanted to greatly expand their influence in Europe and were willing to do so at the expense of everyone else. They were fundamentally opposed to the balance of power doctrine that was Castlereagh's guiding principle.

He sent word to Smith and Jones via Thynne, saying that he wanted to talk to Meriwhether Trelawney. Trelawney came to his bedside that evening. He was only about thirty but looked twenty years older. His cheeks were sunken, his eyes hollow, and he possessed a seemingly limitless appetite for whiskey. Pennywhistle fed that appetite with Glen Livet in exchange for the answers that he needed.

Trelawney responded volubly enough to his grilling, but he could not quite be sure how much to trust the responses of a drunk who had only seen something through his spyglass. The most important thing to come out of the long interview was that the man who had murdered his brother was exceptionally tall and had a face full of scars and burns. It sounded like that face was a close copy of the one that had been haunting his dreams.

The following day he sent word to Smith and Jones, telling them that he needed a diplomatic order of battle for the Russian Delegation to the Congress of Vienna. It was soon forthcoming because the Prince Regent had come through with his official appointment.

He reviewed the list, looking for highly placed Germans in the czar's entourage. He found four names, all listed as imperial aides-de-camp. He sent another message to Smith and Jones, asking if they could have their counterparts in Vienna come up with a physical description of the four men as well as any information on their backgrounds. He told Smith and Jones that the information was critical to deciphering his brother's materials. They had accepted his explanation without question because the intelligence business frequently needed the oddest bits of information to solve a puzzle.

"We will dispatch a fast rider to Vienna this very evening," Jones replied by letter. "You should have what you want in two weeks."

Find the current possessor of the letters and he would find his brother's murderer. His intuition said it had to be one of the four Germans. He realized that his trip to Vienna might be disputed by the same people who had repeatedly attacked him. He needed an edge and began to consider modifications to Lady Leith's carriage. That would involve a number of contractors, but he had weeks of enforced recuperation to look forward to, and they could probably complete the work in that time.

He read everything he could about the current situation in Vienna. The presence of a deranged murderer shocked him. The London papers helped, but he also needed some from Vienna. The trouble was, he did not speak German. Then he recalled that Thynne had studied at Heidelberg University because his mother admired Kant and wanted her son to read *Critique of Pure Reason* unmarred by faulty translation. It struck Pennywhistle that his translations of Clarke's letters were compiling a critique of pure treason.

The clock struck 2 a.m. The door burst open and in stormed a whirlwind in a robe. "I can't stand it no more!" barked an angry Sammie Jo. "You have been ordering the servants around these past weeks like a goddamned overseer on the worst plantation. You have been swearing, which you never do, and have generally sounded angrier than a white-coated man falling into a tar pit! Now tell me, what the hell is going on? You' ain't been trying to exercise, have you? If you have, I will flay the hide off you."

He smiled at her, remembering the Eureka moment. He should have trusted her with this information earlier: her ability to cut to the heart of an issue might well have enabled him to solve the puzzle faster. He spoke in calming tones. "No, Sammie Jo. It is my mind that has been getting vigorous exercise. I finally have some of the answers that I need and believe I know where to go to obtain the rest." His smile turned wry and his voice grew conspiratorial. "Lock that door. We need to talk. What we say must go no further than this room."

They talked until dawn, and then made passionate love.

Chapter Thirty-Three

"I'm pregnant."

Sammie Jo gently whispered the words as the first rays of dawn flooded their pillows. Spoken in the glow of relaxed, post coital bliss, her words nonetheless caused her husband to sit up as violently as if someone had jammed a Congreve Rocket up his backside. A wealth of emotions suffused his face in rapid succession: shock, amazement, relief, and finally joy.

"My God! And I thought I was the only one guilty of keeping secrets! Are you sure? Absolutely certain?"

"Yup, sure as I am that Summer follows Spring. My periods are regular as clockwork, and I have missed three. I didn't want speak earlier because I could not bear to see the look on your face if this turned out to be a false hope— or I miscarried. You are definitely not going to be the last of your line."

Pennywhistle reached over and kissed her long and tenderly. When he drew back, his face was deep in thought. "For all my careful calculations, I had never considered this possibility. This changes everything."

She looked at him quizzically. "How so?"

"I have been selfish; so obsessed with dredging up the secrets of the past and making peace with the dead that I neglected to consider the needs of a future family. While I have a duty to my brother as well as to king and country, I have one to protect my heir as well. The course of action I have been contemplating might well put that heir at risk. My investigations have already made me the target of an assassination attempt. Should future efforts be extended to include you, our child-to-be would be in danger. There might well be wisdom in a cessation of my efforts."

Sammie Jo's face darkened and her brow furrowed. "I think you got it all wrong, Sugar Plum. Instead of changing everything, my pregnancy makes everything more certain. I don't think you were wrong or selfish before because you are a man who lives for duty. I agree that you have a duty to our son or daughter, but that don't include changing your very essence. I understand you want to keep our child safe, but even if you stopped your inquiries, there is no guarantee the bastards behind the attack on our carriage will cease coming after you. Men like that do not give up easy. They think that you have the key to a powder magazine of explosive information, and so you do. If the missing letters contain information half as damning as the ones in your possession, then you are a marked man. But as long as I breathe, anyone who comes after me or our child is going to get a dose of lead that will rearrange his priorities in double quick time."

Pennywhistle frowned. "I want what is best for you and our child."

"And I want what is best for you, Tom, and that don't include retreat. You consider your word of honor a sacred thing, and you pledged it when you maneuvered your future king into giving you the post in Vienna. How would you explain to your son or daughter that you had reneged on a promise to a king out of fear for his or her safety? People consider you a hero, and though I know that don't mean nothing to you, it does affect how future generations will regard members of your family. I know I have a lot to learn about being a lady, but in my time here I have come to see how important a reputation is. I never had much of one back home but I am trying hard to build a good one here and be a credit to your name."

Pennywhistle smiled. "I have noticed your efforts in that regard, but I love you for your character and heart, not your manners."

Sammie Jo nodded. "I would say the same about you, Tom, and it is because of your character that I know what shunning your quest would do to you. It would be a lead weight on your mind, gnaw at you like a beaver never letting go of a log, and be a slow growing cancer of the soul that would waste you away to a shadow of the man I married. You hate mysteries and are like a bulldog once you get your teeth into one. Your nature demands that you keep pushing until you find a solution."

Pennywhistle sighed, "I do so wish I did not obsess about things."

"No," said Sammie Jo thoughtfully," obsessing ain't a bad thing if the cause is just and righteous. Finding out who took your brother's life qualifies. What you do about it is another matter."

"That is the problem, Hawkeye. I have grave doubts about my course of action if I solve the mystery of my brother's murder. My emotions and martial nature demand one outcome: my intellect and the knowledge from the Other Side require quite another. My emotions and nature inform me that my brother's soul demands justice; even if that justice lies outside the bounds of the law. My intellect tells me justice must only be administered within the confines of the law or else lawlessness becomes the order of the day. The Guide's message is that the Universe is about love and forgiveness."

Sammie Jo pursed her lips. "I love you to death, Tom, but you over think things. My mind is a lot simpler than yours; I see fewer options but I see them more clearly. You once told me,'Be sure your right, then go ahead,' and right now you ain't quite sure. You shouldn't try to run someplace when you ain't certain if you want to walk there. You are like a playwright wanting to cast a leading man for his Tragedy but you can't do that until you look close and hard at the people auditioning."

Pennywhistle scratched his head vigorously, as if compelling a reluctant brain to acknowledge that it was sometimes was too refined and educated to see simple truth. He loved his wife for her no-nonsense, practical intelligence. Hers was borne of instinct and Nature: the product of years of observing trees, plants, and animals. His was borne of intellect and academia: the product of learned men, lecture halls, and leather bound books. Curiously, the two functioned symbiotically; in the manner of a bee pollinating a plant.

"My dear," said Pennywhistle quietly,"I married you for your frankness and commitment to truth no matter how hard it might sound. I see in your face that you are just bursting to tell me something that is in direct conflict with your newly acquired lady-like ways."

Sammie Jo sat up and squared her shoulders as civilization faded her face. "God damn it, Tom, my nature is to speak raw: so here it is. I saw your half brother die at your side, and I know what that done to you. I had a grandmother who people said was a witch, mainly because she knew a lot of herbs and used them to help sick folks and animals too. She called each potion she mixed a spell. Right now you need some thinking magic to fix your problems, and I aim to help you figure out the right spell."

"Are you suggesting that I consult a Book of Shadows for some diplomatic incantations?" replied Pennywhistle with amusement.

"I want to be a lady real bad, but not so much that I ever want to become a yellow-bellied, lily-livered, faint-hearted, no-account bitch so in love with liv'n safe and fine that I put my will ahead of my husband's."

"The trouble is, dearest Samme Jo, I don't quite know my own feelings. I want to see justice done but murder is a monstrous thing, no matter how much a person deserves it. This man may well enjoy diplomatic immunity, and governments frown on one diplomat taking the life of another. Such an action could have unforeseen, even disastrous consequences."

"Tom, I think you are putting the cart before the hearse. First you have to find this man, which will require a lot of digging. You are right in thinking that being a diplomat will open a lot of doors normally kept shut; even so, some of those same doors will stay shut to protect other diplomats. But maybe there is a way to kill the murderer without taking his life. If you ruin a man's reputation, take away all that is dear to him, living is a lot worse punishment than death. Think about it. What would be more painful: the guillotine or social solitary confinement for twenty years because you are shunned by all?"

Pennywhistle rubbed his chin in thought. "That is quite an interesting proposition, and one which needs to be explored. You have me realizing that two heads can indeed be better than one."

Sammie Jo beamed. "Two bodies are better than one as well, Tom. We need to explore that proposition directly." She pulled him close as the certainty of their love banished all worry about the future.

*****

BOMBPROOFED

Von Steinwehr was also focused on family at that moment, for he held the newest addition in his arms. He smiled as the newborn cooed softly. "I cannot tell you how happy this makes me, Ingrid. I am so glad that I brought you here and could witness the birth. I was wrong about you being a distraction. In truth, without your direct guidance, I am a ship without a rudder. Having a male heir is a dream come true. I love our daughters, but every ruler needs a successor. My first thought was that we should name him Karl after my father, but I think Alexander would be a better choice."

Ingrid made a face.

"I know, I don't like it much either, but the Czar would be greatly flattered and I need every ounce of his good will."

"Klaus, this new life makes me think it's time for the Edelweiss Executioner to die. What you have done has been terrible but necessary. I have supported your strategy every step of the way and will never be troubled by sleepless nights, but I now believe it is time to reclaim your humanity. Your doppelganger has accomplished his mission and put the city in an uproar. Now you should bring that killer to justice and become the hero of the hour. Von Danniken has made himself thoroughly despised and many in the Hapsburg Court will cheer at his ouster. The fact that Metternich has now come out in favor of Reichenau's return means that you can now pursue your campaign by more peaceful means."

Von Steinwehr sighed in agreement. "I confess I have grown weary of the bloodshed, but there are still a few loose ends to tie up. In particular, the Englishman."

"Are you sure you need him dead, Klaus? Do you even need what he possesses at all? You already have a dozen letters of the alphabet identified. It is just a matter of time before you decipher them all. Your last attempt on his carriage met with disaster and attracted bad publicity. Furthermore, it alarmed him and put him on the defense. It is only by the grace of God that Alexander has not heard of it, since those men were attached to the Russian Embassy. Making another attempt would be pushing your luck to a dangerous extreme."

"As always, Ingrid, you make a sound argument. However, I do not know how long it will take to decipher the remainder of the alphabet, and the agenda of the Congress waits for no man. I need that information as soon as possible."

"Are you sure that's not the mania talking, dearest husband? I will allow your arguments make sense, but you have everything you want right here without the letters, and the prize is within your hand. Why put it all at risk?"

"Because it's the only way to be sure. Besides, the red ledger may have additional material that could prove useful."

"Very well, but as a favor to me, could you wait a week before putting any new plans into action? Play with your children, make love to me, and enjoy your newborn. Show me and your daughters the food and shopping delights of the city. Relax and allow yourself some joy, then see how you feel."

"You have a golden tongue and a heart as warm as it is valiant. I shall honor your wishes. Pennywhistle can wait a week—or even ten days."

*****

Sammie Jo's love for Pennywhistle caused Dale to constantly think of Deborah. He wanted to rush into her arms like the dashing swain of Charlotte Lennox's novel, but both of them were too old for that sort of romantic nonsense. Expecting her to discard a purposeful life when a figure from the dead materialized out of the blue was as presumptuous as it was foolish. Careful planning was called for, just as it was in a military expedition; he needed to lay siege to her logic far more than her heart. He had to offer her and his son a future built on a solid foundation, not vague promises. That future involved the Black Robin.

The trouble was not all of his prize money from the Chesapeake had been paid, and he had not yet submitted his retirement paperwork to receive his pension. He had expected Pennywhistle's assistance on both matters, but since his officer was fighting to regain his health, he had remained silent about both.

The solution arrived in two parts on the same day. A week after he and Grimsby had killed the burglars, Gabriel's salvage money was delivered by special messenger. Normally payment would have taken months, but Pennywhistle's celebrity had accelerated matters.

"Now what is an old man like me to do with all this money?" said a happily perplexed Gabriel. "I know what old Masstuh Tom would do—go on a bout of drinking, gambling, and chasing fancy women. But I had a good woman once and ain't no one can match her. I'd buy her freedom, but I don't know where she is, or if she is even alive."

"You should bank the money first," said Lady Leith, "then invest it in something safe and reliable like government bonds. I'd be happy to help with that."

Dale noticed that Lady Leith held a newspaper under her arm, *The Laborer's Clarion*. "Excuse me, milady, that newspaper—have you read it?"

"I have. I read a great many newspapers. While everyone subscribes to *The Times*, I like to get different perspectives, perspectives that do not represent echo chambers of current government policies." She unfurled the newspaper and glanced at the print. "The views of this man are considered disagreeable by my friends, but I find his views on social matters as refreshing as they are timely. We may have beaten the French, but I fear if some changes are not made we may experience our own revolution.

Gabriel saw the name on the masthead: "D. MacJarrow." He looked at Dale and blurted out, "Say, ain't that your lady friend?"

Lady Leith blinked and started. "You mean the publisher of this paper is a woman? How extraordinary! Do you know her, Sergeant Major?"

"I do. Quite well. It's a very long story."

"I should love to hear it, Sergeant Major, and I have plenty of time. Why don't we all repair to the morning room and celebrate Gabriel's good fortune with some whiskey while you regale us with what must be a very interesting tale."

Three glasses of the Glen Livet relaxed Dale's normally reserved tongue, and over the next two hours he told his story. He left nothing out and did something he normally would never do—he shared his deepest emotions. He realized as he talked how much he truly loved Deborah: she truly was *the one*.

"That kind of love deserves a better ending," said a delighted Lady Leith when he finished. "I want to help, but I have some bad news to deliver. I read this issue of the *Clarion* carefully because I expect it will be its last. The government considers it a seditious rag. A friend of mine who is a confidant of Lord Liverpool assures me that it will be shut down in two weeks."

"That is indeed distressing," said an anxious Dale. "Deborah has probably invested her life in that paper."

"We have two weeks," said Lady Leith firmly. "If her press could be relocated away from London, she could continue to publish. I think the Black Robin might suit. I know you lack

BOMBPROOFED

the funds to purchase, but I do not." She turned to Gabriel. "This might be a good investment for your funds."

"Being part owner of an inn does sounds mighty good; maybe we could add a livery stable. I like the idea of helping out a friend."

"Here is what I propose. Let us make a journey to the Black Robin tomorrow. If it meets expectations, I will purchase it with gold. Gold should get us a lower price. Consider it a loan, Sergeant Major, but one with an open-ended repayment date. Does that sound agreeable?"

"Agreeable is not the word! It is incredible! Incredible!" Dale beamed.

Lady Leith laughed. "It is worth the money just to see you drop your mask!"

The Black Robin exceeded expectations and Lady Leith proved as good as her word. Dale achieved his lifelong dream and Gabriel resolved to make the Black Robin's livery stable the best in all England.

Dale's meeting with Deborah did not go smoothly. When he confronted her, she fainted. After she revived, he related his life and adventures since Trafalgar. She listened patiently —she had always been good at that—but at the end regarded him with affection rather than love. She explained that his apparent death had broken her heart and she had vowed never again to be so vulnerable. She had learned to do without a man, and so his proposal of marriage was not met with the joyful enthusiasm that he dreamed of, but with words he did not want to hear: "I don't know. I just don't know."

In the end, their son decided things. Deborah summoned her child and gently told the lad he was about to receive a shock that yet might be welcome. She explained that she had told him what she had believed to be true, that his father had died at Trafalgar. "This man's name is Andrew... I named you after him because... he is your father."

The boy started, blinked, and finally smiled. "Father?" he said, as if unsure that a Christmas present given him had not been intended for someone else.

"Son," said Dale with enormous pride, "I so wish I could have said that word to you years ago." His eyes teared up. "The love I had for your mother has truly produced a wonderful outcome, but this is so unexpected that I must touch you to believe you are real."Dale gently placed his hands on the boy's shoulders.

The boy stood ramrod straight, imitating the carriage that was second nature to his father. The boy and the man locked eyes, and silently a bond was established. Both seemed to sense that it was not just their faces that aligned, but also their personalities.

Deborah sighed and thought *"Two peas in a pod."* She bowed to the inevitable. "You two need to talk. Why not take a long walk up Leadenhall Street and get to know each other?"

After a three-hour stroll, father and son returned as fast friends. The boy spoke with the firmness of his father mixed with the common sense of his mother. "Mother, you need to marry Andrew. It is not his fault that his death was misreported. You are about to lose everything and he has a safe alternative. I want a father, especially one who has served his country so long and well. I want a home, too. I am tired of the way our landlord keeps increasing the rent. You loved Andrew once; you will do so again if you give it time. Be sensible, Mother!"

Deborah crossed her arms and bowed her head in deep thought. When she looked up her expression was part skeptical and part resigned. "I can't fight both of you. Very well, I accept Andrew, but... with certain conditions."

BOMBPROOFED

Whatever those conditions, Dale could live with them. Their marriage would be a practical contract that enriched and strengthened both parties, far more to do with everyday rationality than heart-pounding passion. Common sense might lack the electricity of romance, but it was a far more reliable foundation for a long marriage.

Chapter Thirty-Four

November in England is usually windy, rainy, and cold, but that autumn England was blessed with what Sammie Jo called an Indian Summer: warm, cloudless days and cool, crisp nights. It was ideal weather for a wedding and a large outdoor reception, and Dale and Deborah determined to take full advantage of this. Lady Leith shone brightly as their wedding planner and happily provided most of the funds for the festivities. Grimsby served as Dale's best man and used his butler skills to organize a myriad details.

Dale and Deborah's wedding took place at nine a.m. on the morning of the sixth, at the 11th century Church of St. Giles in Kingston, eight miles from the much grander Canterbury Cathedral. The ceremony was a simple and dignified Anglican Service, though both principals were mostly strangers to the inside of a church, conducted by Chaplin Chalmers of the Royal Navy—one of the few good men out of a questionable set of clerics.

The interior of the church was decked out in red roses, pink dahlias, and white carnations, and a carpet of crimson velvet graced the path to the altar. Dale wore a scarlet dress uniform that Gieves had tailored at Pennywhistle's request: intended for that ceremony only, since Dale's retirement would become final the next day. Deborah wore a wedding dress of fine white muslin and a soft, primrose-colored shawl

BOMBPROOFED

embossed with flowers of white satin, supplied with the guidance of Senora Castillo.

The Church was packed with people and their attire reflected their varied estates. There was a sizeable contingent of Marine NCOs in their Sunday best uniforms as well as ordinary marines whose uniforms reflected hard service. There were men of industry who had wealth but were poorly represented in Parliament, all assiduous readers of Deborah's paper. There were tradesmen and vendors that Dale and Deborah had dealt with since taking over the Black Robin. There were townspeople who patronized the Inn. Finally there were local gentry, mostly unknown to Dale and Deborah but well-known to Lady Leith. She had included them on the guest list because she felt their good will would prove useful to the newlyweds in the future.

Sammie Jo loved weddings. "I wish our ceremony had not been so small," she whispered to her husband.

"If circumstances had been different, I would have given you a wedding that would have made a Royal one seem meagre," her husband whispered back.

Sammie Jo smiled. "I got the man I wanted and that's all that counts."

Pennywhistle returned her smile. Though her pregnancy was not yet visible, that condition made her positively glow with happiness.

"The two of them don't look like newlyweds; more like they have been married for years," Sammie Jo continued.

"Agreed; what they have is not the mad, passionate love of youth but the more subdued understanding of borne of middle age. I think they are well suited."

"Andrew junior seems to be enjoying this most of all, Tom."

"And so he should. No boy should grow up without a father, and though he is uncommonly mature for his age, I think he is glad that he no longer has to be the man of the house. I think he is also rejoicing in the fresh air and open horizons of the country; a relief after the dirty, crowded tenements of London."

Sammie Jo and Pennywhistle joined the hush that fell over the church as Dale and Deborah said the magic words: "I do."Dale kissed the bride, and his son Andrew had to be restrained from starting to clap.

Pennywhistle smiled broadly. It was wonderful to step away from his own personal problems for a few hours and revel in the joy of new beginnings. Dale had suffered long and hard for his country and deserved happiness. What he was witnessing reminded Pennywhistle that life was about so much more than trouble and turmoil.

He had a lot to be thankful for. His health was improving rapidly and he had resumed regular exercise. He could not yet say he was back to normal but he was getting there. He was going to be a father, and he looked forward to being an active participant in his child's upbringing. Unlike many of his class, he was determined that his child should spend more time with his father and mother than a nanny. Sammie Jo was making good progress socially with Lady Leith's guidance. The Prince Regent's enthusiasm, as well as her exotic background, caused many elite hostesses to place her on their social calendars. Her Spanish riding habit was causing a fashion revolution.

Following the ceremony, Pennywhistle and Sammie Jo chatted with some of the local gentry after Lady Leith made introductions. They seemed eager to talk with him; his reputation as a hero preceded him. Sammie Jo attracted the usual approving glances from the men and the usual curiosity from the women. It was all pleasant enough, though fairly studied and sedate.

Bombproofed

The wedding reception was held outside the Black Robin. The inn was a small two story building that had originally been constructed during the reign of Queen Elizabeth, but an owner in the early 18th century had encased its half timbered core in a coat of white stucco. Its sign featured a dashing masked bandit wielding a sword; clearly inspired by MacHeath in *The Beggar's Opera*. The celebration was a combination of county fair and banquet. It was loud, raucous, and free-wheeling, lacking only twelve lords a leaping; exactly as it was meant to be. Its chief purpose was not to celebrate Dale and Deborah's nuptials but to let the surrounding countryside know that the Black Robin was under new and dynamic management.

The townspeople from both Kingston and the hamlet of Marley flocked to the reception in droves. Dale and Deborah wanted not just their good will but their future business. No invitations were necessary, and people were drawn not just by curiosity but by the promise of good food and drink. Beans, bread, barbeque, and beer constituted the principal attractions. For those with a sweet tooth, several tables were laden with apple pies, fritters, and turnovers.

Pennywhistle deemed Dale's reasoning was sound. The quickest way to reach people was through their stomachs. Many of the townspeople suffered from poor diets which included little meat. Dale's idea was to give them one day where their bellies would be filled with quality food. He wanted to give them all they could drink as well. The upper classes loved their tea, but the lower orders loved their beer. Being English, they consumed quite a lot.

The barbeque represented a large and expensive experiment. Barbequed pork was popular in the southern regions of America but largely unknown in England. The experiment represented a collaboration of inspirations from Sammie Jo, Lady Leith, and above all, Gabriel.

One night at dinner Lady Leith had asked Sammie Jo what she thought of English food. "It's kind of bland, to be honest. It makes me hanker for some good country-style barbeque," Sammie Jo had replied.

Lady Leith inquired, "Just exactly what is barbeque?"

"I can show you, but I will need Gabriel's help."

Two days later, Lady Leith sat down to a meal of slow roasted pork liberally drenched in barbeque sauce. "This is astonishing, absolutely delicious! She proclaimed."How did you do it?"

"I know how to slow roast a pig and was able to instruct the cooks, but the real power is the sauce, and that was all Gabriel's doing."

"And what is in the sauce?" inquired Lady Leith.

"Let's get Gabriel in here to explain it himself." This was speedily done.

"Well, my lady," Gabriel drawled, "I can tell you the ingredients, but the secret is in the proportions and how they are blended. The main ingredients are cider vinegar and molasses. Then there's malt vinegar, tamarind, onion, mustard, and cayenne pepper. I added anchovies to this particular batch as well."

Lady Leith was so taken with the taste that when she was discussing the wedding reception with Dale and Deborah weeks later, she suggested it might be an excellent dish to serve: both delicious and novel. Dale agreed, since he had tasted barbequed pork during his service in America. "In fact,"Dale said thoughtfully, " it could become the signature dish at our Inn. The reception could be its large scale vetting."

The preparations had started well before the reception, because roasting a 100-pound pig took sixteen hours. Seven were purchased, for Dale estimated that he might have to feed as many as three hundred people. The slowly building aroma caused townsfolk's mouths to water well before the reception began. Dale instructed Grimsby to hire out-of-work ex Marines to slice and serve the pork.

Dale spent most of the reception observing its distribution and assessing the effects on taste buds, but he found plenty of time to swap old war stories with fellow NCOs. As they imbibed beer, their stories grew in grandiosity, tempered by lots of Service humor.

Open barrels of beer stood next to the tables where the pork was served. Tin cups and cheap trencher plates were provided. The slices of pork were thick and generous because the Marine servers knew the importance of a "square meal" to a hungry belly. Townsfolk generally slapped the pork slabs onto hefty slices of newly baked pandemain bread that was sweetened with molasses, then sank their teeth in without ceremony. Giant bites were washed down with large gulps of beer.

Dale observed two slightly unsteady cobblers who mirrored the general mood of the crowd.

"Good beer, and the meat ain't bad neither. Did you see the bride and groom?"

"I don't think so, but word is they are running the Inn. If the portions are as generous as now, I might just have to pay that place a visit."

"I don't know what this sauce is, but it's so tasty that I think you could slap some on a piece of shoe leather and make it taste good."

"You got that right. The sauce could be a mender of bad soles."

Both laughed with drunken glee.

A small band entertained the crowd with popular tunes ranging from "Greensleeves" to "The Girl I Left Behind me. "A little later, they supplied music for a group of Morris Dancers. Morris dancing had its origins in druidic times and possessed religious overtones; such dancing was believed to bring good fortune to the events where it was performed. A sword swallower worked his magic while a conjurer worked his. And of course, there was a Punch and Judy show.

Gabriel loved showing off his new livery stable and the horses within. A group of well dressed gentlemen deserted the reception to hang on his every word. "Now, I can make you a right fine deal on this mare. She be real docile and good for riders who are young or inexperienced. Make a fine first horse for your son or daughter." He guided their inspection of the grey horse with a running commentary filled with back country aphorisms. It was much cheekier than one an Englishman would have given, but his listeners seemed amused rather than offended by his novel approach.

Johnny and Andrew talked animatedly well away from the main revelry. Since Johnny had a background in printing, Andrew gave him a tour of his mother's print shop, now located in a barn a few hundred yards behind the inn. Johnny expressed regret that his apprenticeship had been cut short. Andrew replied, "My mother might be able to help with that."

Deborah was having a fine time as well, handing out copies of *The Laborer's Clarion* and explaining her politics to any who would listen. To those who said that printing was not women's work she replied, "Women can do most things as well as men, and many a sight better. Remember, one of our greatest sovereigns was Queen Elizabeth. She turned the tables on the men who said a woman could never rule."

Stars sparkled in Lady Leith's eyes as she chatted with the Earl Grosvenor. She had not seen him for years but had invited him since he owned a considerable estate in the Downs just beyond Kingston. There was a definite attraction between the two, though Grosvenor had really come for another purpose. He had heard that Peter Pennywhistle's body had been discovered and given a burial. Since his son had been Pennywhistle's assistant, he wanted to speak to his brother Thomas to see if he had any information on his son's fate.

As the hours wore on, the reception grew louder and louder as the massive amounts of beer began to take effect. A few arguments broke out as well as few fights, but there was plenty of kissing and fondling as well: young sparks finding hidden corners where they could express their feelings directly with girls they would normally only pass on the street.

A country dance involving at least a hundred people started up opposite the Inn. Sammie Jo recognized it as very similar to the folk dances that moved in large squares back home. She grabbed Pennywhistle's arm and laughed, "C'mon Tom, let's join in!"

"Why not?" replied Pennywhistle merrily.

She and Pennywhistle danced for an hour and laughed with joy as they did so. It was mad, silly, delicious fun. The cares of the world vanished in the energetic movements, and overactive minds quieted as limbs capered and hearts sang. Here class had no place and all people were friends.

When they finished, both were pleasantly out of breath, and Pennywhistle smiled.

"What is it?" inquired Sammie Jo.

"I just realized that right now, I am truly happy. That is a rare thing. I am reminded of something the Caliph Abd el Rahmann said 800 years ago.'I have now reigned above fifty years in victory or peace; beloved by my subjects, dreaded by my enemies, and respected by my allies...'"

"I smell a lecture coming on," said an amused Sammie Jo.

"'... Riches and honors, power and pleasure, have waited on my call, nor does any earthly blessing appear to have been wanting to my felicity. In this situation, I have diligently numbered the days of pure and genuine happiness which have fallen to my lot: they amount to Fourteen.' I believe I have had at least ten; considering my age, I am doing better than he did."

Rittmeister von Gilsa observed the conversation from a distance. He came dressed as a peasant, and though he hated his clothing, he knew his disguise was effective. Strangely, his master had given him no orders to act but told him to merely observe and report. He wondered what was going on back in Vienna, but decided that speculation was pointless. He had bungled the carriage ambush and was eager to redeem himself. Sir Thomas and his wife seemed to be deeply in love; a far cry from his own carefully arranged marriage. The English truly were a peculiar people.

Steven Thynne tapped Pennywhistle on the shoulder. Pennywhistle turned to face him and was surprised at the woman that the cavalryman had on his arm. He usually had one in that position, but they were generally tall and saucy. This one was short and dumpy, though she had pleasant face. Thynne did not look happy.

Thynne spoke in oddly formal tones, very different from his usual hail-fellow-well-met manner. "Sir Thomas, Lady Pennywhistle, allow me to present my fiancée, Lady Sarah Winters, daughter of the Duke of Dorset,"

"It is a pleasure to meet you, Lady Sarah." Pennywhistle spoke in his most courtly tones and bowed deeply.

"Enchanted," said Sammie Jo.

"I am so happy to meet you two, I really am," burbled Lady Sarah. "I have heard so much about you. I read about your exploits in the papers, Sir Thomas! And Lady Pennywhistle, I got myself a Spanish riding habit just like yours! I would so love to talk to you about fashions."

"I should enjoy that conversation very much," said Sammie Jo with an enthusiasm that Pennywhistle knew was feigned. He could tell she felt sorry for Sarah; she recognized that she was socially awkward despite her impeccable social credentials. She had been in Sarah's place, a fish out of water, and knew just how painful that could be. Sammie Jo arched her eyebrows ever so slightly and Pennywhistle returned the gesture with a nearly imperceptible nod of the head that said "Proceed."

"Lady Sarah, why don't we go someplace quiet and have that talk. No point in subjecting our men folk to a subject that would bore them silly. I am also sure they have all manner of men stuff to chat about that would be equally dull to us."

"That is a good idea," replied Lady Sarah.

Sammie Jo took Lady Sarah's arm and the two strolled away, chatting as pleasantly as if they had been friends from childhood.

Pennywhistle waited until they were out of earshot. "This is supposed to be a joyous occasion, Steven, but I have seen happier faces on men condemned to the guillotine. I have my suspicions of what is wrong, but I'd like to hear things from your own lips."

Steven sighed heavily. "I do not want to get married, but my family gives me no choice. One of the drawbacks of being a member of an old titled family is lack of freedom in selecting the woman with whom you will spend your life. Sarah is by no means a bad woman; in fact she is heartbreakingly sincere. She loves me; but I, on the other hand, will never love her. The best I can hope for is that we get on amicably, more in the manner of a brother and sister than husband and wife—after she has produced an heir and a spare, of course. I just hope she will not object too strongly to my having a mistress as long as I am discreet. I admire you for violating every canon of the gentleman's marriage code and following your heart. You certainly have won yourself a great prize."

"Let me guess," said Pennywhistle. "If you told your father to go to blazes, you would be disinherited, since you are a third son, not the heir to his title of Marquis."

"Exactly right, Tom. I confess to a weak character. It would be hard to give up all that money, and, well, have to actually earn a living. Being an officer in the Life Guards is expensive; my mess bill alone far exceeds the salary connected to my rank."

For the next twenty minutes, Thynne talked and Pennywhistle listened. Thynne needed a metaphorical shoulder to cry on, and Pennywhistle was pleased that the cavalryman trusted him enough to grant him the honor. He remembered Carlotta's words from the Other Side, "You have the potential to alter many life paths for the good."

A discreet clearing of the throat from behind caused Pennywhistle to face about. When he beheld a tall, dark haired young man with fine features and an olive complexion, he smiled warmly. It was his stepson. "Nico, I am so pleased you made it!" He faced back toward Thynne and made the introductions. "Steven, this is my stepson, Marco Ruzzini, Carlotta's older boy. He is an exceptional student at Harrow and I am very proud of him. His brother Marko is a midshipman on HMS *Albion*. Marco, this is Lord Steven Thynne, a man who has twice saved my life."

Marco and Thynne bowed, then shook hands. "It is a pleasure to meet you, my Lord."

"The pleasure is mine, young man. You are very lucky to have such a fine stepfather."

"I am well aware of that, my lord. Not many men would formally adopt another man's son, but he gave his word to my mother that he would look after me and my brother. If

BOMBPROOFED

there is one thing in the world that is as sure as the next morning's sunrise, it is that Sir Thomas is a man of his word. I am pleased that his achievements have finally been recognized with a suitable title."

The three talked animatedly for half an hour until a man Pennywhistle had never seen before approached; walking with a step that bristled with authority. He was dressed in an elegant blue riding cloak, but his jockey boots were muddy, indicating that he had just finished a long and arduous ride. "Have I the pleasure of speaking with Sir Thomas Pennywhistle?" The man said formally.

"You do indeed, sir. And who might you be, sir?"

"Gareth Williams, at your service, Sir Thomas. We share two mutual friends. Might I have a word in private, sir? It is most urgent."

Pennywhistle was curious as to who these mutual friends were and decided to grant the stranger's request. "There is a quiet grove of trees two hundred yards over yonder where we may talk without interference. Steven, Marco, will you excuse us?"

The stand of tall elms was as quiet as a graveyard and a fine place for either reflection or a clandestine assignation.

Pennywhistle spoke first. "So, who exactly are these mutual friends?"

"Messrs. Smith and Jones, Sir Thomas. I have a confidential package for you. I was instructed to deliver it to you personally and in complete secrecy. It contains answers to those inquires you made weeks ago."

Pennywhistle sighed as the reason for the cloak and dagger theatrics became clear. He scowled for a split second, annoyed that politics had come crashing back to puncture the very pleasant bubble he had been living in all day. He quickly regained his composure; there was no point in lashing out at the messenger. "I presume you would like me to sign a receipt."

"Yes, Sir Thomas. My masters require proof that you have received the documents."

William produced a small canvas pouch bearing a large red wax seal from under his cloak and handed it to Pennywhistle. Pennywhistle accepted a pencil as well and signed Williams's form.

"Thank you, Sir Thomas. I believe that concludes our business. I wish you a pleasant good day."

Pennywhistle was staring at the envelope with such intense concentration that Williams' departure went entirely unnoticed. He both wanted to open it and hated to do so. He was enjoying peace, and what resided within the paper probably argued for a very personal war. His plans for departing for the Continent were well advanced, though he had not yet decided on what people he would include in his entourage. The contents of the pouch would definitely affect those plans.

A memory sprang unbidden into his consciousness: a recent private audience with the Prince Regent, the day after he had delivered the key, ledger, and letters to Smith and Jones. "Damn me, Pennywhistle, the stuff in those letters..." Prinnie sputtered. "I can't even find the words. Of course, I burned them. They could have sunk the monarchy and made Parliament look like a den of criminals! I should have been told a long time ago, but that ain't your fault. Indeed, I am beholden to you. You say there are more letters like this floating about?"

"Twenty-three more, to be exact. I do not know the name of the possessor, but I believe he resides in Vienna."

"I must have them back! I shudder to think of the damage they might do to Castlereagh's plans for the Congress." The Prince Regent's normally muddy eyes turned clear and sparkling as he reached a conclusion. "And you are just the man to get them. I trust you, and you are already officially accredited as the Assistant Naval Attaché. Now, you will be my personal representative as well. That fact must of course be kept hidden from all but Castlereagh. The fewer people who know the letters exist the better."

Pennywhistle sat down on a log to think. It was so quiet and peaceful in the grove that it made one want to write poetry. A man could lose himself just listening to the background hum and rustle of birds and insects. He wanted to keep this blissful solitude frozen in time, but the twin sirens of duty and family began singing. He closed his eyes for a few minutes and breathed deeply. Though he knew the information inside the pouch could wait until tomorrow, he also knew the power of his curiosity. He yielded to it and broke the wax seal. He extracted a document and began to read with a mixture of trepidation and hope.

After perusing the letter he was thoughtful for a long while. He lost track of time. Sundown comes early in an English autumn; stars began to sparkle in the cloudless sky. He looked up when he heard a familiar voice from behind.

"I did not want to disturb you," said Sammie Jo. "I saw you go off with that blue cloaked fella and from the stern look on his face, I figured he had not come to make merry at a reception, I been watchin' you close for the past two hours and from the frustration that's made a home in your eyes, it looks like you did not find what you wanted."

Pennywhistle's mouth twisted as if he had bitten a stalk of rhubarb. "I have some answers but nothing conclusive. Each answer seems to spawn another question. I am left with four suspects, but the evidence against each is circumstantial and you don't destroy a man on circumstantial evidence. The only thing that strikes me as odd is that the dossiers on three of the men are voluminous but that on the fourth is threadbare."

"'Be sure you are right, then go ahead,' ain't that what you told me?"

Pennywhistle nodded.

"Right now you ain't sure and so you can't go ahead; no matter how badly you want to."

Pennywhistle let out a long sigh of exasperation and motioned for Sammie Jo to sit beside him. "I hate it when my own words come back to haunt me, but yes, I do need to be certain."

She put her arm around his shoulders and squeezed gently. "I have faith that you will figure it all out."

Pennywhistle heard the bells of St. Giles summoning the faithful to recite the Lord's Prayer.

"That faith means a lot to me, Sammie Jo and it reminds that whatever I have to face in Vienna I will not do so alone. The Other Side was right: love is the glue that holds the universe together."

"Amen to that," whispered Sammie Jo as she kissed him gently.

A comet furrowed its way across the sky as the Heavens signaled their approval.

THE END

OF BOMBPROOFED
But Tom Pennywhistle will return in *Attaché Extraordinaire*.

Author's Notes

Bombproofed is fiction, but all of the things that Pennywhistle experiences after his demise are found in descriptions of the Near Death Experiences of people who were medically dead for periods ranging from a few minutes to an hour or more; 10-15 minutes being the most common duration. Some of the accounts are anecdotal, but many experiencers have died in emergency rooms in the presence of doctors, nurses, and EMTs who carefully monitored their lack of vital signs and recorded the data. They all fit the conventional definition of death: pupil's fixed and dilated; and no heartbeat, respiration, or brain wave activity.

Religion appears to play little role in what unfolds. Muslims, Christians, Jews, Buddhists, and atheists sound much alike when recounting their experiences. Exact details vary, since the event includes many specific symbols keyed to the unique spiritual needs of the person involved. Yet the core experiences are remarkably similar. Frequently occurring elements include a fast life review, a loud buzzing noise, a brilliant light that conveys love and intelligence, a long tunnel, and greatly heightened perceptions of sight, color, sound, and smell.

Beautiful landscapes of mountains, streams, and prairies are common, as is some kind of barrier, often a fence or a river, marking the boundary between life and death. The brightness of the light in those vistas is often remarked upon.

Many are greeted by friends and relatives who have already passed.

Experiencers report a complete absence of the pain that brought them to this crossing over and instead feel a sense of comfort and well being. Some are offered a choice of staying or returning to Earth to finish what they have started. Those who make the choice to return usually do so for reasons of family and are sad to leave a place that they find peaceful and lovely.

Experiencers maintain that what they viewed was for the purpose of instruction, not judgment, that they might become better people. Some report spiritual guides, but no one reports spiritual judges. People are asked to judge their own lives to gain a better understanding of how important their lives are in the grand scheme of things. The only painful parts of the life review occur when the person experiences the psychic pain that their misdeeds have inflicted on others.

Profound changes take place in the lives of experiencers in the months and years after the incident. Experiencers often develop new talents, abilities, and interests, switch careers and change personal habits, or find that a fear-based marriage or religion no longer serve their needs. These changes typically take seven years to fully manifest.

The choice of whether to embrace these reports as truth or discount them as fantasy belongs to you, the reader. You can be Fox Mulder and believe or Dana Scully and remain skeptical. I have provided a list of books at the end of these notes for people wanting to learn more and make up their own minds.

I have interviewed four Near Death Experiencers and found their accounts as credible as they were extraordinary. When they spoke, their eyes sparkled with a remarkable light that did not appear to come from this world. The joy and certitude with which they spoke convinced me that their experience had been anything but a dream or hallucination. Much as an explanation from the frontiers of science might trouble die-hard rationalists, Occam's Razor still applies.

Near Death Experience Reading List (All are available online)

1. ***Life After Life,*** by Raymond Moody. The book that started it all. The author coined the term "Near Death Experience."

2. **The Big Book of Near Death Experiences,** by PMH Atwater. This book is the best single source of information on the phenomenon. It is arranged by topic, as you'd expect from an encyclopedia. Atwater is a good writer and careful researcher. She is brutally honest and makes it clear that while most experiencers become better people afterwards, some learn nothing and remain just as corrupt and venal as they were before.

3. ***Closer to the Light, Learning from the Near Death Experiences of Children***, by Melvin Morse and Paul Perry. Morse is an ER doctor who initially disbelieved NDEs, but changed his mind after extensive interviews with children who had experienced them.

4. **Lessons from the Light: What We Can Learn From The Near Death Experience**, by Evelyn Elsaessor Valarino and Kenneth Ring. Dr. Ring was one of the early pioneers of truly scientific research on the NDE.

5. ***On Life After Death***, by Elizabeth Kubler-Ross and Caroline Myss. While not strictly about NDEs, the doctor who devised the famous "Five Stages of Grief" had some unusual encounters with deceased patients that are useful in understanding NDEs.

6. ***Other World Journeys, Accounts of Near Death Experience in Medieval and Modern Times***, by Carol Zaleski. A fascinating, scholarly book that shows NDEs were far from unknown in the past.

Historical postscript

The title of the book springs from a British officer who was relieved of a shilling-size portion of his upper forehead by a shell fragment at Waterloo. Back in London, he replaced the steel plate implanted by the surgeon with one made of silver. Emblazoned on it was the word "Bombproof." The officer lived another fifteen years and was forever known by that inscription.

Pennywhistle addresses Dale as Sar't; this was a common form of address in early 19th century British military parlance. (Misspellings in previous books of the series are the work of the notorious grammar gremlin. The author forgot to banish him by saying his name thrice.)

The *Dapper James* is based on *The Chasseur*; a reconstructed version of her, *Pride of Baltimore II,* was launched in 1988. One of the best-equipped and -manned Baltimore privateers, *Chasseur* took 11 prizes in three cruises and was never sunk. Her second captain, Thomas Boyle, actually did declare the British Isles to be in a state of blockade and caused the Admiralty to recall a number of frigates from distant reaches to engage in her pursuit. Her greatest triumph was the capture of *HMS Lawrence* on February 26, 1815. The War of 1812 was over, but word of the Treaty of Ghent had not yet reached the West Indies.

Sammie Jo's weapon is based on a rifle in the author's possession.

The Black Robin Inn is still in operation and serves excellent meals. Sadly, has replaced its old sign.

Greek Fire was first used against an Arab fleet besieging Constantinople in 673. Though the exact formula the Byzantines used remains unknown, it likely contained substantial amounts of naphtha and quicklime; petroleum may have been used as well. It functioned much like modern napalm, generating great heat and burning on water. According to Professor Leo Damrosch of Harvard, in 2006 a modern reformulation of Greek Fire was sprayed from a large copper tube against a large wooden boat 40 feet away. Amidst a roaring noise and a large cloud of smoke, the wooden vessel was incinerated in a few seconds.

The Clarke scandal was real, but Mrs. Clarke never corresponded with Napoleon. Rather than writing a series of letters, she published her memoirs in 1809, causing a firestorm of controversy that forced the Duke of York's resignation as commander-in-chief of the British Army. Instead of denying that she had been advancing people in the commission queue for a fee, she boasted of it. Her book mentioned nothing at all about the sexual mores of the famous. She was never prosecuted, and enjoyed her notoriety. Her direct descendent, Daphne du Maurier, was fascinated and inspired by her. Du Maurier's novels became the basis for three classic Alfred Hitchcock films: *Rebecca, Jamaica Inn,* and *The Birds.*

The idea of indiscreet letters compromising the royal family sprang from a correspondence carried out in the late 1930s between the Duke of Windsor and Adolph Hitler. The duke was the former King Edward VIII, who had abdicated the British throne in order to marry the divorced American Wallace Warfield Simpson. In the correspondence, Hitler promised to return him to the throne should he prevail in a future war with the United Kingdom. Though the duke was likely more stupid than treasonous, he was not trusted by Churchill, who made him Governor General of the Bahamas so he could be closely watched. At the war's end, Churchill discovered that the correspondence had been stored in a French chateau and dispatched members of the Special Air Service to retrieve the letters.

The real-life bearer of the dispatches announcing the capture of Washington in the War of 1812, Harry Smyth, was knighted.

Cockburn really did take Madison's book of expenses for the year 1810 as a souvenir. His descendants returned it to the Library of Congress in 1970.

The portrayals of Czar Alexander and the Prince Regent are drawn from life. The Prince Regent actually believed that he had fought at Waterloo, and Wellington politely indulged his delusion.

Klaus von Steinwehr is fictional but is named after Baron Adolph von Steinwehr, a Prussian officer who served as a

Union Army brigadier general during the American Civil War.

Pine Coffin and Hoylet Framingham were British officers who served in the Peninsular War.

Brooks Club, founded in 1762, still exists and did not admit women in the 19th century. It was an exclusive establishment where fortunes were made and lost in a single night, and it invented the tradition of black-balling potential members who were not thought to have the right pedigree or manners.

The Congress of Vienna was a real-life game of thrones. The Congress mostly succeeded in its goals of establishing a rational framework for a European peace. Though there were notable conflicts resulting in the unification of Germany and Italy, the Congress successfully prevented a pan-European conflict for 99 years.

To the best of my ability, the descriptions of weapons and tactics are accurate, as are the depictions of Regency London, the Admiralty Board Room, the Washington Campaign, and the investiture protocols.

Information on Regency England

1. **Jane Austen's England** by Roy and Lesley Adkins.
   A well-written and approachable general survey of the era.

2. **Our Tempestuous Day: A History of Regency England** by Carolly Ericson

Excellent material on the manners, morals, and etiquette of the time.

3. **An Elegant Madness: High Society in Regency England** by Venetia Murray

If you want to understand the mindset, perspective, and habits of the aristocracy this is the volume for you.

About the Author

John Danielski worked his way through university as a living history interpreter at historic Fort Snelling, the birthplace of Minnesota. For four summers, he played a US soldier of 1827; he wore the uniform, performed the drills, demonstrated the volley fire with other interpreters, and even ate the food. A heavy blue wool tailcoat and black shako look smart and snappy, but are pure torture to wear on a boiling summer day.

He has a practical, rather than theoretical, perspective on the weapons of the time. He has fired either replicas or originals of all of the weapons mentioned in his works with live rounds, six- and twelve-pound cannon included. The effect of a 12-pound cannonball on an old Chevy four door must be seen to be believed.

He has a number of marginally useful University degrees, including a magna cum laude degree in history from the University of Minnesota. He is a Phi Beta Kappa and holds a black belt in Tae-Kwon-do. He has taught history at both the secondary and university levels and also worked as a newspaper editor.

His literary mentors were C. S. Forester, Bruce Catton, and Shelby Foote.

He lives quietly in the Twin Cities suburbs with his faithful companion: Sparkle, the wonder cat.

If You Enjoyed This Book

Please write a review.

This is important to the author and helps to get the word out to others

Visit

PENMORE PRESS
www.penmorepress.com

All Penmore Press books are available directly through our website, amazon.com, Barnes and Noble and Nook, Sony Reader, Apple iTunes, Kobo books and via leading bookshops across the United States, Canada, the UK, Australia and Europe.

More Books by John Danielski and others below.

BLUE WATER SCARLET TIDE

BY
JOHN DANIELSKI

It's the summer of 1814, and Captain Thomas Pennywhistle of the Royal Marines is fighting in a New World war that should never have started, a war where the old rules of engagement do not apply. Here, runaway slaves are your best source of intelligence, treachery is commonplace, and rough justice is the best one can hope to meet—or mete out. The Americans are fiercely determined to defend their new nation and the Great Experiment of the Republic; British Admiral George Cockburn is resolved to exact revenge for the burning of York, and so the war drags on. Thanks to Pennywhistle's ingenuity, observant mind, and military discipline, a British strike force penetrates the critically strategic region of the Chesapeake Bay. But this fight isn't just being waged by soldiers, and the collateral damage to innocents tears at Pennywhistle's heart.

As his past catches up with him, Pennywhistle must decide what is worth fighting for, and what is worth refusing to kill for—especially when he meets his opposite number on the wrong side of a pistol.

PENMORE PRESS
www.penmorepress.com

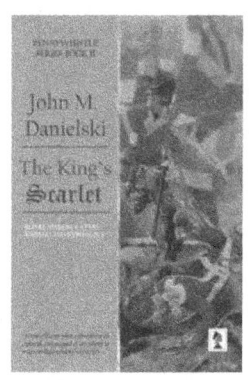

King's Scarlet

BY

John Danielski

Chivalry comes naturally to Royal Marine captain Thomas Pennywhistle, but in the savage Peninsular War, it's a luxury he can ill afford. Trapped behind enemy lines with vital dispatches for Lord Wellington, Pennywhistle violates orders when he saves a beautiful stranger, setting off a sequence of events that jeopardize his mission. The French launch a massive manhunt to capture him. His Spanish allies prove less than reliable. The woman he rescued has an agenda of her own that might help him along, if it doesn't get them all killed.

A time will come when, outmaneuvered, captured, and stripped of everything, he must stand alone before his enemies. But Pennywhistle is a hard man to kill and too bloody obstinate to concede defeat.

PENMORE PRESS
www.penmorepress.com

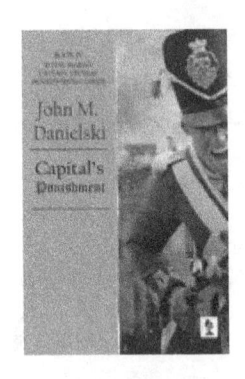

Capital's Punishment
by
John Danielski

The White House is in flames, the Capitol a gutted shell. President Madison is in hiding. Organized resistance has collapsed, and British soldiers prowl the streets of Washington.

Two islands of fortitude rise above the sea of chaos—one scarlet, one blue. Royal Marine Captain Thomas Pennywhistle has no wish to see the young American republic destroyed; he must strike a balance between his humanity and his passion for absolute victory. Captain John Tracy of the United States Marines hazards his life on the battlefield, but he must also fight a powerful conspiracy that threatens the country from within.

Pennywhistle and Tracy are forced into an uneasy alliance that will try the resolve of both. Together, they will question the depth of their loyalties as heads and hearts argue for the fate of a nation

PENMORE PRESS
www.penmorepress.com

BELLERAPHON'S CHAMPION

BY

JOHN DANIELSKI

Deep within each man, lies the secret knowledge of whether he is a stalwart or a coward. Three years an un-blooded Royal Marine, 1st Lieutenant Thomas Pennywhistle will finally "meet the lion," protecting HMS Bellerophon at the Battle of Trafalgar.

Not only will Pennywhistle be responsible for the lives of 72 marines aboard Bellerophon but their direction will fall entirely on his shoulders since his fellow Marine officers consist of a boy, a card shark, and a dying consumptive. If he has what it takes to command, it will take everything he's got.

In the course of battle, he will encounter marvels and terrors; from valiant foes to women performing miracles, from the skill of acrobats to the luck of the ship's cat, from a dead man still full of fight to a coward who has none. He and his marines will meet enemy élan will with trained volleys and disciplined bayonets. Most of all, he will meet himself; discovering just how dark his true nature really is.

Europe will be changed forever by Trafalgar, and so will Pennywhistle.

PENMORE PRESS
www.penmorepress.com

Penmore Press
Challenging, Intriguing, Adventurous, Historical and Imaginative

www.penmorepress.com